Readers Love Ashi

Winging It
"From the terrific world building, the endearing characters and the solid plot and timelines, this book was simply so much more than I could have hoped for."

—The Novel Approach

String Theory
"Ari and Jax are two really vivid characters…I really liked the way things evolved with all the relationships in this story."

—Love Bytes Reviews

Fake Dating the Prince
"If you like fairy-tale romances in a contemporary setting, if you think a flight attendant and a prince might just be a perfect couple, and if you're looking for a highly engaging read full of humorous moments, delightful characters, and a wonderful romance in a special setting, then you will probably like this novel as much as I do."

—Rainbow Book Reviews

His Leading Man
Steve and Drew have a wonderful instant chemistry but thankfully they foster it and don't rush into romance or any I-love-yous. If you don't like insta-love, this book will still appeal.

—MM Good Book Reviews

Babe in the Woodshop
"Watching these two dance around each other was so much fun and created a high level of unresolved sexual tension…I highly recommend this book because it'll have you laughing and full of love."

—Diverse Reader

By Ashlyn Kane

American Love Songs
With Claudia Mayrant & CJ Burke: Babe in the Woodshop
A Good Vintage
Hang a Shining Star
Homecoming for Beginners
The Inside Edge
The Rock Star's Guide to Getting Your Man

DREAMSPUN BEYOND
Hex and Candy

DREAMSPUN DESIRES
His Leading Man
Fake Dating the Prince

With Morgan James
Hair of the Dog
Hard Feelings
Return to Sender
String Theory

HOCKEY EVER AFTER
Winging It
The Winging It Holiday Special
Scoring Position
Unrivaled
An Unrivaled Off-Season
Crushed Ice

Published by Dreamspinner Press
www.dreamspinnerpress.com

HOMECOMING for BEGINNERS

ASHLYN KANE

Published by
DREAMSPINNER PRESS

8219 Woodville Hwy #1245
Woodville, FL 32362 USA
www.dreamspinnerpress.com

This is a work of fiction. Names, characters, places, and incidents either are the product of author imagination or are used fictitiously, and any resemblance to actual persons, living or dead, business establishments, events, or locales is entirely coincidental.

Homecoming for Beginners
© 2025 Ashlyn Kane

Cover Art
© 2025 L.C. Chase
http://www.lcchase.com
Cover content is for illustrative purposes only and any person depicted on the cover is a model.

All rights reserved. This book is licensed to the original purchaser only. Duplication or distribution via any means is illegal and a violation of international copyright law, subject to criminal prosecution and upon conviction, fines, and/or imprisonment. Any eBook format cannot be legally loaned or given to others. No part of this book may be reproduced or transmitted in any form or by any means, electronic or mechanical, including photocopying, recording, or by any information storage and retrieval system, without the written permission of the Publisher, except where permitted by law. To request permission and all other inquiries, contact Dreamspinner Press, 8219 Woodville Hwy #1245, Woodville, FL 32362 USA or www.dreamspinnerpress.com.

Any unauthorized use of this publication to train generative artificial intelligence (AI) is expressly prohibited.

Trade Paperback ISBN: 9781641088053
Digital ISBN: 9781641088046
Trade Paperback published March 2025
v. 1.0

*For the hype team: Amanda, Jeb, and Laura.
Maybe I could do it without you, but it wouldn't be any fun.*

Prologue

Ty didn't even have time to bask in his achievement before it all went to shit.

After years of drifting, followed by as many years of training and hard work, he was finally here—in the ambulance bay at his fire station, in his paramedic uniform, starting his first shift as ambulance commander.

"Try to grin less," advised his friend Stacey, the fire captain—now his direct superior, no more middlemen. "People get weird when you roll up to their broken leg looking like you won the lottery." But she smiled as she said it, so it didn't feel like a criticism.

Ty tried to cut down on the amount of dimple he knew he was flashing. It had taken him until his midtwenties to figure out what he wanted to do with his life, and he'd worked his ass off for it. Now, at twenty-nine, he finally felt like he was where he needed to be, doing what he needed to do. "Sorry, sorry." He pursed his lips, but the smile wanted to come back. "I promise I'm not going to, like, pull a Joker or anything. I'm just happy."

Stacey patted his shoulder. She was almost as tall as he was and built like a linebacker, so Ty was grateful he never had to fit next to her in the back of the ambulance. "You're adorable."

He grinned wider. "It's been said." Mostly by him, but it still counted.

"Just try not to bounce into anything and knock it over on yourself," she said in a way that would have made Ty wonder if she could actually see into his past, but he knew for a fact she'd been present for him doing that at least three times.

He drew an X across the left side of his chest anyway. "Promise."

Stacey rolled her eyes, but again, no hint of mean-spiritedness. "Great. Are you going to be able to sit down, do you think, or are you going to pace until we get our first call?"

Ty would've answered—he didn't know *how* he would've answered, but he would've come up with something clever and endearing—if their coworker, Brandon, hadn't poked his head into the breakroom. "Hey, Morris. Some lawyer here to see you. She's in the front."

What? Ty looked from Brandon to Stacey, who was regarding him with mild disbelief. "Boy, you didn't get sued, did you?"

"I'm going to pretend I'm not concerned that you jumped right to getting sued," Brandon told Stacey.

She flushed. "I'm a little gun-shy after last year, is all."

Yeah, last year had been a mess. Ty cleared his throat. "Uh, I guess I should…?"

Stacey waved him toward the door. "Jason will give you the room."

Great. Exactly what Ty wanted.

He hunched his shoulders and squeezed past Brandon to make his way toward the front of the station. Why would a lawyer be looking for him? And how would they know to find him here?

His thoughts flashed to Myra, and his stomach dropped. Something must have happened to her, and this was how he was finding out. Sure, they broke up five months ago, when she took that Doctors Without Borders posting in Ethiopia, but they were still friends. She'd probably left instructions to contact him if she….

Ty's stomach clenched, and he pushed the thought from his mind as he stepped into the front foyer. "Hey, I'm Tyler Morris, I heard someone is—"

And then his eyes caught on the familiar figure standing by the front doors, and his heart sank.

Eliza Kent's power suit had undergone a handful of fashion upgrades since the last time Ty had seen her in one. But otherwise his father's attorney looked like she had when he was sixteen and she was throwing her weight around a police station in Suffolk, Connecticut, to bully the cops into letting him off a vandalism charge. He ended up getting kicked out of school—not much he could do about that one, since he had smuggled a half-dozen chickens into the principal's office—but he hadn't faced any legal consequences.

Somehow he knew that whatever had brought her here, he wasn't likely to get off so easily this time.

"Ms. Kent," Ty said automatically, through a very dry mouth. "What are you doing here?"

Kent took off her sunglasses and met his eyes. Her voice was heavy when she said, "We need to talk."

Chapter 1

FOR A SOLID ten seconds, Ty was convinced he was hallucinating. He didn't know how else to explain the smokeshow on his father's ostentatious front porch. Ty had seen his fair share of beautiful men, but this was ridiculous—broad shoulders and a lean, muscular body under a *very* friendly henley shirt, artfully mussed dark hair begging for Ty to run his fingers through it, and the kind of stubble movie stars paid big bucks for. With the sun just peeking over the tops of the trees, the guy's skin actually glowed gold, so much so that Ty had to squint to look at him. And his eyes were the color of Ty's father's top-shelf brandy, which Ty had consumed last night in a less restrained manner than was advisable, which would explain the hallucination.

And the headache. Ty felt like death.

But then the guy said, "Hey, uh, I'm Ollie Kent. I'm looking for Leonard Morris? I'm supposed to start work for him today."

Which settled the whole thing. If Ty were hallucinating a guy who looked like this, he wouldn't be asking for Ty's father. And he'd have a way sexier name than Ollie.

Ty blinked, and his eyes focused a little more, and—okay. The guy was good-looking, sure, but now that the sun had risen another degree and Ty's vision had adjusted, he was ordinary enough—too short and round-faced to be a model. He looked like the kind of guy you asked to join your softball team or drank beer with.

Not that Ty planned to consume any more alcohol any time soon.

"Uh," Ty said. He'd been back in town less than twenty-four hours, and it was a *small* town. News traveled fast. He hadn't had to tell anyone else yet. Everyone who lived here already knew. "I'm sorry to tell you this, but he, uh." *He drove his car full speed into a knot of pine trees.* "He died."

Despite his resolve, Ty's voice cracked on the second word.

Ollie's eyes widened and his mouth parted slightly, and Ty could imagine the struggle. He obviously hadn't been close to Leonard, or he would've known about the... accident. Which meant this was super awkward for him, because no Leonard meant no job, but focusing on that when someone had died made you look like an asshole.

"Oh," Ollie said carefully. "I'm sorry to hear that."

Ty snorted without meaning to. "Yeah, me too. Old man's still ruining my life from beyond the grave."

Then he registered the car in the winding circular driveway. Apart from the driver's seat and the seat behind it, it was packed with cardboard boxes.

There was a kid in the back seat, a little boy with Ollie's eyes and a messy head of auburn curls.

Fuck, did his dad ruin this guy's life too? He cleared his throat. "Uh, maybe—do you want to come in? Because I... need coffee." And Advil. So much Advil.

And a shower; fuck, he smelled like bourbon.

Ollie shifted from foot to foot. "I don't want to impose—"

"Come in," Ty said more firmly, because suddenly the idea of sitting by himself in his parents' kitchen, the site of untold childhood scoldings, seemed unfaceable. "Bring your—your kid?"

"Theo," Ollie offered. He smiled with his whole body when he said the name.

So much coffee. "Bring him," Ty said. "I haven't gone shopping yet or anything, but the old man must've had something to eat in there somewhere. I'm pretty sure he didn't actually live on the shattered dreams of his only child. Or we'll order delivery... do you think Uber Eats comes out this far?" There was an IHOP in town. At least, there used to be a decade ago, the last time Ty set foot in the place.

"Uh," said Ollie. He took a half step backward, which was when Ty realized it was pretty weird to invite total strangers into your house for breakfast, even if they looked like they could go totally HAM on a stack of pancakes. "Maybe it would be best if we just came back another day."

Ty had the sudden horrible suspicion that if he let this man out of his sight, he'd evaporate and Ty would never see him again, hallucination or no. Ty couldn't face it—not this big stupid monstrosity of a mausoleum, not breakfast, not the fact that he had to be *presentable* at his father's funeral in less than three hours. Ollie and his kid might be total strangers and they might think Ty was a total freak of nature, and the only thing in his father's kitchen—Ty's, now, oh *fuck*—might be canned milk and maggoty flour. But right now Ty only cared about one thing, and his dignity wasn't it. "Look," he blurted, "I know it's—weird. And we don't know each other. And this is so not how you expected to spend your morning, I mean, clearly." He gestured helplessly at the car, the kid, the boxes. What a clusterfuck. "But my asshole dad just died, and I would seriously love to not be alone in this stupid house for another minute."

For a moment they stared at each other, both—Ty assumed—hyperaware of the tattered remains of his self-respect dying ignominiously on the intricate tile porch between them.

Finally Ollie cleared his throat. "Sure, uh, I guess. One condition?"

Oh thank God. "Name it."

Ollie glanced down and then back up. "Put on some pants?"

Ty's mouth worked soundlessly without input from his brain, and then he finally looked down. Yep, he sure had answered the door in his boxers. Making a real smooth first impression here. "I think I might still be drunk," he confessed.

A smile twitched at the corner of Ollie's mouth. "You think," he echoed.

A literal, actual *sea* of coffee. "All right," Ty said faintly. "Well, uh—I'm just going to… dress. You and Theo, uh, come in and… yeah. Make yourself at home."

Look on the bright side, Ty told himself as he retreated to his bedroom. *This day probably can't get much worse.*

THIS DAY, Ollie thought, standing on the porch as Half-Naked Man disappeared into the house, was already a shitshow.

He and Theo had made the drive up from DC yesterday and checked into a motel. The place was kind of a dump, but it was only for a night. Ollie's parents had tried to convince him to stay with them, but that would've meant Ollie sleeping on the couch and Theo in Ollie's old bedroom in a house filled with people he didn't really know. He figured they could handle a motel for one night. And it had a pool; Theo loved the pool. He didn't care what the room looked like.

But they'd only gotten the room for a night because Ollie was supposed to start work for Mr. Morris this morning—work as a home-care aid, not that Ollie was in any way qualified. When his Aunt Eliza—ex-aunt? She'd been his aunt by marriage, but his uncle had died and she'd remarried; he didn't know what that made her now—called a couple weeks back, he thought she was nuts. Did Ollie want to come be a "companion" to an older man with dementia? Help him with his groceries, make sure he didn't hurt himself, blah blah blah? Then she mentioned the pay, and the fact that the job included housing for himself and Theo, and, well, by that time Theo had finished chemo and Ollie thought a change of scenery would do them both good, so why not?

The answer, apparently, was *because people with dementia die, you idiot*, and now Ollie was in Connecticut with no place to live and no job and a kid to look after.

But he was, apparently, going to get breakfast from a guy who was in even worse shape than Ollie.

He propped the door open with an unnecessarily ornate—and heavy—flower pot and jogged down the steps to the car. Theo opened his door just as Ollie got there. "Hey, buddy," Ollie said. "Small change of plans."

Theo hopped out, pushed his glasses up his nose, and shut the door with both hands. He'd gotten steadier on his feet in the past couple weeks, and he was starting to put on some muscle again. This kid filled Ollie with so much relief and pride he didn't know whether to explode or melt into a puddle.

"Okay," Theo said. "What's the new plan?"

"Breakfast."

Theo squinted up at him. "But we had breakfast at the motel."

Exactly right, and why Ollie wasn't too worried about getting food poisoning from a guy who'd forgotten to put pants on this morning. They could just skip the food part. "You're right, so you don't have to eat anything if you don't want to. But the man I'm supposed to take care of isn't here anymore"—Ollie swerved around the D-word and crossed his fingers Theo didn't notice—"so we're going to go inside and talk to my new friend for a little bit and figure out what to do next."

Like find an apartment and a job. Totally doable with an eight-year-old in tow. Piece of cake.

Ollie made himself walk up the steps behind Theo. The kid was still recovering from chemo, and Ollie didn't want any broken bones, but he also didn't want Theo to grow up feeling like he couldn't do anything without his dad hovering.

For the time being, Ollie was doing his best at hovering unobtrusively when Theo's back was turned, but sooner or later the kid was going to figure it out, and then…. Ollie didn't know what then. He'd burn that bridge when he got there.

"Does this mean we're not going to live here?" Theo asked as they got to the top step. "Because this place is *cool*, Dad."

This place is creepy as hell, Ollie thought, *and I've flown helicopters in active combat.* Which was part of why no one could catch him hovering—one helicopter-dad joke and he'd be toast.

"Sorry, buddy," he said out loud. "I don't think so. But it sure is… interesting."

The place—*house* simply did not apply—was enormous. Cavernous, even. Maybe that was why it felt so cold. The front room had twenty-foot ceilings and an entire wall of windows, but the curtains had been drawn halfway and no one had cleaned the glass at the top in maybe a decade, so it was dark too. The furniture looked like it had come out of a period piece, or an antique catalog, or a horror movie set.

Ollie wasn't even Catholic, and he was still fighting the urge to cross himself.

An antique globe in an old-fashioned wood stand sat next to an armchair. Theo spun it, kicking up a cloud of dust.

Ollie sneezed.

"Where do you think the kitchen is?" Theo asked.

That was a great question. Obviously this place had been built before *open concept* was even a twinkle in an architect's eye. Ollie surveyed the sides of the room, where heavy oak doors were interspersed with equally heavy dark wood paneling—but none of the doors were moving, so there was no way to tell where their host had gone.

Not that he'd gone to the kitchen, probably. Unless he kept his pants there. You never knew with some people.

"I have no idea," Ollie said after a moment. "Maybe we'll just wait here for, uh—" *The guy with no name.*

God, he had to be crazy. Bad enough that he'd gotten himself into this situation, but he'd dragged Theo into it with him. If they got ax murdered this was totally on him.

Ollie was just about to let his common sense override whatever misguided softhearted dumbassery had lured him in here when one of the doors swung open and Boxers Man came back in, this time dressed in fleece pajama pants with smiley-face emojis and a blue T-shirt with PARAMEDIC written on it.

Or, actually, the shirt said CIDEMARAP, because he'd put it on inside-out. Even if this guy intended to brutally ax-murder them, Ollie was pretty sure he wasn't capable of pulling it off at the moment.

"Oh God, you're really not a hallucination, are you?" the guy said. Ollie couldn't tell if he was relieved or mortified.

Ollie looked down at himself. "Not the last time I checked. But it's pretty early in the morning for philosophical debate."

The ghost of a smile flickered across Smiley-Pants-Man's face.

Which reminded Ollie—"Uh, this is my son, Theo." Who was drawing smiley faces that matched the guy's pants in the dust on the globe stand. "Theo, this is...."

"Ty," the guy said, stepping forward. Ollie would've debated about shaking hands when he didn't know where this guy had been, but instinct took over. Fortunately he wasn't sticky. "Uh, Tyler. Morris. In case you didn't grasp the subtext, this is—was—my dad's place."

Theo shook hands too, because Ollie might be new at full-time parenting but he'd managed to get that far.

But he was still eight years old, so he followed the handshake with, "Do you have a dungeon?"

Theo wasn't looking, so Ollie let himself facepalm.

Ty-uh-Tyler-Morris took it in stride, grinning delightedly. "You know, that's a really good question. How about we save it for after breakfast, though, because I made some choices last night that I am going to regret this morning if I don't get some food in me."

"We couldn't figure out which door went to the kitchen," Theo explained in a stage whisper.

Ty laughed like Ollie's kid was the best comedian on the planet, not forced at all. For a split second, the stuffy old room felt bright and lived-in. "All the doors in this place do kinda look the same, don't they? Come on. We'll push 'em all open until we find it."

The kitchen, at least, didn't look like a period piece, even if dishes—clean, from what Ollie could tell—littered half the available counter space. Ollie had done a little research into living with dementia before he told Eliza he'd take this job, so he knew Morris Senior was probably the one who'd taken them all out. He wondered what the rest of the house looked like, if he'd taken everything out of the linen closets and piled his clothes on the floor.

Ollie would've dealt with it, even though picking it up likely would've been a daily task, not a one-and-done. But maybe it was better that he didn't have to. Having stuff all over the place like that had to be some kind of health hazard—tripping, fire. Last thing he needed was Theo breaking a bone.

Which, speaking of breaking things, Ollie had the feeling he ought to get some caffeine into their host before he fell over. Ollie located the coffee maker—miraculously free of countertop clutter or suspicious fuzzy growths—and a canister of coffee and got to work.

"Wow, you are really... just going for it, huh?"

"You did tell me to make myself at home."

"I... did do that, didn't I. I'm sorry. I'm not usually—okay, I actually am usually this much of a disaster." Ty ran a hand through his hair as he dropped into a chair at the breakfast bar and finished in a mutter at the countertop, "At least whenever I'm in this house."

Ollie started to suspect that he'd have to do the cooking if any breakfast was to be consumed. He opened a few cupboards in search of mugs. "What's that they say? 'You can go back home again, but we'd advise against it'?"

Ty snorted and raised his head. "Oh, so the kid gets his sense of humor from you?"

"Yeah, no one's more surprised than me. I definitely thought it skipped a generation."

Theo climbed up onto the stool next to Ty. "What's *that* mean?"

"That means that your daddy needs to start watching his mouth when his kid is around." Ollie ruffled Theo's hair. He might not have the best relationship with his parents, but he didn't want Theo to hate them before they even met. "Your grandma tells bad jokes is all. But don't tell her I said that. You just pretend to laugh, okay?"

Theo nodded gamely. "Okay."

Over his head, Ty met Ollie's eyes and grinned crookedly. Yeah, Ollie's kid was the best. "Knew I could count on you, bud."

Mugs, check. Coffee, check. Ollie poured two and slid one in front of Ty. Ty looked like he might cry.

"Can I have coffee too, Dad?"

"Not unless your aunt Cassie is babysitting." She had it coming after what she'd put Ollie through as a kid. He poked his head into the fridge. Eggs, check. Milk, check. Both passed the sniff test. The deli drawer looked beyond questionable; Ollie wasn't going in there. "Hey, you got flour or bread?"

"Uh, in the little—food garage thing, except…"

Food garage? Oh, in the corner of the counter, a little sliding door lifted to reveal a toaster and a stash of bread and English muffins. Because sure. Plates on the counter, simple carbs hidden away. Dementia logic.

"… I don't actually know how old anything in there is, so…."

Ollie inspected the bread tag. It was within the best-before date, so he shrugged. "No mold. French toast it is." He glanced over his shoulder. "Uh, unless you want over-easy on toast or something?"

The color drained out of Ty's face. "French toast," he said firmly.

"No runny yolks this morning," Ollie said. "Got it." He glanced at Theo. "You want a piece too, bud?"

Theo made a thoughtful face and then said, "I could eat," which he'd definitely picked up from Ollie.

Ty looked like he knew it too, because the crooked grin returned.

"Okay. Coming right up."

For the next twenty minutes, Ollie focused on cooking while Theo played Twenty Questions with their host. Considering how hungover the guy had to be, he had a remarkable amount of patience. Finally Ollie plated up and sat down on the opposite side of the breakfast bar.

"Do you live here by yourself?" Theo asked around half a slice of bread.

Ollie was still working on table manners, which had taken a hit recently. He was pretty sure Theo was getting a growth spurt.

"Uh, not exactly." Ty poked at his breakfast. "I mean. I used to live here when I was a kid, but I don't anymore."

"Cool. Do you have a pool? Do you have a library?"

"Bud," Ollie interjected. "Let Ty eat his breakfast, okay? And you eat yours too, since you asked for seconds."

"Oh, uh, you guys already ate?"

Shit. Ollie looked at his plate. "Kinda thought I'd be starting work first thing this morning, so…."

"Right, yeah," Ty said. "We should probably talk about that? But maybe not with, uh...." He gestured to Theo, who fortunately was focused on following Ollie's instructions to eat his breakfast.

"Yeah," Ollie agreed. On top of losing his mom, moving, and starting a new school, Theo didn't need to worry about Ollie having a job. "Thanks. I'm... sorry about your dad." Even if it kind of seemed like Ty wasn't. Then again, you didn't end up with this kind of hangover because you had simple feelings about something.

"Thanks," Ty echoed, a little hollow. He stuffed a bite of french toast into his mouth, and his eyebrows went up. "This is pretty good, man."

"Yeah, I found real vanilla in the cupboard. Makes a difference. My mom always had the good stuff."

"I guess what she lacks in humor she makes up in taste."

Ollie raised his coffee mug in acknowledgment. Ty had hit the nail on the head with that one.

He tuned out conversation after that. Ty had Theo well in hand, and it had been a minute since Ollie had someone else to occupy his kid. God knew he loved Theo, but he couldn't resist the opportunity to turn over the controls to someone else for a bit. Ollie was still there. Theo couldn't get into any trouble.

And he really had outdone himself with the french toast.

He left Theo and Ty to do their thing while he cleared plates. He'd just turned on the tap to start washing dishes when the timbre of the conversation behind him changed. "Ollie, you don't—jeez, I've taken up enough of your time—oh *shit*."

"Swear jar," Theo singsonged.

Ty apologized profusely, which Ollie ignored. His kid had been raised by a woman who used to be in the Army Corps of Engineers.

"Oh shit what?" Ollie asked, letting Theo's delighted squawk wash over him.

"I am supposed to be at the funeral home in an hour." Ty groaned and rubbed his hands over his face. "And I *definitely* can't drive."

Jesus. This guy needed a keeper worse than his dad had. "You better get in the shower, then," Ollie told him. "It's a twenty-minute drive."

Chapter 2

IF TY hadn't been well on his way to sobering up by the time he got out of the shower, walking into the funeral home would have done it.

The rich half of town had turned out to pay their respects, so the lot was full of black Jaguars and Mercedes and Land Rovers, everything spit polished to keep up appearances. Ty's beat-up pickup wouldn't have fit in any better than Ollie's respectable silver Honda Civic.

"You going to be good?" Ollie asked, as if he hadn't done enough for Ty already this morning by waking him up, feeding and caffeinating him, and practically pouring him into his suit.

Ty puffed out his cheeks and blew out a long breath. "No idea," he admitted. "Thanks for the ride, guys. I guess I'll see you around."

And then before he could lose his nerve, he got out of the car.

He didn't look back.

Just like he hadn't looked back when he left this town over a decade ago.

Reid Funeral Home hadn't changed since they buried Ty's mother. It had the same neutral walls, the same somber décor, the same dark wood furniture. Ty's chest felt the same way now as it had then, like he'd taken a crushing injury that left his broken ribs screaming every time he tried to draw a breath. Back then he'd been grieving his mother, furious at the world for taking her from him and leaving him with his distant, impossible father.

Now his dad was gone too, and Ty didn't know what made him angrier—that he'd had to come back here for this or that he'd never get to tell the old man to fuck himself.

Not unless he wanted to make a scene, anyway, and Ty… didn't have the energy to make another scene today. He'd embarrassed himself enough.

Eliza Kent and the funeral-home director met Ty at the door. The director shook his hand, and Eliza took his arm like he was a frail old lady, or maybe like she'd taken one look at him and calculated how much he drank last night. "Come on," she said in a bracing voice that reminded Ty of his mom. "We'll get you through this."

Ty was installed at the front of the room, near the casket, which was closed. "The accident...," Eliza had told him when she'd come to the station to find him. "It wasn't pretty."

The funeral director had asked if Ty wanted to see his father, assured him they'd reconstructed his face as much as possible. Part of Ty had thought maybe looking would make it final, make it real, and the other half was pissed off that even if he did look, he wouldn't get to tell his father to go to hell.

It was too late to change his mind now.

Ty shook hands with a hundred of his father's nearest and dearest, who offered hollow condolences to his face when he knew for a fact they'd spent his adolescence gossiping about him. Even when Alan Chiu not-so-surreptitiously wiped his hand after shaking Ty's, Ty didn't have the energy to give a shit. He could just about manage to stand upright, and even that he had to credit to a guy he'd literally never met before this morning and who he'd initially assumed was a product of his imagination.

Finally the parade of mourners ended and Ty got to sit down at the front row of the chapel, where everyone was staring at his back as the local preacher talked about his father's impact on the *community*.

Ty kind of wished he were still drunk.

Instead he sat ramrod straight next to Eliza and kept his eyes fixed forward. He did his best to let the eulogy wash through him without leaving anything behind. It was easier than it should've been.

After the service, professional pallbearers lowered his father's casket into the ground. The well-dressed crowd waited for Ty to throw a handful of dirt onto the coffin, or maybe to spit on it. Ty did the former and then wiped his hand on his suit pants like a five-year-old and immediately felt stupid and self-conscious.

At least the old man himself wasn't here anymore to look at him with that perennially disappointed sneer.

The fog didn't clear from Ty's vision until the crowd dispersed and suddenly he found himself standing with his father's lawyer and...

... and Ty's high school football and baseball coach?

Now that he was looking at the guy, Ty vaguely remembered him coming through the condolences line, but he'd been too out of it then to pay attention. But now he was standing next to Eliza in a—a *really nice* suit, which was maybe why Ty hadn't recognized him. He'd never seen the guy in anything other than a track suit or a school polo.

"Uh. Coach Tate?"

Coach put a hand on his shoulder. "How you holding up, Ty?"

"I have had better days."

Coach squeezed, and Ty swallowed an unexpected lump in his throat.

"We have some things to discuss," Eliza said gently. "Why don't you come back to our place for a chat? Henry can make us lunch."

Our place? Ty wondered. *Henry?* The last Ty knew, Eliza was married to a guy named David. He was about to ask, but then Coach Tate put his arm around Eliza's shoulders and the penny dropped. "Wait," Ty said, "you two are *married*?"

"Six years now," Coach Tate said.

"There've been a few changes around here since you left." Eliza put her hand on Ty's arm. He couldn't help but feel like he was being… handled… but it had been a long time since anyone cared enough about him to try it. "Come on."

He spent the ride from the funeral home looking out the window of Eliza's slick SUV. Winter was receding, leaving mud and damp brown-green grass. The trees had started to bud, though nothing had leafed out yet. In Eliza's neighborhood, daffodils were blooming in the garden beds and the tulips had started to come up, though it was a crapshoot on whether they'd get to flower. Ty's mom had always complained about the deer eating the tops off before they opened.

"Kind of dreary," Coach Tate commented as Eliza pulled into the driveway. "What do you think, sandwiches and chicken soup? Homemade. My specialty."

Coach Tate had been a bachelor when Ty knew him. This sudden turn for the domestic threw him for a loop. "Uh, yeah. Sounds great, Coach. Thanks."

Moments later the door to Eliza's home office closed behind them. Ty expected something like his father's study—heavy dark wood and leather furniture, something that felt stifling in its attempt to convey luxury and importance. Instead it was a bright room with a bay window facing the back garden. It was decorated with a menagerie of potted plants and midcentury furnishings. Eliza motioned Ty to one of the two armchairs in front of her desk. He expected her to sit facing him, but she took the one next to his instead.

"How are you doing, Ty? Really. I know this is a lot, and you and your daddy never did get along…."

Ty snorted before he could control himself. "That's a hell of an understatement."

"I know." She patted his arm. It was wild. Ty had never considered her the maternal type. "And I'm sorry. But it's better that we sort out what we can now."

"Uh, Ms. Kent, no offense." How could he put this into words without coming across as ungrateful? "But… what do you mean 'we'? You're—you were—my dad's lawyer. It's not like we're…." Friends? Yeah, obviously not, because Ty didn't have any of those. At least not in this town.

Eliza was quiet for a moment, her dark eyes serious. Then she said, "It's true that I was your daddy's lawyer. But he's dead, God rest him"—she said that the way Southern women said *bless your heart*—"which means I'm *your* lawyer now. And while I can't directly act against his legal will, he's also not here to clarify *how* any of his wishes should be carried out, if it hasn't been put down on paper. Do you understand me?"

The last of Ty's two-day stupor evaporated, and he looked at her with clear eyes as his brain translated: *Fuck your dad.* Not something he'd ever expected to hear from her, even if it wasn't in so many words. "I think so." He paused. "Thanks."

She waved this off. "You're welcome. Now, that being said, your daddy paid my retainer for this year, but if you're planning on getting arrested and I have to bail you out of jail, my rates are going up, you hear?"

And now she was… teasing him? This day kept getting weirder. Ty raised his hands. "Hey, I get you. I haven't been arrested since the last time you had to bail me out. I promise. They don't let you be a paramedic if you've got a criminal record, you know." And his job was the one thing he had going for him. The sooner he got to go back to it for real, the better.

"Yes. About that." She sighed, and in the sudden lines at the corners of her eyes and around her mouth, Ty detected that she *had* actually aged in the ten-plus years since he'd last seen her. "I've been going over the policies your father had in place, but because of the nature of his death, the insurance payouts will be minimal." Translation: nobody wanted to pay because Ty's dad drove himself into a tree, possibly on purpose, when he had already lost his license. Ty was lucky Eliza hadn't said anything yet about someone suing his estate. "There's more than enough money in his accounts and in the house. The problem is with the will, probate, and home insurance."

Of course it was. "That actually sounds more like three problems."

With a shake of her head, she got up from her chair. "You always were smarter than your daddy gave you credit for." She went to a sideboard, where there was a pitcher of ice water and two glasses, and poured one for each of them. Then she sat back down, this time on the opposite side of the desk.

"First problem." She passed across a glass for him, along with a cork coaster. "The will. Your father has named you executor, which you already know. It's a responsibility you can refuse, which I've also told you."

Ty chugged the glass and wiped a droplet of water from the corner of his mouth. The pitcher was still half full; he eyed it hopefully. Dehydration was setting in. He should've packed himself a banana bag—an IV infusion of potassium would be great right about now. "Right," he said. "And you said the executor takes, uh, 5 percent?"

"Typically that's what they're entitled to, although in this case you're also the beneficiary of the majority of the property."

Ty's mouth fell open. "I'm sorry?" He'd been sure his dad would disinherit him.

"There's five hundred thousand set aside for a donation to the Cancer Society." Eliza reached for a tablet at the corner of her desk and thumbed it on. "As well as various endowments. But that leaves a substantial amount of assets, including the house."

Ty stumbled to his feet and poured himself a second glass of water, which he brought back to the desk with him. "Uh. The Cobra?" Ty didn't care about the house, but the Cobra had been his mother's baby, a car she loved driving with her dad when she was a kid. She even taught Ty to drive stick in it.

Ty's dad locked it up when she died.

Eliza cleared her throat. "Donated to an automotive museum."

Ty's heart broke. "Of course he did." Why would he have thought otherwise?

"There's more." Eliza surged forward. "As I said, you can refuse to be executor. It's a lot of work, and a lot of waiting, and you'll be under some scrutiny. Probate takes a long time, sometimes more than a year. Nothing can happen with your father's things until that process is complete."

"What happens if I turn it down?"

"Well, normally the state would perform the service and take its percentage of the estate. However, your father included a clause that, if you refuse the duty of executor…."

Oh boy, Ty thought. Here it comes.

"A second will comes into effect, and the proceeds from the estate will be given to the Alliance Defending Freedom."

Great. "Let's take it as a given that I'm accepting the job of executor." Ty didn't care about the money. Well—okay, he could use the money. He only wanted to refuse it because it had been his father's. But if the alternative to the drudgery of being executor was his dad's riches going to an actual hate group, then no thanks. He'd find the time between shifts to figure out how to handle all this. Once he mentioned to any self-respecting accountant how much he stood to inherit, he'd have people lining up to get paid in a year. "What's the next bad news?"

"The home insurance." She shook her head. "A house like that, it costs a lot to insure. Currently, those payments are set to come out automatically, so you don't have to worry about that. The more pressing issue is that under the current policy, the home has to remain occupied, or the policy will lapse."

"Okay, well, that's…." He shook his head. "I mean it can't be that hard to find someone who wants to rent the place, right? I'll put it on the market for like a thousand bucks a month and…."

Eliza was already shaking her head. "That would require changing the current insurance policy, which can't be done until a whole host of other t's are crossed and i's are dotted. It'll take time. Time you don't have."

His stomach sank and he rubbed the bridge of his nose. "So you're saying what, exactly?"

"The easiest way for you to solve this problem is to move in permanently, or at least until the estate clears probate and you can put the house up for sale."

Fuck. Ty thought that was where this was going. He'd spent more than fifteen years furiously swimming away from this place, but he'd never escaped the chain around his ankle, and now the anchor was dragging him back down. "My job is in Chicago."

The words sounded as flimsy as they felt.

"I know."

It would've been easier if she'd been more like his father—more like he expected. But this unknown, gentle woman who was *almost* familiar just made him want to crumple.

Ty took a deep breath and let it out. Then he washed away the tightness in his throat with another sip of ice water. Finally he put the glass down, wiped his hands on his suit pants, and sat forward. "Take me through the rest of it."

Five minutes in and Ty felt like he should be taking notes. But when he reached for his phone to start making them, Eliza shook her head and said she'd email him a summary.

Ty didn't know lawyers could be saints.

Eliza was just wrapping up a primer on inheritance tax and how it would apply to his father's estate—she was also emailing him a list of questions to ask his father's accountant—when Henry knocked on the door and stuck his head inside. "Lunch is ready."

The scent of a homemade meal sneaked into the office, and suddenly Ty's stomach forgot all about Ollie Kent's french toast. "That smells amazing."

"Well, let's eat."

He thought they might sit in the formal dining room, but instead Henry led him into an eat-in kitchen where they sat at a battle-scarred table. The soup tasted as good as it smelled, and it did the job of chasing away the rest of Ty's hangover as well as any banana bag would have. Henry and Eliza carried the conversation while Ty focused on eating, digesting not only the food in front of him but the mountain of things he'd have to do over the next few months just because his dad was a spiteful old dick.

Ty had never been all that great about staying focused when he didn't have to, though, and it was only a matter of time before his gaze started to wander. The office might've been all Eliza, but the kitchen was obviously Henry's domain. A desk against one wall hosted practice schedules and permission forms, and the wall was full of photos of the high school's athletic teams. Two of them featured a huge trophy, and Ty's stomach twisted.

He should be in one of those pictures. But after his mom died, after his father shut down, after Ty lashed out because it was the only way he knew to get any kind of parental attention, his dad had shipped him off to boarding school. Too bad, so sad for the home team, who were down their star pitcher before baseball season even started. More than one of the guys on the team had hated Ty for that.

Except…. Ty frowned. Except the year on that photo….

Without meaning to, he got up from the table and walked closer to the wall.

Those were Ty's teammates, all right—Jimmy and Carlos and PJ and the rest of them crowding around the trophy, grinning like it was the best day of their lives. And there was Coach Tate, beaming like a proud dad, standing next to—

"Is that *Ollie Kent*?"

Conversation at the table stopped, and Henry and Eliza looked at each other. "You know Ollie?"

"Well, I didn't know he stole my spot on the baseball team." Ty grimaced internally. He hated how that had come out. Ollie hadn't stolen anything. Ty lost that spot through his own stupidity. And Coach Tate was the last person who deserved to be the target of that anger. He put as much into that team as any of the players. "Fuck. Sorry. I just… didn't know, uh, I mean, obviously you had to replace me."

"Nobody was going to do that."

Ty swallowed. He traced his fingers over the trophy, then over Ollie's shoulder. The shoulder that should've been his. He exhaled shakily.

"How *do* you know him?" Eliza asked.

"He showed up at the house this morning." It felt like a lifetime ago now. "Um, with his son. I guess he was supposed to start work for my dad as a… I don't know what you'd call it. A home health-care aide, I guess, except I don't think he's qualified beyond being able to lift a grown man off the floor if he falls down. Adult babysitter? Which, all evidence to the contrary, I don't actually need. But since dear old Dad is dead as a doornail, it wasn't like he could call and say, 'Sorry but you're fired,' so I got to do that part."

There was a beat of silence. Then Eliza said, "I'm going to *kill* that boy."

Ty blinked.

"Eliza—"

"No, Henry. I asked him *three days ago* to set up a phone conference with Ollie Kent"—she whipped out her cell phone and brandished it toward him—"and what did he do? He *emailed an invitation* to my calendar and then never followed up."

Ty put together that *that boy* did not refer to Ollie.

"Albert's a good kid," Henry insisted.

"But a lousy secretary," Eliza finished. "I'd better call him myself and apologize. Having a single father—my *late husband's nephew*—drive all the way up from DC for a job that's disappeared, honestly." She huffed. "I should've double-checked. Excuse me, boys, please." With one last touch to Ty's shoulder, she left the room.

Maybe Ty wasn't the only one who'd been thrown for a loop this week. He didn't get the impression Eliza dropped the ball very often. "Albert?" he asked Henry, for something to say.

"Class of 2022." Henry gave a little wince. "Tore his ACL in the last football game of the season. Goodbye, college scholarship. Eliza needed someone to help out in the office, he needed a job.... Guess I can forget about that second career in matchmaking."

"Career," Ty echoed as the reality of his conversation with Eliza closed in around him. Without his input his legs carried him back to the kitchen table and dumped him in a chair. "Right."

Henry tilted his head at him. "What?"

Of course—Eliza wouldn't have told him anything, even though he was her husband. "Uh, it looks like I kind of have to move into my dad's place temporarily for...." He waved his hands. "I don't know. Insurance reasons I guess." Though in theory, couldn't he roll the dice? If the place burned down, oh well?

Maybe... but if someone decided to sue him because they got hurt, he'd be hosed. Ugh.

"Which means you're looking for a new job," Henry finished, and Ty could see the wheels in his head turning.

"Just don't try to make me Eliza's secretary." They'd kill each other inside a week. "I'm a danger to myself and others if I have to sit still for too long."

"I do remember your teenage years, yeah." Henry tilted his head. "What have you been doing for work?"

Eliza hadn't told him that either? Ty spared a moment to be a little bit glad about that. His job was the one thing he'd managed to get right, and he wanted to make someone proud of him. Nothing ever would've been good enough for his dad, but—"I'm a paramedic. Uh, for four years now. I actually just got a promotion." Which he'd have to give up unless he could con someone into letting him take an indefinite leave of absence. He'd have to talk to his union rep. He could probably get a couple months unpaid for bereavement, but he would still need to work in the meantime. Not for monetary reasons—Eliza had explained he'd have access to some of his dad's accounts as executor—but because he would lose his mind if he didn't have something else to do.

Henry's eyes widened. "Hey, good for you. That sounds like the perfect job for you."

Ty warmed at the praise. "I mean, it's not like I'm a doctor or anything, but it's important, and I-I'm good at it. Keeping a cool head in a crisis. Which, believe me, I know that's ironic because *cool head* is not something any of my teachers would've said about me."

Henry laughed. "No, I think Mrs. Murphy in particular—"

"I did not *blow up* the chemistry lab," Ty protested automatically with a grin, falling into the old banter.

"You did singe off your eyebrows, though."

Ty sniffed. "It was the fashion."

"Uh-huh." Henry shook his head. "Well, if you're bored, I could use another set of hands at games and practices. Someone with good first-aid credentials? Even better. I can't pay you for it, but—"

"That sounds great, actually." Anything to get him out of the house. "Turns out my schedule is wide open."

"Well, I'm sure it'll fill up. You just let me know."

Fill up with what, Ty wanted to ask. By now all his high school teammates either thought he was a loser or they'd forgotten all about him. He was an only child and now an orphan. His parents didn't have much family either. Ty was the last. The closest thing he had to friends right now were Henry and Eliza—a whole generation older than he was—and the stranger who'd seen him at his worst and taken pity on him to make sure he didn't show up to his father's funeral reeking of bourbon.

Maybe he should get Ollie's number from Eliza, call, and… what? Apologize? It wasn't Ty's fault his dad died.

He shook off the thought and refocused on the conversation at hand. "So, baseball. How's the team looking this year?"

Chapter 3

OLLIE ONLY meant to take Theo to the playground. It was supposed to be a nice afternoon where Theo could be a normal kid. A slide, some swings, a merry-go-round that made Ollie dizzy with memory just looking at it—and he flew heavy machinery for a living.

Or he used to.

Unfortunately for Ollie, his sister happened to be at the park with *her* kid, and she *happened* to text his mother a photo, and now instead of a nice Saturday at the park with his kid, he was having a less relaxing Saturday at the park with his kid and his mom.

It wasn't Cassie's fault. She hadn't realized Theo was in the shot.

"Oliver, you know we'd love to have you—"

"Mom." Ollie tore his eyes away from Theo's attempt to swing over the top of the swing set and called upon years of military discipline to keep his voice even. Who knew that would have so many real-world applications when it came to his family? "I'm not moving in with you. We need our own space."

His mother had never met a weakness she wouldn't exploit to get her way. "Your father and I have plenty of room now that your brothers and sisters are out of the house. And it would give us a chance to get to know your son." Ollie had had to physically intervene to keep her from going right over to Theo when she arrived.

"That is not what I meant, Mom." He shook his head. "Besides, Theo isn't ready for that. He lost his mother a few months ago. He's only just starting to trust me, and I've known him since he was born." Not that he'd been there for it. *It's complicated* didn't exactly describe the relationship between Ollie and Theo's mom. They were friends who'd had an IVF baby. As an asexual woman, she hadn't wanted a partner; as a former foster kid, she'd wanted a sperm donor who'd be there for her kid if something happened to her.

Neither of them expected something to happen to her.

"I'm thirty-six years old," she'd said. "I know it's crazy, but it might be my last chance."

Ollie had always wanted a family of his own. Her proposition was a little untraditional, but it worked perfectly for them. While he was deployed, she fostered his relationship with Theo as much as she could. When he was on leave, he stayed with them at their apartment and soaked up Dad time.

And then she died and Ollie got involuntarily separated for dependency.

"He's my *grandson*," his mother pressed—just as Theo took a flying leap off the swing.

Ollie's heart climbed into his throat as his kid sailed through the air, flailing his arms wildly like there was no chance the impact with the ground would crush his frail body. "Theo!"

And he landed on his feet with a broad grin and whooped. "Dad, Dad! Did you see—"

Ollie took a deep breath and willed his organs back behind his rib cage. He wasn't going to be the reason his kid was afraid to live his life. Theo was getting stronger every day. It was Ollie who was really fragile, inside rather than out. "I sure did, bud!" He took a few steps away from his mother and kneeled down so he could look Theo in the eye. "I think your cousin did too, though, and she's a little too young to jump off swings, right?"

Theo turned and looked at Mel, who was furiously pumping her legs like she needed to prove she could swing as high as the cousin she'd just met. "I guess?"

Please let this work. "We wouldn't want her to hurt herself, right? But she looks up to you. Do you think maybe you can save the jumping for when it's just us?"

"Okay," Theo agreed without a second thought, and he went right back to the swing without a care in the world.

Ollie was totally getting the hang of this parenting thing. Of course, the fifteen-second interaction left him feeling like he'd run a marathon, but he wasn't going to let on to his mother. He walked back toward her with his hands in his jeans pockets. "Look, Mom. I know you love him and want to spend time with him. But he barely even knows you right now. He's going to need time—*we're* going to need time, together."

It wasn't that Ollie didn't love and trust his parents. He did. But they were so good at projecting what *they* wanted onto people. He was afraid they'd learn Theo was allergic to bees and never let him play outside. He was afraid they'd learn he was smart and decide he should become a doctor. Ollie didn't want Theo to end up like him, so pressured into choosing the path his parents wanted for him that he signed up to shoot people in another country instead. At least that let him feel like he could make a difference, which was all he really wanted.

It hadn't taken long for disillusionment to set in. He was lucky he ended up in aviation. Learning to fly had probably saved his life.

"But where are you going to live? You aren't working right now. Who's going to rent an apartment to you?"

"I'm a veteran, Mom." He had the equivalent of a year's pay as severance, and it wasn't like he'd had a lot of expenses living on base for the past ten years. "I have enough savings to keep us afloat for a few months while I find a job that'll let me spend good quality time with Theo."

And if he moved into his own place, he'd never have to deal with his parents overhearing one of his nightmares, or the *I-told-you-so*s that would follow. Ollie didn't really believe in God, but he was thankful to *someone* out there that Theo was a heavy sleeper.

"But we could watch him for you—"

"I'm sure you will. I'm not saying I'm not going to let you help." He took her hands. "I'm saying you have to let me ask for it. Okay? Theo and I both need to prove that we can do this."

She sighed heavily. "At least let me make you dinner."

Ollie's frustration must've shown on his face, because she quickly added, "*To go*. Okay? I'll make your favorite meatloaf and you can pick it up. And then maybe next week we can eat together at a restaurant somewhere?"

No, Ollie wanted to say, but he knew it wasn't rational. He would need his parents' help. At some point Theo should get to know them. Allison had wanted that for him. And they were going to have to eat dinner anyway. He couldn't keep Theo to himself forever; it wouldn't keep him any safer, and it would only damage his social development.

"I'll pick up dinner," he relented. "Thank you. And I'll think about the restaurant."

"All right," his mother said finally.

Ollie tried not to sigh. They both knew it was only a matter of time before she wore him down.

His mother left the park to start on dinner, and Ollie spent the rest of the afternoon pretending he wasn't freaking out. What was he doing, really? He'd been a full-time parent for four months. He'd left behind the only adult life he'd ever known to be there for his son, and he'd do it again in a heartbeat.

But he'd never had to find an apartment before. Never had to find a job. Fuck, on Monday he had to register Theo for *school*. Could he even do that if they were still living in a motel?

At least most bills these days could be set to autopay so he wouldn't forget and end up with the water turned off or something.

Those thoughts consumed him as he drove to his parents' place to pick up a truly obscene portion of his favorite dinner, crammed into an overloaded Tupperware container, and a plastic picnic cutlery set and some plates, which made him feel stupid. Of course the motel didn't have dinnerware. He'd have to buy that too, unless he'd somehow managed to pack up Allison's when they were leaving her place.

He barely registered the taste of the food as they ate, even though Theo inhaled his like he had a hollow leg. But his motivation became clear when he finished and looked at Ollie with familiar hazel eyes and asked, "Can I watch cartoons now, Dad?"

Ollie had a strict no-TV-while-eating policy. "Sure," he said. "And then it's time for a bath, kiddo."

Theo wrinkled his nose. "Okay."

The distraction gave Ollie time to scroll through local rental listings on his phone. Ideally he'd like to get a little bungalow, something with a yard for Theo to play in, but that meant working out lawn care and maybe gardening, shoveling snow in the winter, that kind of thing. All that would be fine, except he was already going to be cooking and shopping and doing laundry—the trappings of a civilian life he was still getting used to. An apartment made more sense, at least until he had a handle on all the other life crises he had going on. So an upper unit in a duplex, or an apartment or condo, then. Two bedrooms. Close to the school would be good—Ollie wanted to be able to drive Theo in without being late for work.

Whatever work was going to look like.

He filled out a handful of contact applications asking for viewings and then glanced over to check on Theo. Apparently he'd gotten bored with TV, because the cartoons were still playing, but he had dug out *The Lightning Thief* and was curled up against the headboard of his bed, engrossed.

Ollie had a lot of feelings about that particular choice of book, which was about a kid whose mom got turned to stone, and then went to a camp for demigods, where he seemed to be in constant peril. Ollie was worried that the loss of Percy's mother might hit a little close to home, or that Theo might be upset when Percy got his mother back, because Theo couldn't. But Theo's therapist in DC had said that Theo's love of fantasy and ghost stories might not be a bad thing, that working out his feelings through fiction could be helpful, and that Ollie should let Theo take the lead unless problems arose.

Ollie was pretty sure by "problems" she didn't mean "parental overthinking." He should probably get his own therapist.

But that could wait until after he had a job and a place to live.

Ollie let himself browse Indeed for half an hour before he nudged Theo into the bathroom. He left the door cracked open so he could make sure Theo didn't fall asleep in there while Ollie pulled out his laptop to start updating his résumé.

Truthfully, none of the jobs excited him—at least none of the ones he could do and still get to spend every night with his kid. But Ollie didn't have to like his job; he just needed something to pay his bills. He applied for a job at an armored truck company, one in some kind of warehouse, and a real estate reception position. At that point his vision started to swim.

He poked his head into the bathroom. "All right, buddy, are you clean? I think it's time for bed."

Despite having whined about bathtime, Theo had happily splashed water all over the floor and drawn on the tile with his bath crayons. Ollie recognized a sun, some birds, the swing set from earlier in the day, and Theo's latest fixation, a row of headstones. "Can I read one more chapter?"

"Half a chapter, and we read it together." That way Ollie could keep an eye on it. Back when Theo was recovering from chemo, he'd been too weak and tired to hold the books himself. Ollie would never miss seeing him like that, but the ritual of reading to him had taken on its own importance. For ten years he'd had the military to structure his days. He felt unbalanced without a routine.

"Okay," Theo said with the exasperation only an eight-year-old could manage. "But you have to work on your Chiron voice, Dad, it's silly."

Ollie held up the towel for him to step into. "You like my silly voices."

OWNING A CENTURY-old mansion was a lot of work.

With nothing else to fill his weekend, Ty set about making the place habitable. It took him the better part of a day to go through and organize the stuff his dad had piled up all over the house. Most of it was headed straight for Goodwill or the trash, but every few hours he found a keepsake of his mother's that stopped him in his tracks with fresh grief.

But not for his dad.

Sunday the real work began. Ty took down the curtains and rolled up the carpets. He dragged all that to the sun porch at the back of the house so he could have someone pick it up to be cleaned. Then he pulled the cushions off the furniture and stripped the beds—all eight of them. Anything too moth-eaten to use went into a trash bag. The washing machine went nonstop. He deep-cleaned the kitchen and the bathroom closest to his bedroom, then ordered takeout and passed out in front of his laptop after half a beer.

And then it was finally Monday, and Ty had something to *do*. Thank God.

He showered and shaved and dressed in a pair of his blue work pants and a plain T-shirt. He still hadn't done a proper grocery shop, so he ate leftover takeout for breakfast, brushed his teeth, and then drove to the school. Henry had said there would be paperwork to fill out, and in the afternoon he'd have to stop by the police station for a background check—Ty wasn't looking forward to those memories—but since he had an active paramedic certification in another state, they were pretty sure he wasn't a risk to students.

Embarrassingly, it was only seven thirty when Ty stepped into the office at the school. Sure, he had good memories of this place—before his mom died and everything turned to shit—but seven thirty? Ty was turning into a suck-up in his adulting years.

He didn't have long to feel self-conscious about it, because the woman behind the front desk looked up and caught his eye and Ty almost swallowed his tongue. "Holy shit—Peggy?"

"Tyler Morris!"

Ty barely had time to brace himself before five foot two inches of ballistic human hit him in the chest. Peggy hadn't grown much since high school, even if she was now part of running the place.

"You are the last person I expected to see here again," she said when she'd released her death grip on his rib cage. Then she paled and amended, "Oh God, I didn't mean that in an offensive way, just—uh, I remember you swearing you were never going to come back here, so... I guess you're in town for the funeral?" Her face fell. "Shit, I would've gone if I realized—"

"It's good to see you too, Peggy," he interrupted before she could work herself into a froth. Apparently not everyone in town hated him after all. "It's been a long time. Yeah, I'm here for—well, not only the funeral, I guess. I have to sort out a few things." Like his entire life. He cleared his throat. "Uh, I'm actually here because I need to fill out some paperwork so I can help out Coach Tate?"

"Oh, *you're* the one!" She beamed at him even as she shook her head and retreated behind her desk to find the appropriate folder. "When I heard the rumor, I thought it was going to be Ollie Kent."

There was that name again. Ty told himself he wasn't going to be jealous. He cleared his throat. "I've heard that name a few times. Do you know the guy?"

Oh God, was that a *blush* spreading across her cheeks? "Everybody knows Ollie. We actually dated for a hot minute in high school, if you believe that."

"Why wouldn't I believe that?" Peggy was smart and pretty, even if she'd never had the ego to think of herself as one of the popular girls.

Before she could answer, a man in chinos and a polo shirt breezed into the office. "Morning, Peggy." He collected a folder from his mail slot, saluted her with it, and then breezed back out before she could even reply.

Peggy huffed a sigh and briefly looked around as though she was worried someone might overhear. "I don't know. I mean, jock was never really my type, right? Ollie was so sweet, though. I had to give it a shot. It wasn't a bad breakup or anything, just awkward when he came in this morning and I thought the volunteer forms were for him."

Right, of course—Ollie would have to register Theo for school. Apparently he wasn't wasting any time on that if he'd made it here before Ty this morning. Back when Ty attended, this place only hosted grades seven through twelve, but the town had expanded it to include elementary grades. "Maybe give him a little time before you let Coach rope him into extracurricular commitments."

She laughed. "Oh my God. Henry would be over the moon if he managed to wrangle both of you."

Not much chance of that, Ty thought, with Ollie having Theo to look after. "So I just fill this out and then…?"

"Then I imagine Henry will pick you up and put you on a leash and parade you around like a prize-winning Dalmatian." She slid a pen across the counter. "I would love to chat more, but it's about to be bonkers in here. Catch up this weekend, maybe?" She tapped the paperwork. "I can get your number from the forms if you're cool with it."

"That sounds nice. Thanks." Ty saluted with his folder the same way the teacher who'd come in earlier had, and then got out of the way as Peggy's prediction came true and the office became a bustle of activity. He retreated to the detention desk outside the office. Cramming himself into it at six foot two was a lot harder than he remembered.

He'd only gotten as far as the third line on the form when a familiar voice said, "Tyler Morris. Now this sight does take me back."

Ty worked hard to not jump. He raised his head and pasted on a smile. "Principal Gupta." He hadn't realized she was still running this place, or he probably wouldn't have accepted Coach's invitation to return. At the very least, he'd have picked someplace less conspicuous to fill out the paperwork. "Uh. Hi."

"I don't believe the designers of that desk had you in mind when they built it," she went on, as though it wasn't awkward at all to run into the adult version of a kid she'd expelled. "Why don't you come on into my office? I think I have a chair that'll fit you."

He couldn't read her tone, which left him feeling a lot like the sullen teenager he'd been the last time he walked these halls. But she was in charge here, and if he wanted to help Henry out, he had to stay on her good side.

He didn't like the principal's office any better as an adult than he had as a kid, but at least she couldn't kick him out of school this time. Ty settled into a chair and started to cross his arms defensively. Then he caught himself and forced his palms down against his thighs. *So* much better.

"Coffee?" Principal Gupta gestured to a sideboard that hosted a fancy Nespresso machine.

Ty was stunned into answering, "Yes, please," before his brain could engage.

Principal Gupta wouldn't poison him just to keep him from corrupting the baseball team, right?

She made him a mug, carried it over to the desk, slid it in front of him, and then took her own seat. "I was sorry to hear about your father."

I wasn't, Ty thought, and then felt like an asshole. Fortunately some preprogrammed part of his brain answered out loud instead. "Thank you."

"Although your father and I had our share of differences." She sipped her own coffee. "Now I understand you're volunteering to help our hapless team remember which end of the bat they should be holding?"

Oh boy. Ty moved his mug away from his lips. "Uh, it's possible Coach Tate didn't put it in exactly those words."

"He's a sneaky one." She shook her head. "Anyway, we all appreciate it. It's good to have you back around here."

Maybe you shouldn't have sent me away in the first place, Ty thought, but he managed not to say that out loud either. "Thanks."

"Anyway." She smiled. "I've got to go make the morning rounds, but feel free to use my desk to fill out that paperwork, okay?"

Nothing about coming back to this town was going the way he expected.

He finished the paperwork and left it with Peggy at the desk—she was surrounded by a crowd of four adults and two kids—just in time to run into Coach Tate.

"Ty. You're here early." Henry grinned at him. "Paperwork all done? Great. I'll give you the ten-cent tour."

"Did they move the ball diamond?"

"Oh, I'm sorry," said Henry serenely, "did you have somewhere to be?"

And no. No, Ty did not. He straightened his shoulders. "Nah. Lead the way, Coach."

With half an ear, Ty listened as Henry recounted the past sixteen years of the school's history. Not much had changed apart from a few upgrades here and there and some retirements. Ty only recognized a handful of the teachers.

He got to see the teachers' lounge, which was honestly not as exciting as it sounded when he was a kid, just a painted cinderblock room with some old couches and a bunch of desks and a kitchenette, then the health and phys ed office, which was smaller and smelled like feet but had a mini fridge stocked with Gatorade.

"Somehow this is a lot less glamorous than I remembered," Ty commented.

"Maybe you got us mixed up with your fancy school."

There it was again—another reminder that Ty hadn't been good enough sixteen years ago, and he was only good enough now because he was offering free labor. Suddenly he felt like he was going to throw up. Why was he doing this to himself?

Ty fought the urge to push back, but he could feel the words chafing in his throat now. The more he did it, the harder it got to breathe. Soon he'd be choking on them.

Instead of speaking, he grabbed a random textbook off the shelf behind Henry's desk and leafed through it. The tops of the pages were caked with dust. The thing had to be older than Ty was. "You're not still using this to teach, are you?" he asked. The cover had indicated it was some kind of first-aid book. "Because they changed the compressions-to-breaths ratios for CPR."

"Yeah, they covered that one in our professional development training. The one with the active shooter drills."

Jesus. Ty put the book back on the shelf. "You do not get paid enough."

"Don't think any of us got into it for the money." Henry glanced at his watch. "I've got a class this morning. You want to sit in? Otherwise I've gotta go. The kids get real nosy when you're late."

Ty had no idea why—not why Henry asked, and not why he agreed—but he shrugged and said, "Sure. Lead the way."

It turned out to be a gym class of tenth-grade boys. Henry introduced him as "Mr. Morris, who's going to be shadowing me today," and then went right into assigning warm-up exercises. The class ran two laps at a jog, and then Henry selected kids at random and called out a muscle group to have them demonstrate stretches.

"I love a pass/fail mark," he confided to Ty as they stood against the gym wall. "Nice to be able to give everyone perfect on something, even if they have lousy hand-eye coordination." After each kid demonstrated a correct stretch, he put a checkmark next to their name.

"You probably shouldn't brag about that in front of the English teachers."

Henry grinned. "Mum's the word."

After that they didn't get to talk much, with Henry busy directing the kids through the finer points of the rules of basketball. Ty sat on one of the old wooden benches near the wall, observing.

But that grain of sand kept chafing. Henry treated his students fairly, with an even mixture of discipline and good humor. He didn't put up with bad behavior or kids mistreating each other, but he didn't raise his voice unless he needed to make himself heard over the racket in the gym, and he had kind words for everyone.

All those kids… by now some of them must be on their second or third or fourth chances with Henry. Ty remembered what it was like to be a teenage boy—more attitude and hormones than brains. None of these kids had gotten kicked off the baseball team and expelled.

Ty knew he hadn't been an easy teenager, but he wasn't a bad one either. His mother had just died. Why hadn't he gotten another chance?

And could he really do this volunteering thing without clearing it up?

He couldn't. At ten minutes to the bell, Coach dismissed the kids to change and shower, and Ty shoved his hands into his pockets and made himself get up. If he didn't ask now, he'd stew forever.

"Hey, uh, Coach, I gotta ask—why did you… I mean, after everything that happened." Ty huffed, hating himself as much for needing to know as for his inability to get the words out. "You guys kicked me out of school as a kid, but it's okay that I'm back now? You and Principal Gupta are acting like nothing ever happened. Well, mostly." He couldn't have the rug pulled out from under him again.

Henry frowned. "We didn't kick you out of school."

What was he talking about? "Uh, yeah, you did. I think I'd remember. After the chicken fiasco in Gupta's office? I'm not saying I didn't deserve to be punished—"

"Ty. You didn't get kicked out of school." Henry shook his head. "Principal Gupta and I agreed. You were grieving the loss of your mother, so you lashed out. It wasn't appropriate or constructive, but it was certainly understandable. We decided on a three-day in-school suspension, and you'd have to sit out the first baseball game of the season and clean up the mess the chickens left in the office."

Ty blinked as that uncomfortable grain of sand grew heavy and sank into his stomach. "I don't understand. If I wasn't expelled, then why…?"

Why did I have to change schools? This was the only one in town. Changing schools had meant boarding at Northeast Academy. If he hadn't been expelled, then he wouldn't have had to leave. He could have stayed with his friends. He could have visited his mother's grave. Instead—

"Your father thought it would be best if you got a fresh start somewhere else." Ty didn't know if Henry put the sarcasm in his voice on purpose, but he heard *Your dad thought we were all too soft and this was the perfect excuse to get you out of the house for good.* "I didn't know he told you otherwise. I'm sorry."

Of course. Fuck. Ty should've guessed years ago, but he'd never questioned it. He knew he was a pain in the ass. He'd spent half his life fucking around. It had only been a matter of time before the find out part came around.

He just hadn't expected his own father to be the one to hurry that along.

"Right." Ty cleared his throat. "I, ah, I actually think I need some air. I'll come find you at lunchtime?"

The kindness and understanding in Henry's eyes almost undid him. "Sure, Ty. Of course."

Chapter 4

OLLIE LEFT Theo at the tender mercy of Grace, the student helper who'd been assigned to give him a tour of the school, while Ollie went outside to the bleachers to think about his assessment.

"He's reading at a fifth-grade level," the resource teacher had told him earlier, which made perfect sense because Theo had to be pried away from his books with a crowbar and because he'd spent half his life in a hospital bed with nothing better to do than read. "That's wonderful, but he's a year behind the curriculum in math."

Ollie didn't know how much math curriculum an eight-year-old was supposed to know. Was Theo having trouble with adding or long division? But before he could ask, the teacher went on.

"He's young, so there's every possibility he'll adapt quickly and catch up. But he's also been out of school for a long time. Given that and the fact that he's smaller than other kids his own age, it might be worth placing him in second grade instead of third. It would give him more practice at socialization. And there's no reason the other students need to know he's a year older than they are."

The whole thing made Ollie feel like a failure as a parent. Allison would've made Theo do more math. Then Ollie wouldn't have to make this kind of monumental decision.

He hated the idea of Theo being held back, even if that wasn't *really* what this was. Of course he had gaps in his education. He'd been busy fighting for his life. It didn't mean he wasn't smart.

But kids tended to see things in black and white. Ollie didn't want Theo to feel stupid, or like his dad didn't have confidence in him.

He also didn't want his kid to suffer in third grade because he couldn't keep up with the classwork his peers were doing.

The fog of his thoughts must've been pretty thick, because he was already climbing the bleachers before he realized he wasn't alone.

That figure the third row up, along the side near the forty-yard line, looked familiar. Sure enough, as Ollie got closer, he made out the scar along the jawline and the distinctive profile of Ty's nose. He looked just as lost in thought as Ollie was.

That probably meant Ollie should leave him alone, right? Except if Ollie was being honest with himself, *he* didn't particularly want to be alone right now, even though he'd stalked out to his old sulking grounds to have a think. So maybe Ty didn't either.

In the end he split the difference and sat one row down from Ty, a few feet over. When Ty didn't react to his presence, Ollie offered, "Hey."

Ty's head came up so fast Ollie had to believe he'd been so deep in his thoughts he really hadn't noticed Ollie. "Jesus, you scared me. Uh. Hi."

Whoops. "Hi. Sorry about the ambush."

Ty glanced down at the metal floor of the bleachers and then back up again with a crooked half-smile. "Something tells me you didn't mean to sneak up on me. I guess I was just thinking."

"Good spot for it," Ollie commented.

"Yeah. Did all my best thinking out here in high school. Well." The crooked grin widened, but it still didn't reach his eyes. "At least when I could be bothered to think."

Ollie found himself smiling back a little. "You played football too, right? I know I kind of filled your spot on the baseball team."

"Yeah, how dare you," Ty said flatly, like maybe it bothered him. Then his lips quirked back up again. "I played tight end."

"Well, that's all right," Ollie said. "I was quarterback."

Ty snorted. "Of course you were." He tilted his head. "Registering Theo for school today?"

Ollie heaved out a breath, grateful to have an opening, even if it was weird. Ollie wasn't a *let's talk about it* kind of guy by nature. The Army didn't exactly encourage a sharing-is-caring mentality either, so he was extra used to keeping his mouth shut.

But something about Ty made him easy to talk to. Maybe it was like that magazine article Ollie had read while Theo was in his last round of treatment at the hospital. Some study had shown that you were more likely to trust a stranger after you'd done a favor for them, even if it was something simple like passing them a bottle of ketchup at a diner. Ollie figured helping a drunk, hungover, mostly naked guy get to his father's funeral service on time was a lot more effective than handing someone a condiment.

It definitely helped to know that almost no matter what he said, Ty had no room to judge. "Yeah. He's getting his tour right now, while I came out here to have a crisis about what grade to put him in."

"What, they're just going to let you pick?"

"No. Yeah, kind of?" He ran a hand through his hair. "Uh, he missed a lot of school because he had leukemia, so...."

"Jesus." Ty's eyes widened. "Poor kid."

Ollie blew out a breath. "Right?"

"So... picking a grade?" Ty prompted.

"I mean, I don't think they'd let me put him in eighth grade or anything. He's ahead in reading and behind in math. I have to decide if I'm putting him in third grade with the rest of the eight-year-olds or in second so he can catch up."

Ty was quiet for a second and then climbed down to Ollie's row. "Okay. And?"

"And I don't know what to do." Ollie held up his left hand, palm up. "On this side, I don't ever want to be responsible for holding my kid back. I don't ever want him to feel like his dad doesn't believe in him." He flipped over his other hand. "And on this hand, I don't want him to get bullied for being small or not being good at math. I don't want him to struggle. And I don't want him to feel like there's shame in needing more time to learn."

"Wow." Ty whistled under his breath. "That's a lot to consider. What does his mom think?"

"Ah," Ollie hedged, "she's not really around."

"Where is she?"

The answer slipped out before Ollie could stop it. "Arlington."

Ty's eyes went wide and the color drained from his face. "Oh my God. I'm so sorry. That was so insensitive."

"It's okay," Ollie assured him quickly. "I could've been more forthcoming, I can see how that would've led to follow-up questions. Uh, but yeah. She passed four months ago. That's when I got custody. I mean, we were never together, but Theo knew I was his dad. It's just that when

I was deployed, I didn't really have to be a *father*. Allison said he didn't need more than one parent. We just got to do the fun stuff. And now...."

"Now you get to be good cop, bad cop," Ty finished. "Why don't you ask Theo what he wants?"

"I could." Ollie had considered it. "But what if he tells me and I suddenly realize it's not what's best for him? I'd feel like a dick and he'd probably hate me."

"I guess that's a fair point." They sat in silence for a few seconds. Then Ty said, "Okay, feel free to tell me to shut up, because it's not like I have any parenting experience to draw on. But I've met your kid, remember? Not that I had all my faculties at the time, but he had no qualms peppering a total stranger with questions over breakfast while you were there. Speaking as someone who lost their mom as a kid, you're doing a great job. Whatever you decide, Theo will be fine because he has a great dad."

Ollie's throat went tight. "You don't even know me."

"I know you're the kind of dad who's agonizing over the right thing to do for his kid to a total stranger. That counts for a lot."

Now he couldn't help but smile, but he also needed to deflect. Ollie had never gotten the hang of gracefully accepting compliments. "Total stranger, huh? I've seen you mostly naked."

Ty's laugh was a loud, surprised sound that echoed in the stands around them. "Remind me not to tell you about my misspent youth."

"I'm absolutely not going to do that." Something told Ollie those stories would be hilarious. "Anyway. You know about me now. What were you thinking about so loud you didn't hear me coming? If you want to talk about it, that is."

"Just reevaluating some stuff from my childhood." He shook his head. "Turns out *my* dad was an even bigger asshole than I thought. Good times."

"I'm sorry."

Ty smiled again, though it was a little wistful. "It's kind of nice, actually. My dad being more of an asshole means other people weren't when I thought they were. Hence the reevaluating."

Ollie didn't follow all that, but he nodded anyway. "I guess."

In the distance, a bell rang. Ollie watched his own instinctive reaction play out on Ty's frame as his spine straightened and his feet twitched like they were trying to stand up without input from his brain.

Ty quirked his eyebrows. "Old habits die hard." He got up. "I better go before Henry decides I'm too much of a flake to help the baseball team."

Ollie glanced at his watch as though he didn't know exactly what time the lunch bell rang. "I should go too. I have to tell the resource teacher to put Theo in third grade where he belongs. And then I have to look at apartments while he has his first day of school."

They walked back toward the school together. For the first time since Allison died, Ollie felt like he might actually have a handle on this parenting thing.

WHATEVER TY expected from his first baseball practice, this was not it.

"Coach," Ty said seriously. They were standing in the dugout to watch the boys warm up—well out of earshot of any potentially sensitive listeners.

"Mm-hmm," Henry answered.

"That kid doesn't know how to hold a bat."

"Yeah."

"This is *America*."

Henry gave him a sideways glance. "What, are you angling to teach geography next?"

Smartass. "They can't do the beautiful game like this, Henry."

"I'm pretty sure they're within their constitutional rights to be bad at baseball." There was a beat. After a moment Henry said, "Couple years ago the school started a lacrosse program. It's popular. Season runs at the same time as baseball."

"So all the athletic kids went out for that instead," Ty extrapolated. Henry nodded. "So why even *have* a baseball team?"

Henry gave him a look. "This is *America*."

Fine. Ty probably deserved that. He rubbed the back of his neck. "When's the season start?"

"First game is Friday."

So they had four days to teach these kids enough skills that they didn't die of embarrassment. Ty took a deep breath. "Okay, then. We'd better get started."

Ty was good with kids. His team back in Chicago said it was because he was one himself, but really kids were just easy to like, easy to understand and get along with. All you had to do was talk to them, show an interest in things they liked, listen thoughtfully to what they said. Treat them like people.

Teenagers were not like kids. Teenagers were like aliens. Ty did his best, but having been an alien in the past did not prepare him to deal with them now.

Dustin and Butch—who was all of five foot three and maybe a hundred and ten pounds sopping wet; Ty couldn't make this up—were supposed to be practicing fielding grounders, but they could barely be torn away from their conversation about a girl named Lila. Danny was so distracted looking at the clouds he almost got beaned by a pop fly, and only Ty shouting "*Heads up!*" at the top of his lungs saved him from a concussion.

He didn't catch the fly ball either.

And then there was Jeremy, their aspiring catcher, who took one look at the mask and took an actual step backward. "I'm not wearing that."

Somehow Henry managed to answer without pinching the bridge of his nose. One day Ty was going to figure out how he did it. "You are if you want to play. League rules. Sorry."

"Coach." Jeremy lifted the mask by its strap with one finger. "It's giving Hannibal Lecter."

Never mind—now Henry *did* pinch the bridge of his nose. "I'm way too young to feel this damn old."

Ty turned his laugh into a cough that might've fooled the kids but didn't get past Henry, who skewered him with a knowing glare.

By the time practice finished, Ty was reasonably certain the kids at least knew the *rules* of baseball. He was less convinced they would follow them. When the last of the kids' parents left the parking lot, Ty heaved out a breath and asked Henry, "Do high school games have a mercy rule?"

"Nope."

Jesus.

"You want to come over for a beer?"

"Absolutely."

A beer turned out to come with homemade burgers on the grill and a garden salad in every color of the rainbow. Ty kept Henry company while he cooked, and they made small talk about the goings-on around town. It was nice—normal, like what Ty might've done with his coworkers back in Chicago, except none of them had a backyard this big.

"So," Henry said when they'd loaded up the dishwasher and Eliza had excused herself to go watch her guilty pleasure TV show, "this is the part where I admit to ulterior motives."

"I already signed up for free labor." Ty finished off his beer and set it on the table. "Schedule's still wide open." He'd gotten as far as filing for bereavement leave, so at least he'd have a job to go back to when he returned to Chicago… theoretically. Assuming it got approved and could be extended more or less indefinitely.

Henry set down the bottle of beer he'd been nursing all night. Ty wondered if he even liked the taste or if he kept it on hand as a social expectation. "Thing is," he said, "you remember I told you about Margie?"

"The lady with the cryptic pregnancy?" Ty said. "Yeah, Coach, we were just talking about her five minutes ago. My memory's not that short." Besides, cryptic pregnancies fascinated him. All those people who didn't realize they were expecting until all of a sudden they were in labor? So cool. From a medical perspective, anyway. From a personal standpoint, Ty was pretty glad he didn't have the equipment for it. And from a professional standpoint, helping someone deliver a baby they didn't know they were having was kind of a lot.

Henry nodded. "Yeah. So anyway, she's a part-time teacher. Elementary school health."

The past few years had made Ty a little cynical. "Wow, this state allows elementary school health classes?"

That earned him an eye roll. "It's mostly stuff like the importance of stretching before exercise and why we have to eat our vegetables."

Nobody wanted a class full of constipated fourth graders. "I still don't see what any of this has to do with me."

"Seriously?" Henry was looking at him like he'd dropped an easy pop fly. "We've been shy on substitute teachers since the pandemic. Principal Gupta ran your clearance check. You passed, not that anyone's surprised.

We'd like you to sub in for a couple weeks. We're thinking a crash course in first aid could do the kids some good, and you're well qualified."

They wanted him to *what*? "Jesus, Coach. You kept that one close to the chest."

"You gotta know when to hold 'em," Henry quipped. "Principal Gupta thought it'd be better coming from me."

Well, she wasn't wrong about that, but.... "What the hell," Ty muttered. "I only found out I didn't get expelled this morning, Henry."

"Then it's the perfect time to heal your wounds with your old school. Right?"

I don't think that's how therapy works, Ty thought, but... maybe it did. Maybe if he spent a couple hours a day with some rowdy grade-schoolers it would take his mind off the rest of his life. "What the hell," he repeated. "How bad could it be?"

Henry grinned. "That's the spirit."

Chapter 5

OLLIE KNEW intellectually that there was a housing crisis.

But Ollie did not know that by the time he got to the showings he'd booked, the apartments would already be leased.

"Now, I do have another unit in this building coming available next month," his realtor told him placatingly. "Mrs. Hudson in 3B is moving to Boca Raton for her arthritis."

Ollie considered the possibility of living without a kitchen for another four weeks. His intestines rebelled. Ollie liked vegetables. He liked having a digestive system that was not waiting for the dessert portion of an MRE. A month of restaurants and takeout and his mother's dinners would set his gut biome back four months.

Besides, Theo needed nutritious meals.

"I'm looking to get into something a little sooner than that."

Jenna said, "Hmm," and consulted her tablet. "Well, there's a one-bedroom guest cottage available starting next week. I can contact the owner and see if we can get you in for a showing this afternoon."

Ollie had spent most of his adult life in barracks or in on-base housing. He didn't *need* that much privacy. Theo could have the bedroom and Ollie could get a pull-out couch. Maybe it wasn't ideal, but....

"Sure," he said helplessly. "Let's do it."

The "one-bedroom guest cottage" turned out to be a converted one-and-a-half-car garage. It had a bathroom that would've fit in the back seat of Ollie's Honda, a kitchenette slightly less cramped than a pop-up camper's, a living area big enough for a couch and a TV, and a bedroom that would have to be Theo's, because Ollie wouldn't fit.

The front window also faced the driveway, so every time the occupants of the main house started their car, the headlights would shine right into Ollie's sleeping area.

He sighed. "Do you think they'll give me twenty-four hours to decide?"

Maybe he should just suck it up and buy a house. A kid should have a yard to play in, right? But what if they hated it here? What if Theo's cancer came back and they had to move somewhere that had a specialist? And Ollie might have savings, but he didn't have a job yet—who was going to approve him for a mortgage?

No, buying a house was out of the question for now. Ollie shook hands with his realtor and promised he'd call tomorrow with a decision on the cottage.

He was on his way back to the motel—he had an hour before he had to pick up Theo—when his phone rang with an unknown number.

"Hello?"

"Good afternoon. Is this Ollie Kent?"

"Speaking."

"Mr. Kent, this is Rosa calling from Secure Logistics. We've received your application for the guard position. Are you available to come in for an interview?"

He barely avoided sagging with relief. "I'd love to. What time were you thinking?"

"Well, are you available now?"

The interview went significantly better than the apartment hunt. It turned out to be mostly a formality; Ollie was trained in military operations and firearms use, so he was overqualified to babysit bank pickups. The company only operated during daylight hours, which meant he only had to find a couple hours' worth of childcare for Theo, and the school had a latchkey kids program. Ollie just had to wait for his police clearance to come through and he could start job training tomorrow.

For the first time in months, some of the tension between his shoulder blades unknotted. Theo was in school. Ollie had a job. They had a line on a place to live. It wasn't *perfect*, but it was all they needed for now. Maybe the owners would agree to a six-month lease and he could spend the meantime looking for something more appropriate.

His improved outlook lasted through picking up his kid ("Dad! We learned about *tadpoles*! Did you know some frogs can lay ten thousand eggs a day?"), celebratory dinner at the town's most upscale restaurant (an off-brand Applebee's), a night's sleep (blissfully without PTSD nightmares, possibly because the motel mattress was so awful Ollie couldn't sleep deeply enough to dream), and dropping Theo back at school the next morning.

He went back to the motel and spent another half an hour looking through rental listings. If anything, the offerings depressed him more than they had two days ago.

But he couldn't make himself pick up the phone to call Jenna until he'd done one last drive-by evaluation of the place.

The guest cottage was in a good neighborhood, close enough to the school that Ollie could even walk him in the morning, if he wanted to, and still get to work in plenty of time. It was situated on a boulevard lined with mature oaks. Ollie could just imagine what it would look like in summer when a broad, leafy canopy covered everything. A well-maintained sidewalk boasted chalk art from neighborhood kids—another great sign for Theo.

But as Ollie approached the block the guest cottage was on, his heart sank.

There was a firetruck parked on one side of the street, and dark smoke billowed into the sky.

Ollie pulled the Honda to the side of the road and parked a few houses down.

A crowd had gathered on the sidewalk, several retirees and one young mom with a toddler on her hip. Ollie put his hands in his pockets and leaned in to eavesdrop.

"—not rented yet, thank *God*—"

"What do you think happened?"

The sound of splintering wood split the morning. A cloud of dust and ash went up.

"And that, ladies and gentlemen," said one of the firefighters, "is why you don't do your own electrical work. Leave that stuff to the professionals."

Ollie felt sick. If he'd been a little more desperate, he and Theo could've been in that house.

That settled it. He needed to raise his standards, even if it meant another few miserable weeks at the motel. The alternative was moving in with his parents, and Ollie could not do that.

Looked like the motel was home sweet home for now.

TY'S TWO classes shadowing Henry had not prepared him for the second graders.

This was likely because Henry only taught high school classes, and he knew that if he subjected Ty to seven-year-olds first thing he would flee for the hills.

Ty liked kids, he reminded himself.

Okay, well, Ty liked tigers too, but he wasn't going to lock himself in a room with twenty of them for forty minutes.

He did have an educational assistant in each class, which helped immeasurably. This one's name was Miss Tina, and she knew all the kids' names and the fastest way to get them to listen.

"I also have their IEPs and medical needs memorized," she assured him at two minutes to the bell. "Two peanut allergies in this group, one with epilepsy."

"Wow. Kinda glad I'm a paramedic." Though at the moment a little anaphylactic shock might be easier to handle than keeping the kids' attention for the whole period.

Ty didn't have a textbook for teaching first aid to kids. Hell, if one didn't exist, maybe he should write one. But he certainly wasn't going to have time for that in the next couple of weeks, because it immediately became apparent that he would need all his energy to keep up with the kids… and he only had to teach three periods a day.

Fortunately Ty *did* have a well-developed projecting voice, as well as a lot of firsthand experience keeping a cool head. "Good morning, second grade! My name is Mr. M"—like hell were the kids going to call him by his father's name—"and I'll be your health teacher for the next couple of weeks while your regular teacher is out."

Tina had warned him about the likely influx of questions, and he fielded them for a few minutes because it would be unproductive not to.

And then they got down to the brass tacks of child-appropriate first aid, beginning with the obvious—a primer on when and how to call 911.

Which, naturally, began with a primer on when and why *not* to call 911.

"Okay, so, who in this room has been hurt before?"

Every hand went up.

"What are some of the ways you've gotten hurt? Um… Sarah?" He glanced at Tina for confirmation; she gave him a miniscule nod.

Sarah put her hand down. "I fell off my bike."

"That must have hurt. Did you get injured?"

She nodded. "I scraped my knee. And my hands!"

Ty called on a couple other kids to share their tales of woe. Connor's dog had stepped on his foot. Monique pinched her finger twisting the chains on a swing set. Ty thought the days of that kind of injury were behind them; hadn't everyone switched to rubber-coated chains by now?

"Let's see a show of hands—who thinks Connor should have called 911?" No hands went up. "What about Monique?" Two hands. "Sarah?" Three hands.

God, he hoped they didn't really think that, but he guessed it was his job to straighten them out. "Let's try something else. When *should* you call 911 if someone is hurt?"

Connor's hand went up. "If you break your leg!"

"Good," Ty said. "That's right, if you think you broke a bone, you should call 911. What else?"

"If there's a car accident!"

"If you get bit by a rattlesnake!"

"If you get attacked by a grizzly bear!"

This predictably led to a whole lot more animal-themed disasters. Ty gave up trying to diversify their answers and tried another tactic. "Okay, that's good—lots of good brainstorming there. Now let's talk about why you shouldn't call 911 if it's not an emergency. Can anyone give me a reason?"

Bless Connor, who had his hand up again. Ty waited to see if any other volunteers appeared, but apparently Connor was the only one brave enough to hazard a guess. Or else he just liked talking. "Okay, Connor?"

"Um, one time, when my grandma was at my house, um, my dog peed on her shoes!"

Oh no. This kid was karmic payback. Ty had *been* that kid. He fought the urge to facepalm. "I think we're getting a little off topic. Anyone else? Monique?"

She put her hand down. "'Cause you'll get in trouble?"

Not what Ty was going for, but definitely a primary concern for a seven-year-old. "That's true. If you call 911 and it's not an emergency, you might get in trouble. Can anyone tell me why?"

No takers. Ty elaborated. "What would happen if I called 911 because I scraped my knee and they sent me an ambulance, but then Miss Tina got in a car accident?"

That finally prompted them down the right track, and Ty spent the remaining ten minutes of class (how had so much time passed going over so little material?) giving an introduction on what to say to a 911 dispatcher when you did get through.

The kids were all still riveted to their seats when the bell went.

Miss Tina smiled at him as she herded them out the door toward their next class. "Not bad, new guy. I'm impressed."

"I'm exhausted," Ty said. "I have to do this two more times?"

"Don't worry. I think your next class is fourth grade."

"Teachers definitely do not get paid enough."

The fourth graders got through the 911 talk in ten minutes. Normally that would've been great, but in this case it left him scrambling. Obviously he needed to rethink his lesson plan on the fly a little. Or, like, actually make one.

"Why don't we try some role-play?" the class's EA, Josh, suggested.

Ty shot him a horrified look, thinking *What the fuck, they're nine*, and then Josh went on, "Mr. M will be the 911 operator, and… who can think of an emergency?"

Oh. That kind of role-play.

Every kid's hand went up. Ty went through three demonstrations, and when the kids had gotten the hang of giving their names and locations and details of their made-up injuries (or the made-up injuries of their friends), Ty let them split up into pairs to keep practicing until the class ended.

"I don't know if I'm cut out for this," he told Henry in the teachers' lounge at lunch. "There's a reason people go to college to learn how to be a teacher."

"Tina and Josh said you did fine. Relax," Henry soothed. "It's just another day in paradise."

Ty eyed the couch and wondered if it would be empty enough next period for him to have a nap. He had prep for the next two periods, meaning he could recover… or spend time figuring out how he was going to expand his material for the sixth-grade class he'd have after that.

Maybe he could wrangle both?

The sixth graders turned out to be his least favorite. They didn't respect his authority, they didn't raise their hands, they talked back, they whispered and giggled. One of them, a redheaded girl with smattering of freckles across the bridge of her nose, threw a paper ball at his head. Ty caught it one-handed and redirected it into the recycling bin next to his desk.

"Did you even go to school to be a teacher?" one of the boys in the third row asked.

"No. A fact for which I'm currently very glad." That earned him a few laughs. Maybe this class needed a different approach. "I went to school to be a paramedic."

The kid's eyes lit up. "Whoa! So you've treated people in car accidents and stuff?"

"And stuff," Ty confirmed.

Another kid leaned forward. "Did you ever see anyone die?"

And suddenly they were so fucking young. Jesus. Ty had been that young once. "Yeah," he said. He let the words come out as heavy as they wanted to. "Some of them were younger than you."

Finally the class went silent. The EA looked like she didn't know what to do.

Ty sat on the corner of his desk and resisted the urge to massage his temples. "Look. I can't teach you how to be a paramedic in six weeks. There's just too much to know, and the school board would probably try to put me in jail for traumatizing you. But I can teach you enough about first aid that if you get hurt, or your friends get hurt, or your family member gets hurt, and there's no one else around to help you, you can give them the best possible chance of a full recovery. I can teach you how to help someone stay alive until the professionals get there. But only if you let me."

The redhead and the third-row boy exchanged glances.

The girl nodded.

"Okay," the boy said. "Where do we start?"

TUESDAY NIGHT after baseball practice, Ty did not get invited to beer and dinner.

"It's date night," Henry explained as they walked toward the parking lot. "We get our favorite takeout and watch trashy TV."

He said it like he couldn't wait for that kind of domestic night in. Ty's heart panged in his chest. It sounded amazing.

When was the last time he had a night like that? Before Myra moved away, definitely. Even then, they'd both had busy schedules, both on shift work that didn't always line up. Sometimes they only managed to have breakfast together as one of them was coming off shift and the other one was going on, but those moments felt all the more precious because of it.

But there was no point trying to date now, he thought as he waved goodbye to Henry and folded himself into the driver's seat of his truck. Ty knew himself pretty well. He was an overcommitter. Case in point: He'd signed up to help coach baseball and ended up teaching elementary school. He could not date casually, which meant he couldn't date. He would stay in town until he got as much of his father's affairs settled as he could, and then he would go back to Chicago, where he belonged, where his team needed him. Where he could save lives.

But God, the idea of going home to an empty house—an empty house he *hated*—for the next few months made him feel like he was going to suffocate. He rolled down the truck window and closed his eyes to feel the breeze on his face.

He was just telling himself to get over it when a familiar Honda pulled into the parking lot next to him and Ollie Kent got out of it.

Ty took him in, head to toe, and somehow managed not to say *Hey, rent-a-cop* out loud. But that took all his restraint, which was probably why the next thing out of his mouth was "New job?"

Truth told, Ollie didn't look a lot better than Ty felt. Ty didn't know if that was because the mushroom gray of his uniform was sucking the color out of him or if he'd had a day like Ty had. Maybe worse.

Ollie didn't bother trying to smile. "Gotta make a living, I guess. How was baseball practice?"

"You wanna replace me again?" Surely Ollie knew he'd filled Ty's role on the team when Ty changed schools. "I don't think this team's bound for the championship. Although on the plus side, none of the batters hit themselves with the ball this time."

Ollie actually laughed, and color returned to his face. "I think this is the first time I'm realizing how different it's going to be not having my kid around all the time."

"Lot of changes going around." Ty drummed his fingers on the steering wheel as a sudden thought occurred to him. "Hey, do you and Theo have plans for dinner tonight?"

OLLIE NEVER expected to be invited back to the Morris mansion, but Ty pointed out that he owed Ollie a meal, at the very least, after Ollie had helped him make it to his father's funeral without reeking of booze. Ollie had spent all day in a tin box that felt a little too much like other tin boxes he'd been in, and the idea of facing a meal in public made him want to crawl out of his skin. If he dissociated in Ty's kitchen, at least Theo would have someone to talk to.

"What's for dinner?" he asked in the parking lot.

Ty's cheeks flushed a surprisingly dark pink. "Uh. I actually have no idea what I was going to make. Why don't we ask Theo what he wants, and we can all go shopping?"

Ollie didn't know how he ended up agreeing to that, but somehow it wasn't that bad, trailing his kid and Ty through the local supermarket as they picked up ingredients for a baked pasta—"with homemade sauce," Ty promised—and fresh fruit and ice cream for dessert.

Theo kept up a steady stream of informational chatter about his first full day of third grade, which included even more frog facts and a play-by-play of every joke his new friend Hassan had told. Ollie didn't get all of them and wasn't sure if that was because he wasn't eight years old, because Theo had mangled the punch lines, or because Ollie was just in the wrong headspace to pay attention. Still, he didn't get lost at the grocery store, nobody interrupted Theo to thank Ollie for his service, and the ride in the Honda to the Morris estate was comfortable.

And then Ty was letting them in the front door to his ridiculous house... which looked nothing like the last time Ollie had been there despite the fact that the only thing he could pick out as different was the lack of curtains. Now the front room was filled with afternoon sunlight.

"Wow," Ollie said. "You undecorated."

"Yeah, the Addams Family vibes are cool but not really the way I want to live my life." Ty had taken a few doors off their hinges too, so now they could all go right through to the kitchen. He hefted the paper bag of groceries onto the island counter and then turned around to face Theo. "Okay, buddy, I'm going to get started cooking, but first, do you want to be my sous chef, or do you want to see the games room?"

Theo's eyes went wide. "You have a *games room*?"

"Do I have a games room." Ty shook his head and popped the ice cream into the freezer. "Every creepy mansion has a games room. I'll show you."

Bemused, Ollie followed them on a brief tour down a hallway with actual painted portraits, where Ty pointed out a likeness of his great-aunt

Clementine—"Dad said the song was written about her, but the old man was full of sh—uh, nonsense." Then Ty led them to a broad enclosed sunroom at the back of the house.

"Not what I expected," Ollie admitted.

"Yeah, you thought upscale billiards and snooker, right?"

"This is the *coolest*," Theo said.

Ollie had to admit it was pretty cool. The windows offered a panoramic view of the gardens, which were currently overgrown but in a kind of endearing way. There were beat-up sofas against one wall, interspersed with ancient arcade games like pinball and *Pac-Man*. A bookshelf crammed with books and board games stood in one corner next to a poker table that would seat eight. Instead of a pool table, there was Ping-Pong.

"Dad, Dad, can I play pinball?"

Ollie looked at Ty, who raised his eyebrows as if to say, *What, you thought I'd ask your kid if he wanted to look but not play?* Which was a fair point. "Sure. Just holler if you get lost on your way back from the bathroom, okay? I'm gonna help Ty in the kitchen."

Translation: He was going to hide from arcade-game noises.

"Okay."

Ollie followed Ty back down the hallway.

"Thanks again for inviting us," Ollie said when they returned to the kitchen. "You really didn't have to."

"Look, I'm gonna admit up front my motives aren't purely selfless." He took down a cutting board, pulled a knife from a block, and started to chop onions. "I definitely owed you one. But also…." He set down the knife and gestured around him. "I hate rattling around in this place by myself."

"I get it." It had taken Ollie a while to adjust to living in Allison's apartment in DC and not on base. Sometimes it got so quiet it seemed like the rest of the world had stopped existing, and it freaked him out. He had to open the window so he could hear traffic in the distance. "Uh, can I help with anything?"

Ty hummed noncommittally. "You drink wine?"

Ollie preferred beer, but he wouldn't say no. "Sure."

He uncorked a bottle of red and took out a heavy saucepan, which he doused liberally in olive oil and slid onto the stove. "It's not my beverage of choice, but I need some for the sauce anyway, so…." He took down two glasses and poured generously.

Then he looked up, and Ollie met suddenly serious blue eyes as Ty handed his glass over. "Uh, feel free to tell me if I'm overstepping here, but… you look like you could use a drink. And I'll add the asterisk 'but alcohol is a shitty coping mechanism' because I'm a medical professional and I'm an atheist, so I'm not worried about God smiting me for being a hypocrite."

Snorting, Ollie took the glass. He didn't know much about wine, but this one smelled good. "You're not wrong on either count. I'll stick to the one glass anyway, since I'm driving." And in charge of a kid.

Ty nodded and went back to his chopping—tomatoes this time, then garlic, which he smashed with the flat of the knife. "You can talk about it if you want," he offered, like that was a totally normal thing to say to someone.

But that wasn't the weird part. The weird part was when Ollie said back, "I spent the day crammed into an armored truck, so worried I was going to have a flashback that I tensed every muscle in my body."

He hadn't even tasted the wine yet. The VA should move their shrink headquarters into Ty's kitchen.

For a second he worried he'd fucked it up, that Ty was going to get all sympathetic and ask too many follow-up questions until he ended up chasing Ollie out of the house. But Ty just said, "That sucks. I wonder if the old man kept the Jacuzzi heated," and then turned around and scraped the onions into the saucepan.

Ollie blinked.

Ty didn't turn away from the stove.

Ollie sipped the wine. He was right, it was good, but it certainly wasn't strong enough to explain why he opened his mouth again after he swallowed it. "They're making me carry a gun, which I get is the point of being an armored guard, but I kind of hate it. I've shot enough people. Money seems like a stupid reason to do it again."

As acknowledgment, he got a "hmm," and then Ty pulled out another frying pan and decanted a pound and a half of Italian sausage meat from its butcher paper. "So you don't keep a gun at home?"

Ollie felt like he'd slipped into the Twilight Zone. "I have PTSD and an eight-year-old, so no."

"Okay, good. Guns are a deal-breaker for me."

A deal-breaker for what? Was this some kind of very strange first date? Ollie would've known if he were being asked on a date, right?

Right?

"I've seen too many gunshot patients," Ty elaborated. The garlic went in with the onions. Suddenly Ollie was starving, bizarre conversation notwithstanding. "Especially young ones. I mean, one would've been too many, you know? It's good that you're smart about it. And open."

I'm really not. You're just kind of a human barbiturate. Finally Ollie said, "Is something on your mind, Ty?" because he was going to get a headache if he didn't figure out which direction this conversation was going.

Yet another cooking vessel emerged from the cupboard, this one a deep pot. Ty filled it from one of those fancy pot-filler taps that Ollie had always secretly wanted in his kitchen one day, even though he didn't cook. "I'm getting there, okay?"

Ollie took another sip of wine and figured he might as well relax on the barstool. "Okay."

"Since we're sharing and everything…." Ty dumped the sausage into the hot pan and Ollie's stomach growled over the sizzle of cooking meat. "I told you I'm stuck here, right? Do not pass go, do not collect two hundred dollars. Until I can sell this house, which won't be for a while. Because my oh-so-well-prepared father didn't put it on a transfer-on-death deed, I'm stuck living in it. I have to wait and make sure there are no creditors, which includes, like, the government. I hope the old man kept up the property taxes."

Ollie didn't even want to think about the property taxes on a house like this. "Me too."

"I have an appointment with my lawyer and my dad's accountant on Saturday." He stabbed at the sausage to break it into smaller pieces. "There's enough money in the accounts I *can* touch to hire the best professionals to do most of the work, but it's going to suck anyway." Ty threw back half his glass of wine.

None of that made the eventual destination of this conversation any clearer, but Ollie decided to go with the flow. Ty was providing food and wine. Ollie could listen to him ramble. "You didn't have a good relationship with your dad."

With a soft huff, Ty scraped the tomatoes into the onion pan. "What gave it away?"

"Can I ask why?"

He froze, shoulders tensed; then he turned around and sat across from Ollie at the island. "It's an ugly story."

"I've heard a few of those." *I told you my kid's mom died.*

Ty spun his wineglass in his hands and peered into its depths. "My mom found out she had breast cancer when she was pregnant with me."

Oh. "Fuck," Ollie said. Cancer had almost taken his kid—it still could. He couldn't imagine having to choose to save his partner or his child.

Ty quirked a sad smile. "Swear jar." He shrugged. "Dad wanted her to terminate so she could do cancer treatment, said they could try again after she recovered. Mom wasn't having it. She wanted to carry to term, so she did. Had me and went right into chemo followed by a double mastectomy, radical hysterectomy, reconstructive surgery…."

"So she beat it?" Ollie asked.

"She and Dad thought so. But then when I was eight, doctors found something suspicious on one of her lymph nodes. She fought it for years, but eventually it spread too far. She died when I was sixteen." A thump as one of Ty's feet slipped off the stool and smacked the side of the island. "Dad didn't make it a secret that he thought it was my fault. If Mom had aborted me like he wanted, the cancer wouldn't have gotten as strong of a foothold."

The way he said that, it sounded like Ty believed it too. "There's no way to know that."

"My dad thought he knew everything." He got up again and dumped the pasta into the now-boiling pot, stirred the sauce to break down the tomatoes, and poked again at the sausage. "He blamed me, I acted out like any kid whose mom had died, and he sent me off to boarding school rather than deal with me. The end."

"No wonder you hate this place."

Ty sighed as he rattled through the spice jars, picking certain ones up seemingly at random and sniffing them, then shrugging and replacing them or adding them to the pot. "Not all of it. I like the kitchen—my mom and I used to cook together. And the games room. She started working on it when the cancer came back so she'd have a cheerful place to rest and look at the garden, even if she didn't have the energy to weed it herself. We spent a lot of time there. But when the house is empty, it just makes me think of all the nights I was here alone with my dad when my mom was in the hospital for treatment."

Finally Ollie saw what he was getting at. Should he wait to make sure he was right? It seemed like Ty was having a hard time asking for what he wanted. Ollie didn't want to make the wrong assumption and come across as entitled, or like he was trying to take advantage.

Ty didn't return to the island. His shoulders were pulled in as he stirred the pasta sauce, which now smelled better than any Italian restaurant Ollie had ever been to.

When fifteen seconds had gone by, Ollie tapped his fingers against the counter. "This morning I drove by a place I was thinking about renting, and it was literally on fire."

"Jesus." Ty barked out a laugh and finally turned around. His cheeks were pink from the heat of the stove, and the faraway expression was gone, replaced by something rueful and amused. "Thanks for the opening. You want to move in?"

A sane person would say no. But a sane person wouldn't have wandered into Ty's house that first morning and made him breakfast, and a sane person would not get to partake in whatever glory was going to come out of this kitchen in another forty minutes or so. Ty was already cleared to be around children, and he'd trained as a paramedic. So if Theo had an allergic reaction or Ollie put his fist through a wall, they were in good hands.

Ollie cleared his throat. "Let me just talk to my kid."

Chapter 6

TY TRIED not to overthink things while Ollie went to the games room to talk to Theo. Instead he focused on the sauce. It needed another five minutes, maybe, before the tomatoes broke down to his satisfaction and started to get sweet. Meanwhile, he washed and chopped the fresh basil, took the sausage off the heat, and shredded the cheese.

Theo would want to move in, right? He loved the house when he first got here. Ty would give him the fancy globe he liked so much. Hell, he could have the games room for his bedroom if he wanted… as long as he was willing to let Ty play pinball after school.

Okay, no, he couldn't sleep in the games room.

But this was a perfect solution, he told himself as he spooned the sausage into the sauce. Ollie and Theo would have a place to live, and Ty wouldn't have to be alone. Hell, if Theo had enough toys to scatter around, it wouldn't look anything like the place where Ty had grown up.

He'd drained the pasta and mixed it and the sauce into the casserole dish along with the cheese by the time Ollie returned to the kitchen.

And honestly, now was not the time for Ty to have second thoughts, but he maybe should have considered the fact that Ollie was the kind of man who could look edible in a security guard uniform.

Oops.

Ollie slid back into his seat at the island. "I have conditions."

Ty forgot he ever had a single reservation. He slid the dish into the oven and picked up his wineglass again. "Hit me."

"I haven't had a roommate in a while. I want to make sure we're on the same page."

Ty rummaged in the junk drawer until he produced a pen and a pad of paper. He wrote *Ground Rules* at the top.

Ollie snorted. "I didn't mean literally, but sure, that works. Okay, so rent—"

Oh God, this was going to suck.

He cut himself off midword at the sight of whatever Ty's face was doing. "Wow, that bad?"

Ty groaned and put down the pen so he could scrub his face. "No. Maybe? Let's call the issue of rent 'logistically complicated.'"

When he pulled his hands away from his eyes, Ollie had his brows raised.

"I am living in an income tax nightmare," Ty explained, "and I don't want to make it worse." His dad had died, and Ty was probably going to have to file his income taxes at least twice if not three or four times.

He should've let the hate group take the money.

"Ah." Ollie considered this for a moment. "Utilities?"

"Fifty-fifty," Ty offered.

"Done." Ty wrote it down. "House and yardwork? Do we want to share meals? I'm not much of a cook, but I don't mind it."

Ty tapped the pen against the notepad. "How do you feel about riding lawn mowers? Because pretty soon the grass is going to start growing and there is… a lot of it."

"How much is a lot?"

"Five acres, I think. But only one of them gets cut."

"So you're thinking you do most of the cooking, I do most of the mowing?"

"Works for me if it works for you. And we can sub out as needed."

Ollie nodded, his lips pursed as though in thought. "Okay, what about if my kid starts to drive you crazy?"

"I'll go elsewhere?" What a silly question. "I'm a big boy. I'm perfectly capable of running away. Either in my truck or elsewhere on the aforementioned five acres."

"I meant—you can tell me if he's bugging you, you know? And I'll deal with it. You don't have to. He's not your responsibility just because he also lives here, but…." He blew out a breath. "I don't know, I don't want you yelling at him either."

Ty didn't mean to get stuck on that, but he did. "Huh."

Ollie's pretty eyes went the tiniest bit flinty. "Problem?"

"Oh God, no." Ty shook his head, smiling a little. "It just occurred to me that you might be the first good father ever to live in this house. But seriously, I like kids. I didn't volunteer to help coach the baseball team because I think I'll enjoy watching them lose."

Laughing, Ollie leaned back on his stool. "I take it they're, uh, not very good this year?"

"I asked Coach Tate about a mercy rule."

"Oh man." Ollie reached for his wineglass. "I was thinking about taking Theo to the game this week, but I don't want to traumatize him. Maybe we'd better skip."

"Try the lacrosse team instead," Ty advised wryly. "I hear they're good."

Ollie grinned. "Noted."

"Speaking of Theo, do either of you have any allergies or medical conditions I need to know about?"

"Aside from recent chemo recovery and PTSD?" He tilted his head. "Theo's allergic to bee and wasp stings. He has an EpiPen. Three, actually—one he has with him all the time, one we keep at home for backup, and one at the school office."

Ty made a mental note. Jesus, the poor kid—as if he didn't have enough to worry about. And Ollie had to be living in perpetual fear. But maybe living with a paramedic would help with some of the anxiety. "It's a big house. We should have an extra extra, maybe, when we figure out where the best place to keep a second one is."

Shit—that had just come out, the automatic thought of someone who'd been a paramedic for four years. He hoped Ollie didn't think he was overstepping.

But Ollie's expression didn't hold a hint of offense. Instead his amber gaze had gone thoughtful, and he was tilting his head like he was reevaluating something. Ty felt his ears start to heat up under the weight of it; it made him want to squirm. "That... actually a really great idea. Thanks."

"Uh, no problem." *Deflect, deflect, deflect.* "What about you, though? Anything I need to know about the PTSD? I know it's not always predictable, but if you know you have certain triggers...?"

Perfect deflection—Ollie broke the gaze and glanced down at the countertop. Ty felt simultaneously relieved and disgusted with himself. "I keep it together pretty well when I'm awake. Some days are better than others. Hot, loud days are the worst, but out here in the middle of nowhere, I should be okay."

Four years as a paramedic had made Ty pretty good at hearing the details people didn't say out loud. "And when you're not awake?"

He winced. "The nightmares can get pretty intense. I've been lucky so far—nothing too bad with Theo in the room with me. He has this kind of wheezy snore when he sleeps, so when I wake up from one and I can hear that… it helps."

"Okay. It's a big house, so you can pick rooms that are close together if that's easier for you, or far apart if you want to be able to, uh, wake up screaming from a nightmare without ruining your kid's sleep schedule." Maybe he should let Ollie pick *two* bedrooms. It wasn't like Ty was going to use all of them.

"You're surprisingly chill about this."

"Yeah, well." Ty gave a half-smile. "I might never have been in a combat zone, but I've had my share of nightmares after bad calls." Especially in his first year on the job, when the pandemic had just started and everyone was either terrified or defiant. "If I'm around when you're having a flashback or a nightmare, what's the best way for me to deal with it?"

Ollie was already shaking his head. "Ty, no. It's not for you to deal with, all right? I can handle myself." And then his face got a pinched look, and he closed his eyes and added, "Just—if you can keep Theo distracted, keep me away from him. I don't want him to see me like that."

From the defeat in his voice, it had cost him a lot to ask for that. "Hey, no, Ollie, I wouldn't have asked if I minded, okay? There's a reason I became a paramedic. I'm not, like, trying to play hero or anything. It's just, if I can help, I can't… *not* help."

The tension of the moment broke. Ollie's lips twitched.

"Oh my God, shut up. You know what I mean." Ty rolled his eyes. "If you're going to live here, we're going to be *friends*. And friends don't let friends suffer if they can help it. So tell me what to do."

Ollie snorted. "Bold of you to assume I know what works."

Right. He probably hadn't had anyone around to help him. Ty could do some internet research and trial and error and figure out what worked. For the time being, *stay out of punching range* seemed like a good place to start.

"Anyway," Ollie said, "we kind of skipped the part about your rules. It's your house."

"Unfortunately," Ty agreed. "It's kind of a lot, as you've noticed. The whole second floor is locked, mostly because I don't want to pay to heat it. It's not like I need the space. But it's probably best if nobody goes up there in case there are racoons living in the walls or something." He wondered if he could get the house condemned if there were and skip the whole bit where he had to live here.

"Racoons?" Ollie teased. "Not bats?"

"Don't be ridiculous. We don't have a belfry."

"What even is a belfry, anyway?"

"No idea. I always assumed it was, like, a bell tower kind of thing. Now that I think about it, it's kind of surprising we don't have one. My dad was definitely the type." A big ostentatious tower with a big loud bell in it he could ring so everyone in town knew how important he was. "Anyway, we'll do a full walk-through on the weekend, maybe, because you'll have a better sense of where you don't want Theo going than I do. The regular garage is probably okay, but the pole barn with the gardening and landscape equipment is probably a supervision-only zone for an eight-year-old." Maybe he could incorporate a segment on Household Goods to Leave Alone in his first-aid class.

"Makes sense. I guess that just leaves, uh…."

Was Ollie blushing? Or was it the wine? "Yes?"

Nope—his cheeks went pinker. Definitely blushing. *Fascinating.* Ty figured the Army would've drilled that out of him in basic training. "I think we should have a protocol for if you're going to have adult company."

What? Then the penny dropped. "Oh my God, Ollie, you can say 'sex.'"

He groaned. "Sometimes I forget Theo isn't listening to everything I say."

Yeah, Ty could see how that could happen. "I mean, I'm definitely going to make fun of you for that, but what are we worried about, here? I'm not going to sexile you and your kid."

"So the sex dungeon is soundproof?"

Ty shuddered. "Ollie, please. This was my parents' house." And Ty didn't need to be thinking about Ollie and sex dungeons either.

"I just mean, uh…. God, I'm not a prude, I just don't want to answer any of Theo's questions about why there's a strange half-naked woman in the kitchen at seven in the morning."

"Now who's assuming?" When the question didn't seem to register a reaction, Ty added, "It's just as likely to be a half-naked man." If he had to rescind the offer because Ollie turned out to be homophobic, that would suck, but better to know now.

The only reaction he got was an eye roll. "Whatever. Look, I'm not trying to cramp your style. But I have a kid to think about. There's nothing wrong with casual sex—"

"Casual adult company," Ty interrupted, unable to help himself.

"—but I don't know if I'm comfortable with strangers around my kid, potentially unsupervised."

"No, I get it," Ty assured him. "You don't have to worry, though. I am really bad at casual adult company." Wait a second, that made it sound like Ty was bad in bed.

"I'm never going to live that down, am I?"

"Sorry, Grandma, but I will be mocking you for life. Seriously, though, I was kind of wild when I was younger, and it tanked my self-worth. If I'm sleeping with someone, it's serious enough for you to internet stalk them before you have to worry about Theo meeting them."

Not that Ollie would have to worry about that, since Ty didn't intend to date anyone here when he'd be leaving town as soon as he could.

It did beg the question, though—

"What about you?"

"What, my sense of self-worth?"

"What if you want to get laid, smartass?"

"Then I'll hire a babysitter and go out."

Well… duh. It made sense he'd have to go elsewhere since Theo would be here and that would not be conducive to a casual adult good time. "Good point."

"So is there anything else? You have a rule about which side of the driveway you want me to park on or which days we can drink orange juice out of the carton?"

"You can park in the garage. There'll be so much room once I move all Dad's precious babies into the yard." If he had to live here, at least he'd have the pleasure of watching the luxury car collection slowly rust. He was going to put his father's favorite antique under the mulberry tree to get crapped on for eternity. "And everyone knows that's allowed any day the carton is almost empty as long as you finish it off."

Ollie laughed. "I think I can agree to those terms."

"Okay, then." Ty stuck out his hand. "You got yourself a roommate."

Ollie shook. He was a good three inches shorter than Ty, but his hands were just as big. "You got two."

OLLIE HAD the impression Ty would've been fine with them moving in that night, but he didn't have the energy after stuffing himself with delicious baked pasta, even if Theo fell asleep at the kitchen table during dessert. Ollie bundled his kid into the car and took him back to the motel. Then he had a two-minute shower and collapsed into bed.

After the day he'd had, he expected to wake up sweating from a nightmare of being shelled in a Humvee. Instead he dreamed about driving the armored truck through the halls of Ty's mansion, Theo in the passenger seat next to him as they called out Ty's name. Ollie didn't put a lot of stock in dreams—he knew they were really the brain's way of organizing information. This one wasn't so hard to interpret—their new home was going to be an amazing setting for hide-and-seek. Also maybe Ollie should make a map.

He dropped Theo off at school with his lunch of leftovers, courtesy of Ty, and then delivered himself to work for day two of training.

He changed into his uniform, signed out his weapon from the armory, and met up with his partner, Lucy, in the vehicle bay.

"Morning, Ollie. You're looking chipper."

"Solved my housing crisis." For the first time in a while, he felt like he had a handle on his life. Theo was healthy and back in school. Ollie had a job, and they had a nice place to live. And apparently he hadn't totally forgotten how to make friends. "It's better than therapy."

Lucy laughed. "Oh, he's got jokes this morning. Okay. I'm glad you're in a good mood, because you have a very important job today."

Ollie raised his eyebrows.

Lucy said, "You're going first in Fuck, Marry, Kill."

"Oh God, I wish I'd had more time to prepare," Ollie deadpanned. They didn't listen to music in the truck because it could distract them from being aware of their surroundings, but not talking at all would lead to daydreaming, which wasn't any better. "Where's my clipboard? I need to start making notes."

"Hilarious." She followed him into the kitchen while he put away his lunch, and whistled when she saw the packed container. "Damn. You manage that in a motel kitchen?"

Ollie closed the door. "Nope. The new place came with a personal chef."

As they went over the list of the day's pickups and deliveries, he told Lucy about his moving plans. "Theo's really excited. There's a whole room of games. We had to drag him out of there last night so he'd eat dinner."

"Sounds like you got lucky." Lucy smiled at him. They'd been friends in high school, as much as new-kid Ollie had managed to have friends. "You deserve it, though. I still can't believe you have a kid."

"Lots of people our age have kids." Granted, not usually an eight-year-old and not usually one they'd had out of wedlock with a friend almost a decade older than them.

"Lots of people our age still live in their parents' basements," she countered as she stacked the paperwork for the day and passed it over to him. Ollie looked through it to make sure it was all in order, switched the second and third sets, and handed it back. "Meanwhile you landed a sweet gig as a companion animal."

Ollie wasn't sure if that was more of an insult to him or Ty. "Hey."

"Relax, G-man. It's just sour grapes." She tossed him the keys. "Come on, our chariot awaits."

Lucy had stuck a cotton-candy-scented air freshener to the dashboard in the truck, which might have bothered Ollie except that he could still smell the coppery weirdness of money under that, and it always smelled like blood. The air freshener at least gave him flashbacks to high school instead; it smelled like one of the body sprays that had been popular with teenage girls back then—bright and pink and sugary.

Ollie slid behind the wheel and turned the ignition. "Okay, first set. Fuck, Marry, Kill. Paul at the diner on Main, Tanya at the front desk, or your grandmother."

Lucy let out a scandalized gasp. "Ollie Kent! You twisted motherfucker." She paused for dramatic effect and then asked, "Maternal or paternal?"

"Your choice."

"Hmm." While Lucy thought about it, Ollie took a left out of the garage toward Main Street. They were servicing ATMs today, which Lucy had likened to performing a rectal exam on a bear on an acid trip. Should be fun. "Fuck Tanya, marry Paul, kill Nana."

Now it was Ollie's turn to gasp dramatically. "Your own grandmother?"

"She's ninety-two! She had a good life." She shook her head. "Besides, what, I'm supposed to marry or fuck my grandma?"

"If you had different equipment you could be your own grandpa."

"Funny."

Lucy was doing the actual ATM servicing. Ollie could only watch from the truck since one of them had to stay in it at all times and he hadn't done the training for the machines yet. He kept an eye out for traffic or any suspicious activity, but the most suspicious person in the area was a dog who was unsatisfied with the placement of his pee on a fire hydrant.

From what Ollie could tell from the truck, service calls for this particular bank's ATMs involved ritual cursing of the gods along with the regular expletives. Theo would have enough money in the swear jar to put a down payment on a car. Ollie had the easy job. All he had to do was watch Lucy's back.

He hated that it made his palms sweat. It was only early April. The truck's AC worked just fine. He was in a small town in Connecticut. It was his brain that needed to chill out, not his body.

Damn, that dog could really pee.

With one final middle finger, Lucy finished swapping out the ATM's contents. She stowed the old one in the back of the truck and slammed the door hard enough that the sound echoed off the library across the street. A moment later she clambered back into the passenger seat. "One down, fifty to go. Your turn. Velma, Daphne, or Fred?"

Chapter 7

THEO'S CLASS had another redheaded girl with incredible aim. Fortunately she was easily distracted with the calling 911 role-play. Ty needed a classroom management strategy. So far he was skating by on being the cool new teacher, which wouldn't last.

In the field, it was easy. Ty knew what he was doing. He projected confidence. The people he worked with respected his experience, and the patients generally just wanted someone calm to tell them what to do.

Ty could relate. He was pretty sure that was the appeal of having a life coach.

Maybe he should hire one of those. They would probably tell him to quit this teaching gig—that he was going to be busy enough sorting out his dad's estate for the next two years. But if Ty didn't have anything to distract him from that, he would lose his mind.

That afternoon one of the batters lost his grip and flung the bat directly at a teammate who had been told four times not to stand there. Fortunately Henry had forbidden the use of phones during practice, so the kid was paying enough attention to jump out of the way. No trips to the ER today, Ty thought.

"Hey, hey, Pete! What did we say about throwing the bat?"

Pete was halfway to first base because he was the only guy on the team who could hit worth a damn. "Oh—oh shit, sorry, Coach."

Ty made a mental note to stop by the pharmacy after practice and stock up on Advil, chemical ice packs, and other necessities. "Watch your footing!" Ty yelled back, because the idiot kid was about to trip over the base.

He looked at Henry, but Henry was dead inside. Ty could tell from the hollowness of his eyes. It was a rare talent for a guy to be able to project the idea of facepalming without actually moving a muscle in his face. Henry had missed his calling as an actor.

Meanwhile, the right fielder was still running toward Pete's ball, both because Pete had hit it halfway to the next time zone and because Danny, the fielder, had stubby little legs and hadn't anticipated him absolutely crushing it, even though Pete had never once hit the ball less than two hundred feet.

Ty had the feeling the next few weeks would involve some aspirin for his own headaches.

God, they were going to be so hosed on Friday.

Ty glanced toward the parking lot for what had to be the twelfth time since practice began. Still no sign of Ollie's Honda.

Ty hoped he hadn't changed his mind about moving in. He was supposed to pick up the extra key Ty had made on his lunch break so he and Theo could start moving their stuff before Ty finished with practice. They were going to order pizza to celebrate.

"Hey." Henry put a hand on his shoulder, and Ty startled. "Whoa, easy." He frowned. "You okay? You looked like you were not on planet Earth for a minute, and now you're jumpier than a long-tailed cat in a room full of rocking chairs."

I'm fine, I'm just worried the first friend I've made outside of work in years is going to stand me up. "Yeah. Yeah, I'm okay, just...." Henry's phrasing caught up with him. "A long-tailed *what*?"

"Good thing we didn't tap you to teach listening skills." A second pat of the shoulder and then Henry was off to the outfield, presumably to remind Danny to pay attention to who was at bat.

"Maybe if you didn't talk like a *Howdy Doody* character I wouldn't have to ask you to repeat yourself," Ty grumbled after him.

By quarter after five, they'd wrangled the kids into putting away most of the equipment, and there was still no sign of Ollie. The last few stragglers on the team were heading toward the parking lot to find their rides. Ty did a double take when he saw what was presumably Pete's dad, because he recognized Mr. Chiu from his father's funeral (though, since he wasn't looking at Ty, he wasn't wearing the expression that made him look like he'd just stepped in something foul).

Somehow he ended up in a conversation about left-handedness with Danny and Henry.

"Did you know left-handed women have a 62 percent higher chance of developing multiple sclerosis?"

Henry gave him a concerned look. "Why do you know that?"

"My ADHD was unmedicated for most of my life."

"Ah."

"What about left-handed dudes?" Danny asked.

Ty shrugged and picked up his practice duffel. "No idea." Danny and Henry stared at him blankly until he continued, "ADHD, remember?"

Before Danny could ask about anything else Ty didn't know, like whether this correlation was biological sex- or gender-linked, a shout went up from the parking lot. "Ty!"

Ty's head snapped up, and he grinned as Ollie vaulted over the two-foot barrier around the parking lot, even though there was an opening three parking spots away. He'd changed out of his rent-a-cop uniform today, and Ty automatically clocked how nice his forearms looked with the sleeves of his henley pushed up. Ollie should never wear that greige monstrosity when a nice burgundy did that for him. Putting him in military OD should've been a crime.

"Sorry I'm late." Ollie shook his head. "Got in trouble yesterday because we're not supposed to take the uniforms off-site, apparently, so I needed a few more minutes to change."

"Hey, it's no problem." Ty dug the key out of his pocket. He'd chosen a blank with little yellow smiley faces on it and paired it with a miniature plush bear. His dad would've hated it. "I could've just met you at the house after."

"Yeah, but I'm late for Theo too, which isn't great." He eyed Ty with vague amusement as he held up the key chain, but he didn't comment on the choice. "The company talked a big talk about work-life balance, but shockingly they're not walking the walk. I don't know if I'm going to be able to make it every day before five thirty."

Nobody who was so concerned with being there for his kid should have to sound so defeated that he couldn't make it to the school by five thirty. Ty's dad had eaten dinner with the family maybe once a week and never thought twice about it. At least Ollie *wanted* to be there. "He can always hang out with me," Ty offered. "I mean, I can grab him after school and take him home or he can chill and watch baseball practice." He almost added that he might have to get the kid some antidepressants, but Danny was still there. ADHD medication was good for a lot of things.

Ollie's face lit up. "Yeah? Oh man, I bet he would dig that. Kid loves baseball. Like, every movie he wanted to watch in the hospital was baseball-themed." He jerked his thumb toward the building. "I'm gonna go get him and you can ask him yourself."

What, Ty was going to get *credit* for this? It wasn't like he was going out of his way. "Sounds good."

Henry cleared his throat. "Ollie. Good to see you again."

Oh... Ty had been kind of hogging him, huh? "Coach Tate." Ollie shook his hand. "Sorry, I'm a little distracted, but we can catch up soon? I hear there's a game this week. I gotta go or they're gonna charge me twenty bucks—"

He jogged off toward the school. Ty maybe watched his ass a little.

"Holy shit, Coach M, is that your boyfriend?" Danny asked, impressed. "He is a *snack*."

Henry made a noise like a ticking pressure cooker.

"No, it's not." *And he is a whole meal, kid.* "Aren't your parents here yet?"

"Oh, I'm riding my bike home." Danny opened his backpack—which held enough loose paper that Ty thought maybe this kid could use an ADHD diagnosis too—and shoved his glove inside. "See you tomorrow, Coach Tate, Coach M!"

If Ty thought getting rid of Danny would relieve the sense of scrutiny, he was disappointed. He could feel the weight of Henry's judgy eyeballs on the side of his face. "What?" Ty said testily. He'd kept it together when the kid was in earshot, but now he could feel himself blushing.

"Nah, nothing," Henry said, all casual, and for a second, Ty thought he was going to get away with it.

Then he added, "Just, if you don't want people to know how you feel about him, you should probably stop looking at him like he's your own personal miracle."

Ty was going to die of embarrassment. "I have known him *less than a week*."

Henry slapped his back in encouragement. "I hope you don't play poker, kid."

"At least he didn't call him a DILF," Ty mumbled.

They walked toward the parking lot. "What's with the key, anyway?"

Could Henry maybe just have a teeny tiny cardiac event right now so Ty could escape this situation? No, that was an awful thing to think. Ty could have a ministroke instead.

Sadly, no medical emergency materialized. Ty steeled himself. "I told you, I hate that house. It's huge. I'm not gonna live there alone."

"No, that would be ridiculous," Henry agreed mildly. "Why do that when you could move in a DILF you just met and his eight-year-old kid?"

"Friends don't judge friends, Henry."

"Of course they do. This is what 'I told you so' was invented for. Also beer, which I am making a note to stock up on. I feel like you're going to need it."

Fuck it. Ty deserved the ribbing, and at least he had someone to break his fall. "Thanks, Coach."

OLLIE DIDN'T know what excited Theo more—getting to pick a bedroom from one of seven available or Ty asking if he wanted to be a junior baseball coach.

Theo's eyes went wide as quarters. *"Really?"*

"Absolutely," Ty said as though he hadn't even noticed Ollie's kid falling head over heels in love with him. "Your dad tells me you're an expert. And between you and me, we need all the help we can get." He pushed open the door to yet another bedroom and let Theo wander in to check it out. This one had a double-size four-poster in the same rich dark wood the whole house seemed to be paneled in. Did all that stuff have to be oiled, Ollie wondered? Was it as expensive as it looked? He could probably buy a car for what it cost to panel one room in that stuff.

"Cool. I know a lot about baseball. I can help." Theo launched himself at the bed. He bounced a few times on the mattress and then proclaimed, "I like this one." He looked at Ollie. "Is this one okay, Dad?"

He'd picked one several doors farther down than Ollie had hoped. Ollie could switch the bedroom he planned to use, but the one he'd shortlisted was close to the kitchen and had an en suite bath and a mattress that felt like heaven, and he was trying not to suffocate his kid. It was a good sign that Theo felt secure enough to pick his own room. If Ollie had to sneak in at night to listen to him breathe sometimes, they'd all survive. "You sure you're not going to get lost in that bed?"

Rolling his eyes, Theo whined, *"Dad."*

God, Ollie was five hundred years old, and he loved his kid with every fiber of his being. "Just checking. It's my job as your dad."

He glanced at Ty to include him in the joke, but then he remembered that Ty's father sucked. But if hanging around with Theo and Ollie made him think about his dad, he was hiding it well, because that smile held nothing but fond amusement. "All right, well, that's the hard work done. Are we ready for pizza?"

"So ready."

Ollie thought Theo was going to speed past them both toward the kitchen, but instead he grabbed their hands and dragged them along in his wake.

"I hope you know what you're getting into," Ollie said quietly. He might love Theo with all his heart, but he knew he could be a lot.

But Ty only smiled back. "Are you kidding? He's flying solo. Yesterday I had twenty-five of him at once. I'll be fine." When Theo released them to go look out the window for the pizza guy, he added almost bashfully, "I, uh, I think it's going to be good for me, actually, to have a kid in here who'll get to *be* a kid."

Yeah, Ollie definitely made the right choice moving in here. "I think it's good for him too. He was really standoffish with my parents, so I was worried at first that he didn't want to get attached to any adults after what happened with his mom. But I think he just doesn't know how to have grandparents, or anyone, really. Allison didn't have any family."

That was part of why, when she decided she wanted to have a baby, she didn't go to a sperm bank. She needed someone she knew would be there to step in if something happened to her. She didn't want her kid growing up in the foster system the way she had.

Ollie should've introduced her to his family when they first became friends. Theo could've grown up knowing he had a big family who loved him. But by the time Allison asked Ollie to be a donor, he was about to be deployed, and once she was pregnant, it felt like it was too late, like his family would've gotten the wrong idea.

All he could do now was move forward.

"Yeah, that's—"

Something in Ty's voice brought Ollie veering sharply back to the here and now. Ty looked like he'd seen his own ghost. "What?"

He puffed out a breath that might have been tinged with dark amusement. "I was going to say that's always hard." His words didn't crack, but he hit a hitch on *hard*, like his throat was trying to close up. "And then I realized how right I was. I mean, I've *felt* alone since my mom died. But now I really am the last."

Fuck, Ollie was such an insensitive asshole. Just because Ty hadn't gotten along with his father didn't mean he didn't love him, hadn't held out hope that one day things might get better. "Ty, I'm sorry. That was thoughtless of me."

It wasn't what he wanted to say at all. He wanted to say, *You've got me*. But that was insane. They barely knew each other. And hell, probably the only reason Ty *did* have Ollie and Theo—at least physically—was *because* his dad had died and he couldn't face living here alone.

"Don't," Ty said. "It's not like you don't—let's not have a pity party."

Okay. Time to dial back the emotional intensity. "But we already ordered the pizza."

"I think I still have ice cream left too."

"Shhh, don't say that where Theo can hear you." Not that Ollie wouldn't let him have ice cream, but if Theo found out about it, Ollie wouldn't get any.

They exchanged weak, grateful smiles and were interrupted by a whoop of delight as Theo announced the arrival of dinner.

Ollie had paid online, so he let Theo run to the door to get it.

When he was out of earshot, Ty took the opportunity to say, "So listen, there's something I always wanted to do as a kid and never got the chance, but you're the parent in the house, so…."

Ollie raised his eyebrows.

"Can we eat pizza and watch a movie?"

Why did Ollie suddenly have visions of someone saying that that furniture was for *company*, that pizza wasn't dinner, and that dinnertime was for family—even though he already knew Ty's dad rarely ate with him growing up?

"Theo's going to want to watch *Moneyball*," he warned.

Ty beamed. "That's cool. I haven't seen that yet."

"Also…." Ollie gestured expansively around the living room. He couldn't believe he hadn't noticed earlier. "You don't have a TV."

"Yeah, the old man thought television was for plebs unless the Red Sox were playing. He always watched that in his office. It still reeks like cigars in there, though. I'll pull the TV out and we can put it in the living room."

"You also don't have a TV stand," Ollie pointed out.

"So we'll put the TV on the floor for tonight."

Now Ollie was starting to get a clearer picture. "And sit in front of it like kids at a sleepover?" he guessed.

From the sheepish expression on Ty's face, Ollie was right on the money.

The idea felt safe and wholesome and welcoming. It felt fun too, at least in theory, which was removed from the reality of what Ollie's thirty-two-year-old ass felt like after two hours sitting on the floor. The part of him that was just a guy, that wanted his kid's approval above everything, the one who'd recently lost the closest friend he'd ever sat on the floor to eat pizza with, wanted to say yes.

Unfortunately, Ollie couldn't always be that guy. "I don't think it's such a good idea."

Ty's face fell. "Oh. Yeah, you're probably right."

"It's a school night." Ollie was not prepared for the way the disappointment in Ty's voice cut him. Being a dad had made him soft when it came to saying no, apparently—and he wasn't even saying no. "And I'm not sure he's going to have time for a movie and homework and unpacking and getting to bed on time."

"Ohhh," Ty said again. "I didn't think of that."

"But we could do it Saturday night. Maybe with popcorn instead of pizza?" Ollie didn't want Theo eating a steady diet of takeout. He had barely overcome the urge to feed him nothing but cancer-fighting antioxidants, and that was mostly because he couldn't subject himself to any more of Theo's obnoxious broccoli farts.

"Deal," Ty said. "Can't wait."

Strangely, Ollie believed him.

INSTEAD OF heading right to the ball diamond when the elementary school let out on Thursday, Ty swung by the third-grade classrooms to pick up his assistant.

"Ty!"

"Theo!" Ty high-fived him, then leaned down to stage whisper, "It's Coach M until after practice, okay?"

Theo pushed his glasses up his nose. "Can I be Coach T?"

Ty considered the odds of the high school kids reacting well to that and decided on probably not. "Tell you what, we'll workshop it." He held the door as they walked outside into the sunshine. "So your dad tells me you love baseball."

"It's the best."

"What's your favorite team?"

"Washington Nationals."

Well, he grew up in DC, so that made sense, even if they currently weren't very good. "I *guess* we can still be friends," Ty said heavily.

Theo giggled. "What's yours?"

"Cubs," he said ruefully. Ty's team wasn't doing any better than Theo's. That was good—it would give them plenty of practice with disappointment for the upcoming high school baseball season. "We can suffer together."

A trio of girls with red hair passed by, and one of them waved to Theo. Ty had her and the next tallest in his classes, but he didn't recognize the oldest, except that she was obviously related to the other two. "Friend of yours?"

"Yeah. She's really cool. She likes baseball *almost* as much as me."

"Only almost?"

"Nobody likes baseball as much as me."

Ty led the way into the dugout, which already held Henry, Danny, Peter, and a few of the other players. "Hey, guys. This is Theo Kent. He's going to be my assistant today."

Henry's side-eye gave a monologue on Ty's life choices.

"I didn't know you had a kid, Coach." Danny held out his hand for a fist bump from Theo. "I'm Danny."

Theo bumped it seriously.

"Sadly, I'm only borrowing him." Ty studiously avoided Henry's gaze as Theo went down the line fist-bumping the rest of the team. When he finished, Ty set him up with a clipboard and a score sheet. "You know how to use one of these?"

He didn't, so Ty gave him a quick tutorial and then called Henry over. They were doing a mock game today as practice, with the team divided into two groups. He and Henry set the batting order, and then Ty gave the sheet back to Theo, who studied it like there might be a test later.

The team had just finished arriving and Ty and Theo were in the process of decamping to the visitors' dugout when a woman said, "Theo? Is that you?"

For a moment Theo froze. Then he looked around. Ty guided him out of the teenagers' way but didn't let him out of arm's reach.

The woman who'd spoken was in her late fifties, with curly dark hair and a familiar jawline. Ty could've picked her out of a lineup as Ollie's mother, but Ollie had clearly been right that Theo didn't know what to do with grandparents, because he half hid himself behind Ty rather than step forward to say hello.

Ty turned to Theo. "Hey, buddy, can you do me a big favor?"

Theo looked up and met his eyes, clutching the clipboard to his chest.

"Can you go into the dugout and let everybody know the batting order? We need to get started with practice." Henry's kids were already trickling onto the field to take up their positions.

"Really?"

"Big, loud voice," Ty told him. He caught Danny's eye in the dugout and nodded at Theo. Danny would have the kid's back. "Okay?"

"Okay."

"Theo—" the woman began again, but Theo was already in the dugout. Danny helped him up onto the bench so the team could see and hear him. Once it became clear she wasn't going to get what she wanted, she frowned at Ty. "You didn't have to do that, you know. I'm his grandmother. I'm not going to hurt him."

"Kinda figured," he said. "But it looks like he doesn't know you very well, and I don't know you at all, and you're not on the list of approved adults to pick him up." Which Ty happened to know since Theo was in one of his classes. Ty didn't normally have to contend with parental pickup, because he didn't have last-period class, but he'd peeked at Theo's file in case. "It's not personal."

She looked like she wanted to argue, but her better angels prevailed. "No, of course not. I'm sorry. You're just doing your job. I'd better go pick up his cousin."

Ty waved her off, unsure how he felt about the victory. Either way, Ollie needed to know about it, but that could wait until they were home.

No, Ty reminded himself, not *home*. Home was his rooftop Chicago apartment with his herb garden, a short walk from his favorite gastropub and his station in Rogers Park. Home was Ty's spot on the beat-up couch that Stacey, the fire station captain, refused to get rid of. It was an ambulance with Ty's initials written on the underside of the back bumper in metal Sharpie. It was a crew of people who got him.

"Hey, Morris! Are you gonna get this show on the road anytime this century?"

Thanks for the reality check, Mr. Chiu, Ty thought darkly. He turned back to the diamond and clapped his hands. "All right, let's play ball!"

Chapter 8

OLLIE HAD just changed out of his uniform when the text came through.

I saw Theo at the school today.

He slammed his locker closed a little harder than necessary and sat heavily on the bench. What kind of passive-aggressive…? Did his mom know how that sounded? It was like she was taunting him because she'd seen Theo without his express permission.

He was debating his reply when a second message came through. *I was there to pick up Mel. The baseball coach wouldn't let me talk to him.*

Ollie smiled. Given Ty's relationship with his own parent, he could imagine how he reacted.

I told you. Baby steps. Theo doesn't know you yet.

And he never will if you don't let us see him. Come to dinner Saturday night. We'll have the whole family over.

Oh sure, Ollie would simply bring his kid into a houseful of twelve near-strangers. That was a totally reasonable thing to do. Besides—*We have plans Saturday. But maybe you and Dad can meet us for lunch on Sunday?*

Hopefully she found that a reasonable compromise. Ollie *did* want Theo to know his family. Just because Ollie's relationship with them was strained didn't mean they wouldn't love Theo. Hell, they already loved Theo. They might never forgive Ollie for waiting this long to tell them he existed, but they hadn't forgiven him for joining the Army either, so he was used to it by now.

He picked up his keys and was heading for the door when his phone vibrated again. *Heads-up, your mom tried to talk to Theo today. I sent him to give the kids the batting order. FYI, longest baseball practice of my life. Only got through 3 innings. Theo ran out of score sheet.*

Oh Lord. Ollie made a note to bring a cushion to sit on at the game tomorrow. Those high school bleachers weren't built with comfort in mind.

Thanks for running interference. Should I pick up anything on my way home?

Xanax? Ty suggested.

Ollie snorted and slid his phone into his pocket.

Sadly, by the time the game rolled around the next evening, he wished he hadn't taken that as a joke.

As official assistant to the assistant coach, Theo had the honor of sitting in the dugout with the team. That left Ollie and his dollar-store cushion all alone with no buffer when his parents showed up with his sister and Mel.

Like a pride of lions picking off a sickly water buffalo calf who'd wandered off on his own.

"Uncle Ollie!"

Naturally they sent Mel as their advance guard to catch him with his defenses down. She was six and looked just like Ollie's sister Cassie had at that age—all gap-toothed and pigtailed and cute as anything. She ran up to him and hugged his knees. "Mom says *you* used to play baseball. Are you gonna play today?"

Ollie held back a laugh as he picked her up and plopped her beside him on the bleachers. At least he'd have a little insulation on one side. "Not today. I'm too old. These are the high school kids."

"Oh." She wiggled her butt like somehow that could make her more comfortable on the cold aluminum. "How come Theo is with them? Is he old enough to play?"

"My friend Ty asked him if he wanted to help coach."

Unfortunately he mentioned this just as the adults came into earshot. His mother sat on his right, Cassie on Mel's left. Ollie's father sat in the row behind them, probably so he didn't get dragged into the upcoming battle of wits.

"Ty?" his mother echoed. She was frowning. "Not Tyler Morris."

How did Ollie's mother know his name? Ty had left town before they moved here. "Yeah, that's him."

Cassie sucked in an audible breath.

His mother clucked. "I don't think you should be hanging around with him, Ollie. That boy is a *hoodlum*."

Oh my God, what? In the dugout, Ty was wearing a blue polo shirt, cargo shorts, and a school windbreaker. He was holding a clipboard. He looked like a nerdy dad. "A hoodlum, Mom? Do people still say that? Anyway, he hasn't even lived here in years. Do you have connections in Chicago I don't know about?"

Mom sniffed. "Mrs. Chiu was talking about it at church. Showing up drunk at his father's funeral."

Ah. Of course. Church lady talk. "Doesn't the Bible say something about gossip?" Ollie poked Mel's side until she giggled. His mom couldn't get mad at him if he was making her granddaughter laugh. "What did she do, give him a breathalyzer?" Because he hadn't *smelled* like booze anymore, that much Ollie could attest to.

He desperately hoped his mother didn't ask him when *he'd* made friends with Ty. He'd hate to have to give credence to church lady talk.

"You know Mr. Chiu was good friends with Leonard Morris. I'm sure he's shared stories with his wife. And there were all those rumors that first year that someone tried to burn the school down—"

"Mom. I remember the rumors." Because unlike his mother, Ollie had attended the school just after the incident. "And there was no attempted arson. It was chickens in the principal's office."

"Coooooool," Mel said. "Mommy, can I bring chickens to school?"

Oh, that was not going to help Ollie's case. Cassie caught Ollie's eye over her daughter's head and glared.

Yeah. As a parent, Ollie should know better now. He mouthed, *Sorry.*

"I don't think so, sweetheart," Cassie said. "Chickens are messy, and some people might be allergic."

His mother *humph*ed as though this proved her point. "I just don't think Theo should be spending time with this man. He can't be a good influence. I can't believe the school allows him on the property."

Truly, Ollie was so looking forward to mentioning he'd moved in with this man his mother apparently hated. "I'm pretty sure the same principal invited him back, Mom." And then, sensing an opportunity to soften her up, "Besides, his mother had just died. You can't expect perfect behavior from a grieving kid."

As he suspected, that got to her. The hard lines around her mouth softened. "Oh, Ollie. Of course you have a soft spot for him."

What? he wondered, and then he realized she thought he was sympathetic because his own kid had lost his mom.

"Has Theo been having problems?"

Ollie glanced at his niece, but the game had started, and she and Cassie were getting into it, cheering as Peter Chiu struck out the first batter. "No. I mean, not more than the usual expected stuff." He still had nightmares, and on the drive up from DC, they'd passed a dead deer on the side of the road, and he'd spent five minutes asking questions about what would happen to its body. But they had gotten past most of the argumentativeness and the impulsiveness. "He's starting to make friends. I think the therapy really helps." He still talked to Dr. Vaughn twice a month on Skype.

"I'm glad he's doing well, honey. You're a good dad. I wish—I wish we'd known sooner—"

Damn it. Ollie wished that too, if only because it would have made his life easier now. Two weeks after Allison died, when Theo was still barely talking to him, Ollie had woken up from a fitful nap in a hospital chair to find Theo sobbing from a nightmare that Ollie had died too and there was no one to take care of him.

Ollie had promised that wouldn't happen, that he was safe and healthy, but if something happened, there were people Theo hadn't even met yet who loved him and would look after him. And now Theo was hedging on getting to know them.

Dr. Vaughn thought it might be because he'd decided Ollie couldn't die if he didn't have a backup plan, which made Ollie want to curl up for a nap at the bottom of a bottle of tequila.

"I know, Mom," he said finally. "Things with Allison—it was complicated. I thought if I told you, you'd pressure us to get married, and we weren't ever like that."

"You liked her enough to have a baby with her," his mother pointed out.

Jeez. Ollie's ears burned. "It's not like we did it the old-fashioned way, Mom."

On Mel's other side, Cassie stifled a snicker. So she was multitasking—eavesdropping and watching the game at the same time. Ollie was so glad he could provide some amusement.

"Well, maybe you could use some old-fashioned romance."

They should serve beer at high school sports games. She hadn't even made it five minutes. "Mom—"

"I'm just saying. It's not like you'd be replacing Allison, since you weren't ever *like that*." He should've known she'd throw those words back in his face. He made a note to stop volunteering information in the future. "It might help Theo feel more stable."

Using his kid against him was another low blow he should've seen coming.

The truth was, Ollie's parents loved him. They wanted what they thought was best for him. But that had always manifested in trying to plan his life by other people's milestones instead of what Ollie would have chosen for himself. He was good at football and baseball, so he should have gotten a college scholarship, then either gone pro or put his free education to good use to help send his sisters to school. Ollie liked sports, but he didn't want to play forever, and he didn't have a clue what he might want to do after college. The pressure of trying to decide when he wasn't ready had driven him into the local Army recruitment office.

Somehow that had actually worked out for him, apart from the fact that he was now thirty-two and still didn't know what he wanted to do with his life. But he didn't think it was a good idea to try the same tactic to avoid having his parents arrange his personal life. What would that even look like? Running away to Vegas with a mail-order bride? Joining a religious order and taking a vow of chastity?

Neither option held any appeal. Ollie could do without sex fine, but he wasn't going to pretend to be religious about it.

Unfortunately, the third option was telling his parents the truth, and Ollie had never been very good at that either, at least not when it came to his love life. Especially since he didn't really understand the truth himself.

It had been easier when he was a teenager, a raging mess of hormones attached to a dick that got hard when the wind blew the right way (and frequently when it didn't). But halfway into his first deployment, that constant level of desire faded. Ollie'd thought he was just *busy*. Not dying took up a lot of his time, and it wasn't like he had a lot of privacy. He had more important things to worry about than why he didn't want to hump his CO's leg.

But the itch didn't come back when he was on leave either, not really... not until a few months after he met Darcy, an aid worker in what passed for the local town. That at least reassured him his dick still worked, but eventually the area got too dangerous for civilians, Darcy and her team relocated, and that was the end of that.

It had become sort of the pattern.

"Tell you what," Ollie said finally. "If Theo comes to me—on his own, with no interference from anyone else—and asks me when I'm going to get married, I'll start dating." It would be a long, slow process to meet someone he liked enough to try it with, but he'd *try*.

He could practically see his mother turning the words over in her head as she looked for a loophole, her mouth pulled down at the corners.

She agreed just as the crack of a bat sounded from the diamond. Ollie looked over to see the visiting team hit a triple. He glanced at the count—one out. Could be a long night.

"Great. I'm going to get a hot dog. Anybody else want anything?"

AFTER THE 18–3 loss—and the week of teaching that preceded it—Ty needed the weekend to recuperate.

So it really sucked that he had so much to do.

First, he had an appointment with his dad's accountant. Ty knew enough about managing someone's estate to know that it was about as much fun as a hot-sauce enema, but after sitting with Georgia for an hour, he was ready to hit up the grocery store for a quart of Frank's and take his chances. Unless he wanted to make dealing with this nightmare his full-time job for the next year, Georgia recommended he hire a firm that specialized in the task.

Ty boggled that such a thing existed, boggled more at the price, and then realized it was the smartest money he'd ever spend and signed on the dotted line.

To add insult to injury, he also had lessons to plan. The whole *this is how you call 911* improv schtick was only good for one class worth of material. Now Ty needed to teach kids things like how to clean cuts and administer EpiPens and check if someone was breathing.

Where did he even *start*? What was appropriate first aid to teach an eight-year-old? And how the fuck was he going to test them on it? Oh God, he needed a binder. He needed, like, six binders for keeping track of the kids' grades. His team at the fire station called him Trunchbull behind his back—and occasionally to his face—because he was so strict with the paperwork, but Ty simply knew himself. The ADHD would take a mile if he gave it an inch. He could have six binders filled with kids' grades or he could have a briefcase of indecipherable wrinkled paper scraps. And by *briefcase* he meant *sixteen-year-old backpack unearthed from his childhood bedroom*.

So before he did lesson planning, he needed to shop for *school supplies*, a fact so depressing it made him want to swing by the corner store for booze. Sadly, by this point in his life, Ty could recognize a self-destructive tendency from a mile away, and he lived with a kid now, so he refrained.

Instead he took extra joy in picking out color-coded binders. Rainbow would have been ideal—red for second grade, orange for third, and so on—but the tiny stationery store in town didn't have orange, so he skipped to yellow and compensated for his disappointment by adding coordinating sticky notes.

After perusing all four aisles of the store twice with his arms increasingly tired, he still hadn't found a set of dividers to keep his classes separate.

Which was fine. He could order them from Amazon Prime, right? Even out here, surely it wouldn't take more than two days to deliver them. He could have them ready by Tuesday at the latest.

But sooner would be better, and he wasn't going to resort to ordering online just because he was too chicken to face Mrs. Sanford.

Steeling himself, he made his way to the front of the shop and deposited his haul on the checkout counter.

Mrs. Sanford looked at him from over the wire rims of her glasses, then went back to her crossword.

At least she didn't spit at him. She'd very nearly done that once. "Uh, hi." Ty put on his best public-servant smile. "I'm looking for subject dividers. You wouldn't happen to have any…?"

Mrs. Sanford clicked her pen and marked something on her puzzle. *Slang term*, Ty thought, *five-letter word for standoffish person*. Finally she said, "Back endcap. Aisle two."

Right. "Thank you."

He grabbed what he wanted and returned to the counter.

Mrs. Sanford didn't look up.

Ty cleared his throat. "Thank you, again. Just these, please."

She didn't say a word as she rang him up, didn't ask if he wanted a bag, only turned the till display toward him and announced the total.

Nothing like that small-town hospitality.

Before he knew it, half the day had slipped away and he still had things to do—grocery shopping, laundry, housework. Ty didn't mind cleaning his apartment on the weekend, but his apartment was *tiny*. Cleaning his dad's house was a Sisyphean task. By the time he finished dusting, he had to start all over again.

So it was really nice when he came home to pick up reusable bags and found Ollie in the kitchen, already unpacking groceries.

"Hey." Ollie tucked two cartons of milk in the fridge—two percent for Ty, one percent for Ollie—and closed the door. "How was the accountant?"

"Horrifying." Ty spied a package of pudding cups and immediately snapped one off and ripped open the foil. If he couldn't medicate with alcohol, chocolate was an acceptable placebo. He grabbed a spoon from a drawer. "My father's final"—he glanced around and, not seeing Theo, continued—"fuck-you is that after he's gone, I get to spend three years of my life sorting out his financial shit." He shoveled in a spoonful of pudding. Yep, that was the stuff. "Thanks for going grocery shopping." It looked like he'd even used the list Ty had stuck to the fridge.

Ollie shrugged. "We eat too. Besides, you've got enough on your plate."

Yeah. Ty was starting to get a headache.

No, wait. He'd forgotten to eat breakfast. Or lunch. He probably needed to fix that.

Ty finished the pudding cup and took care of the garbage. Then he stuck his head back in the fridge. "Sandwiches for lunch?"

They were putting the finishing touches on the food when Ty's phone rang. Caller ID read *Chicago EMS*.

Oh good. Another fun way to spend his Saturday.

"You and Theo eat." Ty held up the phone. "I have to… yeah."

"Don't worry, I won't let Theo eat all the pickles."

Ty ducked into his father's office, grimaced at the ostentatious, self-important-looking desk chair, and kicked his feet up on the tufted leather couch instead. "Tyler Morris."

"Commander Morris. This is Field Chief Rivers."

Of course it was Ty's boss's boss. "Chief Rivers, hi. To what do I owe the pleasure?" As if he didn't already know.

"I just wanted to check in with my newest ambulance commander. How are you holding up?"

Ty puffed out a breath. "I'm doing okay. I have a lot of stuff to sort through with my dad's estate, but I hired a company to help out with it. I should be back to work by the middle of June."

Rivers sighed. "Tyler, I asked how you're doing, not when you're coming back."

Right. "Sorry."

"You're supposed to let me get through the pleasantries first," she said reprovingly. "I ask if you got the flowers the department sent, you thank me for the thoughtful gesture, we make small talk about grief for two minutes, and *then* I move in and ask when you're coming back to Chicago."

Ty smiled. He liked his boss so much. She was a straight shooter. "You should just send me the script next time."

She laughed. "I'll keep that in mind. You're really doing okay, though?"

"I'm really okay. You know my dad and I weren't exactly close."

"That doesn't always make it easier."

She was not wrong about that. "No kidding." He wriggled deeper into the sofa. "Anyway, I'm keeping busy. Keeping sharp, even. Got a fancy gig teaching the next generation of paramedics."

"God, please tell me you're joking. Samira's great, but she's not you. The paperwork is *not* the same."

"Relax. An elementary teacher at my old school had a cryptic pregnancy, and they asked if I could teach some third graders first aid for a couple weeks until school's out."

"That doesn't count toward your professional education hours. Just saying."

Ty hummed. "I should see if they're offering anything nearby, since I'm here anyway. Get it out of the way." He had to take a set number of hours of CME credits every year to recertify.

"Nothing locally?"

Ha. As if. "You ever look at a map and try to find this place? We don't even have a fire station. Nearest one's ten miles from here."

"At least I don't have to worry about them stealing you away from me." Ty's disdain for any sort of commute was a running joke in Chicago. He took the L into work, Ubered home if he'd had a long shift, and usually made someone else drive the ambulance.

"They don't even *like* me here." Ty could barely go to the grocery store without getting stink eye. "Believe me, I'll be glad to be back home."

"And we'll be glad to have you. I'll let you get back to your Saturday. You enjoy the rest of your weekend."

"You too, Chief. Thanks."

Chapter 9

THERE WAS only so much weekend to go around, and Ollie wanted to spend as much of it as he could with his kid... but he also had responsibilities.

Which was why, after he stuck his head into the pole barn to check things out, he walked back into the house and said, "Hey, Theo, want to help me cut the grass?"

Theo looked up from the pinball machine and made a face. "Why would I want to help cut the grass?"

"Oh, I don't know," Ollie said, pretending to hedge. "I just thought because it's a riding mower, you might like to learn to drive. But if you'd rather not—"

The pinball machine was left in the dust. "Really?"

"Yeah, really. *But* you can never do it without me there, and you'll have to sit on my lap and do what I tell you. Okay?"

"Can we go cut the grass right now?"

Riding around on Ty's lawn mower with Theo in his lap reminded him of doing this with his dad when he was a kid, back when they lived in their rambling farmhouse in New York State. That seemed so long ago now, but when Ollie asked if Theo wanted to steer, Theo's eyes lit up and brought those feelings right back.

Ollie's parents hadn't done *everything* wrong. There were good times too.

The rest of the day passed in a pleasant haze. The sun was shining, but it was still cool in that early spring way. In the games room, the greenhouse effect made for the perfect atmosphere for reclining on the couch with one of the paperbacks from Ty's mom's bookshelf while Ty and Theo did their homework together at the poker table.

Okay, so Theo was doing homework and Ty was lesson planning. It was nice. Ollie kept looking up from his book to find Theo coloring in his map as Ty researched how not to traumatize grade-schoolers while teaching them first aid, or whatever.

Then, after dinner, Ollie made good on his movie-on-the-floor promise. But he was still thirty-two years old, so he pulled a couch cushion onto the floor to sit on and leaned back against the sofa. They made a bag of microwave popcorn and introduced Ty to *Moneyball*, and even if Theo fell asleep on Ollie's shoulder in the last ten minutes and his ass went numb, it was still the nicest Saturday night he'd had in a long time.

When the movie ended, Ty turned off the TV while Ollie picked up Theo to put him to bed. Sure, he could wake him up and make him go brush his teeth, but he hadn't gotten to do this when Theo was little—pick him up, tuck him into bed already asleep. Soon he'd be too big to carry or too old to let Ollie get away with it. One night without brushing his teeth wouldn't give him cavities.

He turned out the lights and went back to the living room to help Ty clean up the popcorn kernels that had spilled on the floor.

"Thanks for tonight," he said just as Ty raised his head and said, "Thank you."

Their eyes locked for a moment, and Ollie found himself matching Ty's sheepish grin. "I really needed this," Ty said. "Just, I don't know, a night in with a friend doing something… *fun* seems like the wrong word for a movie and popcorn on the floor. Silly?"

"No, I get it," Ollie assured him. "My kid loved it, for one thing, and that's pretty much always going to be enough for me, but you're right. It was nice. *Normal*, maybe? Although," he added, rubbing his tailbone, "if we're going to make a habit of it, I want thicker cushions."

Ty laughed. "Or I could get a media console so we can sit on the actual couch." He scooped up a stray napkin and tossed it in the bowl with the unpopped kernels. "Theo's a really great kid. You're lucky."

"Luckier than you know." Ollie paused as he searched for the right words. "Theo's been through a lot for an eight-year-old. He's already beaten cancer and lost his mom. And he's…. He fought me on going to school the first three days, because he doesn't like being apart from me. And he hated latchkey. He's afraid I'll die and he won't have anyone, but he's also… not afraid to meet new people. It's just, I think he thinks I can't die if he doesn't have any other grown-ups to take care of him. He's been resisting getting to know my parents, and it's driving them nuts." He paused. "But he likes you. That sounds kind of dumb, and believe me, I'm not trying to put anything on you, but it's a relief, you know? It may take time, but he *can* form attachments with other adults."

Or whatever lightning-in-a-bottle combination he'd found with Ty.

They brought the dishes into the kitchen, and Ty loaded them into the dishwasher. "I wonder if it's, like, an identification thing?" He glanced over and lifted a shoulder. "That first day we met, I was not exactly projecting *I am a responsible adult*. And I did just lose my dad."

"I don't know what it is," Ollie said. "I'm just grateful. And with the baseball? He's actually been excited to go to school because there's practice after." Any little bit of guilt Ollie could take off his chest for missing so many milestones in his kid's life, for not dropping everything to homeschool him to make up for it, helped. "So thank you."

Ty ducked his head and blushed when he smiled, like he wasn't used to being appreciated. Ollie couldn't understand how that was true since he literally saved people's lives for a living. Maybe he was naturally modest. "Uh, you're welcome. I'm glad I could help."

After a day like that, Ollie figured he'd have no trouble falling asleep, even if he didn't have Theo wheezing in the same room with him to send him off to dreamland. And he was right; lots of fresh air and the weak spring sunshine, some normal household chores, and about three times as much social interaction as he was used to, and he was out like a light the minute his head hit the pillow.

Ollie had loved flying from the moment he'd first stepped foot on an aircraft. When the ground fell away beneath him and the sky stretched out above and in front and around him, he felt weightless, buoyant. All his problems—his parents, his lack of direction in life, loneliness, indecision—those were earthly concerns that couldn't touch him up here.

Which was pretty weird considering he'd been shot at while flying, but not everything had to make sense.

So when the dusk-bruised sky of Afghanistan filled his field of vision and he felt the helicopter controls under his hands, Ollie thought, *This will be a good dream.* He hadn't been able to fly since he separated from the service. It was maybe the only thing he regretted about leaving. Dreaming about it wasn't the same, but if this was all he could get, he'd happily soak in every moment.

Ollie didn't mind the desert, apart from the sand and the heat. It could be beautiful. At night you could see every single speck of light in the sky.

He was guiding the chopper over a ridge when things took a turn.

First the sun seemed to stutter on the horizon, the last brilliant line of it shaking against the curve of the earth until it reversed course and dragged itself back into the sky.

The wind picked up, buffeting the helicopter with gusts of sand. Ollie's instrumentation flickered. Comms went down.

By the time the sandstorm was on him, the dream had become a nightmare.

Suddenly Ollie was no longer flying solo. "We're taking fire!" In the copilot's seat, Theo yelled into his oversize headset. He turned around and shouted at the row of seats behind them. "Brace for impact!"

Ollie looked back. In the second row on the floor was another Theo, bleeding from a bullet to the chest, the same wound Hernandez had when Ollie medevacked him. A third Theo wearing a combat medic's insignia pressed a pressure bandage to the wound.

Enemy fire impacted the tail rotor, and the helicopter controls heaved under Ollie's hands. *No*, he thought fiercely. *It can't end like this.* The best he could hope for was a controlled crash that might not kill them all. *I'm sorry, I tried my best—*

Something landed on his chest. Ollie opened his eyes.

It was dark, but not desert-sandstorm dark. Sprawling-Connecticut-mansion dark. He forced himself to inhale deeply through his nose, even if his breath shuddered, and focus on the comfort of the mattress beneath him.

In the bedroom doorway, Ty cleared his throat. "Ollie. You good? You were having a nightmare."

Ollie's lungs cooperated more smoothly this time. "Yeah. Thanks." Exhaled. That was a horrible dream, but he hadn't had to live the worst part of it. "What… did you throw something at me?" He squinted toward the hallway. They'd bought motion-activated night lights so Ollie and Theo didn't get lost trying to find the bathroom, so Ty was silhouetted.

"My shirt," Ty said sheepishly. "I didn't want to get murdered."

Of course. Ollie felt around on top of him until he found it. The fabric was still warm from Ty's body. "So you sent your shirt to be murdered instead?"

This was probably the fastest Ollie had ever wanted to laugh after a nightmare. He chucked the shirt back at Ty, who caught it one-handed.

"It worked, didn't it?"

Ollie sat up. "Yeah. Thanks." He rubbed his eyes. "What time's it?"

"Like, three, I think?" Ty answered, muffled as he pulled his shirt back on.

Ollie frowned. "Did I wake you up?" Theo closed his door when he went to bed, but Ollie opened it again when he was turning in, then left his own open so that he might hear Theo better if he needed something. But if he was disturbing Ty—

Ty snorted. "No. There's an owl outside my window, and it's loud as fuck. And then once I was awake, I was thirsty. Just a coincidence."

"Guess you could take a bedroom on the other side of the house for the night," Ollie joked. "Thanks for waking me up, though."

"No problem." He paused. Then, "Hey, want to see if we can see the owl?"

It was better than trying to go back to sleep in a room that smelled like Ollie's fear sweat. "Sure." He got up and cracked the window—might as well air the place out—and then jumped half a foot in the air when the owl hooted. "Jesus, you weren't kidding." He craned his neck, but he couldn't see anything.

"Try from the games room, maybe."

The games room glowed with moonlight, or they wouldn't have been able to see anything. As it was, it took them a few minutes of peering out into the night before Ty finally touched Ollie's shoulder and pointed. "There!"

Ollie followed the line of his arm just as the owl hooted again, ruffling its feathers. A chill went down his spine. "Okay, that's pretty cool."

He could barely make out Ty's grin in the moonlight. "Right? Not so bad to wake up to."

Definitely better than the end of that nightmare, Ollie thought. "Not for one night, at least."

And then another bird landed in the tree next to the first one.

The owls did a very cute face-bumping thing.

Ollie said, "When is owl mating season?"

"Uh. I think it depends on the kind of owl."

Well, yes, probably. "Can you tell what kind of owls they are?"

"No?"

They watched for a moment longer; then Ollie ventured, "We had a nesting pair of barn owls living on our property when we lived in New York."

Neither of them took their eyes away from the tree. "Yeah?"

He nodded. "I was thirteen, so I thought it was pretty cool. But my sisters, uh, well, we kept finding their leftovers. Little headless rodents, shrews and mice and voles or whatever. I guess the brains are their favorite part? And then baby bunny season rolled around...."

The owls silently fluffed each other.

After a moment Ty said, "Do you think turning on the outside lights will be enough to scare them away?"

"They might at least decide to nest farther away from the house, which is good enough for me." Teenage Ollie had thought the decapitated animals were kind of neat, in a gruesomely fascinating way. Adult Ollie didn't want to look at them or clean them up or, crucially, answer any of Theo's questions about the decapitated baby bunny afterlife.

It certainly ruffled some feathers when Ty flicked on the lights that illuminated the garden. Ollie caught a flash of buff-and-brown feathers, and then the birds were gone, leaving the night eerily silent.

"I should get a motion sensor installed, maybe. Or a remote control." Ty yawned and turned away from the window. Then he did a double take when he saw Ollie, now illuminated in the overglow of the flood lights. "Jeez, aren't you freezing?"

Ollie looked down. The adrenaline had worn off, and his fear sweat was cooling on his body, so yeah, actually. He'd gone to bed in a thin pair of pajama pants, and his nipples were trying to secede. "Now that you mention it."

He thought he detected the hint of a flush on Ty's cheeks, but that probably came from having been caught noticing your roommate's nipples were about to fall off. Ty didn't get awkward about it. "I should probably get back to bed. Oh—but, uh, wait up for a minute? There's a throw blanket on the couch if you want to, like, not die of hypothermia."

Bemused, Ollie wrapped himself up like a burrito and sat on the sofa, tucking his feet in so they wouldn't get cold. True to his word, Ty was gone only a few minutes. When he returned, he was carrying a couple of ancient plastic radio-looking things.

He held them up triumphantly. "Found these when I was binge cleaning the other day. Baby monitor."

Ty passed them over like he was bestowing a gift. Ollie untangled his arms to take them. "Uh... thanks?"

Seeing Ollie didn't quite understand, Ty said, "Okay, so, you said hearing Theo breathe helps when you wake up at night. But now he's got his own room, and that's great, but what about you, right? So—baby monitor. It's, like, thirty years old, obviously, but it still works. Just put the transmitter in Theo's room and the receiver in yours. You can keep it turned off until you need it. And since they're like ancient technology, they actually plug into the wall. No batteries."

Ollie wet his lips, suddenly without words. *I met you a week ago.* But it didn't have anything to do with Ollie, not really. He could see that. This was how Ty treated people. He looked out for them. He was a caregiver. How else had he ended up a paramedic?

"Thank you," he said when his voice returned to him. He didn't want to wake Theo tonight with the baby monitor, but knowing he'd have it in the future helped. He already knew he'd be sleeping better in the future. "Wish I'd thought of this."

"Hey, I wouldn't have either if I hadn't found the thing." Ty gave him a bashful smile. "Anyway, I'm gonna see if I can't convince my body to go back to sleep. Night, Ollie."

"Night, Ty."

"Do I HAVE to come?" Theo asked the next day, dragging his feet as Ollie helped him choose a brunch outfit that didn't look like he'd spent three hours playing baseball in it.

Ollie probably should have done laundry yesterday.

"'Fraid so, bud." There—that sweater was decent. Ollie offered it and received a disgusted look in return.

Possibly he should also take his kid clothes shopping.

"Anyway, why do you want to stay home?" Theo had been glued to Ollie's hip for the past six months. "You don't want to spend time with your dad?" Okay, so he kind of figured this was more avoiding the grandparents, but it had to happen sometime. Ollie was not above playing the guilt card.

Theo made a very dramatic eight-year-old noise. "No, that's just—you said Grandma and Grandpa are coming, and I—you don't like them."

Wait, what?

Ollie paused with his hands on a long-sleeve Nats shirt. "Theo, why would you say that?"

Theo rolled his eyes. Ollie had a sudden vision of what he'd be like as a teenager and made a mental note to look into cryogenically freezing his kid before that could happen. "'Cause that's what Mel said. Duh."

Mel. *Mel?* "When did you talk to your cousin?"

"At recess."

The shirt only had one little stain, near the cuff of one of the sleeves. If Theo wore a zip-up hoodie with it, no one would ever know. Ollie held up the shirt and received a nod of approval. "Okay, well, Mel doesn't know everything about me. I love your grandparents." He could've gone with *It's complicated*, but Theo was eight. One piece of the truth at a time. "I thought you weren't ready to meet them yet. You didn't seem like you wanted to."

Theo put on a thorny face. "I can change my mind."

"You sure can." Ollie still wasn't sure how Theo not going to brunch would've saved Ollie from his parents, but it didn't matter. "So, if *I* love your grandparents, and *you* want to have brunch with your grandparents, then can *we* get ready to go have brunch with your grandparents?"

"Okay," Theo said, tugging on his shirt, "but can I get pancakes?"

"As long as you promise to eat some protein with your sugar."

By some miracle, they made it to the restaurant only a few minutes late. The hostess at the front looked vaguely familiar; she smiled when she saw them. "Ollie Kent." She was his parents' age, but she reminded him of one of his high school friends—someone's mother, definitely, but he was having a hard time placing her. "Welcome back to town, sweetheart. Thank you for your service."

Ollie hoped his return smile looked more natural than it felt. "Uh, hi." He never knew what to say to that. *You're welcome?* Ollie hadn't done it for her, or for his country. He'd signed up for the Army in part to escape his parents and in part because he thought he could make the world a better place, and he'd made it home in one piece physically because—well, if he had to hazard a guess, probably because the universe had a sense of humor.

"And this must be your son." Her eyes widened a little. "Don't you look just like your father. Ollie, you're meeting your parents, right? They're right this way."

Ollie's parents were seated in a booth by the front window, which made Ollie twitch—a table would've been better—but the restaurant was pretty full with the after-church crowd, so they'd have to make do. He smiled at the hostess and finally remembered—"Thank you, Mrs. Robinson"—and helped Theo get settled.

"Hi, Mom, Dad. Sorry we're late."

His dad smiled carefully at Theo as his mother waved off his apology. "No, nonsense, Ollie. I remember what it was like trying to get you and your sisters anywhere on time."

"Hello, Theo," Ollie's father said. "I'm your dad's dad. I'm really happy to meet you."

He meant it too—Ollie could tell by the way he said it, but also from the fact that he didn't say something like *I've been waiting for months*.

Theo squinted at him like he was sizing him up and then held his hand out across the table to shake.

Ollie mentally awarded his dad ten points for not bursting into laughter. "Hi."

"Hello, Theo. Do you remember me?"

Theo looked at Ollie's mom and said, "You were at the park. And at the school."

Ollie's dad gave his mom third-degree side-eye, so she apparently hadn't been forthcoming with her husband about that encounter. "That's right. I'm your grandma."

Theo nodded seriously and asked, "Do you like pancakes?"

Ollie could've exploded with pride. Look at his kid, carrying on a conversation with grown-ups without any cues from Ollie. *Everybody* was getting points this morning, even Ollie. A good night's rest could do wonders.

It didn't take long for his dad to cajole Theo into a conversation about baseball—Ollie mentally congratulated himself on the wardrobe selection—and the two of them hashed out Friday night's disaster at length while Ollie's mom looked on with a well-disguised pout because she preferred football.

Ollie thought the introductions went well. His parents didn't overstep any boundaries, even if his mother did give him a look when Theo put in his pancake order. "With sausage, please."

She wasn't the one who'd have to deal with Theo's energy crash and subsequent nap this afternoon, so she could keep her comments to herself. Either Ollie managed to convey as much with his eyebrows, or she decided it simply wasn't worth the argument. Either way, Ollie counted it as progress.

He was so busy basking in the success of the moment that he missed the signs Theo was steering the conversation into dangerous territory until the whole thing hurtled off a cliff. "Dad, can Grandma and Grandpa come over to our house after lunch? I want to show Grandpa my signed baseball."

Two sets of shrewd eyes zinged in Ollie's direction. "Ollie, you didn't tell us you found an apartment! Where is it? Are you going to have a housewarming party? We'd love to get you something."

"I'm impressed you were able to find a backup plan so fast," his dad added. "If you need any furniture, we can lend you some. We still have your old bedroom set from when you were a kid."

And now they were being all *reasonable*. That made Ollie feel like an asshole for not telling them sooner, but he knew the general reasonableness level at the table was about to plummet.

"It's not exactly a backup plan," Ollie hedged. "It's more like, uh, Plan A."

His parents exchanged glances like they had no idea what that meant.

Ollie had been shot at, damn it. He could handle telling his parents he'd moved in with a hoodlum.

But he didn't get the chance, because Theo piped up, "We live with Ty now!"

If he lived to be five hundred, Ollie would never be as brave as his kid.

To his parents' credit, neither one of them said anything to dampen Theo's enthusiasm, although that might have been because he didn't give them a chance to get a word in edgewise.

"My room is really big, and it has a four-poster bed." On his syrup-sticky fingers, Theo ticked off the merits of living with Ty. "There's a big yard, and Dad let me sit on his lap when he cut the grass. It was *so cool*, I even got to drive! *And* there's a whole room for just games, like pinball and *Pac-Man* and Monopoly and poker."

Lord above, Ollie hoped his kid never took up poker. Ollie's parents would never let him hear the end of it.

Then Theo added, "I guess it's not *just* for games. Me and Ty did our homework there yesterday, 'cause of the nat'ral light."

Under the weight of his parents' combined gazes, Ollie felt his spine try to slither down the chair leg. Ollie willed it straight. He cleared his throat and offered, "It's a sun room on the back of the house."

This was obviously not the clarification they had been hoping for. Ollie's mom said, "Theo, why don't you come with me up front and we can pay the bill? You can help me do the math."

Theo looked at Ollie for permission. Ollie could've told him no, but he didn't think that would improve the situation. "It's okay," Ollie said. "I'll be right here."

Maybe he should've let Theo keep believing Ollie didn't like his parents.

Once grandmother and son were out of earshot, Ollie's father cleared his throat. "Son, is there something you want to tell me about you and Tyler Morris?"

"Didn't I just tell you guys Friday that I wasn't interested in dating right now? Did you think I was making that up?" He fought the urge to groan out loud. "I ran into Ty at the school, and we got to talking. The insurance company won't cover the house if it's empty, but he's only in town until the end of the school year before he goes back to Chicago. And the place is huge, Dad. I think he wanted the company."

His dad hummed neutrally. "You seem to have made fast friends with this man."

"We have a lot in common." The words came out before he really thought about them, and even though they surprised him, they rang true. They'd both experienced loss and disappointed parental expectations. They'd both fled this town to try to find their own way. And now they were both back here again. It made Ollie wonder if Ty's temporary teaching job chafed as much as Ollie's driving one.

Another noncommittal noise. "You say that Theo likes him?"

"Theo adores him. Probably because Ty's like a big kid himself. Last night we had a movie night with popcorn and watched *Moneyball*, which, uh, if you and Mom ever babysit, I'm sorry in advance for how many times you're going to have to see it."

Ollie was almost sure his father was going to withhold judgment. He was teetering on the edge. But then he shook his head and said, "You know your mother won't like it. I'm not going to rock the boat by taking your side."

Fuck. "I'm an adult and I can make decisions for myself and my son. Mom doesn't have to live there. Ty—"

Ollie paused as the bell above the door jingled.

"Speak of the devil," his father said.

Personally Ollie thought *the devil* was giving Ty a lot of credit. He was only waiting at the host station. He had his phone out but wasn't looking at the screen—probably getting a pickup order. Somehow he and Theo hadn't seen each other, probably because Theo had begged a handful of loose change off his grandmother to plonk down one of those old-fashioned donation funnels and Ty was staring intently at Mrs. Robinson as if he could will her to notice his existence.

Mrs. Robinson was pointedly ignoring him in favor of having a conversation with her coworker.

"Dad...."

"Isn't it going to hurt Theo anyway, to let him get attached when he's going back to Chicago?"

Ollie flinched. "Well, Dad, he knows damn well that anyone could leave him at any time, seeing as his mother died four months ago, so I think I can trust my kid to feel his own feelings. What's he supposed to do, never get attached to anyone ever?"

With a frown, his father turned in the booth, like he was half shielding Ollie from being able to look at Ty. Mrs. Robinson was still blatantly ignoring him. "People are going to talk, Ollie. About why a thirty-year-old man wants to live with someone else's child."

Oh, absolutely not. "Enough. First of all, Ty has a literal police clearance to work at the school. He also has one for his *real job* as a paramedic, saving people's lives." His hands clenched into fists under the table. "Second, if I hear anyone insinuating anything about queer men being pedophiles, they're going to get a piece of my mind if not my fist." Ollie tried to keep his temper in check, but his temper wasn't having it. "If you and Mom care more about what the church ladies might say than respecting my judgment and authority as a father, that's your problem. I'm not going to make it mine." He stood up and put a couple of twenties on the table to cover their share of the bill. "I'll tell Theo something came up today. You let me know if the two of you can be civil."

Then he turned toward the front of the restaurant and put on a smile for his kid. No reason for Theo to get dragged into this. "You ready to go, bud? I was thinking we'd go find a sports store, pick up a baseball bat—"

"Yeah!" Theo whooped. Ollie's mother looked like she'd bitten a rotten lemon. "Can we go right now?"

"Right now." Ollie kissed the top of his head.

And then, because if he was going to be an asshole, he might as well be a useful asshole, he added, "Oh, hey, Mrs. Robinson—I think Ty here is waiting for a pickup order."

As he strolled out into the spring sunshine, he could feel the eyes of the whole town on his back, but he was starting to think maybe he only cared about the startled blue pair that lived down the hall from him.

Chapter 10

TY DIDN'T have time to drive around aimlessly—there were a limited number of hours in the day, and he still had to do laundry—but he couldn't stomach the idea of going home yet, so he drove to the park and sat alone at a picnic table to eat his sad takeout sandwich. Mrs. Robinson had let it sit in the pickup area so long it had gotten soggy. He understood why she hated him—Tyler Morris, offender of church ladies everywhere—but he thought at least half of it was misplaced anger.

No point in trying to tell someone to stop carrying a grudge they'd held on to for sixteen years. If she hadn't gotten over it on her own by now, nothing Ty could say would change that.

At least his milkshake was still delicious, even if it had half melted. On the other hand, no brain freeze.

But eventually his puttering had to end. He drove home and shoved a load of laundry into the washing machine, went over his outlines for the next two days' lessons, and then sat down in front of his laptop to write an email.

He'd managed to squeeze in half an hour with the fire captain in Holton. Originally he'd only planned to go out there to see if they had any professional education he could sit in on, because their website was broken as fuck and nobody had their direct phone line posted anywhere these days. But instead he got sucked in as Gina lamented the state of the district's EMS services.

"That village you live in might have been small fifteen years ago, but its population has doubled in the past five years. And it's the same with three of the other villages we share services with." Ty didn't know how old she was, but she looked like she was aging as fast as the population was growing. "We've already started losing people because we can't be everywhere at once."

"That sounds like a lawsuit waiting to happen."

"Oh, it gets better." She put her head in her hands and rubbed her face. "Two of the villages in our district petitioned to start their own departments, but they can't because technically they *have* an 'established fire department.'"

"So either the district boundaries have to be redrawn or any new station has to be a substation of this department."

"And building substations is expensive. All new sets of equipment, including the engines, ladders, and ambulances. Why not try hiring more people and see if that works? And let's forget about the fact that we still have to transport them to the emergency."

Ty whistled under his breath. "Don't you just love red tape?"

"I'd love to drive the engine through it," Gina muttered direly. "But anyway, to answer your question—no, we don't have any professional development activities coming up I could invite you to. Because we literally don't have time to organize something like that." She blinked. "Hey, wait, you don't want to organize something, do you?"

At that point Ty made his excuses and scrambled out of the station before he could get press-ganged into service.

But now, well…. Ty might not live in this town anymore, but other people did—people like Ollie and Theo and Henry and Eliza and Peggy. And even the people Ty didn't like still deserved prompt access to emergency services so they didn't die or lose their homes. Part of being a first responder was spotting problems before they turned into catastrophes, and this one was on the fast track.

So he planned to write an email to the town council as a "concerned citizen." He figured he technically was paying taxes here, so his opinion should count. But he hadn't expected to look at the council roster and see Mr. Chiu sitting on the board—and what the hell did that guy need a councilor's salary for? Writing the email now felt pointless, because Chiu was an asshole and would ensure anything Ty said got dismissed because Ty said it. But he wrote it anyway and sent it. Then he put serious thought into whether the wall between the kitchen and the living room was load-bearing and if he remembered where his dad kept the sledgehammer.

It was probably for the best that he heard the crack of a bat from outside and found a better outlet for his feelings. He slipped on his shoes and walked out the back door of the games room.

If Ty's childhood had looked like this….

But it hadn't.

Ty must've missed the lesson on holding the bat and how to swing, because Ollie was pitching now, slow underhand tosses. They were using softballs rather than baseballs, and Ollie had a whole clutch of them at his feet. There was another collection behind Theo, and a few more lying in the grass at various intervals.

"Okay, now try choking up on the bat a little bit. Just like that, good. You ready?"

Theo adjusted his hat—a new one Ty hadn't seen before—his grip, and his stance. Kid was practically ready for the pros. "Ready!"

Ty cheered when he hit a solid line drive back at Ollie. "Nice hit, Theo!"

Ollie jumped out of the way to avoid a straight shot to his nuts. "We're gonna work on your aim, though," he added ruefully.

Theo was giggling even as he accepted Ty's high-five. "Sorry, Dad."

"You want in?" Ollie gestured to Ty. "We've got room for a catcher… or a fielder… or a medic."

Theo laughed again.

Did Ty want in?

"Absolutely. Let me see if I can find my glove." He hoped his dad hadn't thrown it away.

THE WHOLE first week living with Ollie and Theo, Ty had been on alert for disaster. It seemed like so much could go wrong. What if Theo turned out to hate him, or one of them used up all the hot water in the morning, or they didn't like the same food? What if they somehow managed to step on each other's toes in his dad's rambling mansion? What if Ty had forgotten how to live with other people in his space?

And those were only the rational worries. That didn't count things like *What if I run into Ollie when he's just gotten out of the shower and he's wet and only wearing a towel*, which happened to him on that first Wednesday morning. The rest of the thought went *and I can't stop staring or drooling and it makes Ollie so uncomfortable he moves out and I never see him or Theo again*, which didn't happen because despite what Ty's father might have said on the subject, Ty did actually have both self-control and self-respect.

Did he also now have the image of Ollie's muscular chest and shoulders seared into his memory for eternity? Of course, but Ty was a goddamned adult and he could deal with it.

Anyway, the point was, after that first week, it got... easy. Ollie frequently still looked so good Ty thought he was hallucinating—he spent a lot of time outdoors and that agreed with him in a way Ty couldn't articulate—but it didn't take long for that to become the least interesting thing about him. He read Theo bedtime stories (insisting even when Theo claimed, unconvincingly, that he was too old) and did the dishes and cut the grass and yelled at the TV when the Mets were losing, which was frequently. Three of them in the house and none of them could pick a winning baseball team. Someone should figure out the odds on that.

They folded laundry together and ate together and hung out together, and it took no time at all for Ollie to go from *that hot guy I live with* to *the best friend I've ever had.*

And that didn't even make sense. Ty worked ridiculous hours in a high-pressure job that basically forced you to make a surrogate family out of your coworkers because you were going to see them more than you saw your actual family. And sure, he missed his team back in Chicago—Stacey with her wry advice, the rookie's every-other-f-bomb way of speaking, Jordan and his city-slicker homesteading and his homemade bread-and-butter pickles.

Ty had never been tempted to tell any of them about his childhood, beyond *I don't really talk to my dad. It's complicated.* With Ollie it was like he could hardly keep it from bursting out of him, like someone had filleted him open and sewed him up, but the stitches wouldn't hold, and he just kept spilling his guts.

The thing was, he'd started to suspect his guts were poisoned, because every time he did it, he felt a little better after.

Maybe when he went back to Chicago, he could open up a little more with his team. It would be nice to have that kind of unguarded, honest relationship with them that they had with each other—to have people know he was available to babysit, and have someone he could ask to water his plants when he went out of town. This time Ty had brought all his herb pots to the station, figuring they'd get used even if they weren't alive when he got back.

He had to hold on to the idea that he could recreate what he had now in a different setting. He liked working with kids—they kept him on his toes, they made him laugh, they made him think about things differently—but what Ty really needed, what every therapist he'd ever seen had told him, was to be *needed*, and the kids didn't. They'd be fine, or better off, in a real teacher's hands. Real teachers knew what they were doing. Ty was a glorified babysitter, and he was okay with that temporarily, but he was his best self when he could step into someone else's crisis.

He missed being that version of himself, but he knew he couldn't do it here. Ty needed the trust and confidence of the people around him. He couldn't exist in a place where he'd always be his father's fuckup.

Which was too bad, because this town could use an experienced paramedic or six.

All this was buzzing around in the background of his brain one day near the end of April. Baseball practice had been rained out, so Ty had taken Theo with him to get a few groceries instead, figuring he had the extra time, so he'd make something special.

"Do you know what your dad's favorite dinner is?" he asked as they picked up a cart. Ollie'd been getting home later and later, the new job obviously not what he'd been expecting. It was wearing him down, and Ty wanted to cheer him up. "Something he used to order in restaurants, maybe?"

This town didn't have a whole lot of dining options—definitely not compared to what Theo and Ollie would've been used to in DC.

"He used to get buggy beef."

Well, Ty wasn't making *that*. "Do you know what kind of restaurant it came from? What did you order, when he got that?"

"Pad thai."

Okay, so some kind of Asian restaurant, probably. "*Bulgogi* beef?" Ty asked.

Theo's face brightened. "Yeah! That's it."

"Okay." Ty steered the cart toward the produce section. "I can make that."

Buggy beef. He shook his head. Kids were hilarious.

This early in the afternoon, the grocery store patrons were mostly older folks—people his parents' age or older. Ty caught Eliza's eye from an aisle over and waved; she waved back with a smile and then rolled her eyes when she noticed Mrs. Sanford giving him the gimlet.

That would've made grocery shopping at this time uncomfortable, but Theo provided a good buffer. Nobody wanted to outright be a jerk to someone hanging out with a kid—especially hometown hero Ollie Kent's kid.

Theo did not protect Ty from the awkwardness of running into Jake Robinson, but Ty didn't think anything could save you from the mortification of meeting someone who'd been caught with your dick in his mouth behind the school bleachers. A piece of you would die inside and that'd be it.

At least the encounter seemed to mortify Jake too. Ty nodded at him as they passed in front of the pears. "Jake."

Jake cleared his throat and pointedly kept his gaze ahead, like he couldn't be caught speaking to Ty in public. "Morris. Cute kid."

"Thanks. I'm just borrowing him, though."

Even that short of an exchange would probably have the church ladies buzzing. Jake probably knew it too, from the wry smile he managed when their eyes accidentally locked for a second.

Small towns. What were you gonna do, really?

Ty was pretending to consult Theo on which cut of beef to buy when someone shouted for help.

Ty knew a medical emergency tone when he heard one. Instinct kicked in and sent him running toward the shout—and then he remembered Theo.

Theo, who'd lost his mother a few short months ago. Who'd been in a hospital for too much of his life. Who didn't need to see whatever Ty was running to.

Who had been entrusted to Ty's care.

Then he saw Eliza beelining toward him down the main aisle and sent up a silent prayer of thanks to the god of first responders. He met her eye and she nodded. "Theo, hey, have you met my friend Eliza? She knew your dad when he was your age."

"And even younger," Eliza agreed, holding out her hand to shake.

Ty knelt so he could be on Theo's eye level. "Okay, buddy, you know I'm a paramedic, right?"

Theo nodded.

"Someone in the store needs help, and I need to go to them. I need you to stay with Eliza, okay? She's a good friend of mine, she'll take good care of you."

Somehow he managed to wait for Theo's confirmation before he sprang to his feet and booked it down the cereal aisle.

The bystander effect was in full force in front of the Cheerios. Two people in store polos were standing together, both with their phones out, neither dialing. A woman lay on the floor, unmoving, blood pooling on the floor near the edge of a pallet. She must've hit her head when she fell.

Ty was already jerking off his jacket as he got next to her on the floor. He looked up long enough to point. "You"—store employee on the left—"call 911, give them the store's address, and tell them we've got a…." He glanced down. Fuck, that was Mrs. Sanford. "Woman in her midsixties, head trauma, possible spinal injury." He pressed his fingers to her neck. No detectable pulse, so either her heart had stopped or she was tachycardic, and it was racing so fast it couldn't pump enough blood. Based on the fact that she didn't seem to be actively bleeding, he was betting on the former. "Possible cardiac arrest. Breathing is shallow." He started chest compressions.

The store employee Ty had given instruction took a few steps back to make the call.

Ty looked at the other employee, who was wearing a manager name tag that read Christie. "Christie, does this store have an AED? A defibrillator?"

Christie snapped out of her dazed staring at Mrs. Sanford and met Ty's eyes. "Uh, yeah, we—in the break room—"

"Go get it and the first-aid kit now. Hurry."

Even as he told her, he doubted it would be enough. Mrs. Sanford's sternum cracked under his hands.

"Does this store have a pharmacy?"

Phone Guy shook his head.

Ty didn't think so. "Does anyone know this woman? Does she have any medical conditions?"

The growing crowd of bystanders only looked at each other, shaking their heads.

But Ty recognized one of them, and—well, he'd make do. "Jake, I need you to pick up her purse and open it. Go through it, see if there are any medications in there. Nitroglycerin would be great, but anything you find, let me know. Meanwhile if anyone here has aspirin…?"

"I have Advil," offered a woman who couldn't have been more than twenty as Jake dumped the contents of Mrs. Sanford's handbag on the floor.

Ty stopped CPR long enough to check for a pulse. Nothing detectable. He laced his fingers back together and resumed. "No, if it's a heart attack, that'll make it worse. Run to the frozen food section and get me a couple bags of frozen vegetables. Peas would be best but whatever you find, be fast." On the slim chance she was tachycardic, cooling her down could help slow her heart rate, maybe give her heart a chance to recover and start pumping more normally. "I need the ETA on that ambulance!"

"They're saying ten minutes."

Jesus *Christ*. "Tell them to drive faster."

"Jake, anything in the purse?"

"No, nothing! Sorry!"

Christie and Frozen Peas arrived at about the same time. Ty didn't stop compressions, just directed the young woman to put the peas along the side of Mrs. Sanford's face and under one armpit.

"Christie, you know how to use that thing?"

"Um, um, we had a training session on it last year—"

One she wouldn't remember while she was panicking. Ty walked her through it so he didn't have to stop until he had to pull his hands away to cut Mrs. Sanford's shirt open.

God, if she survived this, she would probably send him a bill for it.

The pads went on. How long had it been now since her heart had stopped pumping? Three minutes?

The AED recommended a shock. "Come on, Mrs. Sanford," Ty muttered. *I know you have something to say about how I ripped your shirt off in the grocery store.* "Everybody get back—*clear*!"

Her body arced as electricity raced through it.

The AED did not detect a pulse.

Ty swore and went back to compressions. Ten, twenty, thirty. No pulse. Time to shock her again. "Clear!"

When the on-duty paramedics finally arrived, Ty had sweated through his T-shirt from the effort of the compressions and the pool of blood had stopped spreading.

He gave them a rundown of the interventions he'd tried and let them take over, but by that time they all knew it was a lost cause.

The ambulance didn't run the siren as it pulled out of the parking lot.

The crowd dispersed.

Ty heaved a long breath and fought the urge to wipe the sweat off his forehead. He had blood on his hands and soaked into the knees of his pants. At least he was wearing dark-wash jeans today.

"Um," said Christie, who was the only other person left in front of the Cheerios, "we have a staff washroom in the back, if you want to wash up."

With a little luck, he could get there before Theo saw him. "I would really appreciate that."

He texted Eliza as soon as his hands were clean, and she brought Theo to the back of the store to meet him as he emerged, as presentable as he could make himself.

"Thank you," he told Eliza feelingly, "for looking after him while I—"

To his utter shock, she cut him off by pulling him into a hug.

For a second Ty didn't remember what to do with his hands. Then, after a moment, he folded them around her. "My clothes are kind of—"

"Shut up and hug me, Ty."

"Yes, ma'am."

After a moment she pulled away and patted his cheek. "You're a good boy. And so's this one." She put her hand on Theo's shoulder. "Though between you and me, I think he deserves some ice cream."

Ty cracked a smile. "Well, that makes two of us."

"Two who deserve ice cream?" Theo said. "Or two people who think I deserve ice cream? 'Cause that's actually three."

"All right, all right." Ty smiled at Eliza and steered Theo to the frozen section—the long way, so they could stay far out of sight of the war zone in the cereal aisle. "New plan. What about frozen pizza and ice cream for dinner?"

"And we can do bulgogi tomorrow?"

Tomorrow they had a baseball game. Ty was pretty sure the meat had to marinate for a while, and he'd lost his enthusiasm for grocery shopping. "Maybe Thursday."

He got them both home and set Theo up with his homework in the games room while Ty went to have a very fast breakdown in the shower.

Theo hadn't asked him any questions, at least not about what Ty had been doing. Based on his level of calm, Ty would bet he didn't know a woman had died in the store today. He did ask why Eliza wasn't still Ollie's aunt, or how that worked, which Ty admitted ignorance to. He didn't have any personal experience with relatives beyond parents. If he had to guess, it had more to do with Ollie's family not having moved to town until after his uncle was dead than anything.

But just because he hadn't asked this afternoon didn't mean he wouldn't ask. News was bound to get out. Sooner or later Ty was going to have to explain—

Fuck. He needed to text Ollie.

He closed the toilet lid and sat down as he pulled out his phone. Where did he even start with that? *Hey, remember how you trusted me to look after your kid? Well today he almost got to watch someone die because of me.*

But it was a small town and gossip traveled fast. Ollie needed to hear it from Ty before he heard it from anyone else. *A lady had a heart attack while Theo and I were at the grocery store today. I asked Eliza to look after him so I could go do CPR. I don't think he saw anything but I wanted you to know.*

There. Now he could sit here on the toilet with his guts churning while he waited for Ollie to text him back and tell him he had fucked up and they were moving out and he was going to be alone again.

Ty's hands shook. Dealing with a death on the job was easier. The uniform let him keep some distance between Ty and Paramedic Morris. Not that he hadn't done first aid while off duty before, but he'd never done it in his hometown.

He'd never lost a patient while a kid he was looking after was within spitting distance.

He felt like he might puke.

Finally the phone vibrated. *Oh my God. Is she ok? Are you ok? Is Theo ok?*

Ty blinked suddenly stinging eyes. Ollie wasn't mad at him—yet.

Mrs. Sanford didn't make it. I'm fine. That much was, if not exactly true, then only a little white lie. *I don't think Theo knows she died.* But he would find out, if not at school tomorrow, then probably sometime this week.

I'm really sorry. I know he's been asking a lot of questions about death since his mom passed. I hope this isn't triggering for him.

His hands were still shaking when Ollie's reply came through. *Like you said, he doesn't know yet. But even when he finds out, it was going to happen sooner or later. People die.* Then, before Ty could think of another way to frame this mess as his fault, *You were doing a good thing. Theo will understand.*

Something inside Ty unclenched. Okay, so Ollie really wasn't mad. Good. That was—good. *I hope so*, Ty wrote back, and then he turned the shower heat up as high as he could stand and tried to melt the guilt from his shoulders.

He'd done everything he could. Right? Mrs. Sanford had been bleeding from a head wound on top of her cardiac event. He couldn't have done anything else to save her. He only had one pair of hands. Maybe if he'd gotten the aspirin from the store's first-aid kit, if he'd crushed that up and gotten it into her system—

Had he not done it because she treated him horribly?

No. He wouldn't have let her die. He'd done everything he could. Some people couldn't be saved.

The patch of dried blood on his thigh turned pink and washed down the drain. He willed his guilt to go with it. It didn't work, but it was worth a shot.

He got out of the shower and put the clothes he'd been wearing in a garbage bag. It wasn't like he couldn't afford new ones, and he didn't want to deal with the bloodstains. He didn't want to look at the evidence. He'd never wear them again even if by some miracle it did all come out.

Then he dressed in sweatpants and a T-shirt and took the garbage bag out to the garage. Not that he thought Theo might go through the garbage or something, but… just in case.

But something was weird when he returned to the house.

"Theo?"

There was a decisive *snap* from the games room, followed by the sound he'd heard before—a stifled hiccup of a noise, all the more distinctive for the fact that Ty hadn't heard it in years.

The unmistakable sound of a boy trying to hide his tears.

Had Theo found out what had happened? Had he been crying the whole time Ty was in the shower. "Theo, are you—"

He stepped into the games room to see Theo holding an iPad to his chest, the cover closed tightly over it. The source of the snapping noise, no doubt. Theo's eyes were red-rimmed, his cheeks streaked with tear tracks, even if his skin was dry now.

"Hey," Ty said gently, feeling awkward and out of his depth. But he couldn't leave Theo alone. He pulled out the chair next to Theo at the poker table and folded himself into it. "Is, uh, is everything okay?"

Theo's chin crumpled as he curled his lips inward, biting down on more tears or whatever words he wanted to say.

"It's okay," Ty backpedaled. Hell, who was he kidding? He'd known this kid for two weeks. Theo wasn't going to just spill his guts—

"Do you ever miss your dad?"

Or, okay, he was totally going to spill his guts and Ty was going to have to find a way to navigate that conversational minefield.

Really, he should've seen this coming. Theo had lost his mother. A kid didn't simply get over that. And he knew Ty had just lost a parent too. Of course he wanted to talk about it with someone who'd been through the same thing.

Ty wanted to answer his questions in a way that felt sensitive and helped him process his grief, but he didn't want to lie. "It's complicated, for me."

Theo put the iPad on the table. "How come?"

Loaded question. Ty let out a slow breath and considered his phrasing. "You know how your dad plays baseball with you, and reads you stories, and eats dinner with you every night?"

Theo nodded.

"Well, my dad—he wasn't like that. We didn't spend a lot of time together, even before my mom died. But then she did, and…." He pursed his lips. He didn't want to speak ill of the dead, even if his father deserved it. He didn't want to do that in front of Theo, who was looking for someone to relate to. And so instead he admitted out loud, for the first time, something he'd always suspected, and gave his father the grace no one had ever given Ty. "I think every time he looked at me, he saw my mom, and that hurt him because he missed her."

With a heavy sniff, Theo looked around and—yeah, okay, Kleenex, they needed Kleenex before that snot trail made its way to his mouth and Ty gagged. He used his long reach to snatch the box off the top of the bookcase and offered it.

Theo blew his nose with the volume of a foghorn, because he was eight years old. Right. Ty needed to refocus this conversation. This was about Theo's grief, not his. "But it's okay if you miss your mom. Everybody—everybody experiences grief differently."

Theo swiped his eyes with the snotty Kleenex. Ty fought down a twitch. "Miss Eliza said she likes to talk with Uncle David's family 'cause they knew him too, and it helps her feel like part of him is still here. But nobody here knew my mom. And it makes me mad, because I'm—because they have that and I don't."

Oh, kid. Ty's battered heart tried to break again. "Your dad knew her," he pointed out gently. "You know he'd talk to you about her if you wanted. I know that they weren't *together*, but they were friends. He loved her. He misses her too." And if Ty knew anything about Ollie, it was that he'd walk through fire for his kid.

Theo ducked his head and dropped the Kleenex on the table. Ty took the opportunity to whisk it out of reach before Theo could give himself pinkeye. "But I don't—I don't want him to think he's not good enough. I know he's trying really hard."

No kid should have to carry this inside them. Now *Ty* needed a Kleenex. "I don't think he would think that," he said around the lump in his throat. "But if you want… if you want, you can talk to me about her. I didn't know her, but I can listen."

There was a scrape and a clatter as Theo stood up too quickly and knocked the chair over. And then Ty had a crying eight-year-old in his lap and tears in his own eyes, and they were wrapped up in a hug that felt like family, the kind of hug Ty hadn't experienced since his mom died. He was on the other side of it now—the adult instead of the child—but it grounded him just the same.

When they'd both gotten control of themselves, Ty snatched a tissue from the box for each of them and dabbed his eyes. "Okay, I think we need a new plan. First, we're going to wash our faces."

Theo nodded.

"And then we're going to make cookies."

"Before dinner?" Theo asked. "What about homework?"

Ty extended a hand toward the door and let Theo precede him into the hall. "Sometimes we have to take care of our hearts before we can take care of our brains, so we're going to make cookies. My mom's special recipe. And maybe you can tell me about your mom. Only if you want. Okay?"W

"Okay."

They stopped by the linen closet and Ty got them each a fresh washcloth. Something about the moment felt fragile, and he didn't want to let Theo out of his sight just yet, so he led them through the master bedroom—unoccupied since his father's passing—and into the master bath, so they could each have their own sink to wash up.

When they were safely ensconced in the kitchen, Theo on a chair so he could better reach the counter, Ty thought he was prepared for more emotionally heavy stuff. After all, he'd invited Theo to talk about his mom.

But he wasn't prepared for Theo to say, "Hey, Ty?"

Ty got down the flour and sugar. "What's up, kiddo?"

"Does it...? Is it bad that I get mad sometimes? 'Cause my friends still have their moms? Or 'cause Miss Eliza has people who remember Uncle David?"

Ty huffed out a breath and made a note to measure the chocolate chips with Theo's heart, rather than his own. "No, buddy. You're not bad, okay? It's okay to have feelings. It's not nice to take your feelings out on other people, though. But you're not doing that, and even if you did, I think people would understand it's because you're hurt."

Theo nodded and flipped open the latch on the flour canister. He didn't look up when he asked, "Do you ever get mad? 'Cause of Dad and me. Does it make you sad?"

Kid, we literally just stopped crying. "A little bit, sometimes. But mostly it makes me really happy, because you deserve a dad who pays you lots of attention and spends time with you. Every kid should have people who love them like that, Theo. And it's good for me to see that and to remember I should've had that too and it's not my fault that I didn't."

After a moment of contemplation, Theo nodded. Then he said, with the kind of gravitas only an eight-year-old could manage, "Feelings are hard."

Ty startled into a laugh. "You said it, kid." He plopped the egg carton on the counter next to the stand mixer. "Now, pass the sugar."

Chapter 11

OLLIE ENDED his shift on edge after Ty's message about Mrs. Sanford, so he was primed for panic when he closed his locker and saw a new notification on his phone.

But this time Ty hadn't just sent a text, he'd sent a picture: Theo passed out on the couch, head pillowed awkwardly on Ty's knee. In the background, the TV showed a still from *Moneyball*.

So just a heads-up but I don't think we're getting our homework done tonight.

Without thinking, Ollie touched the phone screen, as if he could move through it into Ty's weird old-man living room and squeeze in at the other end of the couch with Theo's feet in his lap.

God. He should be there. Someone had died, and his kid had almost seen it because Ollie had to work. And now it was—fuck, it was almost six. So much for a family-friendly company. Ollie's ass, legs, and shoulders ached from too many hours in the driver's seat of an armored truck. His heart ached for his kid. Obviously something had hit home for him today.

And that didn't even touch the complicated tangle of things he felt that someone else was there making sure Theo got what he needed. Gratitude, yes. Envy, certainly. Guilt. Pride, a little, because Ollie had navigated that all by himself, making friends with someone with such a generous heart, someone Theo obviously loved and trusted already.

None of those explained the peculiar tug in his chest, the sensation almost like barbed wire wrapped around his heart. Ollie rubbed his sternum distractedly and put his phone away. He wasn't going to ask Ty to explain whatever happened by text, and a phone call might wake Theo. They could figure things out in person.

When he got home, the television volume was on low and the smell of baked-from-frozen pizza filled the front room. Ollie left his boots by the door and his keys and wallet in the second bowl on the console table. Then he poked his head around the side of the couch. Theo was stretched out fully now, covered by the throw blanket from the games room. *Moneyball* was still playing on low volume; Ty must've set it to play on repeat or something.

Ollie wandered into the kitchen, where Ty sat at the island, half hidden behind an enormous plate of chocolate chip cookies. A mug of hot chocolate steamed in front of him.

Ollie cleared his throat as he sat across from Ty. "So the pizza I smell, that's dessert?"

Ty gave him an anemic smile and nudged the plate over a few inches. "Been that kinda day, I guess."

Off a long exhale, Ollie said, "Yeah." He paused. Picked up a cookie. Then, "I really hate my job."

He punctuated the statement by biting down. The chocolate chips were still molten, and the chewy, buttery crumb soothed something deep inside him.

"Honestly?" Ty sipped his hot chocolate. "Same."

Frowning, Ollie shoved the rest of the cookie into his mouth. After he swallowed, he said, "I thought you liked the kids."

"I love the kids," Ty clarified. "I'm just not built for sitting still, or grading things, or wrangling twenty-five eight-year-olds at a time. And I don't want to be out of my real job for so long that I get rusty."

Ollie glanced at the timer on the stove—still another three minutes on the pizza—and took another cookie. "Is that what happened today?"

Ty huffed and spun his now empty mug on the counter. "No. I think—there wasn't anything anyone could've done for her, short of installing a pacemaker or putting her on blood thinners long before this. But I...."

Ollie waited him out.

A gusty exhale. "I caught myself wondering after if I'd done everything I could. I know—I *know* I did. I only really wondered because Mrs. Sanford was such a.... She was not nice to me. And I resented that. But I still tried my best to save her." He lifted one large shoulder in a halfhearted shrug. "It's easier to deal with when you're wearing a uniform."

"I know something about that."

They exchanged meaningful glances and then, by unspoken agreement, dropped the subject when the timer dinged. Ty pulled out the pizzas and set them on the stovetop to cool.

"You never get deep dish," Ollie commented. "I would've thought living in Chicago…."

Ty tossed an oven mitt at his head. "If you need a spoon to eat it, it's not pizza."

"True." Ollie glanced at the kitchen door, which he'd propped open with the heavy pink rock salt slab Ty said was for cooking meat on. No movement from the living room. He sighed and opened the drawer for the pizza cutter. "So, not to jump from one difficult subject to another, but uh…."

"What happened with Theo this afternoon?" Ty finished as Ollie sliced the pizza.

"Kinda killing me, I won't lie." He winced. "Poor choice of words."

Ty handed Ollie a plate. "You'd think it would've been the medical drama, but actually it was Eliza. Well, talking to Eliza. I asked her to look after Theo while I—anyway. I guess she told him about being married to your uncle, and how she still talks to your family because they remember him, and he got jealous because no one here knew his mom to talk about except you, but then he felt bad about being jealous, and he didn't want you to think you weren't doing a good job."

That little monologue just about took Ollie out at the knees. His fingers felt suddenly nerveless. He was glad he hadn't put anything on his plate yet, because it clattered loudly to the counter as his hand spasmed.

"Ollie—Jesus, Ollie, are you okay?"

The barbed wire around Ollie's heart constricted until it felt like something had to break. Then Ty put a hand between his shoulder blades and the tension snapped. Ollie let out a shaky breath. "I'm okay," he said, faintly, and then again, surprised that he meant it: "I'm okay. Just, you weren't kidding when you said it was a rough afternoon." He turned to meet Ty's gaze.

Ty's shoulders were up around his ears, and his cheeks were red—shame, not embarrassment. "I'm sorry we didn't get to the homework. I know it's not my place to say what's important—"

"Wait. Are you seriously apologizing right now?" Ollie said disbelievingly. "For taking such good care of my kid that he could open up to you like that?"

Ty's flush deepened. He flicked his gaze up to meet Ollie's eyes. "Um."

"Come here," Ollie demanded, and opened his arms.

It shocked him how easily Ty went into them.

More shocking was how good he felt there.

Ty melted against him like he didn't have a spine. He snaked his arms around Ollie's waist and sagged into him like no one had hugged him in years. Maybe no one had.

Come to think of it, Ollie couldn't recall the last time he'd hugged anyone other than Theo. But his body remembered what to do—arms wrapped around Ty's broad shoulders, head leaned against the side of Ty's, breathe deeply. Ty smelled like he did in the mornings, of vanilla lavender bodywash and coconut shampoo; he must've showered after the grocery store. Ollie took a deep breath and then another before he realized that at some point he was supposed to let go.

But Ty didn't seem like he was in a big hurry for that, so he didn't.

Ollie had hugged people who were taller and broader than him before, of course. Not as many since he became an adult, but he'd served with guys who were taller than his six feet and broader too. But he'd never hugged any of them like this.

He wasn't sure he'd ever hugged anyone like this.

Finally Ty took a shaky breath and raised his head, and Ollie forced his arms to soften and let go. "Um." He was bright red now, and blotchy, his eyes a little too bright, but he smiled crookedly. "I guess you're not mad about the homework."

"Good guess," Ollie said dryly. He helped himself to a few slices of pizza and sat back down at the island, trying not to shiver and wondering if they'd left a window open somewhere. It was warm in the kitchen. He had no reason to feel cold.

Ty served himself some pizza, poked his own head out into the living room, and must've decided the same as Ollie had—that Theo could sleep for another half hour or so before they fed him—because he slouched back to the island. This time he sat at the corner next to Ollie, so their knees almost touched. "Your kid is pretty great, you know."

The chill disappeared. "Yeah." Allison did most of the work, but Ollie had contributed too. "I got lucky."

"*Lucky?*" Ty snorted. "Ollie. One minute your kid was crying about having no one to talk to about his mom and the next he was worried it made me feel bad to see you doing your World's Best Dad routine."

Ollie ignored the heat rising in his face and somehow managed to swallow the bite of pizza he had in his mouth. He thought he'd done a good job making sure Theo knew he could talk to Ollie about Allison if he wanted, but obviously he needed to be firmer about it. Or gentler. Gentler? "Does it?"

Ty made an indecipherable noise. "*See*?!"

Ollie didn't.

Apparently Ty didn't actually expect him to; he shook his head fondly. "Never mind." He shoveled in another bite of pizza.

But maybe the sound had woken Theo, because a moment later he appeared in the doorway. "Dad."

Ollie scooped him into his arms before he could think about it. "Hey, buddy."

And then he couldn't make himself put him back down again. He sat with Theo in his lap instead.

"Did I miss dinner?"

"Uh, nope." Ty stood and loaded another plate, which he set down next to Ollie's. "Plenty to go around."

TUESDAY THE team had an away game. Ty couldn't decide what was worse, the 13–2 loss, or the fact that he had to get on the bus with the kids afterward and go all the way back to the school instead of just getting in his truck to go home.

To make matters worse, there was nothing else to do in a small town on a Tuesday night, so the visitors' section was decently full anyway. Ty couldn't tell if he felt persecuted because he couldn't save the team from themselves or because he couldn't save Mrs. Sanford. Either way, his skin itched throughout the game. He couldn't help but feel like everyone was looking at him.

On top of that, there was some kind of teenage soap opera happening in the infield. Pete and Paolo, the catcher, were okay; Paolo and Danny, the first baseman, were fine. Pete and Danny seemed to be giving each other the cold shoulder.

As the team traipsed back into the dugout after a brutal five-run infield, Ty muttered to Henry, "Do we ask them about it?"

Henry's expression read Cynical Old Man. "Absolutely not. If we ask and they tell us, we might be obligated to mediate."

Okay, well, Henry probably needed his pension, so *he'd* have to mediate, but Ty? "*I* could ask," he pointed out. "What're they gonna do, fire me? This job doesn't even pay for groceries."

"But then you'll know and have to keep it to yourself," Henry pointed out, and that sounded awful, so Ty didn't ask.

In the bus on the way home, he had Theo next to him, trying to do his math homework while half falling asleep against Ty's shoulder. Ty was glad he was doing it now, because his nose told him Theo needed a bath tonight.

He shot Ollie a quick text when they got back to the school. *On our way. Did you get dinner by any chance?*

He got back a picture of an enormous pot of spaghetti. *It's not fancy but you won't starve.*

You're my favorite, Ty sent back, and his stomach growled all the way home.

Ollie sent Theo off to shower as soon as he cleaned his plate. Then he puttered around the kitchen with Ty doing dishes, even though he'd cooked so it was definitely Ty's turn.

"I can handle this," Ty promised through a yawn.

"Uh-huh," Ollie said good-naturedly. He elbowed Ty in the ribs. The hug on Monday must have broken the physical-touch dam, because the boundaries of personal space had been redrawn in the past few days. Ty wasn't complaining. Human contact was important for mental and emotional health, and God knew he and Ollie could use all the serotonin supplements they could get. "Go sit down on the couch. You're missing the Cubs game."

OLLIE HAD thought his parents would cave in a day or two. He knew how much they wanted to build a relationship with Theo, and he wanted that for them too, but not at the expense of Ollie being second-guessed over every decision he made about Theo's well-being.

But by Thursday, he still didn't have an apology, and he was starting to wonder if he'd lost objectivity.

Am I making too big a deal of this? he texted Cass on his lunch break. *Be honest.*

He didn't get a reply until two hours later. *Hell no. Stick to your guns. Do you know how many arguments we had about Mel being baptized?*

Cass's husband was Jewish. They'd agreed Mel could make her own decisions about religion when she was old enough. Ollie could imagine how that had gone over with their parents. *And you still speak to them?*

They get three strikes a year and if they use them all we don't come for Christmas.

He whistled under his breath. *I might have to try that one.*

Good luck!

Ollie was going to need it—both with his parents and with the commute home, because construction season was upon them. At the rate they were going today, he'd barely make it home in time for Theo's bedtime. To make matters worse, their usual truck was being serviced, and the seat in this one had spent its previous life as a medieval torture device. He already knew he'd have to take muscle relaxants to sleep tonight, which meant he could expect the nightmares to make an appearance. One day he hoped to be able to once again rest his mind and his body simultaneously.

But when he eventually did make it home, the scent in the kitchen almost made him forget how cranky he was.

He stopped in the living room, where Theo was curled up on the couch with his nose three inches from his book. Ollie kissed the top of his head and accepted a distracted reverse half hug in return, then carefully pulled the book farther away from Theo's face so he didn't end up with a headache.

Urged on by his stomach, he continued to the kitchen. "Okay, two questions: What are you making and when can I eat it?"

Ty scraped something warm and garlicky from the wok onto a serving dish. "Bulgogi beef, and it's ready now."

Ollie might cry. "Seriously?"

He smiled. "A little bird told me it was your favorite. Well, he actually said 'buggy beef,' but we got some context and sorted it out. I was going to make it Monday, only Monday ended up being a word I can't say unless I want to contribute to Theo's college fund."

Ollie got down a trio of pasta bowls and opened the rice cooker. "At least cursing is more fun than selling a kidney."

By now they moved around the kitchen, in and out of each other's space, in a kind of dance. Ollie knew what Ty would do next—remove the hot pan from the burner, wipe up any splatters around the stove, get the pitcher of water and carton of milk from the fridge. Ollie weaved in and out, grabbing napkins and cutlery and the bottle of gochujang Ty would forget about until he was three bites in and then return to the fridge for.

"Theo! Dinner's ready!"

He came into the kitchen with the book still in front of his face and would've tripped over his stool if Ollie hadn't plucked the book away.

"Dad!" he protested. "I just got to the good part."

"You can talk to us for five minutes so you don't get soy sauce all over your library book." Ollie slid his bowl in front of him. "Besides, Ty obviously worked hard on dinner. Doesn't it smell great?"

Heaving the kind of sigh eighteenth-century poets could only dream about, Theo dragged himself onto his barstool. "Yeah, I guess."

Ollie winced—Ty had obviously gone to a lot of trouble—but when he looked over to see Ty's reaction, he was hiding a smile.

Theo proceeded to eat his dinner so fast that Ollie didn't think he could even taste it. So much for talking to Ollie and Ty. He barely had time to breathe. "Thanks, Ty." He stood up and put his plate and fork in the dishwasher. "Can I be excused to go read now?"

Fuck it. How mad could Ollie be that his kid liked reading?

"Okay, but try to keep the book more than two inches from your face, all right?"

Ollie could tell Ty was laughing at him, but at least he did it behind his hand, where Theo couldn't see him.

When Theo had decamped to the living room, the laugh slipped out as the two of them got up to start cleaning. "That kid," Ty said ruefully. "Barrel of laughs. I needed that."

"Yeah?" Ollie chucked a detergent pod in the dishwasher. "You have a tough day too? Were the sixth graders mean to you again?"

Ty snapped the dishtowel at him. "They're always mean. No, this time it was Mr. Chiu. Old friend of my dad's. He sits on the town council now because I guess venture capitalism doesn't keep him busy enough or whatever."

Lots to unpack there, Ollie thought. "Where did you run into him?"

"Oh, I didn't." Ty slammed a cupboard door a little harder than necessary. "But on Sunday I had a conversation with the fire chief at the station in Holton, because I was hoping I could pick up some training while I'm in the neighborhood. Except no such luck, because they're so overrun with calls because of how much the population has grown, they can barely do that, never mind keep everyone up to date on their skills."

"Sounds bad."

"I thought so too. So much so that I wrote an email to the town council *even though* I knew Mr. Chiu was on it and hates my guts."

Ollie waited for the other shoe to drop.

"And then Mrs. Sanford had a heart attack in the grocery store on Monday."

The dots were there, but Ollie didn't connect them until Ty added bitterly, "Which Mr. Chiu pointed out was 'convenient timing' in his email reply to me this morning."

Holy shit. "He really implied—"

Ty gave him a tight, mirthless smile and raised his eyebrows.

"What the hell is wrong with this town?" Ollie wondered. "Genuinely. Should I take my kid somewhere else? Is there something in the water?"

"Metaphorically speaking," Ty offered, "I think my dad poisoned the well."

"Did you tell Mr. Chiu to go to hell?"

This time Ty's quirked lips held a trace of real amusement. "I told him any further communication should go through my lawyer."

"Ha." Ollie smirked. "Taste of his own medicine." Then he turned to put the wok away and froze as his whole back seized. "Ow. Fuck."

Ty took the pan before he could drop it and gently slid it into the cupboard. Then he turned around. "Whoa, hey, are you all right?"

Wincing, Ollie rolled his shoulders, trying to loosen whatever demonic muscle spasm had its claws in his trapezius. "Fine, kind of." His body had never betrayed him like this when he was in the Army. Maybe he needed to find a regular gym to go to just to make sure his joints stayed lubricated. "It's bullshit that the warranty on your body expires the minute you turn thirty and then everything immediately falls apart."

Ty laughed. "Wow, and people call *me* dramatic."

Ollie stuck his tongue out, but he could only hold the face for so long before he had to go back to working out the stiffness in his back. "God. Might have to be an early night."

"Actually… if you're okay leaving Theo with the baby monitor, I have an idea. We'll just be right outside." He paused. "On the deck."

A second later the pieces fell into place. "The hot tub?"

"Apparently my dad had a standing service call. Guy was here yesterday. Everything good. Water's at 102."

"Wow. I am not used to thinking nice things about your dad."

Ty grinned crookedly. "Guess there really is a first time for everything. Meet you out there in five?"

"Yup."

Ollie double-checked Theo didn't want to join them, but as he'd expected, he was too busy plowing through the last three chapters of his book to be bothered with something so trivial as a hot tub. He brought out the baby monitor—he should rename that if he was going to talk about it out loud—his phone, a towel, and a beer from the fridge, right in time for Ty to open the cover.

The sun had gone down, and the tub lights illuminated the steam escaping into the cool night air. The tension in Ollie's shoulders eased just looking at it.

"The beer's not gonna help your shoulder," Ty chided, but he said it wryly, because he had one of his own.

"Yes, Doc," Ollie agreed. "I promise to drink three glasses of water before bedtime."

"Well in that case, Dr. Morris prescribes sitting in the hot tub with the jets on for half an hour." Grinning, he pulled his shirt off and climbed into the hot tub.

Ollie couldn't follow fast enough.

The hot water stung skin that had pebbled to goose bumps in the chill. The scent of bromine prickled his nose. Ollie took a moment to close his eyes and tilt his head back against the padded side of the tub and let the simple pleasure of it wash through him.

Then Ty turned the jets on, and Ollie about flew across the tub into his lap. He braced his feet on the floor and pushed back into the massage and only barely held back a sound that was not appropriate for the occasion. "Okay," he said after a second, when he had better control of his vocal cords, "I have got to get me one of these."

The soft hiss of escaping carbon dioxide as Ty pried the top off his beer. "Why would you need your own?"

Ollie opened his eyes to find Ty staring at him with furrowed brow, like it didn't occur to him that Ollie would ever move out.

Which Ollie didn't know what to do with. Sure, Ty had asked him to move in, but Ollie had figured it was temporary. Ty made no secret of the fact that he needed to go back to Chicago, to his real job and his real life. He was only here out of necessity—and he had the house for the same reason. He was great with kids, but it wasn't his *purpose*, and he knew it.

Something deep inside Ollie sparked with jealousy at that, but he pushed it down.

"Uh." Ollie pried the cap off his own beer to give himself a few seconds to scramble for an answer. "I kind of thought... I mean, you're going to sell the house eventually, right?"

Ty's expression cleared. "Oh. Yeah, I guess. I wasn't thinking that far ahead. It's probably going to be a while. You're good housesitting for me for a couple years, right?"

Ollie tried to imagine the place without Ty in it—just him and Theo rattling around in this unnecessarily huge house, waging an eternal war against the dust bunnies. His entire extended family attempting to move in because he "had the space." No one to make homemade bulgogi and suggest they watch movies on the floor.

Thinking about it made his chest tighten. He cleared his throat and tried to play it off. "I'll think about it."

That wide, uncomplicated smile. "That's all I ask." Like Ollie was considering doing him a huge favor, living here for free.

This stupid town didn't deserve Tyler Morris.

Ollie was trying to think of a safer topic of conversation when Ty started rolling his shoulder. "Hey, where's your back tightest? If it's lower than your shoulders, you mind trading? Mine's acting up."

Ollie ached pretty much everywhere, so he stood up. "Sure."

As Ty turned around, Ollie's gaze caught on a slash of smooth pale skin beneath his shoulder blade. A smudge of black ink above his left pec. Another in red on the inside of his right elbow.

Ollie didn't realize he was staring until Ty said, "I swear none of the scars are from my parents." He paused and then added, "The tattoos either."

Ollie settled as deeply into his seat as he could and told himself it was the water making his cheeks feel warm. "Sorry. Didn't mean to stare." Then he shook himself out of it, reached for the beer near him, and stopped. "Actually I think we have to trade these too."

Laughing, Ty handed over Ollie's bottle. "You're probably confused, right? Didn't know being a paramedic was so dangerous?"

"Kinda wondering if you got into it because you had a lot of personal experience sewing yourself up," Ollie admitted before raising his beer to his lips.

"Well, only a handful are from the job. The shoulder thing—got stabbed in a bar fight."

Somehow Ollie managed to swallow without spraying beer into the hot tub. "Seriously? What was it about?"

"No fucking clue, man. I was a bouncer at the time." He shook his head. "Only a couple of my tokens are from the job I have now. This one"—he pointed at the slight puckering around his jawline—"was the first and almost last injury I ever got as a paramedic."

Ollie shivered involuntarily and pressed back deeper into the power of the jets. Ty was right, this side was better for his back. "What happened?"

"OD, first week on the job. Should've known better, but I panicked."

Ollie raised an eyebrow.

"Before administering Narcan, always check to make sure the patient doesn't have a weapon." He winced. "Or in this case, a broken bottle. They can wake up disoriented, still high, angry that they're *not* still high…."

"You saved somebody's life and they *stabbed you in the face*?"

"I mean, I don't think it was personal. Kind of a gut reaction."

"Still." Ollie tried to imagine that happening to him and still wanting to help people afterward. Nope. He was too cynical. "What else have you got?"

The tattoo on his chest was a compass rose, not perfectly vertical but with the axis tilted so it pointed over his shoulder. The right forearm smudge was a Maltese cross for the Chicago Fire Department, with a smaller six-pointed star of life inside. There was a scar half hidden by the hair of his eyebrow—"Hit my head on a glass table as a kid," Ty said with a crooked smile, like *What can you do?*—and a burn mark on the inside of his left ankle from "sitting on a motorcycle wrong."

Ollie could only blink at that explanation.

"That was my preparamedic days," Ty assured him. "Believe me, you see one motorcycle accident from my end of things, you never want to be on the other. Actually I don't even want it from my end."

Without thinking, Ollie brushed his thumb over the smooth skin of the burn. When Ty did show-and-tell, he got up close and personal with it.

Ty shivered, and Ollie let his foot go.

"All right, I showed you mine." He leaned forward and then paused. "Uh, unless you have, like, PTSD or military-related trauma about them, I guess."

"About what? Scars? I don't have any tattoos."

Ty blinked, suddenly ramrod straight again. "Wait, seriously? I didn't think they let you out of the military before you had some ink on you."

True, most of the people Ollie had served with had something somewhere. But Ollie had never felt like he fit well enough to want a reminder on his skin forever. "Guess I'm lucky they didn't look that close when they discharged me, then."

Ty laughed. "Guess so. Okay, no ink, then, but...."

Only now Ollie was thinking about it, and—"No scars either."

Ty's jaw dropped. "What?! You were on active deployment."

"I got shot *at*," Ollie said. "Nobody hit me. Got a couple nasty bruises from bumpy landings. Nothing that left a mark." Other than on his nightmares.

He should've expected Ty would lean into the bit. "No way. I don't believe it." He gestured as he rose from the water. "Come on, stand up. I want to see. The Army might not've looked too close, but I am determined."

Something about it felt ridiculous, but it had been so long since Ollie felt like he *could* be silly. First sitting on the floor to watch a movie, and now this. He didn't have to be serious with Theo all the time—kids needed someone to joke with—but it was different to play along with his kid. He stood up and spread his arms at his sides, raising an eyebrow as he did.

The night air was cold after the heat of the tub. The wet hair on his arms and the back of his neck stood up, and his nipples pebbled, which made him feel... strange.

Only for a second, though—the next he was back to mild amusement as Ty lifted his arm farther to peer under it.

"There's gotta be something." Left arm back down, right arm up. Ollie hoped his armpit didn't stink. Ty basically had his nose in it. "Childhood chicken pox?"

"Never got it."

Ty spun him around to examine his back. "Acne scars?"

"My mom does not fuck around with skin care."

"You played *sports*," Ty protested. "You never fell down, skinned your knee?"

"Sure, but scabs heal."

"Crabs?" Ty asked, half humor, half desperation.

The idea made Ollie laugh out loud. "Are you deranged?" What kind of infestation would leave lasting marks?

He barely heard Ty mutter, "It's starting to feel that way." Then he opened his mouth and his eyes caught Ollie's and Ollie could *hear him thinking*. Ty's entire being was broadcasting the extremely personal question he was about to ask. It was practically bursting out of him. "Wait, are you—"

"*If* I was," Ollie interrupted, because he wasn't committing to answering, "would it count as a scar?"

Ty held his gaze for a moment and then broke it, admitting, "I don't count it as one of mine. Maybe I should, though."

Zero personal boundaries. Just casually mentioning to your friend that you were circumcised. Ollie shook his head fondly and they both sank back into the water.

"I give up," Ty said. The long line of his arm stretched out as he reached for his beer. Hell of a wingspan, Ollie thought, absently tracking the flex of muscle under inked skin. "You are flawless."

"Definitely not." Ollie glanced over at the hot tub settings and wondered if he should turn the heat down, but no, it was at a normal setting. "All my flaws are on the inside." He thought Ty knew him better than that by now.

Ty pulled his right arm across his chest with his left, stretching out the muscle. "I'm not sure your inability to cook counts as a flaw," he teased.

But Ollie resisted the pull back toward silliness. "How about my inability to make a decision for myself?"

"What?" Ty furrowed his brow. "What are you talking about? You agreed to be a sperm donor for your friend. You *joined the military* out of high school. Those are huge decisions."

Shaking his head, Ollie reached for his beer. He slid his thumbnail under the label and scraped up some of the glue and paper. "Joining the Army was my way *out* of making a decision. I wasn't ready to figure out the rest of my life, but I didn't want my parents to figure it out for me. I was just buying time. I figured I could at least make a difference while I did it, but that didn't turn out the way I planned."

"Okay, well, what about Theo, then?"

Another head shake. "That was never really—Allison didn't ask me to help raise him, you know? I mean sure, she wanted me there as backup in case, but she just wanted the, uh—"

"Baby batter?" Ty supplied, batting his lashes.

Jesus. "I can't believe they let you around children." He flicked water across the hot tub. "That's different from deciding I wanted to be a dad."

"But you *did* decide that," Ty pointed out. "That was part of the original agreement, right? And anyone can see how much you love Theo."

Reluctantly, Ollie admitted Ty had a point. "Theo was the easiest decision I ever made, I guess. It never felt like I decided. And he's also the best thing I've done, but I've only been his dad for a few months. Doesn't seem like I should get to take credit for him."

Ty's empty bottle made a *thunk* as he set it on the edge of the hot tub. "Not this again. Are you angling for another pep talk?"

He wasn't—he really did *feel* like he was doing a good job with Theo, even if the rest of his life was a shambles. He hated his job, he hadn't exactly found a home of his own, and his parents weren't talking to him for reasons so stupid Ollie couldn't even put them into words.

But he wanted *something*. He just hadn't put his finger on exactly what.

In reply, Ollie shook his head. "No, sorry, I think I'm just in kind of a weird mood."

"Hot-tub drunk?"

"On half a beer?"

Ty's foot nudged his under the water. "Alcohol hits the bloodstream faster when you're in the hot tub. Medical fact."

Ollie could have made a joke about that—Ty had finished his drink; did that mean he was white-girl wasted?—but he was thinking about the press of Ty's foot against his, both purposeful and casual. Reassuring. *I'm here. You're a weirdo, but I like you.* It was so close to what he wanted.

Are you angling for another pep talk? He replayed the words in his mind and let himself feel his own answer. *No, but a hug might be nice.*

Which was—not new, exactly. They touched each other all the time now. And people *needed* touch; Ollie knew that. Even in the military, where machismo dominated, people touched: back slaps, high fives, hugs. Friendly touches.

He and Ty were friends. Hell, Ollie didn't think he'd ever had a closer friend. It didn't mean anything.

Ty's foot bumped against his more forcefully. "Earth to Ollie. Come in, Ollie."

He startled out of his musings to find Ty watching him with that patient, perpetually amused half-smile. "Shut up," Ollie said automatically.

Ty raised his hands. "I didn't say anything. Although if you space on me again, I might cut you off. Clearly you can't handle hot tub beer."

Ew. "First of all, 'hot tub beer' sounds like something frat boys would brew in unsanitary equipment—"

Ty cackled.

"—and second—" Ollie raised his right leg out of the water. "I forgot. Your footsie game reminded me."

"Footsie—" Ty protested, flushing. But he must've understood what Ollie was getting at, because he caught his calf. "What exactly am I looking for, here?"

Ty had big hands, which Ollie had noticed before, but noticing felt different when one of those hands was supporting his leg behind the knee, thumb on the outside, fingers brushing sensitive skin.

Ollie made himself take a steadying breath. "Front of my shinbone." He reached down and felt for the mark. It was a little too dim outside to go by sight alone, and Ollie had enough hair on his legs to make the task difficult. Finally he felt the slight divot. "Fell out of an inner tube in the Grand River camping with my parents. I would've been about eight? Flipped over in the rapids and smashed my leg on a rock."

His heart stuttered in his chest when Ty leaned down to try to get a better look. His face was so close to Ollie's skin now his warm breath was tickling the hair on Ollie's calf. Maybe the beer *had* gone to Ollie's head, because for a moment, he could've sworn Ty was going to dip his head and kiss it better.

And Ollie? Ollie wanted him to.

Finally the pieces connected. This was not the most intense friendship of Ollie's life. Or it *was*, but it didn't end there, not on Ollie's part. This was the clicking tracks at the top of a roller coaster. It was the lurch of the helicopter as the landing skids left the ground. It was the exhilaration of staring down a fast-flowing river.

This was the last chance to bail out before the inner tube capsized and sent him tumbling down the rapids—maybe by himself, but maybe, if he was lucky, with the dork holding Ollie's leg like he was Cinderella's prince fitting a slipper.

Ollie didn't bail out.

"Well, look at that," Ty said after what felt like an eternity. He glanced up at Ollie with that gentle smirk, and he rubbed his thumb over Ollie's scar just briefly before he let go. "Turns out you're a real boy after all."

Ollie clamped down on a sharp breath. He'd never thought twice about it before—Ty had always been affectionate, and he'd always ribbed, and he frequently made Ollie feel like the most important person in the room.

Somehow it hadn't occurred to him until now that this might be Ty flirting with him.

Ollie allowed himself a smirk of his own as he planted his feet firmly on the ground. "Did you think I was just Ken?"

Ty's laughter rang through the night. "You're a ten anywhere, Ollie Kent."

Sitting across from him, Ollie felt like one. But as the night settled back into comfortable, companionable quiet, he wondered, *What now?*

It was the beginning of May. In a couple weeks, school would be done for the year and Ty would return to Chicago to go back to his life. And Ollie would be here with Theo.

He might not be speaking to his parents at the moment, but he didn't think it would be fair to uproot his kid again so soon. Theo was just starting to make friends. He even liked school. His math teacher had emailed Ollie this week to say how far he'd come in the past two weeks. Ollie had already promised to sign him up for softball camp this summer.

Ollie didn't know where that left him and Ty, but if he'd learned anything from his mistakes, it was this—he wasn't going to let life make the decision for him this time.

Chapter 12

IF THERE was one thing Ty had learned about teachers, it was that they would sell a kidney to get out of lunch duty.

Technically Ty worked half-time. That meant he didn't get a paid lunch, so they couldn't schedule him for duty. Ty should probably take less pleasure in putting his feet up in the staff room and making a show of unwrapping his sandwich while whichever schmuck trudged outside like a condemned prisoner, but sometimes you had to enjoy the little things.

"*Please*," Jason Kim begged. "I will do whatever you want. Seriously. I will wash your truck. I'll bring you lunch for a week. I'll enter the grades for all your classes into the report card system you hate."

Ty put his feet down and leaned forward, because if there was one thing he'd learned teaching, it was that the program the school used to track grades hated him. It crashed at least once every time he opened it. "I'm listening," he said intently. "But first… why?"

Now Jason looked hunted. "Really?"

So it had to be *juicy*. "I'm waiting." Ty took a bite of his sandwich and chewed slowly.

"Fine!" Jason looked over both shoulders and around the whole room—not without reason; the only thing teachers loved more than they hated lunch duty was hot gossip—and lowered his voice to a whisper. "I want to take Peggy out for lunch, okay? Off school property. But I've got lunch duty the only day she's available."

Damn, he'd hit Ty in the softest place possible. He'd suspected Jason had a thing for Peggy ever since the whole saluting-with-the-morning-mail thing, and he'd caught Peggy blushing afterward enough times to believe the two of them had a decent shot at happiness, and Ty *loved* love.

Ty was especially weak for love after the significant looks that had been exchanged last night in the hot tub. He could've sworn he saw—*felt*—something flickering back at him in Ollie's warm brown gaze. Something that hadn't been there before.

But he could be imagining it. It wouldn't be the first time. Plus, talk about lousy timing—Ty literally had a call with his boss in Chicago on Monday to figure out his return-to-work schedule. And either way, he had to live with Ollie for a few more weeks, so he needed to get his romantic fix vicariously rather than hope a magical teapot was about to sing him a classic Disney love song.

Oh fuck, he lived in a creepy old mansion and he'd conned Ollie into moving in with him. Did that make him the Beast?

The townspeople did kind of hate him. It was probably only a matter of time before they stormed the castle.

"So will you do it?" Jason asked.

"I—am I allowed?" Ty replied. "I mean, you're gonna be entering all my grades and maybe my report card comments too, if they let me do it, but we probably have to make sure it's not violating some union agreement or something."

Jason's face fell. "Fuck, I don't know, I'll have to check. But if it's cool—"

"I'll do it," Ty said. "Not for you, though, just FYI. Because Peggy deserves a nice lunch date."

Jason broke into a grin that knocked at least five years from his face. "Ty, you are the best. Seriously. I'm going to enjoy entering those grades for you."

Ty had been in the middle of a bite and almost choked on his sandwich. "You're a weirdo, Jason. So, where are you taking her?"

"There's only two lunch restaurants in town, and one of them is McDonald's."

That did narrow it down some. "Oh, hey—" Ty put down his sandwich and put on his most serious eat-shit expression. "I guess I have to give you the talk, don't I? As the resident health education specialist, I mean. Remember to always use protection, and lube is your friend."

"I am afraid to ask how many of your lunch dates have involved lube."

Ty snorted. "I did once spend what was *supposed* to be my lunch break teaching a probie how to patch an oil leak on an ambulance. She didn't even buy me dinner first."

"The probie?"

He grinned. "The ambulance."

Jason was shaking his head when the overhead speaker crackled to life. "Ty, are you in there?"

Something in Peggy's tone had Ty dropping his half-eaten sandwich back onto the wrapper. She never used his first name over the PA, even when she was buzzing him in the teachers' lounge. "Yeah, what's—"

"It's Theo Kent. He's been stung by a bee—"

Ty was out of his chair before he even finished processing the words. "Where is he?"

"Main office."

"Has he taken the EpiPen?"

But he didn't wait to hear the answer. He sprinted out of the staff room and down the hallway, dodging occasional children, grateful that most of them were outside enjoying recess. He didn't want any more obstacles between himself and Theo.

He burst through the office door like a madman.

Theo sat in one of the orange plastic chairs by the front desk, his skin pale and waxy. His tear-tracked face had swollen, and his breath rasped audibly over the hum of the school's decrepit air-conditioner.

For a heartbeat Ty's personal feelings threatened to overwhelm his professional training.

Then Theo wheezed, "Hi, Ty," and he snapped back into action.

"Hey, buddy." Ty went to his knees beside him and automatically put his fingers on his wrist to check his pulse. Too fast, but not *oh fuck* fast. "Heard you found some bees." He glanced up at Peggy. "Has he taken the EpiPen?"

"Just the oral Benadryl and the albuterol," Peggy answered calmly. "We were hoping that would take care of it, but he was stung multiple times."

No kidding. Ty kept his voice soft and comforting and looked Theo in the eye. "Sounds like you had a bad day. Can you show me where you got stung?"

Theo held out his arm first. Two prominent red welts stood out from the surrounding flesh, and a spotted rash had spread from wrist to shoulder.

"Did you get the stingers out?" Ty couldn't see anything, but the stings were so swollen it was hard to tell.

Theo wiped his nose on the back of his hand. Ew, but not the time to reprimand him; it wasn't his fault he was snotting all over the place. "I think so."

Ty grabbed a Kleenex from the front desk, met eyes with Peggy, who nodded, and then returned his attention to Theo. "Okay, that's good. Ms. Peggy, can you get Theo a cold cloth to keep the swelling down?"

"Am I going to have to go to the hospital?" Theo's lip trembled.

"That depends how fast the Benadryl works, okay?" If he didn't start breathing easier in a few minutes, or if his condition got worse, they'd have to use the EpiPen, and he'd definitely have to go. "Try to take a few deep breaths for me, all right? Nice and slow."

The rasping did not improve, but it didn't get worse. Ty looked over at Peggy again. "Did you call his dad?"

Her expression made him stand up and take a step away from Theo. He wasn't in immediate danger.

Peggy lowered her voice. "We tried to reach Ollie, but his phone's going straight to voicemail. Nobody's picking up the office phone at his work either. We think maybe he should go home with you. We'll get coverage for your classes."

Ty was the only other person with permission to take Theo off school property. "Yeah, of course. And I'll keep trying Ollie."

But before he could even let Theo know he was just going to grab his stuff from the staff room, Theo said, "*Ow*! Oh no!"

When Ty turned his head, Theo was slapping at his shorts. Ty's heart stuttered in his chest when a small yellow-and-black body fell to the floor.

"Theo—"

The wheezing increased as his airway tightened further. At least one more sting, maybe two, and Theo's body was throwing everything it had at the bee venom.

"Get the epi and the albuterol!" Ty stepped forward just in time to catch Theo as he listed sideways off the chair. Theo was fumbling at the pocket of his cargo shorts, but his fingers were swollen. Ty ripped open the snaps holding the pocket shut and grabbed the tube. He flicked the cap off and jammed the spring-loaded tip against Theo's thigh.

"Peggy, call 911."

Theo's wide, tearful eyes met Ty's. "Don't… make me… go to… the hospital," he pleaded.

Ty's heart broke as he held the inhaler to Theo's mouth. "I'm sorry, buddy, but we need to get you checked out by a doctor."

Everything got exponentially worse when Theo started crying in earnest. Between his restricted airways and the hitching of his sobs, he definitely wasn't getting enough oxygen.

"Get me his backup epi and the first-aid kit!" Ty didn't want to have to give him another dose—his heart was racing as it was. He also didn't want Theo to pass out or for mucus to further obstruct his windpipe.

He *really* didn't want to have to cut a hole in Theo's throat so he could breathe, but better that than the alternatives.

Peggy handed him the kit. "911 says the ambulance is three minutes out."

"Okay, thank you." Ty put the kit on the floor next to his knees. "Theo, buddy, I need you to listen to the sound of my voice, okay? Everything is going to be fine. I'm going to stay with you the whole time, all right? Ms. Peggy gave me the rest of the day off. Wasn't that nice of her?"

The hitching slowed but didn't stop. Ty was going to have to try harder.

"Come on, Theo." Ty squeezed his hand. "I need you to help me out, okay? I know it's hard right now, but breathe in with me. We're going to breathe in for a count of three." Four would be better, but he didn't think Theo could make it to four right now, and setting him up for failure could make things worse. "Here we go. One, two, three. Hold it for a second. Now when I stop squeezing your hand, you're going to breathe out."

By the time the paramedics arrived, Ty had talked Theo down from his panic. He was still obviously upset, and he struggled when they put him on the gurney to load into the ambulance, pulling at the oxygen mask over his face with one hand and reaching for Ty with the other.

"Leave the mask on, buddy. Don't worry, I'm coming too."

The paramedic in charge—Brent; Ty recognized him from the Mrs. Sanford fiasco—sized him up. "This your kid, Morris?"

"Uh, no, but close enough." Ty gestured back toward the office. "Peggy can get you the paperwork to show I'm allowed to pick him up, if you need it." He didn't know the local policy on nonrelatives riding along with minors, or whether he could technically act *in loco parentis* since he was only an emergency supply teacher.

Theo clenched his hand tighter into the fabric of Ty's shirt.

"Think Theo here made the decision for me. Let's load up."

It was strange to ride in the ambulance as a passenger and let others do the work taking care of Theo. All Ty had to do was talk to him and try to keep him calm, which was more difficult than he expected. Having other professionals present gave Ty's brain the space to freak out.

By the time they arrived at the hospital, Ollie still hadn't answered Ty's texts. Maybe he was on the phone with Peggy? Ty could only hope. He trailed along behind the gurney into the ER, but a nurse stopped him before he could follow Theo behind the curtain.

"I'm sorry," the man said firmly, "but if you're not family, I can't allow you back there right now."

Shit. Ty had expected this. "I understand, but—"

"Mr. Morris here is Theo's teacher," Brent put in.

Ty fished his school ID out of his wallet and handed it over along with his driver's license. "We also live together. His father's my... roommate." Talk about an inadequate word, but hedging over the right one wouldn't help him. "I know you can't tell me anything, and I can't make medical decisions, I just—he's a kid, and he's scared, and I promised I wouldn't leave him alone."

The nurse glanced from Ty's IDs to Brent and back before returning the cards. "He's here for observation after an allergic reaction, yes?"

Ty's paramedic mode activated. "Yes. The school administered 25 milligrams of diphenhydramine and two doses of albuterol." He wasn't sure of the dosage on that, so he fished the inhaler out of his pocket and handed it over. "And 0.15 milligrams of epi"—he checked his watch—"seventeen minutes ago."

The nurse blinked at him, then at Brent.

"I'm also a paramedic," Ty added, because yeah, he probably should've let Brent do his job.

"Tell you what," the nurse said. "It's not like this ER is particularly private. So why don't you stand on this side of the curtain where Theo can hear you while we have a doctor check him out, and then when we move him for observation you can sit with him until his guardian arrives."

Ty's shoulders sagged in relief. "Thank you."

The nurse smiled. "Patient care doesn't end with physical health. You know that." And then he disappeared behind the curtain.

Ty made sure Theo knew he was right there—"I'm just going to make some phone calls, buddy. You'll hear my voice, all right?"—and then started scrolling through his list.

First he left Ollie a voicemail. Peggy had probably done that already, but Ty had more information now, and he wanted to cut any possible panic off at the knees.

Then he called the school.

"Hey, Ty. How's our patient?"

"He's okay. The doctor's looking him over now, and then they'll probably move him to observation for a couple hours. I'm guessing no luck with Ollie?"

"No." She sighed. "And either their dispatch office is on the world's longest lunch break, or they just never answer the phone."

Shit. "Okay. Hey, uh, hypothetically, since I'm a teacher, would you be able to give me Cassie Kent's number? For reasons?"

"Absolutely not," Peggy said cheerfully as Ty's phone pinged in his ear. "Good luck with that."

"Thanks, Peggy."

BY TWO o'clock, Ollie had serious regrets about forgetting his cell phone in his work locker. He couldn't check last night's baseball scores, and he didn't have *2048* or *Angry Birds* to distract him while he waited for Lucy to return from whatever errand she was on. Not that he should be playing phone games—he was supposed to be watching out for signs someone was going to attempt a robbery—but you could only maintain vigilance on small-town streets for so long before your brain started longing for physical death to go along with the lack of stimulation.

They were parked outside their five hundred and twelfth stop of the day, a pawn shop in Holton. Ollie had one eye on the mirrors and one on Lucy for trouble, and was going through the alphabet making a list of the most absurd fake ice-cream flavors he could think of in order to keep himself awake.

It was possible that the fact that the air-conditioner in this truck was still only half working had an impact on his activity of choice. Ollie was desperate for a Popsicle.

He'd made it to G for the second time—Georgia Peaches, Pralines and Cream—when the dormant part of his brain noticed a change in Lucy's body language. Ollie snapped to attention as she finished up her exchange with the shop manager and used her key to open the passenger door.

"Here." She shoved her phone at him. "I'm going to put this in the back and then we can go."

Blinking, Ollie looked down at the phone, which seemed to be mid-call from a number Lucy didn't have stored. He raised it to his ear. "Hello?"

"Ollie, holy shit. Finally. Where are you? Why haven't you been answering your phone? We've been calling for an hour."

The stress in Cassie's voice went straight to Ollie's blood pressure. "I'm at the pawn shop in Holton. Working. I accidentally left my phone in my locker. What's going on?" Something awful occurred to him. "Oh God, are Mom and Dad okay?" They might not be talking right now, but he didn't want anything bad to happen to his parents. If they got into an accident while they weren't speaking to Ollie—

"They're fine. Well, everyone's fine now, just worried about *you*—"

"Cassie." If it wasn't his parents, that meant—"What happened?"

"Theo got stung by a bee."

Ollie's chest went hollow, and her words rang in his ears.

"—a couple of bees, actually, I guess. They had to use his EpiPen. The school couldn't get hold of you. I guess they had to send him to the hospital."

Miraculously, Ollie didn't drop Lucy's phone. "And he's—Theo's—"

"He's freaking out about being in the hospital, but he's fine otherwise, Ollie, I swear."

He swallowed and tried to will his heart to slow back to a normal rhythm. "Okay. Okay. Thanks. Uh. Wait, we've got—the trucks all have radios. Nobody tried to call the office?"

Cassie made a derisive noise. "We *all* tried to call the office. Nobody picked up."

The news did not improve Ollie's blood pressure. "Okay. Um. I'm going to—we'll have to go back to the depot so I can switch cars, but can you let them know I'll be there as soon as I can?"

"Of course."

A moment later Lucy climbed back into the cab. "You need me to drive?"

Obviously Cassie had briefed her already. Ollie's hands shook. "Uh. Would you mind?"

Lucy did not mind, so Ollie spent the drive back to the depot with his eyes closed, concentrating on his breathing and trying to convince himself Theo was fine. He would recover, though Ollie would be beating himself up for forgetting his phone for years to come.

He practically bolted out of the truck when they arrived. He went inside long enough to retrieve his phone, brushed off his manager's pointed question about why they weren't still out on their run—"Sorry, my kid's in the hospital, I gotta go, Lucy will fill you in"—and drove to the hospital on autopilot while nightmare visions of Theo, alone and scared, competed for his attention.

He couldn't believe this had happened. He'd worked so hard to be a good father, to try to make sure he was always there when Theo needed him. Now he felt like the world's biggest fraud. He'd failed his kid. Maybe his parents were right about him needing more help.

Somehow he held it together enough to ask someone at the nurses' station how to find Theo's room.

The hospital hallways stretched out before him like an effect from a horror movie, but finally he found 218. The door was open. He stuck his head in.

Theo was asleep, his chest rising and falling steadily in a way Ollie would never take for granted. He was hooked up to a pulse-ox monitor, but no IV. All his stats were normal. His color was good. Aside from his sweat-matted hair, he looked perfectly healthy, none the worse for wear. The relief of it almost took Ollie out at the knees, even as guilt welled up in the place anxiety had vacated.

He was supposed to be there for Theo, and he'd let him down. He'd been in the hospital with no one to comfort him—probably scared as well as alone—

"Oh, Ollie—thank God. Did Cassie finally get through to you?"

Ollie turned around.

If Theo looked none the worse for wear, the same could not be said of Ty, who looked like he'd just come off a three-day bender. Ollie didn't think stress could make your beard come in any faster, but he could swear Ty's face was scruffier than normal for this time in the afternoon, and he had dark circles under his eyes. In his left hand he held a phone charger, still new in the box; he had a half-empty paper cup of coffee in the right.

"I called about a hundred times, but my phone died half an hour ago. Probably shouldn't have spent my prep this morning watching

YouTube videos about weird birds. Anyway, Peggy sent me Cassie's number earlier in case she had a better way to reach you, but when Theo fell asleep, I hit up the gift shop—"

Finally Ollie found his voice. "You've been here the whole time?"

Ty tilted his head like the question didn't make sense. "I wasn't going to let the school send someone else—"

The guilt flowed out again, but this time something warm and bright filled the vacuum. Of course Ty hadn't let Theo be alone and scared. Of course he'd kept calling Ollie until his phone died, and called in reinforcements when he couldn't get through. Never mind that he and Cassie barely knew each other and the town thought he was a *hoodlum*—that would never stop Ty from making sure Theo was looked after.

"—even if he is giving me the silent treatment," Ty added, half wry, half hurt, and still twice the speed of his normal speech.

Ollie glanced from Ty to Theo, who hadn't stirred. Before he could ask why Theo would do that, Ty went on. He was talking even faster now, like he was worried Ollie might be angry if he didn't explain before Ollie could get a word in.

"He tried to make me promise he wouldn't have to go to the hospital." He grimaced but didn't pause long enough for Ollie to interject. "I couldn't do that, obviously, especially after the second bee got him."

Ollie had a hundred questions—how many times had he been stung, how bad had things gotten, whether they could expect his next reaction to be worse—but Ty didn't give him an opening to ask. That made sense, kind of, since Ty had had several hours to get worked into his anxiety spiral, and Ollie had only had a fraction of that. "Ty—"

"I mean, it's hard to blame him for not wanting to go to the hospital." Ty's hands got in on the talking, and he gestured around at the sterile walls painted an overly cheerful pastel green, the industrial window with its scenic view of the parking lot, the monitoring equipment beeping softly in the corner.

"Ty—"

"Given his history and everything—"

It dawned on Ollie that if he wanted Ty to stop talking, he would have to physically make him. And that was what he intended to do—raise his hand, put his finger over Ty's lips, and finally let out the *thank you* that was blistering the inside of his mouth.

Except that somewhere between his brain and his arm, his heart intercepted the message, and instead of putting a finger to Ty's lips, he pulled Ty in with one hand on his waist and the other on the back of his neck and pressed their mouths together.

Something electric zinged down his spine. Under his hands, Ty stilled and then shivered. Ollie had caught him mid-word and his lips were open, and when Ty breathed a tiny noise of surprise, Ollie *tasted* it.

He wanted more.

Before he could chase after it, Ty pulled back, just the slightest pressure against Ollie's right hand. He didn't go far, only enough to look into Ollie's eyes with his own, blue irises sharp with curiosity and want. Ollie watched them flick down to his lips, and then he didn't know which of them had moved, but they were kissing again, Ty's hands in his hair and on his ass, his chest firm against Ollie's, his mouth wet around Ollie's tongue.

Something thunked, and Ty inhaled quickly. Oh. That was Ty's skull hitting the wall. Ollie had pushed him into it in his enthusiasm. But Ty didn't pull away, and some long-banked fire in Ollie's chest roared to life and surged through him—the compulsion to learn all of this man, every tattoo and scar, every bruise and ticklish spot, all of the secret places that made him gasp and beg and moan.

And then the speaker overhead crackled. "Paging Dr. Robinson. Please check in at the nurses' station."

This time the noise Ty made was kind of a whimpered laugh, as the metaphorical cold water washed over Ollie and he drew back.

Ty licked already wet lips and Ollie immediately wanted to kiss him again. Just not here, in his son's hospital room, where anyone could see them, when they hadn't had a chance to figure out *anything*, when they hadn't even—

"Um," Ty said. His cheeks were very pink, the apples plumped by a shy, unrestrained smile. Any moment now he'd say something like *Aw, shucks*.

Ollie adored him.

"You, um, wanted to say something?"

Did he? "Uh." Ollie tried to remember what had been going through his mind a minute ago, but he came up empty. His cheeks went hot. "I forgot."

Ty blinked rapidly a handful of times and curled his lips over his teeth, but Ollie could still see the smile threatening, and he only lasted a second before a laugh burst out of him.

Ollie snickered too, but he covered his mouth with one hand so Theo didn't wake up to find his dad howling with laughter in his hospital room. Ollie didn't want him to get the wrong impression. Except the harder he tried to keep it in, the louder Ty's suppressed laughter got, until finally Ollie grabbed his arm and pulled him into the hallway, where they both collapsed against the wall until they could breathe again.

"We're a pair, huh?" Ty commented, smiling vaguely up at the fluorescent lighting.

I hope so, Ollie thought. He reached over and threaded his fingers through Ty's. "I remember what I was going to say."

Ty turned to face him.

"Thank you, for being there for Theo. I was beating myself up pretty good, knowing he was in the hospital by himself because the school couldn't get in contact with me and I don't have my parents listed as emergency contacts. And then I got here and you told me he'd never been alone."

Ty swallowed audibly. "Oh."

Ollie didn't know if he could put the rest of it into words, never mind do it in public without making a scene—more of one than they made already, holding hands on the floor outside his kid's hospital room—so he didn't try. He squeezed Ty's hand instead. "Maybe when we get home we can talk?"

The look Ty gave him promised a lot more than talking, but he just said, "I'd like that," and Ollie let himself bask in that smile for a few seconds before his ass reminded him he was sitting on a cold tile floor.

"I tried to tell you," Ty said quietly when they'd dusted themselves off and returned to the room. "He might be kind of upset when he wakes up."

Right. Some of the things Ty had been trying to say when Ollie's brain had refused to accept any input aside from *kiss him, you fool* might actually be important. "You mentioned the silent treatment?"

"Yeah." He glanced at Theo and then lowered his voice further anyway, even though he was still out like a light. "He was really upset he had to go to the hospital, and he kind of blamed me. I'm not taking it personally, though. Last time he was in the hospital without a parent, his mother died."

Jesus. No wonder he freaked out. Ollie was glad he interrupted; he didn't think he would've had the nerve to kiss Ty if he'd been processing that.

"I should probably wake him up, you think?" He cleared his throat. "You know… reassure him I'm still alive."

The look Ty gave him made it abundantly clear he knew Ollie needed reassurance as much as Theo did, but he didn't call him on it. "I'll give you guys a minute."

Ollie almost told him not to go, but if Ty stayed, it would be for Ollie, and Theo deserved an explanation one-on-one. He waited until Ty had stepped into the hallway before touching Theo's hand. "Hey, buddy. You want to wake up?"

Theo inhaled deeply, and his eyelashes fluttered. "Dad?"

He sounded normal, if sleepy. His eyes were a little red-rimmed, but that could be the allergies. (Ollie knew it wasn't allergies. But he was having a day and he needed to lie to himself for a minute. He could have a breakdown about it later.)

"I heard you had kind of a rough day."

Theo's lip wobbled, but he didn't cry. "Why didn't you come sooner?"

Ollie was scum. Ollie was lower than scum. Ollie was the thing scum scraped off its shoe. "I'm so sorry. I forgot my phone in my locker and didn't have it on me. Your aunt Cassie had to find my coworker's phone number so she could tell me what happened."

Theo narrowed his eyes. "Like a detective?"

"Just like that."

This was apparently cool enough to take the heat off for a moment. Only for a moment, though. "Can we go home now? The nurses treat me like I'm a baby."

Ollie frowned and instinctively looked up to find a nurse he could stare down. Theo's room was still devoid of other adults. "That's not very cool of them."

"And my stings are itchy and they keep telling me to 'be a big boy and don't scratch.'" Even with his still-swollen face, the twist of his mouth conveyed his extreme offense. "I'm eight. And it's itchy. And there's nothing to *do* here, Dad, and Ty didn't bring my bag, so I don't have my book, so there's nothing to think about except *scratching*."

"We will get you some good lotion and extra-strength Benadryl," Ollie promised. "And maybe a doctor can write you a prescription for the really good stuff. And tonight we'll all watch TV together, no homework, okay? Or play board games or something until you're ready for bed, to keep your mind off it."

His talk with Ty was going to have to wait until Theo was in bed anyway.

Theo pursed his lips. "Can it just be us?" he said plaintively. Oh, there was a pout underneath it. That was bad news.

"Well, I don't think I can kick Ty out of the living room," Ollie said, trying to sound reasonable. He really *couldn't*—though Ty would probably voluntarily banish himself—but he also didn't want to set that precedent, especially without getting to the root of Theo's problem. "But of course you and I can hang out." He paused. "Did something happen to make you mad at Ty? Is it because he forgot your backpack?"

The pursed expression became a flat-out scowl. "I don't want to talk about it."

Ooookay, then. "We don't have to talk about it right now," Ollie hedged. "But I do have to give Ty a ride home since he came here with you in the ambulance."

For a moment Theo slumped dejectedly into the pillows. "Fiiiine." And then, just as quickly, he sat up and reached for the pulse-ox monitor. "So we can go now?"

Ollie caught his hand and lowered it back to the bed. "Hold your horses, bud. We need to see a doctor first. I want to make sure I take good care of you so we don't have to come back, okay?"

An extremely dramatic sigh. "I *guess*."

"That's the spirit." Ollie ruffled his hair and then bent down to kiss the top of his head. "I'm so glad you're okay. You had me really worried."

He'd almost pulled away when Theo's arms wrapped around his neck. "I'm sorry I made you worry. I thought you might be mad at me."

Ollie wanted to pull back to see his kid's face, because he had to be joking, right? But he couldn't make himself do it. Theo sounded miserable, and Ollie needed this hug. "Why would I be mad?"

Theo sniffled against his chest. "'Cause you said—when we left Anacostia you said you never wanted to see me in a hospital again."

Oh God. "Theo—" Ollie did pull back now, and he wiped a tear away from his son's cheek with his thumb. "I said that because I wanted you to be healthy. I'm not mad that you had to come back. It's not your fault you got stung by a bee, okay? And even if you did something to make it your fault, like, I don't know, kicking a beehive or something, I would never stay away from the hospital to punish you for it. I love you *way* more than I hate hospitals."

Theo wiped his eyes and nose with the back of his hand. Ollie tried not to grimace too loudly and handed him a tissue from the tray table. "But I don't have to stay overnight again, do I?"

"Ty didn't seem to think so. Let me track down a doctor and we'll find out for sure."

Chapter 13

IT WAS after dinnertime when they finally got Theo sprung from the hospital. Ty took a moment to say a silent prayer of thanks that Ollie was driving, because *his* brain had been experiencing total paralysis for the past three hours.

Ollie had kissed him.

Not, like, a chaste kiss of gratitude or anything either. Well—okay, so the first kiss had kind of felt a little bit like *shut up*, but in a good way.

The second one had tasted like the rest of Ty's life.

But could he have his cake and eat it too? (Put a pin in that *cake* thought for later.) When the school year was almost over and Ty's bereavement leave was almost up and he was expected back in Chicago?

Could he leave and keep Ollie?

Could he keep Ollie and stay in this messed-up town, where people treated him like a delinquent because he couldn't be the son his father wanted?

And what about Theo? Until today Ty would've held out hope that Theo would accept him into this little ready-made family with open arms. Ollie would never put his own wants before Theo's, and Ty would never want him to, but—

"How come the police are at our house?" Theo asked from the back seat, and Ty's mind spun off in a totally different direction.

Ollie put the car in Park—the police cruiser was blocking the entrance to the garage—and he and Ty exchanged looks. "I'll get Theo settled, while you…?"

Ty sighed. Based on probabilities alone, the cops were here for him. "Yeah."

At least the weather was nice enough that he didn't have to feel the slightest bit of guilt not inviting them inside.

Ty closed the car door and made his way over to the two uniforms sitting in their squad car. They got out as he approached, and he was surprised to recognize Jake Robinson on the passenger's side.

The other cop was a fortyish woman he didn't know. She had her hair pulled back in a severe bun, and her sharp green eyes seemed to bore right into him as she approached. "Tyler Morris?"

Well, at least she wasn't reaching for her gun. "That's me." He glanced over her shoulder. "Jake."

Jake offered a pained half-smile. "Ty."

"My name is Sergeant Rosewater. Is there somewhere we can go to talk?"

They'd sent a *sergeant* out here for this? Ty glanced from her to Jake and then back. "Patio's pretty comfortable this time of year." Plus it wasn't located inside his house. Ty didn't have anything to hide from the police, but he wasn't taking chances.

Besides, on the patio Ollie and Theo wouldn't be able to eavesdrop. Ty didn't have anything to hide from them either, but that didn't mean the whole scenario wouldn't be upsetting.

"So," he said when they had settled into his dad's conversation set. "What brings you out here, Sergeant?"

"I'd like to take your statement about the incident at the grocery store on Tuesday."

Oh hell no. Ty schooled his face into neutrality. "The incident? You mean Mrs. Sanford's heart attack?"

Rosewater exchanged a glance with Jake. "That's correct."

"I gave my statement to the paramedics on the scene," Ty said. "Jake was there. He can tell you."

"I did," Jake muttered.

Rosewater's expression remained neutral. "Regardless, we're here to follow up with inquiries into a potentially suspicious death. This is just routine."

"Sergeant." Ty leveled her with his most jaded and over-it stare. "I have been a licensed paramedic for four years. Don't insult me. Mrs. Sanford's death was in no way suspicious, and if this is routine, the Suffolk police force are either spectacularly incompetent or ridiculously overfunded. As I've said, I gave my statement on the scene. If you're looking for anything more than that, it'll have to wait until I call my lawyer."

Rosewater might as well have been made of stone for all the reaction that got him. Jake tried to give Ty a commiserating look over her shoulder.

It didn't take a genius to figure out what was going on—not with Alan Chiu on the town council, and not with the way things ran in Suffolk. Ty didn't realize people still got run out of town. Part of him wanted to find it funny. Hell, part of him *did*. This was Connecticut in the twenty-first century, not the old west.

"Mrs. Sanford's body has been sent to the medical examiner's office for autopsy."

Was he supposed to be scared? "Where they'll confirm she died of natural causes, specifically a heart attack," Ty said levelly. "Sergeant, I don't know what you've heard about me, but I can guess who has a bug up their ass that I haven't skedaddled like a kicked dog. If Alan Chiu wants to round up a posse, let him. It's not going to change the truth."

It was only going to make Ty's last couple weeks in Suffolk miserable. But hey, once he left, Chiu could declare victory over the godless heathen and go back to his self-important life.

That finally got a reaction out of Rosewater—the hint of a twitch around her mouth. Ty had worked in emergency services long enough to recognize the signs of local politics at play.

Jake cleared his throat. "You weren't on duty as a paramedic," he said, gaze fixed carefully above Ty's right shoulder. "So no investigation into your professional conduct can be made."

Ty knew that.

"However, the paramedics called to the scene will also be questioned as to why the response to the call took so long."

"Were they supposed to break the laws of physics?" *Someone* was playing some kind of stupid game here.

"There will be a town hall meeting on the topic next weekend," Rosewater continued. She was looking over Ty's shoulder too. Were they trying to weird him out or something? Or—

From behind him came a fluttering sound. Jake and Sergeant Rosewater ducked. Ty didn't understand why until a sudden breeze wafted through his hair as a shadow passed overhead.

Something struck the deck between him and Sergeant Rosewater, and Rosewater stumbled back a step.

Ty only avoided the blood spatter out of sheer luck.

He stared at the headless rabbit. He'd done some poking around online after Ollie mentioned the habits of the birds in his childhood.

This particular bird was a hawk, he thought, and not an owl. Apparently some birds of prey preferred brain matter and would discard the rest of the animal.

He raised his gaze to meet Rosewater's. "I think that bird wants you to get off my lawn."

Jake was biting down on a smile, but Rosewater only sighed and handed him a folded piece of paper. "Details of the inquiry," she told him. "Your presence is requested."

You are cordially invited to jump into the frying pan, Ty thought grimly. "I'll call my attorney." He turned away to go back into the house. "I trust you can find your own way off my property."

He was pretty sure he heard Jake's muffled laughter as he reached for the door.

What a day. First Theo's medical emergency, then Ollie giving Ty a heart attack with that kiss, and finally the fuck-you-ever-after of cops on his doorstep. Ty wanted a beer and a mind-wipe.

No. Ty wanted another kiss. *Several dozen* more kisses, to start with, and progressively less clothing with each one. Although a quiet Friday night in, watching network TV squashed on his couch with Ollie and Theo would make a pretty good consolation prize. Too bad Theo wasn't talking to him. And Ollie had to put him first, of course. Ty had a shitty day, but he was a grown man. Theo had a major medical and emotional trauma and was only eight. Not to mention Ollie probably needed to be with his kid right now.

But maybe after Theo fell asleep they could have that conversation. Ty still didn't have any idea where it might *go*, but sometimes he didn't know what he wanted until he said the words out loud.

He toed his shoes off by the door and slunk through the house to the kitchen, where he poured himself a glass of smoothie from the fridge. He'd eaten too much questionable junk from hospital vending machines today, and he felt gross. He didn't hear Theo and Ollie, so they were probably having a quiet father-son talk with the door closed somewhere. Maybe Ollie could figure out how to get Theo to forgive Ty, and then they could indulge in Ty's pathetic watching-TV-as-a-family fantasy.

He finished his drink, put the glass in the dishwasher, and then tiptoed toward the bedrooms.

Ollie's bedroom door was open, the lights out, bed made with military precision. Ty crept toward Theo's room, straining his ears for the sound of voices.

Nothing.

He kept his own bedroom door closed, not because he valued his privacy but because he felt like he should, with a kid who wasn't his in the house. The empty bedrooms had their doors closed too. Then Theo's, open a few inches with light spilling out into the hallway, even if it was still silent.

Ty knocked softly and peered in.

Ollie and Theo lay on the four-poster bed, fast asleep, Theo curled in toward Ollie's chest like an opening parenthesis. His fingers were clenched in the fabric of his father's shirt. Even on that big bed, even cuddled up together, they somehow managed to take up all the available space. It was hard not to feel like it was some kind of metaphor.

Ty rubbed his sternum like that might remind his heart to keep beating. Then he padded down the hallway to the linen closet and pulled out a couple throw blankets. It was supposed to get cold tonight, and Theo and Ollie had passed out on top of the covers.

He covered each of them with a blanket, turned on Theo's desk lamp, and flicked off the overhead light. Then he returned to his own bedroom and sat on the bed with his face in his hands.

What the hell was he going to do?

TY RAN out of the house on Saturday like his ass was on fire.

He'd slept fitfully the night before. Between talking to the police and not-talking with Ollie, he couldn't get his brain to settle. Add in his anxiety over Theo's silent treatment, and he didn't think anyone could blame him for leaving the house before Ollie and Theo woke up. He walked to the school to retrieve his truck.

The whole thing backfired on him when he returned home to find a note on the kitchen table. *Gone to Cassie's to help set up for Mel's birthday party. Talk later?—Ollie X.*

"This is just mean," Ty said out loud to the universe. It was one thing for him to avoid his own problems and quite another for the universe to take the decision out of his hands. Now that he *couldn't* have that talk with Ollie right now, it was the only thing he wanted to do.

Instead he had to attend an end-of-year cookout with his coworkers, pretend his heart wasn't wherever Ollie was, and hope desperately that he wasn't being too greedy, grasping for more when Ollie had already given him so much.

What if Ollie changed his mind?

Ever since his chat with Ollie the other night, the atmosphere in the house felt charged. Ty kept catching Ollie *looking* at him. It was driving him crazy. And it felt unfair—he'd *just* managed to convince himself he could be Ollie's normal platonic friend he lived with, at least for a few months.

Ty could not be Ollie's normal platonic friend if Ollie was going to look at him like that.

Hell, Ty wasn't sure he could move back to Chicago if Ollie kept looking at him like that.

For the first time in over a decade, it felt like someone looked at him and saw someone they liked. Someone they wanted to build a life with.

Unfortunately Ollie seemed to want to make his life in a town that had ground Ty's self-worth into dog shit and then used a stick to scrape it off their shoe. Plus, Ollie had never once mentioned being attracted to men. That would've come up, right? So maybe Ty was imagining things. Or maybe Ollie had an incipient sexuality crisis on his hands. Did Ty want to get involved in that? (Dumb question. Ty would absolutely be all up in Ollie's sexuality crisis, lending a hand or mouth or dick or whatever body part the situation called for.) And on top of those issues, they had Theo to consider. Ty was by no means a parenting expert, but he was pretty sure his dad dating right after his mom died would've sent Ty into an absolute rage tornado.

He couldn't be responsible for turning sweet, sensitive Theo into a seething ball of angst. That would do terrible things to his karma. It was bad enough he wasn't talking to Ty right now.

"Hey," Peggy said from across the picnic table. Around them, the not-quite-end-of-school-year staff party ebbed and flowed. This year Jason Kim was hosting; his family had a fruit farm with a small event space. Ty would've loved it if he could convince himself to take any of it in.

Maybe he and Ollie should come back here with Theo.

Maybe Ty shouldn't count his chickens before he asked if they wanted to peck in his yard. Or something.

Peggy continued, "This is supposed to be a party, and not the pity kind."

"Yeah," Henry put in, knocking his elbow into Ty's. "Cowboys don't cry. What's going on?"

For a moment Ty didn't know where to begin—Henry might maintain there was no crying in baseball, but he infamously cried at graduation every year, and also Ty wasn't a cowboy; he didn't even ride the lawn mower.

At least the question knocked him out of his Ollie-and-Theo spiral.

And then Peggy said darkly, "This better not be about Alan Chiu."

Henry's expression went thunderous. "Is he still giving you a hard time?"

Oh good—a whole new pile of anxiety. "That asshole." On the other hand, no need for Henry to get worked up. He should watch his blood pressure. Eliza would kill Ty if she lost a second husband. "I mean, he's trying to run me out of town, naturally. Cops showed up at my house last night to get a statement. Didn't take a genius to figure out they were there doing his bidding. I told them I wasn't talking to them without my lawyer." Which—fuck. Ty took out his phone. "So I guess I have to call your wife. Again."

The sun returned to Henry's face. "I love my wife."

Peggy caught eyes with Ty and just *barely* rolled them before returning to the subject at hand. "So anyway, what, Chiu's trying to pin Mrs. Sanford's heart attack on you or something?"

"That's my guess." If not legally, then at least in the court of public opinion.

"What does this guy have against you?" Henry wondered. "Did you seduce his wife or something?"

"I haven't even been in town in over a decade," Ty protested. Then, just to be sure, "Wait, who's his wife?"

Peggy rolled her eyes. "Let's take it as unlikely that you randomly ran into this woman in Chicago and slept with her and he somehow found out about it. And since I'm assuming sixteen-year-old Ty wasn't in the habit of sleeping with people old enough to be his parents—"

Ty recoiled. "Ew."

Even Henry looked a little green. "Let's forget I suggested it."

If only it were so easy.

"The point is," Peggy said, "why's he hate you so much?"

"I don't know. I'd understand it if I benched his kid or something, but Peter's the best player on the team. It's not like we're going to hamstring ourselves worse than we already are." The closest game this season had been a 6–3 loss. "Maybe he's mad I have more money than he does. Well, the estate. It's technically not mine yet."

Henry and Peggy exchanged looks again. "It's not the craziest theory I've ever heard," Peggy allowed.

"No," Henry agreed, narrowing his eyes. "What's weirder is that it's getting to you."

Ty squirmed under the scrutiny. "It's not weird to hate it when people try to run you out of town."

"Ty, believe me, we're all aware of how, uh…." Henry faltered.

"How desperate you are for people to love you," Peggy supplied, and reached for Ty's hand across the table when he tried to put it over his face.

Henry opened his mouth like he might amend the statement, then carried on instead. "But that never bothered you when the people who didn't like you were assholes."

Peggy picked up a potato chip and used it to punctuate her sentence. "You *loved* pissing off assholes. Actually, I know for a fact you still love pissing off assholes, because I've seen you book it for the copy machine whenever you see Jenny coming"—Jenny Darel had despised him as a teacher and made sure he never forgot it—"and I've heard you whistling afterward." She crunched the chip, licked salt from her thumb, and then seemed to think for a moment. "Something's changed, though, and I don't blame you if it's different with Alan Chiu…. What's Ollie think?"

And just like that, the innocent topic had circled back around to the place Ty's brain always ended up lately. What *did* Ollie think? Did Ollie think he'd made a horrible mistake last night and want to let Ty down gently? Did Ollie think it was a problem that people in this town hated Ty for no discernible reason?

It definitely *was* a problem. Currently it was a problem because it was making Ty's life annoying and running up his legal fees, but it could become a problem that made Ollie think twice about wanting to be the constant Ty built his life around. A problem that made Ollie not want to kiss him again.

Ty deflated. "Ollie doesn't know yet."

"Oh." The way Henry said it had the hair on the back of Ty's neck standing up. Just… knowing. And smug. Dare Ty even say patronizing.

"Oh," Peggy repeated in the same tone, meeting Henry's eyes. "I thought it was a weirdly political agenda that had you looking at that apple tree like it could unravel the mysteries of the universe, but—"

"It's Ollie," she and Henry chorused.

Ty needed better friends. Friends who wouldn't do this to him. "Shut up," he hissed. He didn't need the whole faculty knowing what a disaster he was. Aside from Ollie and his students, they were the only people in town who actually liked him.

"Oh please," Peggy said. "Sweetie. Everyone knows already. You moved the man in with you after meeting him one time. You're a walking lesbian joke."

That didn't seem fair. There hadn't even been a U-Haul involved. "It's not like that," Ty protested, his face flaming because it was exactly like that and he hadn't even known it until a few days ago. "And it was twice."

Henry snorted. "Whatever you say, Ty. So why haven't you told Ollie about the thing with Chiu? The latest thing, I mean."

Because I would rather talk to him about kissing me some more. "Because he and Theo had a long day yesterday. They were asleep by the time I kicked Jake and Sergeant Rosewater off the back porch. Still out cold when I left this morning."

Peggy and Henry did that look-exchange thing again. Peggy leaned forward. "Asleep where?"

"In bed!" Off their smirks, Ty huffed and added, "*His own bed*, guys. Or actually Theo's bed, because they fell asleep on top of the covers while I fended off Chiu's dogs. Metaphorically speaking. If I'd woken up with my arms full of that beautiful man this morning I would not be at this stupid party."

"You tucked them in, didn't you?"

Ty was going to give Peggy so much shit if she went out to lunch with Jason. She'd never know what hit her. "Can I plead the Fifth?"

"Have you talked to him about his feelings?"

Could they go back to talking about how everyone hated Ty? That seemed like more fun. "You said *cowboys don't cry* two minutes ago and now you're asking if we've talked about our *feelings*?" When Ty was agonizing over the fact that they hadn't had a chance to talk about their feelings? That was just mean.

"Talking is not the same as crying," Henry said patiently. "You're mooning, but you're also happier than I've ever seen you, small town politics notwithstanding. So why haven't you asked said beautiful man if he wants to join you in bed?"

Peggy turned an incredulous look on him before returning to Ty. "Maybe don't open with that."

"How many queer men have you dated?" Ty asked, because in his experience that was how it went a good 50 percent of the time.

She threw a grape at him.

"No, she's right, though." Henry leaned over, picked the grape off the ground, and wrapped it in his napkin. Probably concerned a dog might come along and accidentally poison itself. "You wouldn't want Ollie to think you just want his body."

Ty could not believe he was having this conversation with his former coach and a friend he'd barely spoken to since high school. Life came at you fast. "This is great, you guys, but your concerns are so… basic. Surface-level stuff."

Peggy and Henry exchanged looks. "So what *are* you worried about?"

"Okay, well, for one thing, I'm supposed to go back to Chicago in less than two weeks." He ticked the items off on his fingers as he went. "Are we really going to start a relationship long-distance? What are the long-term implications of that?"

Peggy opened her mouth, but Ty went on before she could answer.

"Or, what if Ollie decides his family sucks as much as mine did and we decide to make a go of it in Chicago? And then it doesn't work, and we've uprooted Theo for no reason?"

"Uh, Ty—"

"And Ollie resents me forever for driving a wedge between him and his family?"

"Ty—"

"They hate me, by the way," Ty went on. Was that the third finger or the fourth? "So, like, imagine I stick around here instead of going back to Chicago. I'm independently wealthy now." He shivered as though someone had walked across his grave. Probably his dad's ghost. "Like, I could do that and stay here with Ollie. But everyone here loves him as much as they hate me. What if everyone decides he's guilty by association? And then the teachers start treating Theo like a criminal—"

"I think you know us a *little* better than that by now," Henry said, but Ty kept talking over him.

"—and he doesn't get into college, and he ends up broke and living in a rat-infested apartment in New Haven, addicted to scratch-off tickets?"

Ty ran out of fingers on the first hand.

"Were you planning on writing him out of your will?" Henry said. "Because I know how much that house is worth, kid."

Hunching his shoulders, Ty stared at his paper plate. A carpenter ant had scaled the side and was investigating his potato salad. "Or what if Theo isn't ready for Ollie to date, and he gets upset because he thinks I'm trying to replace his mom? He's already mad at me because I made him go to the hospital. Or what if he *is* ready and I'm a shitty stepparent? It's not like I had a great example to follow."

Peggy reached across the table and put her hand on top of his. "Hey, come on. You're great with kids."

"Plus," Henry broke in, "you need to make up your mind on how far in front of the horse you're putting the cart."

Peggy plucked a strawberry from her plate. "Henry's got a point. I mean, maybe you should kiss him first."

Ty had always had fair skin. Right now he could feel the flush rising up his neck to gradually fill his face, like a real-life cartoon.

Peggy dropped the strawberry. "Wait, you *already kissed*?" Ty buried his face in his hands. "Excuse me. Here we are trying to give you a pep talk and you're withholding *critical information*."

"Well it's not like I can just go around *telling people Ollie kissed me*, Peggy. I don't usually enjoy outing people. Especially when I don't even know if they're into guys."

"If he kissed you, that's probably a pretty good indicator."

Guys who had been married less than ten years should be less smug, Ty thought.

"Let me guess," Peggy said. "You haven't talked about Ollie kissing you either."

He pushed his plate away so he could fold his arms on the picnic table and lay his head on top of them. "We haven't had five minutes alone together since it happened."

"So I've got a wacky question," Henry said. "Let me know if it's too out-there." He paused for dramatic effect and then said, "What the hell are you doing here, Morris? Go get your man."

Chapter 14

WHEN OLLIE woke up, it was to Theo's knee connecting with his thigh.

"Ow," he said sleepily, and blinked his eyes open to find Theo staring back at him.

"Sorry, Dad."

What was he doing here? What time was it? What *day* was it? Ollie rubbed a hand over his eyes. "It's okay, buddy. I guess we fell asleep early last night, huh?" He didn't remember getting up to get these blankets. Actually, he didn't know if he'd ever even seen these blankets before.

Ty must've brought them, he realized, whenever he got done talking to the cops last night.

God, what had Ollie done, coming back to this town?

"Yeah. But we can get up now, right? Mel's birthday party is today, and we still have to get her a present."

Shit, and Ollie had promised his sister he'd help set up picnic tables and games and stuff goodie bags or… something like that. He needed to get up and get his ass moving.

Ideally he'd get to talk to Ty first. "We gotta get up," Ollie confirmed, throwing off the blanket. "You get dressed while I shower, okay?" Ollie's time in the military had at least taught him the value of a two-minute shower. He'd probably be done before Theo. Maybe he'd get a few minutes with Ty before he had to leave.

But a search of the house—unshaven, hair still wet—turned up nothing. Ty must've gone to the school to pick up his truck.

Which was fine. Ollie was not going to freak out about it. They could talk later.

He stopped himself from texting Ty about that. Nothing good ever came from a *we need to talk* text. He wrote a note instead, then spent thirty seconds debating whether he should draw a heart next to his name. Too forward? Too fast? He wrote an X instead and grabbed his keys from the counter. "Theo. Time to go."

Picking out the correct toy took approximately seventy-five years, in part because Theo kept getting distracted by things *he* wanted, and Ollie had to continually remind himself that it was a bad idea to assuage his parental guilt over yesterday through material gifts. "Your birthday's coming up too," he pointed out after the fifth very cool toy that would be discarded under Theo's bed in three days while Theo shoved his nose in yet another book. "Why don't you make a list when we get home later?"

Fortunately, or unfortunately in this case, Theo's attention was as easily taken up by the task of figuring out what Mel might want. With about ten minutes to go before Cassie sent out a search party, Ollie put two toys behind his back and made Theo pick a hand.

He arrived at the house just as the frazzle entered full swing. Cassie opened the door before he could knock, made a dramatic shushing gesture, and then joined them on the front step instead of letting them in. "Mel hardly slept all night, she was so excited about the party. She's having a nap now or she'll be an absolute bear the whole time. Why do people have kids, again?"

Ollie blinked at her, then looked pointedly at his son, who was standing *right there*.

"Think how boring life would be without them," he said, and then jabbed his fingers under Theo's armpits to coax out a squawk of a laugh.

"Dad! That's cheating."

"It's not. Dads always get to tickle. That's the rules."

Cassie smiled at Theo. "I think he used that same rule when we were kids, except he said *brothers*."

Ollie wiggled his fingers at her. "You're not too old."

"You just keep in mind that I know where Mom keeps the pictures of you on that sheepskin rug. And naughty brothers' kids get drum kits for Christmas."

He lifted his palms. "I yield."

Cassie put Theo to work helping her stuff goodie bags while Ollie set up ring toss and clipped plastic tablecloths to picnic tables. Crepe paper streamers went up above the doorways. Balloons were tied to mailboxes and fence posts. By the end of it, Ollie was wondering if kids still went to Chuck E. Cheese for birthday parties these days. Maybe that clip-n-climb place out on Front Road. Hosting a party at home seemed like a lot of work.

And God only knew what'd happen if the kids tried to play hide-and-seek in the Morris mansion. Ty kept insisting there wasn't a sex dungeon, but Ollie wouldn't put it past the place to have actual skeletons in a closet somewhere.

On the other hand, he could see Ty's face as he hopefully offered to host. He'd say something about bringing in a petting zoo and mention his dad had never let him rent a bouncy castle, and then on Theo's birthday somehow there would be balloon animals and face painting and possibly some kind of carnival ride.

He had to be devastated Theo wasn't talking to him, even if he'd put on a brave face about it. People who loved like that didn't take rejection easily.

"Penny for your thoughts," Cassie said quietly from his elbow after he finished hanging the piñata.

Ollie inhaled sharply and then made himself hold his breath for a count of four and let it out slowly again, sending the panic with it. He knew she'd only startled him because he'd let his guard down, and that was good—that he felt like he *could* let his guard down somewhere outside his house. It was just... funny, maybe. Ty never sneaked up on him like that.

Sneaking wasn't really his strong suit.

"Ollie?"

Oh. He was smiling now.

"That's a good look on you." Cassie bumped his shoulder. "You want to tell me who put it there?"

Little sisters were so nosy. "I think you'd have more fun guessing."

She laughed and teased, "I don't know, I mean, aside from Theo, there's only one person you spend your time with—"

Despite more than a decade in the military, Ollie was helpless to stop the flush.

Cassie stopped. "Holy shit, really?"

Which, well…. One side effect of Ollie not dating very much was that he hadn't bothered telling his family he wasn't exactly straight. He figured he'd tell them if it ever had any bearing on his life.

He hadn't intended to do this today, but it would be weird to walk it back now.

"Ollie!" Cassie smacked his shoulder. "What the hell! You never told me you were... bi?"

He wrinkled his nose. "I don't really label it. I don't know, it's more like… I'm not attracted to a lot of people, so when I am, gender is kind of a nonissue." He'd mostly dated cis women, but when *mostly* could be counted on the fingers of one hand, that didn't mean a lot. "I've never dated a man."

"You like Ty a lot, huh?"

"Enough to come out to my sister."

She squeezed his bicep. "I'm glad you did. And for what it's worth, anyone who puts that look on your face is worth keeping around."

"Thanks, Cass."

"That does explain why he was so frantic trying to get hold of you yesterday. Talk about going above and beyond. I thought maybe that was, like, the school pushing that, but he was with Theo the whole time? No wonder you like him. He must like you a lot too." Ollie didn't know how to interrupt that no, that was just Ty, that Ty would've done that for anyone because that was who he was. He didn't think he could do it without coming across as lovestruck. Plus that would invite follow-up questions. Fortunately, before the moment could feel awkward, she added, "And that butt. Seriously. Who could blame you?"

Well now Ollie was blushing for a whole new reason. "Cass!"

"Tell me I'm wrong."

She wasn't wrong. Ty had an amazing ass. But Ollie only wanted to touch it because it was his.

Miraculously, she let him get away with not answering out loud, even if they both knew his silence was damning. "So how long have you been seeing each other?"

Shit. "Um. We're not. Exactly. Officially."

Her eyes widened. "Please don't tell me you're dumb enough to try friends with benefits with someone who makes you smile like that."

"We didn't even kiss until yesterday."

She took one look at him and immediately figured it out. "Nothing like having your kid in the hospital to remind you what's important?"

"Something like that."

"You gonna tell Mom and Dad?"

Fuck, they'd probably be here later today. Ollie was willing to put up with their presence for Mel's sake, and Cassie's, but…. "Do you think I have to?"

She snorted. "It's a small town, Ollie. You cannot hide the most scandalous relationship in Suffolk from church-lady gossip. And you know how much Mom loves gossip."

"Not really looking forward to that conversation, especially when we're not really talking." He paused. "Although on the other hand, the reason we're not really talking is they were assholes about Ty, so at least they won't be too surprised."

"God." She shook her head. "You want a cupcake before the party starts?"

Did he want to slather his feelings in fat and carbs? "Absolutely."

It wasn't a bad way to spend a morning, or wouldn't have been if he hadn't had other things he desperately wanted to be doing. But then twelve thirty rolled around, the parents started arriving with their kids, and any wistful thoughts of Ty got shoved on the back burner along with things like the need to pee and conversation that went deeper than sports and the weather and whose turn was it to hit the piñata.

Ollie had just enough spare brain power to realize that he never wanted to host a party of this size without at least two other adults riding herd, and then he got swept up watching Theo and Mel plot an absolutely cutthroat strategy in capture the flag.

Maybe he should've tried harder to encourage ring toss instead of kids' war games.

But everyone seemed to be having a good time, even Ollie, who eventually had to slink into the shadows next to the house and hunch there, overstimulated. He already knew he was going to crash hard again tonight. There was too much going on. He swore he'd had better stamina in the Army. But any kind of work was different from this chaos.

He was still standing against the house, eyes and ears peeled for distressed shrieking—not easy to differentiate from regular kid shrieking, so he was happy for the practice—when his parents showed up.

He caught his father's eye, then his mother's, but no acknowledgment passed between them. They didn't come over to say hello, and Ollie didn't move from the house.

"So this isn't going to be awkward at all," Cassie said, sidling up beside him.

"I could leave," Ollie offered. Now that their parents had arrived, the kids would have plenty of supervision. "Come back for Theo later."

Even as he said it, he knew he wouldn't unless Cassie asked him to. He could just about cope with having Theo out of his sight, but only because he stayed within shouting distance.

Obviously Cassie knew better too, because she snorted. "Yeah, right. Anyway, if anyone's leaving, it's Mom and Dad. They didn't blow up thirty balloons this morning." She waited a beat. "I hope Ty appreciates your lung capacity."

He let his head fall back against the brick. "Cass—"

"Anyway, you can't leave now. He'll be here any minute."

The words washed over him like a bucket of cold water. "What?!"

She gave him a sheepish look. "In hindsight I probably should've just sent you to pick him up so you could have that chat away from prying eyes, but I didn't think Mom and Dad would be showing up for another hour."

Ollie had spent too much of his life in undesirable situations to panic now. He only wished he'd taken a little more time to think about what he wanted to say.

Shit, what *did* he want to say? Figuring out what he wanted was easy. Deciding what to say to achieve it, not so much.

Cassie's phone buzzed in her pocket, and she pulled it out. "Doorbell cam," she said. "You wanna get that?"

Ollie did, in fact, want to get that.

He still hadn't figured out what to say when he opened the door.

There was a bouquet of flowers on the other side. It had legs.

It had hands too; one of them was holding an outrageously sized gift bag stuffed to bursting with tissue paper. Presumably it also held a present. Another, smaller bag nested inside it.

Ollie remained speechless.

"Um," said Ty's voice from behind the flowers. "Hi? I'm… um."

While Ollie's brain scrambled for words, his hands went into action. He plucked the bouquet out of Ty's hands and held it at his own side so he could see Ty's face.

"Hi," Ty repeated, a little breathlessly this time. He was flushing—he flushed so easily and looked so good doing it, it suddenly made Ollie crazy. How pink would he get if Ollie kissed him again? If he—no. He needed to focus. Talk first.

"Hi, Ty." Ollie didn't bother trying to play it cool. That was a game for kids. Instead, he smiled and lifted the flowers. "These are nice."

"Um," Ty said again. The flush deepened. Was Ollie imagining that he could feel the heat radiating from his face? "They're for your sister. Hostess present. Since I'm crashing the party and—yeah."

Ollie looked at the bouquet. He didn't consider himself an expert in flower-buying, but he'd certainly bought flowers for hosts before. Never anything this elaborate, though. What was that, a hundred dollars' worth? More?

In his entire life, Ollie had been completely, perfectly sure where he belonged only twice. Once when he cradled his infant son in his hands. The second time at the controls of a helicopter on his first solo flight.

He was sure of it now too. He belonged between Ty and the rest of the world, protecting him from anyone who couldn't see his worth.

Finally he remembered it was his turn to speak. He cleared his throat. "Wow. Are you planning to eat all the cake yourself?"

"Shut up." Ty ducked his head, but he was grinning. Ollie stepped back to let him in.

"And you brought a birthday present too?"

"Ollie, you can't show up at a kids' birthday party without a gift. It doesn't matter if you're not invited. Even evil fairies know that."

Ollie led the way into the dining room, where he rummaged around Cassie's hutch to find a vase big enough to contain the entire greenhouse Ty had carted over. "And you're this town's version of the evil fairy?"

Ty laughed too. "Uh, I guess. If the shoe fits."

"I think that's a different story." He set the flowers and vase on the table. He could get water for them later, after they'd—just, after.

Before he could say anything, Ty added, "I brought something for Theo too. Apology gift, since I sort of—well, for yesterday."

Ollie was going to veto that one. Theo didn't need to get the idea that adults could buy his forgiveness, especially when the adult in question had acted in his best interest. But that was okay; there were plenty of other reasons to give Theo presents. They could think of one later. Right now, though—"What?" he teased. "You didn't bring *me* anything?"

But Ty wasn't laughing anymore. He'd gone serious, cheeks still pink, bright eyes shining. "Me," he said simply. "I—Ollie, I brought you *me*, I—"

Ollie's fingers went numb. "It's enough." He stepped forward and took Ty's perfect face in nerveless hands. "It's more than enough, Ty, it's everything—"

Talking, something in Ollie's upper brain reminded him. They were supposed to be talking.

But talking could wait until after Ollie had his fill of Ty's mouth. He tasted like strawberries and smelled like summer, and when their lips touched, sensation roared back—the heat of Ty's skin and the soft prickle of his stubble and the strange, not unpleasant way his body fit against Ollie's. Solid. Reliable.

Ollie had never felt so grounded in himself, so sure. How could he feel like that when having Ty so close made his heart race, made him… probably unsafe for a kids' birthday party, now that he thought about it. He was going to need a minute to cool off.

Kissing Ty was a paradox, apparently.

Finally Ty made an embarrassed sound against Ollie's mouth and pulled away. He'd flushed again, but this time it left his eyes and lips dark too. That… hmm. Ollie might need *two* minutes, actually. "Okay," Ty said, breathless again. He ran a hand through his hair and Ollie's hands itched to follow it. "Good—good talk?"

"I really need to stop kissing you in public. Semipublic." Heh. Semi.

Ty caught his eye and snickered.

Damn it. Ollie poked him, but he was grinning too. "Stop, come on."

"Well, which one is it? Stop or—"

Ollie put a hand over his mouth.

Ty's gaze went, if possible, even darker. The heat of his breath against Ollie's palm was… something Ollie was not going to think about at his niece's birthday party. He cleared his throat and pulled his hand away. "We still have a lot to talk about. *Actual* talk," he clarified.

"Yeah." Ty was still smiling. "We're already doing everything backwards, though. What's a few kisses between guys who live together?"

God. "Well, when you put it like that," Ollie said, and then he put his hand on Ty's belt and reeled him in for another one.

He was learning the shape of Ty's smile under his lips when the sound of something breaking sent him halfway to a flashback.

He stepped away from Ty and put his shoulders against the wall, chest heaving. For a moment he kept his eyes closed and concentrated on grounding himself in the present. He could hear his own breathing and the hard edges of voices—Ty's and someone else familiar, though Ollie couldn't process the words. The scent of buttercream frosting reached his nose. The coolness of the wall at his back seeped through his shirt.

Then a hand curled around his own, and Ollie snapped back into his body.

"—do you think you're doing?" his mother said, and Ollie wished he could snap back out of it, but no. His place was between Ty and the world, not on the sidelines with his head in the sand. "Ollie, you're not—"

Ollie squeezed Ty's fingers and shot him what he hoped was a reassuring look. "Not going to have this conversation with you at this volume while pretending Ty isn't standing right here?" he suggested.

His mother sputtered. She'd dropped a plate of cake—that was what had shattered, and the frosting had splattered onto her pedicured toes. Why was she using a real plate? Cassie had specifically bought paper ones for the party. They had little baseballs on them.

"You can hardly blame me for being *surprised*—"

That was a bit rich. "Can't I?" Ollie countered. "Dad had no trouble jumping to all kinds of conclusions the other day at brunch. I'd have thought he'd have shared them with you."

Fuck, he hadn't meant to say that in front of Ty. He didn't deserve to have to hear that Ollie's father had implied he might be a pedophile. Life had been cruel enough to him already.

She frowned. "Is this why you've been avoiding my calls?"

And… Ollie's mother wasn't that good of an actor. She really had no idea why Ollie had been avoiding the two of them as a pair.

He didn't know whether that made him angrier or… something else. Sadder? More tired? All of the above.

He didn't have the energy to have that conversation now *and* the one he wanted to have with Ty later, so he said, "We're going to go get some water for the flowers Ty brought for Cassie, and then we're going to give Mel her gift and eat some cake. Meanwhile maybe you can ask Dad why I haven't spoken to you in weeks." He paused. "Oh, and your grandson is fine, by the way, after multiple beestings that landed him in the hospital yesterday. But thanks to Ty, he's out there running around with the other kids. Like he should be."

Let her stew in that for a while. Ollie grabbed the vase in his free hand and tugged Ty toward the kitchen. "Come on. You like cake, right?"

Chapter 15

Ty thought kids were nuts at school, but at Mel's birthday party, he experienced a whole new level of elementary-aged, sugar-enabled shenanigans.

They didn't see Ollie's parents again after they presented Cassie with the flowers, and Ty didn't dare ask. If he didn't know details, he didn't have to feel guilty about driving a wedge between Ollie and his family.

Though frankly if his mom was that upset about Ollie kissing a man, Ollie was better off without her.

A kid's birthday party wasn't exactly the best time to talk, but for once in his life, Ty didn't feel the need to push. No one had ever stood up for him the way Ollie had. That said plenty.

And if the words *it's more than enough—it's everything* rang pleasantly in his head all afternoon while he ate cake and hot dogs and never strayed out of Ollie's orbit, well, Ty could hardly be blamed.

Early in the afternoon, Theo ran out of steam in a spectacular fashion that almost resulted in a meltdown over the last strawberry cupcake. Ty figured he had earned some grace by virtue of having spent most of the previous day in the hospital. Ollie staved off tears by offering, "Okay, bud, tell you what. I think I've had enough of people's company for the day. Why don't we head home and put on *Moneyball*, and maybe if we're lucky, Ty will make us pasta for dinner?"

The last thing Ty wanted was more carbohydrates, but pasta was easy, and he could make a salad too.

Theo's lip wobbled a moment, but he got it under control before any mortifying tears could fall at his younger cousin's party. He looked hesitantly at Ty, like he didn't want to ask for anything from someone he was still mad at, or maybe he was embarrassed about giving him the cold shoulder all day.

"O-*kay*," he said finally as he pressed half his face against Ollie's stomach, "but I want extra parmesan."

Ollie caught Ty's eye and gave him a slight smile.

"I think we can manage that," Ty agreed.

They drove home separately, so Ty took the opportunity to stop for more cheese, just in case, and a bag of baby spinach. When he walked in the side door, the house was quiet—no *Moneyball* on the TV and no Theo anywhere. He put the groceries in the fridge and meandered into the games room.

"Hey."

"Hey." Ty dropped next to Ollie on the sofa, then thought *fuck it* and leaned right into him. Ollie slid an arm around his shoulder like he'd been handed a script. Ty might never get up. "Theo pass out?"

"Carried him inside like a sack of potatoes," Ollie confirmed. He tugged a little until Ty was more or less using him as a body pillow. *Hello*, Ty thought, as his dick decided it liked where things seemed to be going.

Then Ollie's hand slipped from Ty's shoulder to his chest, fingertips brushing a nipple through his shirt, and scratch that, all of Ty loved where this was going, and could it get there a little faster?

His breath hitched.

He knew Ollie heard it—felt it—because he suddenly went very still. Like he was holding his breath.

Talk, Ty commanded his mouth. Nothing came out. His throat was dry.

Instead he put his hand on top of Ollie's. That helped—he could keep that warm, steady pressure in the center of his chest instead of near any danger zones that would inevitably derail him. "So just—to be clear." He wondered if Ollie could feel the scared-rabbit thump of his heart. "We're doing this, yeah? For real. For...." His nerve deserted him. This whole town hated him. His own father hadn't wanted him. Why would Ollie?

But Ollie deserved better than Ty's doubt. He'd been proving that for weeks. Maybe Ty deserved better too. He swallowed and made himself finish. "For keeps."

"Ty." Ollie shifted underneath him, and suddenly they were both sitting up straight, facing each other. Ollie's hand had moved from Ty's chest to the side of his face, like Ollie was afraid Ty might bolt. "You think there's any other way I'd do this?"

No. No, he didn't. Not really. Ty's low self-worth could never hold up against his faith in Ollie.

He shook his head.

"You and me." Ollie had Ty's face framed in both hands now. "And Theo. Everything else is just details."

Ty wet his lips, swallowed against a dry throat. "You should kiss me." Now and for the rest of his life.

Ollie's whole body curled up in a smile, and a second later he'd pulled Ty back into his lap and they were kissing like the rest of their lives could wait.

Weeks of pent-up emotions heated fast. Ollie let out a sharp breath when Ty settled his weight down, and Ty was reaching for the back of the couch to steady himself and take some of the weight before Ollie took his lower lip between his teeth and put his hands on Ty's ass and pulled him in farther.

God, Ty couldn't remember the last time he'd kissed like this. His lips prickled with stubble rash and his head spun faster every time Ollie's tongue brushed his. He was making soft, needy noises between kisses, awful sounds that should have mortified him, but he didn't care. Not when he could taste Ollie's desire, feel the evidence between his legs. Not when he had Ollie's hands under the back of his shirt, on the meat of his thighs, clawing their way up his inseam to unbutton his shorts.

Ty didn't know how he did it. Most of his concentration went to kissing, breathing, and not coming in his pants before Ollie could touch him. At one point he heard the pop of seams ripping. But he didn't have to move from Ollie's lap, didn't have to give up the heat of his body or the wet of his mouth to suddenly have that warm, callused hand wrapped around his dick.

Oh God, this wasn't going to take long. Ollie rubbed his thumb over the head of Ty's cock, and Ty could *feel* the reaction going through him as if in slow motion. Even his throat tightened; his mouth watered and his nipples went hard and his asshole clenched and—

Ollie broke the kiss, breathing hard, his mouth wet and swollen, his eyes dark. He looked down at his hand, at the head of Ty's thick cock in his fist. His other hand tightened on Ty's thigh.

Ty balanced on a knife's edge. He didn't have the leverage to move beyond frantic hitches of his hips, and even if he did, he was caught watching Ollie watch him.

"Ty." Ollie's voice was raw. Ty hadn't even gotten to touch him yet, but he sounded wrecked. Like he was the one strung out in *Ty*'s lap. "God, you're…."

What? Ty wanted to ask. His tongue wouldn't cooperate. He licked his lips and looked down. Ollie never missed a beat; his hand never slowed. But now he'd changed his grip so the head of Ty's cock pointed toward Ollie's chest.

"Ollie." Ty's whole body thrummed with electric current. "I'm gonna come"—*all over you*—"I—"

"Yeah?" Ollie encouraged, breathless. "Do it."

"Okay," Ty said weakly. His balls clenched and his breath stuttered and his eyes rolled back in his head as his release poured out of him, over Ollie's fingers and up his shirt, spattering on their shorts. Still Ollie didn't stop, not until Ty was gasping and panting and had to pull himself out of his grip. That left him heaving for breath braced above Ollie on the couch, with Ollie covered in Ty's come and eyes black with lust and an erection straining the front of his shorts.

Ty wanted to faceplant in his lap. Before he knew it he was scrambling to get bloodless legs under him, half falling off the couch, reaching for Ollie's fly as his knees hit the carpet. "Ollie, can I—"

Ollie pushed Ty's hands away so he could stand and shove down his shorts. "Jesus, yes."

Ty had never been a religious guy. But, like, he could make an exception, probably. Because the way he felt now, with Ollie's hand in his hair guiding him forward, with the scent of Ollie's arousal in his nose, with Ollie's perfect flushed pink cock in front of his face? Ty felt pretty worshipful.

And the way he felt with Ollie's dick in his mouth and Ollie's hand on his neck and Ollie's whispered *fuck*s and *like that*s and then, when Ty closed his eyes and pushed forward until he was holding Ollie in the back of his throat and sucking, swallowing, a soft, strangled *ah*—

Ecstasy.

Any other day, Ty would have wanted to take his time, draw it out. He wanted to learn exactly how to take Ollie apart with his mouth. Right now Ty just wanted him to come in it.

He got his first warning when Ollie tugged sharply on his hair, pulling Ty away.

"Close," Ollie gasped, as though Ty couldn't tell.

Ty flicked his gaze upward and pushed deep again, pointedly. Ollie's thighs trembled under his hands and his balls jerked against his chin as he came down Ty's throat.

Finally Ty pulled off to catch his breath and wiped his mouth with the back of his hand. Ollie's cheeks had a dark red flush, and with his shorts open and his shirt stained, he looked debauched, even shell-shocked, like Ty had really sucked his brain out through his dick.

Ty let the satisfaction of that wash through him for a handful of seconds, and then his calves complained about the blood flow situation and he stretched out on the floor to fix the problem.

Ollie poked his head over the couch to look down at him. "Did we kill you?"

"Rumors of my demise have been greatly exaggerated." Ty flexed his feet. "Pins and needles are pretty nasty, though. Figured I should wait until I can feel my legs before I try to stand on them."

Laughing, Ollie flopped onto the couch and smushed his face into the cushion. "Would hate for the rumors to turn out to be premonitions."

Ty grinned up at the ceiling. His calves still felt like they were covered in fire ants, but worth it? Oh yeah. "See, you get it. That's why I keep you around." He propped himself up on his elbows. "So, like, don't take this the wrong way, because I am zero percent complaining. But this idea I had of you as someone who at least *thought* he was straight is not totally jibing with the fact that you have definitely touched someone else's dick before."

Ollie laughed again, a sound so loose and happy Ty wanted to roll around in it. "You're the first guy I've been with," he said. "But, uh, a couple years ago I ran into someone I had served with. I didn't recognize her at first—she transitioned after her second tour finished—but then I did, and we decided to catch up over drinks, and one thing led to another…."

"I think I'm kinda jealous how easy you were for this woman," Ty said when it became clear Ollie wasn't going to offer up any more details. Maybe Ty should have asked him out for drinks instead of just offering them in the hot tub?

"Hey!" Ollie dropped a throw pillow on his head. When Ty flung it away again, Ollie was grinning. "She was a lot more assertive than you.

We were two and a half drinks in, and the bar was getting too loud to talk, and she said, 'Listen, I'm going to cut to the chase. You're hot and I'm horny. You good with the original plumbing?'"

Ty cackled and pulled himself to a sitting position. "And that *worked*?"

"Well." Ollie was flushed again. "From my perspective, *she* was hot and *I* was horny. And I kind of had a thing for her before, but I wasn't going to pursue that when we were enlisted together."

"Opportunity knocked and you answered." Ty shook his head. "Teach me not to ask for what I want." He folded his arms on the couch cushion. "So you're… bi? Pan?"

"Eh." Ollie scrunched his nose. "I haven't dated enough people to pick a more specific label. Sample size is too small. Let's go with 'queer.'"

"'Kay." Was Ty grinning like an idiot right now? Probably. But what was he supposed to do? Pretend this wasn't the greatest thing to ever happen to him? Ty was not that good of an actor. "And now you're my…?"

"Boyfriend," Ollie decided. "Although as you pointed out, the whole living together thing… I know we skipped a lot of steps in that respect. I don't want to move *everything* too fast."

"No, that's good, I-I'm good with *boyfriend*," Ty promised. He was so, so good with *boyfriend*. Ollie was his *boyfriend*. Oh God, Ty was going to be so embarrassing about this. "What're we telling Theo?"

Ollie swore sharply like he'd just remembered other people existed, sat up straight, then looked around the room and down at himself. "Way more than we probably want to if we don't clean up," he said ruefully.

Okay, yes, this was not the ideal way to break the news to Ollie's kid. Especially since he was kind of mad at Ty already. Groaning like an old man, Ty heaved himself to his feet. "All right, fair point," he said. "Priorities. First, unfortunate decency. Then talk."

Ollie shook his head and reached up with one hand to yank Ty down into a kiss. Ty only just caught himself on the back of the couch, or he'd have ended up back in Ollie's lap, probably making their mess several orders of magnitude worse. Ty imagined him licking the taste of himself out of Ty's mouth and shivered pleasantly.

Then Ollie released him. "*Now* we can shower." He paused. "Probably separately, though."

The master shower was more than big enough for two, but that wasn't how Ty wanted Theo to find out either. God, he hoped Ollie didn't want to wait too long. He licked his lips, hoping he didn't come across like a stupefied pigeon and very much aware it was a lost cause. "Right. Yes. Shower."

He heard Ollie laughing behind him as he turned around and almost tripped—his ripped shorts had tangled around his ankles—but the sound didn't bother him.

Ty might not get everything he wanted, but he was pretty close to having everything that mattered.

OLLIE TOOK the world's quickest shower, changed into clean clothes, and tossed the soiled ones in the washing machine. He figured he'd wait for Ty to start the load, but… yeah. Yet another way he did not want Theo to find out Ollie and Ty were together now. Unfortunately, there seemed to be a lot of them.

When he was in the laundry room, he spied the bottle of air freshener on the shelf and figured better safe than sorry—Theo loved the game room; if he went in there and asked *what's that smell?* Ollie would die—and went slightly overboard until the whole place reeked like fake laundry smell.

Then he opened the windows to compensate.

Ty had never taken a military-length shower in his life, or at least not in the past five weeks. Ollie looked forward to deprogramming himself a little further with Ty's assistance and encouragement, but meanwhile he figured he had time to start thinking about dinner. He'd eaten more than enough junk at Cassie's, which meant Theo had eaten his body weight in refined sugar. Grilled cheese and carrot sticks? Yeah, that would work.

He was buttering the bread when he heard Ty in the doorway behind him. Ollie liked that about him; he never sneaked. Even at night, when Ollie was in bed trying to sleep, if Ty got up for a midnight snack, he didn't tiptoe. He had heavy footsteps and a long stride, distinctive enough to recognize. Maybe he was just oblivious that he was kind of loud. Ollie thought not, though; he was probably loud on purpose because he knew Ollie hated being startled.

Ty cleared his throat. "Hey."

"Hey," Ollie replied, smiling automatically. "You hungry?"

Ty raised his eyebrows, grinning. "Just ate."

Ollie turned back to the frying pan. "Guess I walked into that one. But seriously, you want a grilled cheese?"

"The answer to that question is always yes." He slid into a seat at the breakfast bar.

Ollie could've guessed. Ty was a good cook; you didn't bother getting good at something like that unless you liked to eat. He nudged the first sandwich over with the spatula and wiggled a second one in beside it.

"So." Ollie looked over his shoulder in time to see Ty hook his ankles around the legs of the breakfast bar stool. His loose athletic shorts left a lot of leg on display. Ollie was probably in danger of burning the grilled cheese; it had been a while since his libido had anything to do.

But both of them liked their grilled cheese almost black, so it would work out okay.

Ty smiled when he caught Ollie looking.

"So," Ollie echoed. "Talking?"

Ty's lips twitched. "Talking." He ran a hand back through his shower-damp hair and laughed softly. "Uh, where do we even start?"

Ollie blinked. "We already did the difficult part, didn't we?" He prodded the first sandwich, which was still tragically golden, and then let the corner of the bread flop back down to cook properly. "What else is there?"

Ty cleared his throat. "I mean, I'm supposed to go back to work in Chicago the week after next."

Right, Ollie knew that. "Are you not ready?" It struck him that Ty hadn't exactly done a lot of... processing. Everyone grieved differently, but he wasn't sure Ty had done any of it at all, apart from make decisions based on what would have pissed his dad off the most. Sure, they hadn't gotten along, but some kind of catharsis was still in the cards, right?

Ty's brow creased. "I meant we're not exactly going to be in the same place, so...."

"Huh."

"What?"

Ollie shook his head. "No, you're right. I just never thought about that part of it." Off Ty's incredulous look, he hastened to add, "Every relationship I've ever had, I was in the military at the time. Long-distance has kind of been the default."

"Oh."

Ollie waited a moment for it to sink in, but Ty's frown didn't soften, so he prompted, "Ty?" But before he could ask what was up, the answer occurred to him. "I'm still going to miss you."

Ty made a wry face. "Sap."

Ollie wasn't that either, or at least he hadn't ever been before. Something told him he'd have to get better at saying things out loud if he wanted to keep Ty out of the panic spiral he seemed determined to fall into. "What's your schedule usually like? Do you do three twelves, or…?"

"Two twelve-hour days, then two twelve-hour nights, then four days off. I should actually be able to be here almost half the time, with travel." He shook his head ruefully. "I guess I can afford that kind of thing now. Although I hate to think what it's going to do to my carbon footprint."

You could just quit your job, Ollie almost said. It wasn't like Ty needed the money. But he didn't think it would be fair to say it. Besides, Ty obviously thrived as a paramedic. He loved his coworkers. Ollie had a job, but Ty had a calling. "Maybe you can plant a forest or something."

Ty brightened at the idea. "Now we're talking."

Belatedly, Ollie remembered the grilled cheeses, which were now delightfully carbonated. He flipped them over. "That's the distance down." Though Ollie realized now he'd have to look into camps for Theo for the summer, with school ending. Why hadn't he thought about that sooner? Too distracted, probably. "What else is on the list?"

"Elephant in the room. Or elephant in his room, I guess."

"Theo? I mean I know he's loud going up and down the stairs," Ollie joked, "but name-calling seems a bit extreme."

"Ha ha." Ty made a face, but he was fronting. He'd pulled his shoulders in and hunched down, as though he were more likely to get what he wanted if he made himself small. "He's your kid. I don't want to overstep, but I've been his caregiver. Now I'm also your boyfriend, but I'm not his parent."

"Okay, I admit that's a—" *Minefield*, Ollie wanted to say, but his mouth clacked shut and he shivered, then shook it off. "—a challenge. But Theo likes you, and he's a good kid. And it's not like anything's really going to change. You always defer to me when I'm around, and when I'm not, you're in charge. Not because you're my boyfriend, but because you're his... unpaid babysitter."

"At least I'm not going to be his teacher anymore," Ty said wryly. "I think I was starting to develop multiple personalities."

Ollie poked into the pan once more. "Well, call up the hungry one, because these are crispy."

He plated the sandwiches, turned off the burner, and then hooked his foot around the leg of the bar stool next to Ty's to pull it out. When he sat, he made sure their knees bumped. He knew Ty wasn't done panicking about Theo.

Sure enough, Ty only made it as far as dipping one corner of his sandwich into his ketchup puddle before he asked, "So we're telling him, right?"

"Yeah, of course. Wait, were you worried I wanted to keep it a secret?"

Ty flushed. "I mean you didn't exactly say, you know? And I know it's complicated, especially because he just lost his mom, so I'd get it. But also, I... I don't think I can be chill about you, so he's gonna notice."

I don't think I can be chill about you. Ollie didn't think Ty had ever been chill about anything in his life, but the words still made him feel like he'd stepped out of a frozen wasteland into a grassy sunlit meadow. "Ty, I kissed you in front of my mom. There's no chill here."

The flush deepened. "That was an accident."

Ollie bumped their knees together. "Do I have to do it again?" Normally PDAs weren't his thing, but needs must.

"Oh God, please tell me you don't have a kink about that."

Ollie dropped his sandwich onto the plate. "Ty! *Gross.*"

"Just checking." The joke had relaxed him, though. The tension in his body had melted and he was leaning into Ollie like he needed help staying upright. Ollie had to lean back, or they'd risk toppling the bar stool. "That still leaves the question of what we're telling him and when and how."

"It's not a *we* this time, I don't think." Ty had done a lot of emotional heavy lifting with Theo as it was. Ollie would never forget that, and he would never be able to repay the kindness Ty had shown his kid. But that was the thing—Ty would never expect repayment or even see his actions as anything beyond common human decency, and would likely say he enjoyed spending time with Theo and having difficult emotional talks and—

Ollie needed to stop that train of thought before he melted into a puddle.

Before Ty could feel excluded, he went on. "You do so much for him, and when he's not being a scared eight-year-old, he knows that. I love the bond you have. But you've only known him a couple weeks. Hell, *I've* only been his real parent for less than a year. I owe it to him to tell him one-on-one and give him a safe space to have big emotions about it."

When he finished, Ty was leaning on his elbow, totally ignoring his perfect grilled cheese to gaze at Ollie like he was made of newborn puppies. "What?"

"You're just a really good dad and I'm into it. Not in a sexy way."

Ollie gave a self-deprecating snort, even as his ears heated at the praise. He picked up his sandwich again. "I'm making shit up as I go."

"You're letting Theo lead. I don't mean to tell you how to parent. I mean you let his reactions inform your decisions about what he needs."

"Why do you know so much about parenting?" Ollie deflected.

"I don't," Ty protested. "I know a little. We had a slow shift a couple months ago and someone left out a book about child-led parenting. I was curious."

Of course he was. Even though he had no kids of his own, no partner, no nieces or nephews. Part of Ollie wondered if he'd picked it up thinking maybe the book would tell him why his father had treated him so poorly, though he might have done that without consciously realizing it. "Okay, well, as much as I like to think I'm paying attention, I probably need to take the lead on this one. Even if I'm not sure exactly where to start."

"We could do some research," Ty suggested. Then, his cheeks bright red, "You could, I mean. There have to be resources out there for how to talk to your kid about dating someone when they've recently lost a parent. Maybe his therapist?"

Ollie's heart did some kind of fancy dance move in his chest. It must've shown on his face, because Ty asked, "What?"

"I'm just—I'm not sure whether to be angry at the whole fucking world or if I should shake someone's hand." He couldn't seem to figure out what to do with his own. "How have you been single until now? Why has no one married you?"

Ty flushed a furious red to the very tips of his ears and ducked his head, but he couldn't hide the way the words affected him.

Ollie was probably getting ahead of himself, though. "Don't answer that, it was rhetorical. I'll count it as one of my blessings."

"Ollie!"

Okay, now he was almost purple. Obviously he needed some exposure therapy to get better at taking compliments, because Ollie had plans. Someone so sweet and thoughtful and kind should know how much better he made everyone else's lives simply by being in them. "Ty," Ollie replied. He touched their shoulders together, gently this time. "I mean it. I could have gotten through the past two months without you, but not like this. Not—I've been happy. Barring a few speedbumps, Theo's been happy. And we have you to thank." *Please get used to hearing that.*

He didn't think Ty could flush any deeper without causing himself permanent damage, so he stopped there. Baby steps, or something like it.

"He deserves it," Ty said immediately. "You both do."

"So do you." Ollie backed off with his touch and ate a few bites of his sandwich while Ty processed. He had no illusions that they were finished with this conversation. He was kind of surprised Ty hadn't shown up in the kitchen with a checklist.

After a minute, Ty had collected himself enough to speak again. "Okay, so, uh, here's another question with no wrong answer. Obviously we're not going to be sharing a bed until you talk to Theo, but… after that?"

Oh.

"It's weird," Ollie said meditatively as he used his crust to sop up the last of the ketchup on his plate. "Because I haven't ever done that, actually."

Ty spun his stool to face him. "What, seriously?"

"I've been in the military my entire adult life. I spent most of that time deployed or on base. When Allison died and I had to come home, it took three weeks before I got used to sleeping in her queen-size bed. Most of the time I slept better on a cot in Theo's hospital room. And not just because I could keep an eye on him, you know?"

Ty hummed and stood up with his plate, gesturing to ask if Ollie wanted another sandwich. He shook his head; fruit and vegetables were the next order of business. Ty pulled out the containers of precut carrots and cucumbers and one of washed berries out of the fridge and set them down between their places. "I'm not actually good at it," he admitted.

Ollie tilted his head. "At… sleeping in the same bed as someone else?"

Nodding, Ty sat down and popped a strawberry in his mouth. When he'd swallowed, he said, "It's, uh, sometimes I can't get my brain to shut up. If the person next to me doesn't fall asleep quickly, I'll wonder if I'm moving around too much, breathing too loud. Or what if I fall asleep first and I snore and my partner gets mad at me."

Ollie was starting to understand that he had maybe only scratched the surface of an untapped well of self-esteem issues. "I don't know what I'd be like to sleep with. I woke up mad at myself this morning because the PTSD nightmares can get pretty bad, and what if I accidentally hurt Theo in my sleep?"

Ty paused with a carrot stick halfway to his open mouth. He set it back down on his plate. "If we try to sleep in the same bed, neither one of us is going to get any rest, huh?" He said it lightly, but Ollie felt the weight behind the words.

"We'll just have to wear each other out the first couple times, maybe, so we're too tired to think about it." That got a smile. "And then once we've proved we can do it, it'll be a piece of cake." He stopped and thought about it. "But I mean, I can't control my PTSD any more than you can control your anxiety. I think we have to accept that it's possible we might have to kick ourselves, or each other, out of bed." He gestured toward the house. "It's not like you don't have the room."

Ty managed a weak smile. "Yeah, I guess. But it's not very romantic."

It would be a lot less romantic if I snapped your neck in your sleep, Ollie thought, but that was extreme, maybe. He had no reason to think he'd do that. He didn't need to scare Ty off, and he didn't want to seem overly defensive. "You can make it up to me," he said instead, which earned a laugh and a coveted loosening of Ty's shoulders.

Good.

"Yeah, I can do that." Ty pulled Ollie off the bar stool and slid his hands into the back pockets of his jeans.

Ollie hadn't meant *right now*, but… well. He did have some lost time to make up for, especially if Ty was going to be leaving next week. And it felt *good*, cozying up to Ty in the kitchen, sharing body heat, trading kisses that weren't going anywhere with Theo likely to wake up at any moment.

And maybe Ollie had never really missed anyone before. Maybe he was used to the people he cared about being absent from his life. But maybe he'd just never had someone like Ty to miss. He had the sneaking suspicion that he was about to find out.

Chapter 16

SUNDAY MORNING Ty woke up groggy and disoriented, half convinced that the whole week had been a dream. But when he reached for his phone on the bedside table, he encountered the note he'd written himself the night before.

Yes, Ollie is your boyfriend now.

And *that* was a nice thought, even if it would've been nicer with Ollie next to him instead of the note. Ty loved a cuddle. But he was pretty sure Ollie would still cuddle with him, even if they never managed to actually sleep in the same bed.

He let himself bask in it for a few minutes, but eventually he had to get up. He had plans to make, things to do, people to talk to. He needed to figure out a strategy for this stupid town hall meeting next week, which meant not only talking to Eliza but rescheduling his flight to Chicago. He'd have to talk to his captain about his return-to-work date.

First things first. If he was going to tackle a to-do list that long, he needed a good breakfast.

The kitchen was empty when he entered, though he had no illusions that Ollie was still asleep. Yesterday morning had been the outlier for sure; Ollie was a horrifying morning person through and through. Ty went warm to his core when he saw there was fresh coffee in the coffee maker, even though Ollie had been leaving him coffee for weeks. That had been his friend Ollie. This was his *boyfriend* Ollie.

His boyfriend Ollie who was currently outside cutting Ty's grass, apparently. Shirtless, wearing a ball cap and aviators. Ty needed to put some food in his belly, because the sight was making him lightheaded. Fortunately he had a lot of yard, so there was plenty of time to make himself something to eat and then sit outside with his second cup of coffee and watch the world go by.

Ty was surveying the dishwasher and fridge to determine whether Ollie had eaten anything substantial for breakfast when Theo shuffled into the kitchen.

They hadn't exactly made up the night before. Theo had been grumpy and tired and discombobulated from too much sugar and too much sun and too much excitement. But he hadn't bristled at Ty's presence either, when the three of them retired to the living room to watch baseball before bed. Ty had relegated himself to the armchair so Theo wouldn't have to choose between being close to his dad or avoiding Ty.

He knew he was doing the right thing, getting out of the way, but he missed the way things used to be.

Maybe now was his chance to fix it. Ty cleared his throat. "Hey, buddy."

For a few seconds he thought Theo was going to ignore him. Then he climbed up on one of the barstools. "Where's my dad?"

"He's out cutting the grass." Ty contemplated the fridge, trying to keep his cool. Theo speaking to him voluntarily was progress he didn't want to call attention to. "What do you think he'd want for breakfast?"

Theo was quiet for a minute. Ty didn't know if the kid had spotted his trap and was deciding whether to fall into it or if he was actually considering Ollie's breakfast preferences until he said, "Pancakes."

Ollie was definitely more of a bacon and eggs guy.

"I can do pancakes," Ty said as he reached for the egg carton. "Are you hungry?"

A beat. Then, "Yeah," said cautiously, like he wasn't sure he was allowed.

"Well, that's a relief. I don't know how to make pancakes for two." He set the milk jug on the counter and took out the butter.

Theo was quiet for another minute.

Then, to Ty's horror, came a telltale sniff.

He froze with the broken eggshells still in his hand. What was he supposed to do? He couldn't be the one to bridge the distance between them, not when Theo was still mad at him, but he couldn't just sit here and let him *cry*—

"Please don't be mad at me," Theo wailed.

Ty dropped the eggshells in the sink and turned around. "I'm not mad," he promised. "Theo, I was never mad at you. I was worried."

Theo's face had gone a blotchy red, stained with tear tracks. "But I was mean to you."

What could he say to that? It was true. Ty was pretty sure he shouldn't discourage Theo from taking responsibility for his mistakes. "You did hurt my feelings," he said as gently as he could. Theo cried harder. "But I understand you were scared."

For a second he thought maybe that was the wrong thing to say—Theo's face screwed up even further, like he was about to blurt that he hadn't been *scared*—but then he nodded miserably and wiped his nose on his arm. "I'm sorry."

"Apology accepted—oof." Ty exhaled hard as Theo launched himself off the stool and wrapped his arms around his waist. He could feel tears and snot seeping through the fabric of his shirt, but it seemed like it would be cruel to complain about it, so he just settled his arms around Theo's shoulders and hugged him back. "I'm glad we made up. Do you want to help make pancakes?"

He and Theo had three full stacks warming in the oven by the time Ollie came in from yardwork, shoulders red from the sun and the rest of him glistening in a way that was way too pornographic for nine in the morning while under child supervision. "Smells good in here," Ollie commented, glancing back and forth between Ty and Theo with his eyebrows slightly raised.

Ty nodded that yes, they'd made up, and Ollie smiled.

Ty needed him to put a shirt on stat before he caused a cardiac arrest.

"Ty and I made pancakes," Theo announced unnecessarily. "And we waited for you."

"You did?" A slightly evil light went on in Ollie's eyes as he advanced toward Theo with his arms wide open. "That's so nice of you. You deserve a—"

"Noooo," Theo squawked, but he realized far too late.

"—great big hug," Ollie finished. He scooped Theo against his chest.

"Gross!" Theo fought against the hug, laughing and squirming. "Let me go! Dad, you're all sweaty!"

"I'm just trying to thank you," Ollie said innocently.

Then his eyes went to Ty—far too late for Ty to escape. He didn't have time to take a step back before Ollie grabbed him in his free hand and reeled him in too.

At some point in the struggle, Ollie had let go of Theo, or else Theo had escaped, and now Ollie had Ty in his clutches. Ty should probably try to get away. He should probably find this kind of gross. But Ollie smelled like freshly mown grass and clean sweat, and his skin was slick under Ty's fingers. The upshot of it all was that now Ty was desperately horny and thinking about Ollie fucking him behind the garage after breakfast.

"Thank me by showering," he yelped, trying to push away as Theo giggled, oblivious.

Ollie must've noticed Ty's semi, because when he let go, the light in his eyes had darkened into the kind of promise they'd be waiting hours to keep.

"I guess I can do that, since breakfast is such a swanky affair in this joint." He turned to go, giving Ty a perfect view of the way his damp shorts clung to his ass.

Ty took a steadying breath and made himself focus on Theo. "So, what do you think—maple syrup, or jam?"

Unfortunately, as much as he wanted to get started on that after-breakfast fantasy, real life intruded. Ty barely had the dishes stacked next to the dishwasher when Ollie's phone rang, and he grimaced.

"Mom?" Ty guessed.

"Yeah." Ollie's face went stony.

Great. "You good?" Ty asked.

"Guess we'll see."

OLLIE TOOK the call in the games room while Ty cajoled Theo into doing the cleanup with him. He'd been tempted not to answer, but he knew the longer he put it off, the worse it would be.

He didn't know what to expect, so it surprised him when his mother said, "Your father is sleeping on the couch."

He blinked and settled onto the sofa. Then, remembering the day before, he sprung back up again and sat at the poker table. "I guess he told you what he said."

"After a lot of beating around the bush," she said bitterly. "Ollie, I'm sorry."

He rubbed the skin under his eyes. "Me too. I didn't mean to cause problems for you and Dad."

"No, honey. He did that all by himself."

That didn't stop Ollie from feeling guilty about it. He cleared his throat. "Are you going to be okay? I mean, not just you, but you and Dad?"

"That depends on your father too."

God. "Mom—"

"Ollie," his mom cut in. "I'm a grown woman. Your father is a grown man." She paused. "And so are you. I'm sorry we've—*I've*—overstepped. You're doing a great job with Theo. He obviously adores you, and he's thriving even though he must miss his mother."

"We both do." He took a deep breath and released it slowly, noting with relief that the tension he'd been carrying finally seemed to be ebbing. That made sense, probably. Allison had wanted Theo to have a safety net in place if something happened to her. Ollie had felt like fighting with his parents was letting her down. "Listen, if you need some space or some company, I'm sure Ty wouldn't mind having a guest."

Despite the situation, that made his mother laugh outright. "Sweetheart, I'm not about to butt into your nesting situation right now. Maybe when you're a little more… established." Ollie's ears burned at the implication. "If your father is uncomfortable, he can leave. I'm quite capable of ignoring him."

Well, she would be. She'd certainly perfected the cold shoulder. "All right."

"But I wouldn't say no to tea, maybe?" she added hopefully. "And perhaps you can introduce me to your Ty properly this time."

Ollie's heart stuttered. "You would want that?"

His mother made a noncommittal noise. "What I want is to be a part of my son's life. My grandson's life. If that means playing nice with your young man—Ollie, I've hardly seen you in more than ten years. I'm sorry that I've gotten things wrong. I'm probably still going to get things wrong. But I want to try."

"Okay." Jeez, did this room not get any air-conditioning? He could barely breathe. "Okay, we can try." Then he added, "Uh, but we haven't told Theo about us yet, so maybe give me a couple days?"

She tutted teasingly. "Oh?" But the pause she left afterward felt reproving. "Why not?"

Well, here was the test—could she really learn to respect Ollie's authority about his kid, or was he about to get an earful on a topic he'd never expected? "I want to do it the right way—talk to his therapist, get some resources. He just lost his mom. Even though we weren't together, I don't want him to feel like I'm replacing her, or worry that I'm not going to be around as much, or... whatever kids who've lost a parent worry about when the remaining parent starts dating."

For a few seconds she was so quiet he thought they might have been disconnected. "Mom?"

She inhaled audibly. "I'm just—thinking. I know your father and I made mistakes with you and your sisters. But you turned out well. I'm proud of you."

He leaned heavily on his elbows. "Thanks, Mom."

Several minutes passed before he got up to return to the kitchen.

In the meantime, Ty and Theo had tidied away the dishes, and Theo had planted himself on the living room floor with a book in front of him. Just looking at him in that position made Ollie's spine and shoulders hurt, but Theo seemed unbothered.

Ty wasn't in the living room or the kitchen or his bedroom. Finally Ollie found him sitting on the steps of the back deck with a mug of coffee, staring into the middle distance.

Ollie sat one step below him so he could lean on Ty's knees. He didn't even think about the intimacy of the gesture until he was relaxing into it, trusting Ty to support him. It hadn't even occurred to him that Ty might not want to be Ollie's back rest.

Ty scritched his fingers over Ollie's scalp in a way that made Ollie's bones turn to Jell-O. "Was your phone call as fun as mine?"

"It was good, actually," Ollie said, leaning into his hand like a cat and trying not to lose all motor control. The halfhearted scalp massage felt like something he should be paying for. "Mom wants to make up." He didn't feel confident enough in the possible outcome to share details yet, but it was nice to have good news for once.

Of course, the downside of the good news was that, hey, at thirty-two he might actually be responsible for his parents divorcing.

Fuck it. He wasn't going to ruin the magic of Ty's fingers by thinking about that. "Who were you talking to?"

"Eliza." Ty took a sip of his coffee and then set the mug down so he could put *both* hands in Ollie's hair. Ollie had discovered religion. "I'm supposed to go over there later today so we can sort out this thing with Alan Chiu."

No wonder he was brooding. "Sucks," Ollie offered. "You want any help? Moral support?" He might not be ready to tell Theo yet, and he might not be ready to trust his mom with his kid unsupervised, but Cassie would probably take Theo for the afternoon if he asked. Or maybe he'd want to spend some time with one of his school friends.

"Not yet." He combed his fingers from front to back, sending delightful tingles down Ollie's neck and spine. He probably looked like he'd stuck a fork in an electrical socket, but as long as Ty never stopped doing that to his head, he didn't care. "I'm pretty... yeah."

Upset, Ollie guessed. Maybe he was the one who should be doing the comforting? He turned his head and looked up. "Bad?"

"She thinks I should move my return to Chicago back a couple days just in case." Ty's usual cheerfulness had abandoned him. "If he tries to call my training into question or say I acted in a way that harmed a patient... I don't know. It *shouldn't* affect my work, but anytime people with money are involved...."

Ollie hated this for him. He absently pressed a kiss to the inside of Ty's knee. "I wish I knew what this guy's problem was."

Ty snorted. "You and me both. I'm starting to think he might just be an asshole with a hard-on for power."

"He wouldn't be the first." Ollie had thought he'd signed up to fight people like that, but he'd served with a few of them too. They were everywhere, which made him angry. At least it made some kind of sense when evil people set themselves up as despots in areas with scarce resources. You could almost think, *Well, that kind of selfishness makes sense when there's not enough to go around*, even if it was morally deplorable. But it wasn't like Connecticut was experiencing any kind of scarcity, unless it was a scarcity of decent people with backbone. "You want me to punch him for you?"

Ty barked out a laugh. "No. I can punch my own villains, thank you. Which I won't be doing because that might *actually* affect my ability to do my job. Gotta keep that police record clean."

"Ugh." Ollie made a face. "I'll be your alibi. 'I didn't see anything, officer.'"

"You can't get arrested either. You have a kid to look after."

"You think I'll get caught?"

He shook his head. "I think I'm a lousy liar and I don't want to take you down with me."

Reluctantly, Ollie conceded the point. "I guess that's fair." He'd have to think of a legal, untraceable revenge plan and keep it to himself so Ty couldn't accidentally confess for him. "Is it bad to say I was looking forward to sneaking around with you all day?"

"Awful," Ty told him seriously. "Especially since I have to go figure out stupid legal things."

"I'll make it up to you later." Even if they had to sneak back to their own beds afterward.

"You better, after the show you put on this morning."

"What, cutting the grass?" Ollie asked innocently.

"Looking like you're about to star in a Corbin Fisher video," Ty muttered.

Ollie grinned. "*Co*-star."

Ty laughed. "Oh, I'm sorry. You're so generous to share the spotlight." He heaved himself to his feet and reached down to pull Ollie up too. "I better get going to Eliza's or I'm going to be at it until school starts tomorrow."

Considering the mixed start to the day, Ollie went into the afternoon feeling cheerfully optimistic about life in general. He sent off an email to Theo's therapist and grilled some hot dogs and veggies for lunch. They ate under the giant patio umbrella on the back porch, and then Theo asked for some batting practice in the yard.

He thought his mother might drop by, whatever she'd said, but she didn't. At around three Cass sent a message saying their mom had come over and was going to stay there and let their dad reap what he'd sown for a night. *Good for her*, Ollie thought, and he said as much to Cass.

He and Theo had settled in the games room, Theo begrudgingly doing homework despite the fact that school would be out in three days, Ollie flipping from book to book in Ty's mother's collection before literally choosing a book for its bright nineties-comic-style cover art.

Sadly, it didn't occur to him until he flopped onto the couch that this room might not be great for his ability to concentrate on things that weren't thoughts of Ty. But he wasn't going to leave. He had some kind of idea that this time together, working on independent projects, *counted* for something, parenting-wise. He didn't want to banish Theo to do homework by himself in case that made him associate school with punishment.

The book quickly sucked him in anyway, painting a vivid picture of a fantasy world comically like earth. Something about it felt familiar, like a worn childhood blanket wrapped around his shoulders, comfortable and broken in. It seemed like only moments had passed when Theo said, "Dad?" and Ollie looked up to realize he'd read fifty pages.

Blinking, he marked the page with one of the coasters from the coffee table and sat up. "What's up, buddy?"

"Are you gonna get married again like Percy Jackson's mom?"

Ollie took a moment to sort through his reaction to that, because he didn't quite know where to start. Well, no, he did—shoving down the panic that somehow Theo had found out about him and Ty before Ollie told him anything. No point jumping to conclusions. He took a deep breath and began with the obvious. "I've never been married before."

Theo put down his pencil and turned in his chair so he was facing Ollie. "Why?"

Talk about a loaded question. Ollie considered a handful of responses—*I never found the right person*, or *I was focused on my job*—and discarded each of them for being less honest than he wanted to be. "Most adults want to date someone for a while before they get married to make sure they get along well enough." Okay, that was an oversimplification. "And I haven't really had time to date someone like that."

"'Cause you were a soldier?"

"Exactly."

Theo digested this for a second before continuing, more hesitantly, "Did you and Mom not get along well enough?"

Oh. That was where this was going. Maybe Ollie should have expected this. He and Allison had always promised to be totally open about how Theo came into the world, allowing for child-appropriate omissions, but this was the first time Theo was asking Ollie about any of it. Maybe he thought Allison had lied?

Ollie sent up a silent prayer of thanks into the universe that Allison had been as straightforward as people came. "Your mom and I were best friends, Theo, but she never wanted to get married to anyone."

Theo frowned in thought. "Like Annabeth's mom in *Percy Jackson*?"

Thank God for his kid being an avid reader. "Just like that."

Unfortunately, the questions did not end there. "Did you want to marry her?"

What was in this kid's homework that turned him into the Spanish Inquisition? "I loved your mom a lot, Theo, but it wasn't a romantic kind of love. I was happy being her friend. But when she asked me if I wanted to be your dad...." Ollie pursed his lips and considered his next words. "I always wanted to have a family, and I couldn't do that by myself when I was in the Army. But your mom gave me the chance to be a dad, and that was the best thing anyone ever did for me. I will always love her, and I will always miss her, okay?"

"Okay." But if he'd expected this to assuage Theo's curiosity, he was sadly disappointed. "But you still want to get married someday?"

Ollie wondered if guilt could give you hives. Did Theo know something about him and Ty? Why couldn't Theo have asked him this tomorrow, when Ollie had professional advice on how to handle it? "Yeah," Ollie hedged. "If I find someone I get along with well enough—and someone *you* get along with well enough. You're my number-one guy, remember?"

Theo rolled his eyes. "I know, Dad." He slid off the chair and rearranged himself on the carpet near Ollie's feet.

"And—if I ever do get married, whoever it is, I'm not going to let anyone try to replace your mom."

Nodding, Theo plucked at the decaying carpet. Ollie couldn't quite get a read on him with his face bowed like that, but he didn't think Theo was on the verge of tears. He seemed thoughtful but calm. It struck Ollie how much growing up his kid had done in the past seven months, between beating cancer and losing his mother and starting a new school, even getting caught up in math class. He was resilient and brave. Ollie couldn't take credit for much of it, but that didn't stop him from swelling with pride.

When Theo looked up, Ollie found he was right—no tears, no red-rimmed eyes, just a serious expression and a slightly furrowed brow. "Will you tell me about her?"

"Of course!" The syllables fell over each other trying to escape his mouth, pushed out by relief. Theo's therapist had told him he'd ask when he was ready, but Ollie was starting to wonder. Now all he had to do was hold it together while talking about his dead best friend. He patted the couch beside him and waited for Theo to climb up. He didn't sit in Ollie's lap—he was too old for that, apparently, which sucked a little because physical comfort came a lot easier to Ollie than talking—

but he pulled his legs up onto the cushions and turned his body toward Ollie's so his shin touched Ollie's thigh. "What do you want to know?"

"When did you start being friends?"

"Oh no, you're going to make me do math?" Ollie joked. Theo giggled. "I was—I guess I would've been twenty-two, so more than ten years ago. Your mom was a little older, almost thirty, I think. I didn't know that right away, though." Allison would've smacked him good-naturedly for revealing her age, just for show.

Theo pulled a pillow into his lap. "How come?"

"Well—did your mom ever tell you *how* we met?" Off Theo's headshake, Ollie smiled. "It was a book club. When you're deployed, you're either really busy"—trying not to die—"or you're bored. But our base had a good internet connection, so I went online and found a book club. We would all read a book a week, and there was a discussion board—like Twitter, I guess, but all private, and just for talking about books—and we'd all talk about what we liked and what we didn't."

"So you didn't know that Mom was in the Army too?"

"Not at first. And she was already out by the time we started talking to each other. We were never deployed together, but it was nice that she understood what the life was like. Once we realized we had that in common, we started emailing too. Your mom was really smart—good taste in books too."

"She read a lot when I was in the hospital," Theo said. "But I don't remember the books she read just for her. What did she like?"

Ollie thought back. "Oh, almost everything—thrillers, mysteries, science fiction. But her favorite was fantasy." His eyes were naturally drawn to the book on the table. He picked it up and considered the author's name and the cover. "Actually, I think we might've read a book from this series together. I probably still have the notes she sent me."

Theo sat forward, eyes wide as saucers. "Do you still have the books?"

He shook his head. "I had the e-book versions—much easier to get when you're deployed—and I think I lost my e-reader in the middle of my second tour. But I have the titles somewhere. We can look them up at the library. Not all of them are good for kids," he warned, "but some of them are. We'll read those ones first, and we can do the others when you get older."

"And we can read Mom's notes?" Theo asked hopefully.

As if Ollie could deny him anything. "We can absolutely read Mom's notes," he agreed. "As long as you promise to try not to repeat any of the bad words at school or baseball camp." Allison had elevated profanity to an art form.

"Can we start right now?"

Nice try. Ollie was 100 percent sure Theo had not finished his math homework. "We can start soon. After school's out, okay? I need to read the books again to make sure they're okay first."

Theo heaved out a huge sigh. "Fiiiine." But he grinned, so Ollie knew he was being dramatic for effect.

Ollie ruffled his hair. "I love you, kid."

Theo batted his hand away but then did a faceplant in his chest and wrapped his arms around him. "I love you too, Dad."

Some days Ollie really felt like he had a handle on this whole parenting gig. But for the most part, he was pretty sure his success could be attributed to all the groundwork Allison had laid.

"I'm gonna finish my homework," Theo when they released each other. "Is Ty gonna make dinner tonight?"

Was that a jab at Ollie's perfect grilled cheese, or did he just want to know when Ty would be home? Ollie picked up his phone and sent a quick text. *You home for dinner?*

ETA 40 min, I'm bringing bbq. Make a salad?

That somewhat answered Ollie's unwritten question about how things had gone with Eliza. He sent back a thumbs-up emoji and set a timer so that he didn't get too sucked into his book.

He'd washed all the veg and was in the process of shredding carrots because Ty thought slices were too crunchy when Theo shuffled in.

"All done with your homework?"

"Yeah. It was easy." He pulled a chair up to the counter.

"Easy? Weren't you doing your math?"

"Yeah, but I'm good at word problems." He climbed up so he could stand at Ollie's elbow.

Ollie handed him a carrot to peel. "Careful to move *away* from your fingers, all right? No bleeding all over the place before Ty gets home."

Giggling, Theo took the peeler. "But I can bleed all over the place *after* Ty gets home?"

"I'd prefer if you didn't." Ollie made a face to make him laugh harder. "But if you're going to do it, do it when Ty's around to patch you up."

"Ohhh-kayyyyy," Theo sighed and then ruined it with another giggle.

Ollie reached for the cucumber, grinning.

"Dad? Do you know why Ty's in trouble for trying to help the lady at the grocery store?"

The grin crumbled into ash. Ollie dismembered the cucumber. He did, in fact, know why. What he didn't know was how to explain it to his son without destroying his faith in humanity. "Kind of," he hedged.

Ollie steadied the chair while Theo reached over to wash his hands. "Did he do something wrong?"

"No, buddy. But you know how Twyla wasn't invited to Mel's birthday party because sometimes she's not very nice?" A year ago, news of Mel being excluded from Twyla's birthday party, to which every other classmate had been invited, had reached Ollie across thousands of miles of scandalized, outraged mother.

Theo painstakingly peeled exactly one strip of skin off the carrot, then went over it a second time before judging the job sufficient to move on to the next section. "Yeah."

"Well—some grown-ups never grow out of that."

It took Theo until he'd finished peeling the carrot, his tongue sticking out between his teeth in concentration, to respond. "So Ty has a bully?"

Okay, so Theo understood perfectly what Ollie was still grappling with. That meant he was doing a good job as a father, right? That was what he was choosing to believe today. "Kind of. Sometimes people don't like us and make our lives miserable for no reason."

Theo handed Ollie the carrot to shred and picked up a second one. "Is that why Ty is going away?"

It would look like that to a kid, wouldn't it? "No," Ollie said. "He just has to go back to his job in Chicago." When the carrot had been shredded until he could shred no more, he broke the remainder in half and popped one in his mouth, setting the other aside for Theo.

"So if we stood up to his bully and got him to stop, Ty wouldn't stay?"

Something in Ollie's chest pinched. "I wish it were that easy, kid."

Frowning, Theo ruthlessly gouged away the carrot skin. "But Ty is rich. Everyone says so. He doesn't have to go to work. Why can't he stay here?"

The something unpinched and became a bruise. Ollie hadn't let himself ask that question. After all, why would Ty want to stay when people treated him like this?

But not everyone did. Theo adored him. Henry and Eliza liked him. The kids on his baseball team looked up to him. And Ollie—

Ollie wasn't going to be the guy who asked him to stay when he didn't want to.

"His team in Chicago needs him," he said finally. "And so do the people who live there. You know Ty—he likes to help people."

Theo scowled. "I don't know why he wants to help people when it gets him in trouble."

Ollie finished off the last of the salad preparation and swept the veggie bits into a paper bag. Ty was militant about compost.

Then he let himself feel the impact of the words and turned to help Theo off the chair. "Hey, come here."

He was pretty sure Theo didn't understand why Ollie was hugging him like his life depended on it.

"Dad? Are you okay?"

No.

Despite his resolve to be truthful, Ollie let himself tell a tiny white lie this once. "I'm okay. I just need a minute to think about words, all right?"

Theo looked up with his arms still wrapped around Ollie. He had one eyebrow cocked—a trick Ollie had never mastered and one that made him look uncannily like a younger version of his mother—and an extremely dry expression for an eight-year-old. "You're weird, Dad."

Snorting, Ollie released him. "Okay, here's the thing." He pressed his lips together. "Everyone has power—all different kinds of power—and we can use that power to make a difference."

Theo climbed up onto a barstool. "Even me?"

"Especially you." Ollie ruffled his hair. "You're young and you're smart, so you have lots of time to decide what kind of difference you're going to make. Ty uses his power to try to help people who are hurt, but it doesn't always work. Sometimes people blame him for that and he gets in trouble. But he tries anyway."

"Why?"

Because he is kind and brave and ungodly stubborn. "Well, you'd have to ask him to know for sure." Ollie smiled, though that felt bruised too. "But I think it's because he'd be really sad if he stopped believing he could make the world a better place. And that's what I want you to remember, okay? Just because things are hard sometimes, or they don't turn out the way you want, that doesn't mean you should stop trying."

Please never stop trying, kid.

An eternity passed before Theo nodded, apparently accepting this explanation. Ollie was halfway through letting himself relax when Theo asked, "Is that why you joined the Army?"

The words hit like a sledgehammer to the solar plexus.

Ollie wanted to say no. God, worse than that, he wanted the *answer* to be no. He wanted to cling to what he'd told himself for more than a decade, that he'd joined the Army because he didn't know what else to do with his life but he knew he wanted to make his own decisions.

That was only a tiny sliver of the truth. Ollie hadn't signed up to get shot at just to avoid his parents controlling his life. He hadn't been that naïve.

He'd been a different kind of naïve. Sure, you could change the world by shooting people. Maybe someone could even change the world for the better that way. Lord knew there were people who needed shooting.

But Ollie didn't want to be the one pulling the trigger.

"Yeah," he admitted.

And then, thank God, there was the sound of the side door busting open and a sudden gust of smoky-barbecue-scented air. "I'm home," Ty announced.

With wide eyes, Theo looked at Ollie and said, "Oh my God. I am *so hungry.*"

"See," Ollie said, "he's making the world a better place already."

Ty entered the kitchen in time for this remark, arms laden with so much food Ollie had to wonder how he managed it all. He stepped forward and grabbed a tray before anything could fall.

"You were talking about me?" Ty asked, fluttering his eyelashes as Ollie set the food down and removed the foil to reveal mac and cheese for seventy-five. But there was a real question underneath. Ollie shook his head. They hadn't had *that* talk yet.

"About how that man who doesn't like you is a bully," Theo said, sliding off the barstool. "Did you get cornbread?"

Gasping, Ty clutched his chest. "Oh my God. I forgot." But he only lasted a fraction of a second looking at Theo's heartbroken face before he caved. "Just kidding, I obviously got cornbread. What do you take me for?"

Ollie still felt a little like a walking bruise, but sitting with Ty and Theo and eating his body weight in smoked meat and cheesy pasta soothed the ache. Afterward Theo conned them into a game of catch.

Ollie didn't get to grill Ty on his long day with Eliza until everyone was showered and Theo was in bed, having insisted he wanted to read for ten minutes. He was passed out with the light on when Ollie went to check on him two minutes later.

Ollie flicked the light off, pulled the door mostly shut behind him, and joined Ty in the living room.

"So." He flopped down next to Ty on the couch. He looked… unfairly good. His shirt was clinging to him with the moisture from his shower, and his skin was pink and fresh. Ollie wanted to bite the scar on his jawline, or maybe just rub his stubble against Ty's. "How was your day, honey?"

Ty shook his head. "Better than yours, by the look of things. Everything okay?"

"Couple deep conversations with the kid." Nothing Ollie wanted to think about right now. "I feel old. Distract me. Are you going to sue Alan Chiu's pants off?"

"Nah. There's nothing in there I'm interested in." He gave Ollie a quick once-over, not exactly blatant but not subtle either, like he was testing the waters. "*Your* pants, on the other hand…."

For some reason the back of Ollie's neck went hot. "What about them?"

Ty put a hand on the bend of his knee. That was hot too. "Well, I don't know. I'm hoping they don't need legal action, but you did say it's been a long day…."

Grinning, Ollie kicked his feet up on the ottoman. The motion dislodged Ty's palm, moving it higher up the inside of Ollie's thigh. "I gotta be honest"—he let himself look over at Ty; two could play the once-over game, but he let himself linger a little longer—"if you're trying to get into my pants, I don't think they're gonna fit you."

Ty grinned back. "What if I let you into mine, then?"

Ollie laughed out loud. What a fucking day he'd had—what a week—and here he was with his boyfriend on their couch, laughing at stupid pickup lines and suddenly desperately horny.

"Hey." Ty pouted theatrically. "Was that a yes?"

Instead of answering, Ollie rolled over on the couch until he had Ty pinned between his thighs. He caged him in with his arms on the back of the sofa and leaned down to brush the side of his nose over Ty's, their mouths a whisper apart.

Ty's eyes went dark and his breath went heavy.

Ollie said, "Maybe."

Ty surged up and wrangled him into a kiss that was half passion, half laughter, and 100 percent mutual enthusiasm. The difficult parts of the day fell away under the onslaught of something almost giddy, until only the press of their bodies and the mounting urge to act on the fire simmering in his blood remained.

He was in the process of discovering whether Ty liked his lip gently bitten—conclusive yes, if the desperate moan and the arch of his hips were any indication—when Ty gasped, "Bed?"

And—okay, right, yes. The last time Ollie did this, he wasn't the primary caregiver of a third grader. Bed, or more specifically a room with a door that closed, sounded like a great idea.

Sneaking down to Ty's bedroom reminded Ollie of being a teenager caught up in a whirlwind of hormones and first kisses. They kept laughing softly and cursing under their breath as they ran into doorways, tripped on the trail of clothes they were leaving in their wake.

Admittedly, Ollie hadn't had a lot of sex in his life, but none of it had been like this, so easily joyful. He followed Ty onto his mattress, *oof*ing when Ty somehow elbowed him in the ribs. He caught Ty's apologetic snicker in his mouth and pinned his wrists above his head, just to keep him out of trouble.

It didn't work, of course. Ollie promptly forgot about holding them there because he was too busy touching Ty everywhere—the thick waves of his hair, the sensitive sides of his neck, the dip of his collarbone. When he applied his mouth to the inside curve of Ty's pectoral muscle, Ty gasped and scored his nails lightly over Ollie's bare shoulders, and Ollie shuddered so hard it startled him into stillness.

He looked up and caught Ty's eyes, gone wide and black and curious in the darkness, and said, "Let's come back to that later," and tasted Ty's breathless laughter under his tongue as he left a biting trail downward.

He was teasing his thumbs over the V of Ty's pelvis, watching the muscles jump as Ty squirmed at the attention, watching Ty's hard cock leak against his stomach and debating whether he had the confidence to put his mouth on that next, when Ty kneed him in the shoulder.

He was grinning, red-faced and sheepish, as he offered Ollie a bottle of lube. "Not that I don't appreciate the enthusiasm, but no telling how much time's on the clock."

Ollie bit him on the thigh, half convinced Ty was trying to let him off the hook for his inexperience. "I'm not doing a speedrun." But, well, he *was* trying to be more honest. "This might be kinda sloppy."

If Ty had a smartass remark about that—and Ollie would've bet money he did—he never managed to make it. All that escaped him as Ollie licked a stripe up the underside of his cock was a strangled animal sound.

It didn't sound like a criticism. Ollie did it again, bracing his body over Ty's to keep him from wriggling, and then pinned his dick against his stomach so he could mouth his balls while he scrabbled one-handed for the lube.

This time the noise Ty made was louder, higher pitched. "No fair—*fuck.*"

Fair? Ollie flicked open the cap and pulled his mouth away from Ty's groin. The temperature change made the skin of his balls contract, or maybe he was just that sensitive. "Are there rules I don't know about?"

"Yeah, you're not—Jesus." Ollie lifted Ty's thigh over his shoulder to give himself better access. "Not supposed to look that good and make me feel this good at the same time—"

Ollie pressed a biting kiss to the top of his thigh and squeezed a handful of slick over his fingers. "I think you might've been doing sex wrong."

"Excuse you—"

Ollie pushed a finger inside, shivering in anticipation at the way Ty's body clung to him, velvety and hot.

"—just because I've never fucked someone as hot as you—"

"Flatterer." Jesus, Ty must not be counting himself. The way he looked spread out like this, his skin a canvas of art he'd chosen and adventures he'd lived, evidence of the lives he'd changed, saved, lost. He should be in some kind of pornographic museum, except no, because Ollie didn't want anyone else to see him like this. "Or are you fishing for compliments?"

Ty clenched down as Ollie curled his finger. "Not compliments I'm trying to catch here."

Cute. "No?" He added a second digit. "What're you using for bait?"

"Oh my God," Ty laughed, and suddenly Ollie was the one biting back a groan, because he way he tightened around Ollie's finger—Ollie wanted that on his cock, and why wasn't he moving faster, again? His dick wanted to know. "I *thought* I was using premium-grade Shut Up and Fuck Me, but I think I might've grabbed a pair of white New Balance sneakers and a grill by mistake, 'cause all I'm catching is dad jokes—"

Ollie pushed in a third finger, mouth suddenly dry. His comebacks had deserted him. All his blood had pooled in his dick and higher brain function had gone offline. He stared at his fingers disappearing into Ty's hole, transfixed at the sight, the sound of it, the smell of lube and sex. He licked his lips as Ty's cock jerked and blurted precome onto his stomach, raised his left hand and smeared his fingers through it, then wrapped his fingers around the shaft and stroked.

Planting his feet on the bed, Ty arched his whole body off the mattress, keening in his throat like he'd been struck by lightning. Like Ollie made him feel so good he'd lost control of his body. "Ollie," he pleaded. "Come *on*." His voice broke.

So did Ollie's restraint. He withdrew his fingers, wiped them carelessly on his thigh, and reached for the condom, suddenly aching. When he drizzled more lube on his wrapped dick, his hands shook enough that he spilled on the sheets.

"You're fucking *unreal*," Ollie rasped, without realizing he was going to speak, and Ty went scarlet from hairline to shoulders.

Oh God, if he was going to react like that, he was getting compliments whether he fished for them or not. Ollie knelt up on the bed and pulled Ty's thighs over his. Goose bumps broke out on his chest as his erection brushed against the curve of Ty's ass.

"Ollie," Ty protested, or begged, or—Ollie didn't know, but whatever he was asking for, he was going to get it.

"The way you look." He took himself in hand and lined up, intoxicated by the heat of Ty's body. He paused with the head of his cock just touching Ty's hole, felt it twitch against him. "The way you want me, it makes me feel insane."

With a shudder, Ty tried to push his ass down, like he couldn't wait. Ollie barely held him still. "Fuck, c'mon."

"Yeah," Ollie agreed nonsensically, and thrust inside.

Ty made some kind of sound—a gasp or a moan or a curse. Ollie didn't hear it. His world had narrowed and darkened and focused, and sound had fallen away. There was only the perfect heat of Ty's body, the rictus of pleasure etched into his face, the unexpected squeeze of his fingers between Ollie's.

Ollie didn't remember moving his hand, didn't remember Ty moving his.

Sound returned to the world in a crash of thundering heartbeats as blood pounded in his ears. Sweat dripped between his shoulder blades. Without his conscious input, Ollie's hips jerked.

Ty's fingers squeezed tighter. His other hand clawed its way to Ollie's waist, then up to his shoulder. Nails scored across the back of his neck, and Ollie bowed into it, his mouth falling open.

"Ty."

His stomach clenched. The pressure around him had every nerve in his body primed for pleasure.

He wanted to see Ty's first.

"You're beautiful." Ollie had no more control over his mouth than he did of his hips. Both were working without him now, intent on wringing every perfect note they could out of Ty's perfect mouth.

Beautiful was a stupid compliment. Ollie knew that. But he didn't have any other way to describe how it felt to watch someone else beam with pride when his kid hit a baseball. What else would he call someone who invited a perfect stranger and his son to live in their house and made them feel like they were doing *him* a favor? Was there another word for a person who made every day brighter, warmer, more worthwhile?

It didn't matter if the compliment fell short. Ty flushed darker anyway, almost writhing into the mattress. His eyes were hooded, pupils wide. Spit glistened on his perfect mouth.

"You're so fucking hot. I want to make you feel so good." Words kept falling out of him. His hands had gone to autopilot too. He released his grip on Ty's fingers and pressed his thumb to Ty's lower lip. He wanted to kiss him.

But he couldn't bend like that and fuck like this, and he wanted to give Ty what he needed. "Ty, tell me how to touch you, baby."

He didn't expect Ty to exhale hard against his thumb and hook his long legs around Ollie's back. *Ollie* might not be able to bend for that kiss, but Ty could bend fine. He curled his body under Ollie and pulled in with his thighs, and holy *gods* he was perfect. "Like this," Ty said, half begging, as if he needed to, as if Ollie hadn't just been waiting to give him everything he wanted. "Just—*yeah*."

Ollie could read the play from here. He let his lips touch Ty's in a series of fleeting, sipping kisses, all he could manage while thrusting into him, short, sharp jabs of his hips that punched ridiculous, obscene sounds from Ty's lungs. They sounded as good as Ty felt around him, hot and slick. The air tasted like sex. Even the slight rasp of Ty's stubble under Ollie's lips when their kisses broke sloppy lit up Ollie's brain like a drug.

He couldn't last like this. His orgasm was clawing its way up from his balls, coiling like a spring, but Ollie fought it back. Not yet. Ty first.

"Like this?" Ollie breathed, nearly into Ty's mouth.

Ty keened in response and ran his nails over Ollie's scalp again. Ollie was a little worried he was going to develop a Pavlovian response that made it impossible to get a haircut in public. "Like—"

He dug his heels into Ollie's ass, pulling him in tighter, directing his thrusts.

And then something *clicked*. Autopilot disengaged. Ollie had learned the terrain. He knew the controls.

Ty had shown him what he wanted, and now Ollie could give it to him—deliberately, consciously, continuously. The way he deserved. "There?" he asked, but he knew. He knew by the tension building in Ty's voice and body, by the sharp stinging pain from Ty's nails on his back.

And thank God, because Ollie couldn't last much longer.

"God, you're so good for me." Okay, he still wasn't in control of his mouth, but Ty didn't seem to mind. Ollie got a hand under Ty's thigh and pulled his leg higher, deepened the angle just so. Ty's face went slack and his eyes closed as his body tightened. He had to be close. God, please let him be close. "Wanna make you come, baby, how—tell me how to make you—"

He never got to finish the sentence. Anything else he might've said was lost in a shocked, almost hurt noise from Ty, and then his body clamped down tight and something hot spurted between them because Ty was coming *now*—Ollie was fucking it out of him, thick white ropes of it. Ollie made a sound of his own and slid his hand between them, wanting to make it last and last, until finally Ty twitched *away* from his touch instead of into it.

Ollie did that. *Ollie did that*, and now he was hurtling toward his own orgasm, half out of his mind with pleasure.

"Ollie." Ty's voice was gravelly, low. Wrecked. He ran his fingernails up the back of Ollie's neck again, into his hair, tugged him down. Kissed him.

Ollie's orgasm shook out of him. He poured the sound into Ty's mouth, trembling everywhere, in his shoulders and his knees and his lungs. The world went gray and fuzzy.

Touch returned first—the sensitive squeeze of Ty's hole around his softening dick, the warmth of his breath against Ollie's cheek, and the slow, purposeful tease of fingernails over his scalp. The rest came back all at once, so that Ollie was blinking at Ty's hazy blue eyes and pink cheeks and smelling their sweat and hearing Ty's soft, almost disbelieving laugh.

"The earth moved for you too, huh?"

Ollie didn't have words yet. Gingerly, he reached down to grip the base of the condom and pulled out. He rolled over. Then he flailed for a Kleenex from Ty's nightstand, flung the condom on it, and lay there for a moment, breathing at the ceiling.

His other hand was holding Ty's again.

Finally he said, "I didn't know it had stopped."

Ty turned to look at him—Ollie heard the rustle of his hair against the sheets. After a few seconds, he decided he was brave enough to meet his gaze.

"Until I met you," Ollie clarified. He couldn't have said *when* his world stopped, though it had probably been before Theo's mother died. Maybe when he entered the service.

Ty flushed a deep, charming almost-purple. Ollie leaned closer until their noses touched each other's cheeks. It was more intimate than a kiss, somehow.

When Ty blinked, Ollie felt the flutter of his eyelashes. "You're just a big romantic sap, aren't you?"

"Shhh," Ollie said. "It's cuddling time."

They should get up and shower, and Ollie should go back to his own room. In case Theo had a nightmare, or *he* did.

But not yet. Right now he wanted a few more minutes to bask in the scent of Ty's sheets and listen to their heartbeats and feel it, really feel it, as the world around them spun on.

Chapter 17

IF TY thought the kids were excited about the upcoming end of the school year last week, it was nothing compared to today. Frankly he couldn't blame them. He was chomping at the bit to get out of this place too. The air-conditioning couldn't keep up with the burgeoning summer heat, and green grass and blue skies were calling for everyone to head outdoors, where at least you could get a breeze.

But a classful of chattering, hyperactive kids couldn't bring him down—not even when he took Jason's lunch duty. To be honest, lunch duty improved his mood, since it meant he was outside in the beautiful weather instead of in the soulless, windowless teachers' lounge.

And then Henry found him and made everything even better.

"So, last game of the season this weekend. Are you ready?"

Ty polished off the last of the water in his insulated bottle and stuck it in his side shorts pocket. Were cargo shorts particularly fashionable? No. Did he care about that? Once upon a time he would have, but right now he was just happy to have a place to store various elements of his lunch. "Are we ever ready?" The team had gone unvictorious—Ty had actually had to come up with an antonym for *undefeated*. And the last game of the season was against the top team in the area.

"We might be this time." Henry raised his travel mug to his lips. He was being intentionally cryptic and Ty was not going to fall for it.

Ty fell for it. "Oh?"

The tiniest hint of a smirk appeared at the corner of Henry's mouth. "Rumor has it the reigning champs have the mumps."

Ty was a medical professional. He had Seen Things. He could barely walk down the produce aisle at the grocery store without having flashbacks to the things people put inside their bodies. The hardware store? Forget about it. One look at a Maglite and he was back in an ambulance speeding down Highway 41, biting his lip so he wouldn't make a joke about the sun shining out a seventeen-year-old's ass.

It still took him a moment to digest Henry's words. "Excuse me?" He blinked. "There's a vaccine for that."

He knew better. He did. After working as a health teacher at a public school, he *really did*.

"Tell it to those kids' parents," Henry said wryly.

"I am pretty sure that would get me fired."

"You're leaving anyway. Might as well get the last word."

A tempting prospect, for sure. But Ty already felt like he was being run out of town, even if his return to Chicago had nothing to do with Alan Chiu and whatever flashlight-size bug had crawled up his ass. Besides, he was in too good a mood to spoil it with a fight. Summer was here. Soon he'd get to go back to his real job. And he had Ollie. The timing sucked and the details were fuzzy, but Ty had never clicked with anyone like this, and he wasn't going to let a little distance ruin it.

Especially not after last night. He shivered pleasantly thinking about it.

"I'll take that under advisement."

They ambled around the schoolyard together, supervising vaguely. Ty had never had yard duty and, if he was honest, was not particularly motivated to make sure he did it properly. Walking in aimless silence suited him fine. Occasionally a child ran up and requested permission to go inside and use the bathroom, which baffled him. What was he going to do? Say no, you have to pee behind a bush?

But while Ty was lost in his own world of sunshine and Ollie Kent's kisses, Henry was obviously somewhere else, because after a few minutes of what Ty thought had been companionable silence, Henry said, "Seriously, kid, you're killing me."

Startled, Ty glanced over. "What?"

"Are you kidding me? After the way you ran out of the staff party on Saturday?" Any minute now Henry would start pulling out his hair. "You're just going to keep me in suspense? Eliza will kill me if I don't come home with details."

What? "You're going to blame this on your wife? I was at your house *all day yesterday*. She could've asked me herself."

"No, she couldn't. Ollie's her nephew. Kind of. Can't mix business and personal."

That was the biggest load of horseshit Ty ever heard; everyone in this town was all over everyone else's personal business. Henry was making excuses for his own curiosity. Ty gave him the eyebrow.

"Ty," Henry said plaintively.

Ty shoved his hands into his pockets and grinned at the sky.

Finally Henry laughed at him and shook his head. "Good for you. Does that mean you're sticking around?"

Why did everyone think that? "I still have to go back to Chicago." Where he lived? Where his job was? Where people didn't mistrust him on sight because he locked a bunch of chickens in an educational building one time when he was sixteen?

Henry raised his hands in surrender. "Hey, it was only a question. I don't blame you for going back." He paused. "I just thought, you know…. Ollie Kent seems like a pretty decent reason to stick around."

Ty couldn't have stopped the smitten expression from spreading across his face if his life depended on it. "Yeah." Except now he kind of sounded like a dick, because—well, he wasn't sticking around, exactly. He would commute back and forth for his four-off, but what if…?

"Ty." Henry clapped a hand on his shoulder. "It'll be okay."

It totally would. No point borrowing trouble. Tonight Ollie could tell Theo what was going on, and they could… plan a life. Together. Apart sometimes, sure, but people made it work.

By the time Ty picked Theo up at the end of the day, he had almost convinced himself he wasn't nervous.

"Hey, Ty!" Theo schooled his face and voice into something solemn. "I mean, Mr. Morris."

"I will be so glad when you don't have to call me that ever again." Ty grabbed his backpack, because he could, and slung it over his shoulder. "Did you have a good day today?"

"Yeah. We got to play baseball in gym class."

"That *is* a good day," Ty agreed. Maybe sometime this summer he and Ollie could take Theo to a real game. If Ollie was up for bringing Theo to visit in Chicago, they could see the Cubs. Ty had a connection with someone who worked in emergency services at Wrigley. He could totally leverage that into good seats. He should look up when the Nats would be in town.

On the drive home, Theo gave him the play-by-play. If he never made it as a pro baseball player, he'd be a pretty good color commentator,

Ty thought. Assuming he didn't become a famous writer or an astronaut or something. Listening to the breakdown didn't require a lot of input from him, so he mostly just hummed in the right places and thought about dinner. They still had plenty of leftover barbecue, but what would be the best way to heat it up without drying it out? And he should probably go heavier on the vegetables this time. They'd polished off the mac and cheese the night before—

The train of thought screeched to a halt when the garage door opened and he saw Ollie's car in its spot.

"Cool, Dad's home early," Theo enthused. "Ty, do we have time for batting practice before dinner?"

All Ty's mental alarm bells were ringing at full volume.

So were the notifications on his phone.

"Uh, not sure, kiddo." He pulled his cell out of his pocket. Three texts, all from Ollie's sister.

Hey, do you know where Ollie is?

I heard some news through the grapevine at work and he's not answering my texts.

I'm sure he's fine, just... let me know if you see him?

Ty looked at Ollie's car in the garage, thought about the way he'd left work on Friday, and made an educated guess.

"Uh, maybe?" Ty said after a moment, realizing Theo was still waiting for an answer. "Hey, bud, can you do me a favor? Can you go around the back of the garage and water the tomato plants? It's been pretty hot, and I don't want to lose them before they even give us any fruit."

Blessedly, Theo didn't ask why, which gave Ty five minutes to go inside and make sure Theo wasn't about to walk in on... he didn't know what.

He pushed open the side door. "Ollie?"

"Here."

The voice came from the kitchen. Ty followed it and found Ollie sitting at the breakfast bar, staring at a beer bottle.

It was open but still full, condensation puddling on the counter. Ty didn't see any empties.

Ty cleared his throat. "Are you okay? Your sister's freaking out."

Without taking his eyes from the beer bottle, Ollie said, "Fine."

Ty glanced out the window. Theo was still unraveling the hose so he could reach the tomato plants. "Okay. Cool-with-being-normal-around-your-kid fine or maybe-I-should-get-him-out-of-the-house fine?"

Ollie flinched. His eyes flicked to the clock on the microwave. It read 3:58. Ty hoped he wasn't planning to sit there watching his beer until five, when it was warm and flat, before he drank it.

The muscles at the corner of Ollie's jaw bunched. "I'm not going to hurt anybody. I'm not *unsafe*."

Translation—not a PTSD episode, just unfit for company.

"I didn't ask if you were unsafe. I asked if you want Theo to see you like this or if you'd rather he not. You have about three minutes before he gets tired of watering the tomatoes."

Sooner or later Theo and Ollie would both have to learn how to deal with Ollie's bad days. But maybe that didn't have to be right now, today. Maybe today Ty could act as a buffer.

After another moment of muscle bunching so intense Ty wondered if Ollie had dental coverage, he finally relaxed a fraction. A long breath escaped him and he dry-washed his face with both hands. This time, when he took them away, he looked Ty in the eye. "My mom's with Mel today. You could take him to Cassie's. She'll be happy to have him."

Good, Ty thought. "Okay. I'll be back in twenty minutes."

He made a detour to Theo's bedroom for a pair of pajamas and a change of clothes, in case, as well as his baseball glove. Then he grabbed a fresh toothbrush from his own bathroom cabinet and stuffed everything in a duffel bag.

Theo met him as he got to the door. "Change of plans," Ty said cheerfully. "You're invited to spend some time with Mel. Think you can teach her how to throw a better pitch?"

Theo looked at Ty, then back at the garage. Ty had left the door open, and the taillights of Ollie's car were still visible. "Is Dad okay?" he asked.

"He's okay. Just a bad day," Ty assured him. "He doesn't want his mood to rub off on you. Why don't you go give him a hug, and I'll take you to see Mel and your grandma?"

God, he hoped that was the right move. On the other hand, he couldn't imagine a hug from Theo making Ollie feel *worse*.

A few minutes later they were pulling up to Cassie's house. Ty had texted Cassie while Theo and Ollie were saying goodbye, and Ollie's mother and Mel were waiting for them on the front step when they pulled up.

Theo and Mel ran off toward the backyard before Ty even made it out of the car with Theo's bag. He grabbed it from his trunk and met Mrs. Kent on the walkway.

"Um. Thanks for taking him," he said awkwardly. He hoped this didn't make her think Ollie couldn't take care of Theo on his own or that Ty didn't want to help when things got tough. "I know it's last-minute."

Mrs. Kent took the bag almost as stiffly as Ty held it out, but her face stayed soft. "It's no trouble. I'm delighted to have more time with my grandson."

"He's pretty great," Ty said. He hoped she could tell he meant it. "His dad's not bad either."

For a moment she just looked at him, and then she smiled. "They're lucky to have you, I think."

A shriek of laughter from the backyard split the afternoon, and they both turned instinctively toward the sound. Mrs. Kent shook her head. "I think that's my cue. Tell Ollie… well. Maybe give him a hug for me."

Ty swallowed thickly. "I can do that."

The drive home passed in a blur. He parked in the garage on autopilot. Keys in his pocket. Shoes by the door.

Ollie hadn't moved from the breakfast bar in the kitchen, though now the clock read 4:23 and his beer bottle was half-empty.

Fuck it, Ty thought. He needed some indication of how fucked-up today was. He opened the fridge.

Just a six-pack, one bottle missing. Good. Ty grabbed one for himself and opened it, but he didn't sit down. That would make looking at Ollie awkward, and he had a feeling he was going to need to pay attention.

Finally Ollie said, "I got fired."

"Yeah, I kinda guessed." Based on the fact that he got home before six thirty and the intense sexual tension between him and his beer bottle. "They tell you why?"

He snorted. "For leaving in the middle of my shift with no notice."

"The middle of your shift where your kid's school and all your family members called the office because they couldn't get ahold of you and they never once picked up?"

A muscle twitched in Ollie's jaw. "Same one."

"Can they do that?"

"I'm—I was—still on probation. Or I was. They can do whatever they want." Another swig of the bottle. It had one-third left now.

"What the fuck." Ty uncapped his bottle. "I could call Eliza, if you want. I mean—she's your aunt actually, so—"

"No."

Okay... maybe Ty was approaching this the wrong way. He took a sip from his own bottle. "Look... you hated that job anyway, right?"

Ollie grunted.

"So what's the problem?" Ty didn't get it. It wasn't like this had been Ollie's dream job. It kept him away from Theo all the time. The air-conditioning in the truck broke regularly. The pay sucked. The hours were terrible. It wasn't like Ollie needed the money.

"Aside from my parents being right about me?"

Whoa, whoa—what? Didn't Ollie just make up with his parents? Or at least his mom? Ty took a quick swig and put the bottle down. "Ollie—"

Ollie put both hands over his face and dry-washed it again. "What am I even doing if I can't raise my kid and hold down a job? With all the help I'm getting?"

Ty's mouth went dry. Ollie didn't really think like that, did he? "I think you're being kind of hard on yourself. Didn't you mention the other day this company was having trouble retaining their employees?"

"Yeah, because people *quit*." There were bags under his eyes that hadn't been there yesterday. "And they still fired me, so what does that say?"

"Well, for one thing, they've got their priorities backwards. Not to mention they lied to you when they hired you."

Ty was getting frustrated, and the words came out sharper than he intended. But they finally seemed to get through, because Ollie dropped some of the attitude and groaned.

"I know. I know. I'm sorry. I just—I thought I finally had everything sorted out, things were going my way, you know? Sure, I didn't love my job, but Theo was doing well. I had you. And now...."

"Hey, I get it."

Ollie shot him a look.

"Okay, I *don't* get it. Not exactly." Ty's dad not wanting him after his mom died wasn't the same as being rejected for prioritizing your kid. Ty kind of thought his situation was worse, but Ollie wasn't exactly in the mood to be reasoned with right now. "But it isn't the end of the world. There are other jobs. You can take some time to figure out what you want, you know? Go back to school if you want to. That was the whole point of going into the Army in the first place, right?"

"And do what?" He shook his head. "I'm thirtywhatever years old. I don't want to start over. But I don't—"

I don't want to shoot anyone.

Ty didn't know how he knew, but he knew. "—and I can't be a pilot and be there for my kid."

"So why not take some time off? It's not like I'm going to kick you out of the house." Actually, wouldn't that be kind of amazing? "You could spend all the time you want with Theo. And you wouldn't have to take time off to come see me in Chicago. I can show you around. We can take Theo to see the Nats when they're in town—"

"Ty. I'm not just going to, what, sit around all summer on my ass."

"Why not?"

Ollie was getting red in the face now. "Because I'm—I can't. I need a job. I'm not going to be a—a—"

"Stay-at-home parent?" Ty suggested.

"A freeloader."

"What the fuck." Ty gestured around them. "Hello. When's the last time I cut the grass? Never. When's the last time I did all the dishes? I don't remember. Let's not even talk about folding laundry, okay, because I never remember to do that and somehow it all gets put away."

"I need to make money, Ty."

"Literally why?" Ty was on the verge of pulling his hair out. "You could stay home and make macaroni art for the rest of your life, and unless you developed a taste for gold-plated pasta, we'd be fine."

He knew as soon as the words came out that it was the wrong thing to say. First, he'd gone and revealed far more than he intended. They'd been dating for less than an entire weekend, and here was Ty casually dropping a *just let me support you for the rest of your life*. That was desperate even for him.

And second, it sounded like he thought macaroni art was all Ollie would be good for.

Ollie knocked back the rest of his beer, slammed it on the breakfast bar, and stood up. "I am not going to be a freeloader just so you can—move us all to Chicago or whatever. Theo is my kid. He's mine to take care of."

Ty reeled back, stung. "Maybe you should fucking do that, then," he snarled. He put his half-empty beer in the sink. The last thing he needed right now was alcohol. He was going to go—somewhere. His room. Ollie wouldn't bother him there. "Your mom sends her love, by the way," he added, because if Ollie wanted to be a petty bitch, then Ty would match his energy.

Then, seething, he stormed out of the kitchen.

It wasn't until his bedroom door closed behind him that he let himself wonder if he'd just fucked up the best thing that ever happened to him.

OLLIE KNEW he was being an asshole. He knew exactly where the conversation was going to end up when Ty walked in the door, and he steered toward the cliff and put his foot on the gas like he was in a demented version of *Thelma and Louise*.

All day he'd been itching for a fight. Well, now he'd had one, and he didn't feel any better.

He dumped the rest of Ty's beer and rinsed out both bottles, then took them outside to the recycling bin.

The recycling bin that was full of the little yogurt cups Theo liked, because Ty always bought those ones even though they were more expensive than the other kind, and Ty's smoothie bottles, and the folded-up boxes from Ollie's granola.

In case Ollie didn't already feel like a dick, here was a visual representation of what could have been his family in the trash.

Was there anything in his life he *hadn't* fucked up? Because of his choices, his parents might be getting divorced. He'd lost his job. If he'd managed to push Ty away from him for good, Theo would never forgive him. As a bonus, they'd probably have to move—not because Ty would kick them out, but because staying would be so awkward Ollie would never be able to sleep again.

If he were any kind of decent person, he'd apologize right now and do his best to fix the things he broke. But he wasn't the only one who needed to make amends. Ty's macaroni art comment was going to sting for a while.

That had hit a little too close to home.

If the only way Ollie left his mark on this world was through his kid, would that be enough? It *should* be enough. He could never tell Theo otherwise. But he didn't think it was wrong to want more either.

Did that make him a bad person?

No, that wasn't what made him a bad person. The way he'd reacted to a kind, sincere, *generous* offer, no matter how poorly worded… *that* made him an asshole.

Ollie had made peace with being queer. It had strained his relationship with his parents, but he could live with that. He accepted his PTSD and the past he couldn't change as part of himself, and he'd had plenty of time in therapy while Theo was recovering from cancer to sort out his shit. He might never be *done*, and it might never be easy, but he could live with that too.

And the whole time he'd been in therapy, the whole time he'd been focused on being there for Theo until he was better, he didn't work and he didn't worry about it. He stayed in Allison's apartment, set aside Theo's Social Security checks, and focused on getting himself into mental shape to be a full-time parent.

He had a security net. He had a nice place to live. It had been weeks since anyone insinuated he couldn't take care of his kid, unless he counted himself in his argument with Ty just now.

He'd called himself a freeloader. But the term he really wanted to use was *kept man*. He felt emasculated. And that made him feel sick to his stomach, because he *knew better*. Having a job was not *manly*. Having this particular job had been a lot of things—tedious, ridiculous—but *manly* had not been one of them.

He didn't feel emasculated because he didn't have a job. He felt that way because another man had offered to support him. And that was… not great.

Fuck, Ollie had a headache. He should eat something and figure out when Theo would be home—*if* Theo would be home.

Which would mean talking to either his mother, his sister, or Ty.

He'd resigned himself to picking up his phone and braving a conversation with his mom—she didn't have to know he and Ty had a fight—when there was a crash of breaking glass from somewhere in the house.

Ollie forgot all about his phone as the adrenaline hit his system. "Ty!"

He bolted toward the bedrooms in time to see Ty emerge, looking as startled as Ollie felt. His eyes were wide and his skin blotchy and red.

"That wasn't you?" Ty asked.

Another tinkling noise, this one quieter.

"Office," Ollie barked. Without thinking about it, he grabbed the baseball bat Theo had left leaning against the wall in the living room.

Truly, he wasn't thinking about it. If he had, he'd have realized that he wasn't exactly wearing Kevlar. He had a T-shirt and a pair of sweatpants and a kid-size baseball bat against whatever the fuck was happening in the office.

But when he pushed open the door, it turned out not to matter. A figure dressed all in black was already legging it over the porch and out to the orchard. Shattered glass from the window littered the floor and desk.

Behind Ollie, Ty stepped into the room.

"What the fuck," Ollie said, bewildered. "Are you okay?"

"Fine." Ty stepped into the room. "You?"

"I was in the kitchen." Thank God Theo wasn't home.

"Uh. What do we do? I mean…." He gestured at the window. "We can't leave it like that, right? Except I guess we have to call the police?"

Ollie managed not to snort out loud. "The police who hate you?"

For a few moments no one spoke. Eventually Ty said, "I probably have to tell them, at least, right? Make a report? I'll have to let the insurance company know…."

And here Ollie'd thought the day couldn't get any worse. "Did your dad keep valuables in here or something?"

"How would I know?" Ty rubbed a hand over his face. "I only came in here long enough to grab the TV."

Because he hated his father, and the feeling was apparently mutual. As the shock wore off, Ollie's practical nature kicked back in. Whatever had happened earlier—whatever happened *later*—right now they had things to do. "You call the police," he said. "I'll heat up dinner."

Chapter 18

As Ollie had predicted, the police didn't exactly inspire confidence that they were even going to pretend to investigate.

"Probably just some kids playing a prank," Jake suggested. And this was the cop who actually *liked* Ty. "They ran off when they realized you were home."

That or they were driving home a point that Ty wasn't welcome here, and breaking the window was the exclamation mark on the whole thing. "I'm guessing you're not going to dust for prints."

"Did they actually take anything?"

Honestly, Ty had no idea. He doubted it. Whoever had broken in wouldn't have had much time between breaking the window and Ollie opening the door. "I'm not even sure they actually came inside."

Jake winced. "That makes it vandalism, not breaking and entering. I can't waste resources on that. Sorry."

"Not like I expected different."

Ty knew better by now.

"But look," Jake went on, "I'm off in an hour. I could come back, help you clean up?"

Ty looked at him. He was earnest. One might even say hopeful.

Yeah, of course, why not. Ty just had a fight with Ollie, so the universe was allowing him one more person in town who didn't hate his guts and wanted to bang him. Somehow he managed to smile politely. "Uh, thanks, but I think we got it."

He really should have finished that beer.

Ollie had driven off in Ty's truck when Jake had arrived. Ty didn't know what to think of it and didn't have any spare brain cells to speculate. Now, as Jake left, Ollie returned. He pulled the truck around to the backyard and pulled something out of the bed.

Ty slid on a pair of flip-flops and went out to join him.

It was a piece of three-quarter-inch plywood, already cut down to size to fit the window. Ollie must've taken measurements while Ty was talking to Jake in the kitchen.

Ollie leaned the wood against the side of the house and wiped his palms on his jeans. "You have a hammer in the garage or something, yeah?"

Oh good, so they were going to continue to ignore the elephant in the room. "Yeah." He hoped Ollie bought nails.

They spent the last of the daylight boarding up the window. Ollie pulled a pair of work gloves from somewhere, which Ty thought was unfair. If he was going to look that sexy, they should make up first. Unfortunately, it didn't happen that way. They worked mostly in silence apart from the necessary phrases. Ty didn't even get to make a joke about getting nailed.

But it wasn't *awful*. He was still pissed, and he thought Ollie was too, but the raw edges had scabbed over. By the time they finished, Ty was sore from standing on tiptoe to hold the boards in place and drained from the rest of the day, but he didn't feel like he had to run back to his bedroom to hide.

Could they get away with postponing the dissection of whatever had happened earlier?

"Listen," he said when they had put the tools back in the garage and Ollie, blessedly, had taken off the gloves, "I'm tired and sore and everything sucks, and I'm going to sit in the hot tub with a beer." Ollie had bought the beer, but fuck it, it was Ty's fridge. "You're welcome to join me."

Ollie looked at him like he'd grown a second head. After a moment he said, "I-I need some time. I'm not ready to talk about tonight."

As if. "I would probably fall asleep in the middle of it anyway."

Ollie waited a beat as if he were making sure Ty was serious. Then he shrugged. "Yeah, okay."

Awkward or not, the hot water felt good. But Ty got half a beer in and stopped, conscious of the way the temperature made him metabolize alcohol. The last thing he needed was to get a little too loose and somehow end up in another fight. He still had to go to work tomorrow.

Somewhere overhead, an owl hooted.

"If that thing drops a headless rabbit in here," Ty threatened.

He had his eyes closed, but he heard Ollie strangle a laugh.

Nothing was fixed. But maybe it wasn't all the way broken either.

OLLIE TOOK Theo to school Tuesday morning.

Ty could've taken him—he had to go anyway—but if Ollie was going to be unemployed, he was at least going to be a more hands-on parent than he'd been the past two months.

Last night had been… bad. Ollie barely slept, and not only because the sound of shattering glass had apparently triggered his PTSD. The stupid owl was at it all night too, calling out at three in the damn morning until Ollie was fantasizing about taking a trip to Bass Pro Shop first thing and sitting up all tomorrow night in a fucking deer blind. The house was in the middle of nowhere. Ollie was a good shot. No one would hear it.

Probably firing a gun would not help his PTSD, but it might make him feel better in other ways.

Not sleeping much had consequences—namely, a lot of time to sit and think about why he'd acted like an asshole. Ollie could stop sleeping, but he could not stop thinking, and that was a problem. Thinking did not help.

So he dropped Theo off at school, and then he went back to the house, which was huge and empty. No convenient owl presented itself.

Ollie decided that if his brain couldn't make itself useful, at least his body could, and he got out a broom and a dustpan and set to work cleaning Ty's father's office.

He only meant to pick up the glass. He didn't want any of it getting tracked into the rest of the house where someone might hurt themselves. He put on his work gloves to pick up the big pieces, and then he knocked the jagged edges out of the window and collected those too. He swept. He used a little dustpan to get the small pieces. He vacuumed.

And then it seemed like he couldn't stop.

The office was the one room on the main floor Ty didn't seem to have touched, apart from moving the TV. It still held all his dad's files and stacks of items and hoards of whatever the man's deteriorating mind thought was important at the time. It wasn't Ollie's business. He should probably stick to the task at hand and keep out of it.

But he couldn't. Cleaning… it helped. The more he focused on the task, the less he thought about his problem with Ty, which was actually his problem with himself. With his mind concentrating on something else, his subconscious was free to beat itself against the wall until enlightenment dawned on him.

And a small part of him that he was studiously ignoring pointed out that if Ollie went through this room, if Ollie read the stupid documents and put them in piles and decided what might be important, Ty wouldn't have to.

Whatever else Ollie had going on in his brain, he didn't want Ty to have to face his father's office. He couldn't take back the shit he said last night, but he could spare Ty this additional pain.

Besides, it wasn't like he had anything better to do.

When Ty and Theo got home, Ollie was still at it. Reams of paperwork covered all the surfaces in the room and had spilled out into the hallway.

The side door opened, and a breeze picked up the top few pages of one of Ollie's piles. He reached out automatically with his left hand to keep it from creating more of a mess. "Close the door, please."

"Uh…. Dad?"

The door closed. Ollie carefully collected the displaced papers and put them back where they belonged. "Hey, bud."

"What are you doing?"

There was a careful silence behind him. Ollie could practically feel Ty weighing the same question.

Slowly, Ollie stood, dusting his hands on his pants. "I had the day off," he told his kid. He couldn't quite bring himself to look Ty in the eye yet. "So I thought I'd organize the office."

The silence stretched a little longer. Finally Ty asked, "Into the hallway?"

Yeah, Ollie maybe deserved that. But when he glanced up, Ty didn't seem angry, just bewildered.

Which was also fair. Now that Ollie had broken out of his fixation, he became aware of all kinds of muscle aches. His knees felt bruised. "Uh… well. I ran out of space."

Ty picked his way through the various stacks and peered into the office. He said nothing. Ollie… kind of didn't remember what it looked like in there right now. He was a little afraid to check.

After a few seconds, Ty backed out again, his expression carefully blank. "So you did."

The back of Ollie's neck felt weirdly hot. "Your dad, uh, wasn't the most… organized. Toward the end." Duh, that was why Eliza had originally hired Ollie to help. "It was kind of a mess in there."

"As opposed to how it is now." Ty nodded. His eyes were wide.

"Hey," Ollie protested weakly. "There's a method to my madness."

"I'll take your word for it." Ty paused as though searching for words. "Can we, maybe—move some of your madness to the dining room table so we don't trip over all this going to the bathroom in the middle of the night?"

They didn't use the dining room for anything anyway. "Okay, yes. Good idea. Uh."

Ty was still looking at him like he might do something weird, like tap-dance or explode. He raised his eyebrows fractionally.

Fuck it. Ollie reached toward him. "I'm stuck, okay? Give me a hand to get up."

The three of them made quick work of moving the piles. If Ty was curious about what was in them, he didn't let on, and the lack of interest spread to Theo, who barely looked at them. Ollie, meanwhile, had taken all day to go through them for a reason. He kept getting drawn into Ty's father's weird business empire, trying to track the different ventures, what exactly the man *did* for a living. Owned things, it seemed like. A little light venture capitalism. Silent business partnering.

Ollie felt like Alice falling down a rabbit hole.

"Dad, I got the new *Percy Jackson* at the school library today."

Ollie raised his eyebrows. "There's only three days of school left and they're letting you take out books?"

"Mrs. Aster made an exception." Theo gave him big, pleading puppy-dog eyes. "Can I go read now? I want to finish before I have to give it back."

"Yes, go." Like Ollie was going to say no to his kid reading on purpose.

When he'd gone, Ollie raised his eyebrows at Ty.

"I maybe suggested I could make sure he brought it back before the summer," Ty admitted.

Theo was going to stay up too late trying to finish the book. That or he'd be reading at recess, during lunch, and in the car on the way to school. Maybe all of the above.

Ollie would have to be kind of a dick to be mad about that. "Special treatment from the teachers." He smiled vaguely, hoping he was still allowed to tease. "The other kids are gonna think he's a brown-noser."

Ty rolled his eyes. "He's been going home with one of the teachers for six weeks. I think that ship has sailed."

"Ah… yeah. True." And there was that awkwardness again. All Ollie's fault, and he still had only half understood what was wrong with him, but he knew he owed Ty an apology. "Listen… I'm still working through some things. But I want to apologize."

Ty glanced back toward Theo's room, as though to ensure he wasn't eavesdropping. His face was drawn. "Look, it's… fine. Just forget it."

"It's not *fine*."

"No, I-I minimized your feelings. I didn't listen. I—"

Like he wasn't listening right now? "Ty."

He shut his mouth with a click. His cheeks were red. He wouldn't meet Ollie's gaze. He was looking instead at the piles of paperwork on the dining room table—pieces of his estranged father's life.

Everyone who'd lived with Ty in this house had left him—died or rejected him. Ollie never should have forgotten that.

No wonder Ty didn't want to talk. He was probably afraid Ollie would leave him too, and take Theo with him.

Ollie was such an asshole. "I do need to apologize," he said gently. "You have been more than generous—you have been so good to Theo and to me, and I threw it in your face—" His voice got stuck and he had to stop. After a deep, shaky breath he began again. "I would have been up a fucking creek without you. Just because I'm insecure about that doesn't mean I get to take my problems out on you."

Somehow his hand had found its way around Ty's and was squeezing it, like that would help his meaning sink in.

He watched Ty swallow. Then his mouth worked soundlessly. From the sharp sound he made when he finally inhaled, he might have forgotten to breathe for a moment there. "You're—insecure."

Did Ollie stutter? Surely Ty hadn't missed it.

He dropped Ty's hand and opened his mouth.

"I mean you're—" Ty made a flailing gesture to encompass Ollie head to toe. Ollie's ears burned. "Like—high school star athlete to actual war hero? Town's golden boy. Incredible dad."

Something in Ollie's stomach curdled. "The first time someone died in front of me I couldn't even look him in the eye." Chavez had been twenty-three and terrified, bleeding out from shrapnel from an IED.

Ollie had tried to stop the bleeding. He just didn't have enough hands to apply pressure everywhere. He'd focused on that and ignored Chavez's labored gasps. For a moment he'd ignored Chavez slapping at Ollie's side too, until he realized nothing he could do would save his friend and finally held his hand.

If he expected Ty to balk at this, he should've known better. His expression softened, but he didn't flinch. "You would've been what? Eighteen?"

"Nineteen," Ollie admitted.

Ty nodded. "The first time I lost a patient, I threw up in a planter on the Magnificent Mile. Do you think less of me?"

What Ollie thought was that he'd like to go back in time and give that version of Ty a hug. "It's not the same thing. I let him die alone."

"Everyone dies alone. You were a kid, Ollie. Probably scared out of your mind. Give yourself some grace for that."

Could he do that? Maybe. But he couldn't accept the title. "I'm not a war hero. I hate—I hate when people say that. I'm not proud of the things I did over there. Shooting people should never be heroic." Acts of heroism shouldn't give you nightmares for the rest of your life.

Ty tilted his head. "I mean, I'm assuming you got shot at too. But, uh, I get it. I won't say that again."

Some of the nervous tension Ollie had been holding in, a tightness in his stomach, eased, and he realized he'd been clenching his abs to the point of soreness. His mouth felt suddenly dry. "It's hard to hear, sometimes." Now the rest of it, Ollie. "Especially when it's you who's been pulling my ass out of the fire since I came back to town."

That made him flush and step back. Because he could handle all the horrible truths about Ollie without flinching, but God forbid anyone should say a kind word about *him*. "Ollie. You and Theo saved *me*."

Ollie blinked. No—Ty had given them a home, given Theo an adult he could rely on, someone to have Ollie's back. Someone to be there when Theo went into anaphylaxis. Someone to save them from Ollie's lackluster cooking or death by takeout cholesterol. Someone to wake Ollie up in the middle of the night if he had a PTSD nightmare. He swallowed. "Ty, come on. Of the two of us—"

"*You saved me first.* This house?" Ty said. "I grew up here, and I haven't felt welcome or at home in over a decade. I came back and drank myself into a stupor the first night and would've missed my own father's funeral if you hadn't shown up. You think I would've lasted five minutes in this town without you? You're the only one here who even likes me."

"I *love you!*"

Ollie didn't mean to say it. He certainly didn't mean to half shout it like they were having an argument. But he wasn't going to take it back—not with Ty looking at him like *that*, eyes and mouth soft with shock. Usually he flushed a blotchy red, but this was an almost dainty pink.

Ollie had stunned him into silence.

"I love you," he repeated urgently. "You are kind and hot and you help people, and half of this town wouldn't spit on you if you were on fire, and it fucking kills me. They should be falling over themselves to hand you the world on a silver platter. I feel like I'm insane."

The flush crept higher on his cheeks, now a pale rose.

Ollie could not fucking shut up. "And I also feel like an asshole," he went on, "because I hate that for you, but it means I get you all to myself."

Ty pressed his lips together as though to hold in a sound. Ollie hoped it was a good one. He didn't know what would run out first, Ty's silence or his own words.

"And I hate that I still want more."

That was it, apparently—his throat had swollen tight. Nothing more would come.

His hands were shaking.

"Ollie...."

Fuck. Ollie blinked. The tightness in his belly had returned. "Please say something."

Ty's hands covered his. The shaking did not abate, but Ollie felt more grounded. More sure. "You should want more."

That—wasn't what Ollie had expected. Was Ty going to let him down easy? He'd never thought—

"You deserve *more*," Ty said. But his voice held the same earnest urgency Ollie had felt, pouring his heart out, so maybe Ollie should just hold his breath and hold Ty's hands and hold on. "I want you to have everything—a home and a family and a, a *partner* and—and something you do that's just for you, because it's satisfying. Because I *love* you."

The tension dissolved again. This time it almost took Ollie's knees out with it. "Okay." He felt lightheaded. "So just—so we're clear. The partner is you?"

Ty's laugh matched the flush on his cheeks. "Yeah, Ollie, the partner is me."

"Okay," Ollie repeated. His face hurt now, instead of his stomach; he was smiling too widely. He probably looked like an idiot. He sounded like one too. "Okay."

"I'm sorry I, um, worded that badly the first time around."

Ollie laughed too, and it sounded as insane as he felt. "I mean. I'm kind of glad you did. I was… not in a good place. What if my mood ruined a perfectly good love confession?"

"Oh, well." Ty nodded. Ollie had moved his hands to Ty's face. He didn't remember doing it. It was like he was possessed and the demon in charge of his body just wanted to touch Ty everywhere. "In that case I'm so glad I fucked it up."

Ollie kissed him. Objectively it was not a good kiss; they were both grinning like idiots. Subjectively, it was the best kiss of Ollie's life. He felt like a helium balloon. He might float away at any moment, except Ty's hands on his waist and his on Ty's face kept him happily tethered.

He probably could've spent the remainder of the afternoon there, kissing his boyfriend—his *partner*—and forgetting the rest of the world existed, except a small voice came from the doorway to the dining room.

"Dad, do you know what this word means?"

Ollie blinked and the world returned to focus. Ty was definitely blotchy red now, his skin hot under Ollie's hands. His grin had not disappeared, although it had taken on a definite tinge of embarrassment.

"Uh," Ollie said as he turned around.

Theo handed him the book. "That one." He pointed. "Mem…?"

"Membrane." Ollie handed the book back. "It's like a kind of skin."

"Membrane," Theo repeated. "Cool. Thanks, Dad."

Ollie became aware, suddenly, that Ty still had his hands on his waist. That Ollie had only turned his torso to take the book from Theo and the rest of him was still oriented toward Ty like a flower toward the sun.

He was afraid to move more, now, in case he called attention to it. Was Theo going to say something? Or…?

He cleared his throat. "You're welcome."

"Hey, Dad?"

Not even two inches away, Ty's stomach started jiggling. That fucker was laughing. He was holding it in, sure, but Ollie could fucking *feel it*. "Mm-hmmm?" Ollie asked, dying inside.

"Is Ty your boyfriend?"

Ollie licked his lips. Did he have beard burn? Did he have, like, drying spit on his face?

And did he have to answer this question? "Yeah, bud." He paused. "Um, is that okay with you? This isn't how I wanted to tell you."

Although hey, at least they had all their clothes on.

Theo scrunched up his face. "Are you going to kiss in front of me all the time?"

Ty made a noise. Ollie stepped on his foot. "Um, maybe little ones. But not—not *all* the time. Sometimes we'll just watch baseball together or eat dinner and stuff."

Theo nodded like he was considering this very carefully. "Is Ty still moving to Chicago?"

Oh no. Ollie didn't *want* to answer that one. He glanced up at Ty, pleading with his eyes.

Ty took half a step away from Ollie and turned toward Theo. "Kind of. I won't be working the same way I work here, though. I usually work four days and then have four days off, so I can come visit when I'm not working."

"Like when Dad was in the Army?"

"Exactly, except I'll be home for a little bit of every week."

Ollie thought that was kind of a lot to promise—Ty still had a life and friends in Chicago, and what if he got sick, or someone else did, and he had to cover a shift? But he wasn't going to object.

"But *we're* not going to move to Chicago," Theo clarified. His lower lip stuck out a little, confirming Ollie's suspicion that this was a statement and not a question.

"That's right. We might go to visit, if Ty invites us."

Ty said, "The Nats are playing the Cubs at the end of August." He glanced at Ollie, shrugged helplessly, and blushed again. "I have three tickets behind home plate, if you know anyone who might want to come—oof."

Theo rammed him full speed and wrapped both arms around his waist. "Oh my God! Really? That's *so cool*! Dad, we can go, right? Since you got fired and stuff."

Jesus. Ollie reached one hand out to the back of a chair to steady himself. This conversation was giving him emotional whiplash. Ty put a hand on his shoulder too, and he managed to breathe. "Where did you hear that?"

"At school. Jordan heard it from Megan, whose mom works with a lady at your company." That face scrunch again. "I guess maybe it's not your company now." The scrunch became a crumple. "They said you got fired 'cause of me. Did you?"

Ah, fuck. Ollie glanced up long enough to meet Ty's eyes, and he gave a slight nod and quietly left the room. Ollie pulled out a couple of chairs and gestured for Theo to sit next to him. "I did lose my job, yeah, but not because of you, okay? I only took that job because they promised me that they believed family should come first. It turned out they broke their promise. *That's* why I got fired, not because of you."

For a kid who'd had a lot thrown at him in the past five minutes, Theo was doing a remarkable job keeping an even keel. "Are we gonna be okay? Are we gonna have to move again?"

"We are going to be great," Ollie promised. And then—well. Fuck. He might as well. "I might even take some time to decide what I want to do next. I don't want you to worry about that, okay? I have savings from the Army, and your mom put aside money just for you." Ollie wasn't touching that—that was for Theo's college, or for a down payment on a house one day—but if it helped ease his anxiety now, Theo should know it existed.

Theo leaned forward, all trace of concern gone. "So we can go to Chicago?"

Ollie's mouth opened. Wow, he'd really walked into that one, huh? "Yeah," he said helplessly, "we can go to Chicago."

TY LEFT Ollie and Theo to their conversation and retreated to the kitchen to start dinner prep. Or at least that was his plan, but after two minutes, he hadn't managed to do anything other than stand in front of the fridge with a stupid smile on his face.

If he wanted to keep his fingers, he had better leave the cutting board alone, so he retreated to the games room to process.

Ollie loved him.

Ty dropped down onto the couch and put a hand to his lips.

Ollie loved him, and Theo seemed to be okay with the two of them dating. Ty was pretty embarrassed they'd been caught making out like teenagers, but it could've been worse. And at least the important parts of the conversation had been over by then.

Ollie loved him.

He just couldn't stop thinking it. Ty had had relationships before, lasting ones even, people he thought he could spend the rest of his life with. Now the idea seemed absurd. His previous vague daydreams of what his future might look like had seemed real and clear and tangible at the time, but compared to the vision he saw now? It was like comparing a television show broadcast on an old aerial antenna on a tube TV to an IMAX movie. Before, Ty could barely hear the dialogue over the static; now he could smell the popcorn.

And if he couldn't tell exactly where the movie was set, that would come with time. Right? Everything was coming up Morris.

Well, no. Not everything. Ty was still going to have to show up in front of Alan Chiu and defend himself for trying and failing to save someone's life. The whole idea of it soured his stomach. It was one thing to suspect your whole town hated you and another to face the prospect of knowing it for sure.

Well—no again. Not the *whole* town.

Ollie loved him.

A knock at the door made him look up with a smile. "I'm not exactly looking for privacy."

"Didn't want to startle you. You looked lost in thought."

Ty moved over on the couch so Ollie had room to sit next to him. "I may have been building castles in the sky." Which reminded him. "Hey, if you get a regular pilot's license, we can get you a plane and you can come pick me up from Chicago."

Ollie gave him a wry look. "You are not buying me a plane."

"Well, I'm definitely not buying you a helicopter. Those things are death traps." Could a helicopter even fly from Connecticut to Chicago, or would it have to stop to refuel?

"Do you promise?"

Ty would not promise. He didn't know what a helicopter cost. Maybe someday they'd engineer one that didn't make him fear for Ollie's life. He decided to change the subject. "Everything good with Theo?"

"Yeah. I think, uh, probably some of the gossip around town tipped him off. And it's not like much is going to change for him."

True. Ty cleared his throat. "Well, that's—good. I actually meant about the job thing, though. Not us."

"Ah." Ollie wiped a palm over the back of his neck. "Well, as someone recently pointed out to me, I have the time and financial security to figure out what I want to do with my life, so now that I'm done freaking out about that… I told my kid it's what I'm going to do. Call it accountability."

Ty grinned, his chest swelling with pride. Look at Ollie finally doing something for *himself*. "Yeah?"

"Yeah." He paused. "Although my more immediate future is probably focused on fixing the office. Um. Sorry."

Oh, as if Ty cared. He waved this off. "It was already a disaster. My mess is your mess."

Wow, that sounded kind of romantic. What was a home—a family—if not a shared mess?

Ollie kissed him again, this time soft and sweet. "Thank you."

Chapter 19

OLLIE STILL didn't know how he was supposed to figure out what he wanted to be when he grew up, but he had never been one to shy away from doing the job in front of him. Right now that job was sorting through… stuff.

Ty's father had kept *everything*. At one point in his life, that had probably been a good thing. Ollie imagined businesspeople needed to keep all kinds of records. But somewhere along the way the disease in his brain had taken over, and now he had his attendance badge from the 1996 Republican National Convention in the same file folder as an investment agreement for a greenhouse operation signed in 2015.

He more or less had the important stuff separated out now, with the junk mail and trash in one box and the personal things set aside to go through later, and he was sorting the business things into files. Most of them had been intact, at least; only a few had been of interest to the later Morris.

The greenhouse operation papers were everywhere—in two different filing cabinets, on the bookshelf, in a briefcase, and under the desk. Ollie tried not to read them beyond identifying them—he felt like they were Ty's personal business—but every now and again he got sucked into what felt like a soap opera for rich businessmen.

For example, in the early nineties, Morris did several hundred thousand dollars' worth of business dealings with someone named Applegate, and then all those partnerships were dissolved and some kind of lawsuit ensued. Unfortunately it had either been settled out of court or Morris had lost the paperwork afterward, because Ollie couldn't figure out who won that battle.

In 1995 Morris had gone into business with Alan Chiu instead. It seemed like half the town had come to him with their business ventures. He'd held people's mortgages, owned property to rent, even lent money (at punitive interest) so people could pay their medical bills.

By lunchtime on Wednesday, Ollie was half convinced Ty's father hadn't died in a car crash, someone had murdered him. Who *wouldn't* want someone this obnoxious dead? Maybe the townsfolk of Suffolk all actually hated Ty because they couldn't hate his rich dad out loud or he'd call in their debts.

Finally he emptied all the misfiled cabinets—two in the back seemed relatively untouched—and the desk drawer and was ready to start putting things back in order. He turned to pick up the water bottle he'd left on the floor—and stopped.

There was a corner of paper sticking out from under the filing cabinet behind the door. Ollie must've missed it. Frowning, he reached down to pick it up.

It was a legal-size envelope, stamped and mailed, bearing the house's address and Ty's father's name. The return address was a law firm in Bridgeport.

At some point it had been opened, so Ollie didn't think it was illegal for him to look inside. He lifted the flap and pulled out the papers inside.

Ten minutes later, he put down the papers and pulled out his phone. "Eliza? Yeah, hi, it's Ollie. Do you have an hour free this afternoon? Or maybe tonight? It's important."

WEDNESDAY WAS the last baseball practice of the year. Even if they were playing a team that consisted entirely of the three loners who hadn't managed to get the mumps, Henry thought the kids should be prepared.

Danny and Peter Chiu still wouldn't look each other in the eye, which could not be good for Henry's blood pressure. It wouldn't help their odds of winning a baseball game either, but unless someone came up with a miracle cure for mumps, that probably didn't matter.

No one got seriously maimed, and Ty had an hour's distraction from the looming specter of Saturday's town hall meeting, which at this point was all he could hope for.

"I'm sorry we didn't put on a better showing for you, bud," he told Theo as they made their way to the car. "It would've been nice if we could've won a couple."

"It's okay," Theo said seriously. "The Cubs get paid to play baseball, and they lose all the time too."

Ty cackled and unlocked the doors. "Who's been teaching you trash talk? That was good."

"Grandma."

Even better. "I thought she didn't like baseball."

"I think that's why she's so good at trash talk."

"Could be."

The drive home passed mostly in silence, with Theo leaning his head against the window and Ty humming along with the radio.

When he pulled into the driveway, there was an unfamiliar truck parked behind the house. The hair on the back of Ty's neck stood up, but Theo just said, "What's Grandpa doing here?"

If that was Ollie's father's truck, at least Ty didn't have to worry about another potential vandal attack. Probably. Ollie's dad didn't hate Ty enough to break his window, right?

He clicked the button to open the garage and maneuvered inside. Whatever Ollie's dad was doing here, he was doing it without Ollie; the Toyota wasn't in its space. "I don't know. Let's go find out." He pocketed his keys and led the way around to the back of the house.

What Ollie's dad was doing appeared to involve Ty's office window and a new pane of glass. Jake was there too, helping lever it into place. Replacing a windowpane evidently took two people.

For a second, Ty honestly couldn't think of anything to say.

"Uh," he managed after a moment. "Hi."

"Hey, Ty," Jake said cheerfully. As if Ty hadn't rejected his advances two days ago. "Just about done here."

Mr. Kent pushed a small metal pin in next to the glass, then did the same on the other side. Ollie had said his father had a construction company at one point, if Ty remembered right. "Had a free afternoon, and Maureen said you could use some help."

She did?

Ollie's parents were speaking to each other again?

"Oh," Ty said after a moment. "Well, I appreciate it. Let me know what I owe you for the materials and labor."

"No, no. I had a piece of glass in my garage, just had to cut it down." He didn't quite meet Ty's eyes, and Ty had no idea what was going on. He felt like he'd stepped sideways into an alternate dimension. "Theo. You want to learn a skill? Come over here and I'll show you how to seal a window."

Ty slowly backed away, giving Jake a little wave. He didn't want to come across as unfriendly, but he did want to figure out what was happening. He pulled out his phone to text Ollie. *Your dad is fixing the window???*

The little checkmark indicated the message had been delivered, and then it changed color. Seen.

A moment later Ollie replied. *Oh good, I thought he might not get to it until tomorrow.*

Ollie was going to pretend this was normal? That he and his dad hadn't been engaged in a sort of cold war for weeks?

Did he have a come to jesus moment or something, he wrote.

I don't think Jesus was involved. Mom might have been.

That explained nothing. But fine. Let Ollie keep his secrets. *Where are you? Going to be home for dinner?*

Sorry, boss. Top secret mission. Eat without me. But I'll be home in time to tuck Theo into bed.

Pause.

And you too.

Frowning, Ty put his phone back in his pocket. Well, if Ollie was busy and Jake and Ollie's dad had spent their afternoon doing repairs to Ty's house, he probably owed them dinner, at the very least. He walked back around the house to make the invitation.

OLLIE DIDN'T want to spend the days leading up to Ty's de facto trial essentially AWOL. He and Ty both knew Ty had done nothing wrong, unless you counted assuming other people had basic human decency, but that didn't mean Ollie couldn't see the specter of the town hall meeting weighing on him.

Ollie couldn't fix that.

What Ollie *could* do was take care of the other things in Ty's life.

Getting the window fixed proved easier than he thought. Ollie couldn't *ask*, and his father couldn't offer. Ollie had to hold the grudge until his dad made things right. The family politics made the whole thing trickier than it had to be. Ollie had to arrange for his father to find out about the broken window from someone else and hope he decided that fixing it might be a good first step in building goodwill with Ollie and, by extension, his wife.

Fortunately for Ollie, Peggy knew everyone in town and was far more Machiavellian than Ollie could ever hope to be. All he actually had to do was be home at the right time to give his father access to the office so the initial piece of glass could be set into place.

Sure, it almost made him late for his after-school meeting with Peggy and Jason, but it was worth it.

By the time Ollie got home, dusk had fallen. Theo and Ty were in the living room, watching the Tigers beat the snot out of the Cubs.

"Uh-oh, baseball? Shouldn't you be reading your book?" Ollie teased.

"Dad, I'm over halfway done. I've been reading during the commercials."

"What?" Ollie walked over, ruffled his hair, and grinned when Theo made a face at him. "No homework?"

"Dad," Theo protested.

Ty turned his face upward to look at him. "You're in a good mood."

"Mmm." He was, actually. Ollie hadn't felt this bone-deep contentment—sexual encounters with Ty not included—in…. He didn't want to think about how long. It would only depress him. He leaned over and pressed a smacking kiss on Ty's mouth, upside-down. "Unemployment agrees with me."

"Gross," Theo said from the armchair, but he didn't actually sound upset.

"Uh-huh," Ty said, obviously skeptical. He made room for Ollie on the couch and then promptly shoved his feet into his lap, but he didn't ask any other questions. Ollie's nonanswers from earlier had had the desired effect.

"How was practice?"

"Nobody died."

Any other day it might've sounded light. On a day when Ollie knew Ty had been obsessing over Mrs. What's-her-face, that was black humor at its finest. Ollie rubbed his hand over one of Ty's ankles, then the arch of his foot. "Always good news."

"Danny and Peter won't look each other in the eye, so that's a good sign of team togetherness."

"Paolo says they used to be best friends," Theo piped up. "But now they don't talk to each other."

"Did Paolo have any insight?" Ty asked. "Because Henry forbade me from getting into it, and I am dying to know the tea."

"He forbade you?"

"He said I might learn something we'd have to tell their parents."

"He said I was too young to understand." Theo rolled his eyes. "People always say that, but what they really mean is they don't want to explain it."

Theo really was too smart for his own good. Ollie pressed his thumb into the arch of Ty's foot.

A barely perceptible shudder went through Ty's body, and then he went a little limp. After a deep, gusty sigh, he gave Ollie a heavy-lidded look.

Maybe the foot rub should wait until after Theo had gone to bed.

When he had—when they'd turned the game off and fended off complaints, and when Ollie had enforced the "ten more minutes of reading" bedtime rule and was sure Theo was sound asleep—Ollie coaxed Ty into his bedroom and spent half an hour getting a crash course in blow jobs.

Neither of them made a move to get up afterward; they simply lay together in the soft blue of twilight, Ty scratching his fingers over Ollie's scalp while Ollie lolled on his chest, feeling like an indulgent cat.

"You're not going to tell me what you were doing today, are you?" Ty said after a long, pleasant silence.

Ollie turned his head enough to press a kiss to his sternum. "Not today. That all right?" He lifted his gaze.

"The suspense is killing me." But he made the complaint around a yawn, and there was a smile under that.

Good. Maybe that would keep him from worrying about Saturday.

Ty's nails skittered down Ollie's scalp to his nape. "You going back to your room?"

Ollie should. God knew the last thing Ty needed was one of Ollie's PTSD nightmares to worry about. "In a minute."

"Hmm. 'Kay."

Neither of them moved until morning.

Chapter 20

WHEN HE was very young, Ty loved the freedom that came with the end of the school year. It meant pool parties at his friends' houses and long days riding his bike around town, nights stargazing with his mother on the back deck, state fairs and ice cream and sleepovers.

Then his mother died and Ty was shipped off to boarding school, and suddenly summer break meant long months alone in an empty dormitory, knocking out the requirements to graduate early because he needed something to occupy his time or he'd lose his mind.

The relief and joy Ty felt on Friday when the last bell went and he never had to be a teacher again was like being a little kid times one million—magnified to the power of no more marking ever, divided by the number of times Ty would have to ask a kid to stop chewing gum in class.

"Why do you look like that?" Henry teased as they packed up the last of their things in the athletic office. "Did you hate the kids that much?"

"I love kids," Ty said seriously. "But teaching is fucking bullshit."

Henry snorted. "Amen to that."

"Long hours. Low pay. Administrators." Ty shuddered, and he and Henry said together, "*Parents*."

They laughed as the athletic office door closed behind them.

"So you're really going back to Chicago?"

Ty glanced at him. He was serious, but also just curious. "That was always the plan."

"Sure, sure." Behind them the hallway lights were flickering off for the last time this school year. Their footsteps echoed. "But plans change."

Subtle the man was not. "Say what you want to say, Henry."

"All right." He paused at the heavy exterior fire door. Bright sunshine poured through the narrow rectangular windows. "You could have a life here if you wanted it. I know you think you have to go back to Chicago because—I don't know. But you don't. You can choose."

Ty swallowed.

He wanted that promotion. He'd worked for it for years. Being a paramedic gave him something to cling to when the world didn't make sense. These past few weeks, living in his father's house, hearing his ghost list Ty's failures one after the other, sometimes echoed by the town's other residents, he'd clung to that job.

The job that said he did something right. He did something important. The job that recognized him for it.

He had to choose that for himself, didn't he? Didn't he owe himself that much?

"Yeah," he said, noncommittal, and pushed open the door into summer.

Ollie picked Theo up that afternoon, partly because Theo had somehow strewn his personal belongings across three different locations and the lost and found and needed time to collect them, and partly, Ty suspected, because he could. Ty didn't actually run into him, but he didn't need to; the trail of moony-eyed teachers gave the game away.

A few of them gave Ty calculating looks afterward, so obviously word about *that* was getting around too. As long as everyone still loved Ollie, Ty told himself he didn't care what anyone thought about him.

Unfortunately, with the game tomorrow and the rest of the week booked up, tonight he couldn't just go home and relax. He had an appointment with Eliza at her home office to go over their strategy for the town hall meeting tomorrow.

"I'm not on trial," Ty pointed out.

Eliza raised delicate eyebrows over her reading glasses. "Not yet," she said. "And we'd like to keep it that way, so pay attention."

"They don't have a case, you said."

"Doesn't mean he can't make your life miserable, which he already has. Just because he doesn't have a case doesn't mean he can't have someone bring charges. I don't think he's got an ADA in his back pocket, but I don't want to find out. Do you?"

He sighed. "No."

"All right, then. Now, I'm not going to show up to this thing acting as your lawyer."

That sent a jolt through him. "What? Why not?"

"Because you're not on trial, and showing up with a lawyer makes you look guilty of something."

"It makes me look like I'm not an idiot," Ty muttered.

She offered a slight smile. "That too. Now, just because I'm not going as your lawyer doesn't mean I'm not going. I like hot gossip as much as the next small-town church lady."

"You don't gossip!"

"Not with or about my clients," she agreed serenely. "But I'm only human, so I *will* be asking you about my nephew when we're off the clock."

Everyone in this town knew everything about everybody else. He should know that by now. "Okay, so I'm showing up solo." A hollow pit opened in his stomach. Of all the things he hated, of all the things he feared, standing on his own was near the top of the list.

Eliza shook her head. "Not *solo*. Bring Ollie. Everybody loves Ollie. People see you with him, they're going to want to see the same things in you that he does."

In Ty's opinion, it was more likely to work the other way around. People would wonder if Ollie had a secret criminal side or something. Especially since he'd lost his job. "Are you sure—I mean, he just got fired. Isn't that going to, like… make people think he's untrustworthy or something?"

"He did get fired," Eliza agreed placidly. She seemed very smug all of a sudden. "Thanks for bringing that up. Because Ollie got fired for being a good father. Everybody knows his child was in the hospital. Word travels fast around here. Public sympathy is strongly on his side. And if the two of you bring Theo in with you…."

Ty loathed the idea of using Theo as political clout. He wrinkled his nose.

"Believe me, I know. I understand the reluctance. But this is how the game is played. And don't you think he'd want to help you too?"

God, he'd been here five minutes and he already had a headache. He pinched the bridge of his nose. "All right. What else?"

"Are you sure you don't want to come to the game?" Ty asked for the third time that morning.

For the third time that morning, Ollie shook his head. "I've got a few things I want to finish up around the house, but I'll meet you at town hall. I won't be late. Promise."

Ty exhaled, anxiety pooling in his stomach.

"Hey." Ollie touched his arm. "I was going to—if you need me to come, I'll be there. It's not like any of my stuff is time sensitive."

No, Ty was being ridiculous. What could Alan Chiu even do to him anyway? Nothing. Certainly nothing was going to happen at the baseball game. Alan Chiu probably wouldn't even show up even though his own kid was pitching. "It's fine," he said, as much to reassure himself as for Ollie. "But when it's the only game we win all year and you miss it, it's your own fault."

Ollie kissed him briefly. "I'll take my chances. Theo! Are you ready to go?"

"Ready!"

And—oh. Okay, maybe Ty didn't *need* Ollie with him. Because he had Ollie's kid dressed in Ty's old baseball jersey from about a hundred years ago. It hung down past his waist and the sleeves covered his elbows. Nothing bad could happen to Ty if he had Theo with him dressed like that.

He cleared his throat. "Wow, nice outfit. Where did you find that?"

"I found it in the basement earlier this week." Ollie shot him a small smile. "I was looking for more paperwork."

"I can't believe you braved the centipedes."

Ollie took a step back, feigning horror. "There are *centipedes*?"

Ty shot him a look. "Did you find any? More paperwork, I mean."

"A bit. Your dad was a pack rat. As evidenced." He indicated Theo's shirt.

"I can't believe he kept that." More likely he hadn't known it existed. "My mom must've put that stuff away before she died."

"But it's okay if I wear it?" Theo asked.

"Course. Like I said, looks good on you." And now they would roll up at town hall together with Theo wearing his support for Ty right on his back—keen political machination on Ollie's part. "We really do have to go, though."

It never ceased to amaze Ty how the whole town would turn out for a baseball game even if the team hadn't won all year. Obviously the town needed to put in a trampoline park or something. Maybe a movie theater even.

The visitors' stands, on the other hand, were nearly as empty as the visitors' dugout. From the looks of things, Central High had tapped their JV team to fill out their numbers. A couple of the guys were barely taller than Theo.

Three of them were girls, although Ty knew better than to underestimate them based on that. Either one of them had the mumps, or she had a wad of chewing tobacco stuck in her lip.

Ty watched her spit into a bottle.

Okay, then.

"Play ball!" the umpire yelled, and Ty turned his focus to the game.

Even with a skeleton crew, Central High played a tight game. But Pete's pitching kept them off the scoreboard. Ty's kids eked out a run in the second inning and two in the fifth.

In the top of the seventh, Tobacco Girl hit the ball deep into left field with two runners on base. Two outs. Ty bit his lip as it went right over the fielder's head and Tobacco Girl took off at a run.

The runner on third crossed home plate just as the fielder caught up with the ball. He fired the ball toward second base—far too late to catch the second runner rounding third, but they had a hope of getting Tobacco Girl.

Riley missed the catch. Tobacco Girl made for third. On first base, Danny stopped the ball and sent it blistering toward third.

"Out!"

Jesus. Somehow Ty unclenched the knot in his stomach. This game might actually be worse for his blood pressure than the stupid meeting afterward.

"I've got Tums if you want them," Henry offered sotto voce.

"Fuck off," Ty muttered, conscious of Theo two feet to his left, carefully marking the runs scored on a clipboard. Then, "Yes, please."

Central held them scoreless to end the seventh, and then it was their turn at bat again.

"C'mon, Petey!" Riley encouraged from third base.

"I'm going to throw up," Ty said. He'd never been this nervous *playing* a sport.

Henry passed him another Tums. This time Ty took it without comment.

The kid walking up to the plate now looked like a minor leaguer. He had five o'clock shadow at eleven in the morning and shoulders that wouldn't fit into Ollie's Corolla.

"Who is this kid?" Ty muttered for the fourth time that game.

"I keep telling you," Theo said patiently, which didn't bode well for him not having heard Ty's cussing, "his name is Jeff Bridges."

Ty *knew* what the clipboard said. But how was he supposed to believe that kid's actual name was so appropriate?

Jeff Bridges If That Was His Real Name dragged his bat through the dirt. He squared up to the plate. He spat over his shoulder the way he had the first three times he'd batted.

Henry signaled to the fielders, in case they'd forgotten. His first hit had gone just fair down the first-base line, not quite over the fence—Central's first run of the game. Second was a pop fly, caught out center field, but after that Central's coaches got gun-shy and opted for the safe route—an infield grounder to get on base in the hopes someone else could bat him home.

With the game on the line, it was do-or-die time. Ty expected the kid to swing for the fences.

"You can do it, Pete!"

Ty blinked, startled to realize the encouragement came from Danny. "Aren't the two of them still—"

Henry stepped on his foot, like he thought Ty might jinx it by saying it out loud.

Pete wound up and released the pitch.

"Strike one!"

"Attaboy, Pete! You got this!"

Pete's cheeks flushed, either with the heat or the pressure or the encouragement.

"Strike two!"

Not Really Jeff Bridges spat again. He waggled the bat. He narrowed his eyes.

Crack.

It happened almost too quickly to see. One minute Pete was releasing the ball. The next minute he was flat on the ground, clutching at his throat.

Not Jeff Bridges didn't even run. He dropped the bat, his face white with horror. For the first time, he looked like he belonged on a high school baseball team.

Ty was running, though, almost before Pete hit the ground. "Henry, get the first-aid kit! Danny, call 911. Riley, sit with Theo." The last thing he needed was for his kid to see this.

He skidded to his knees in the dirt, already reaching for Pete's neck even as he fished out his pocketknife. "Hey, Pete, try to stay calm, okay? I'm going to check out the damage and then I'm going to help you breathe."

Pete's eyes were wide and terrified, and their time was limited, but Ty needed to keep him from panicking if he was going to have to do what he thought he'd have to do.

Pete let Ty coax his hands away from his throat, where the ball had struck him straight on below the chin. The impact had left a round red welt, but he'd been lucky enough to take the hit high. Ty had a little room to work.

"Okay, Pete, I need you to do two things. First, can you wiggle your feet?" Ty wouldn't be able to see his toes inside his shoes.

Both feet moved in the dirt just as Henry set the first-aid kit down next to him.

"Good, that's good, Pete. Okay, now I want you to take a very slow deep breath if you can. Got it?"

Pete nodded infinitesimally, but his chest barely rose. Ty could see him start to panic.

Ty flicked open the pocketknife without looking up at Henry. "Give me an iodine swab and the straw from one of the water bottles."

Henry set the supplies on Pete's chest and took off at a run for the dugout.

"Okay, Pete, you're doing fine. You're going to be able to breathe in a minute. Try to relax. This is probably going to hurt, but it's important to stay still." Ty didn't want to wait until he passed out.

Pete gave him a weak thumbs-up. His lips were turning blue.

Ty ripped open the iodine swab and wiped it over the skin just above the kid's collarbone. He scrubbed his hands and then the blade of the knife and then carefully cut an incision deep enough to reach the trachea and used his finger to open a hole.

He sensed more than heard Henry arrive next to him with the thick plastic straw. Ty cut it down, swabbed that too, for whatever good it would do, and carefully inserted the straw into the hole.

Pete's chest inflated as his starved lungs got access to oxygen at last. The panic left his eyes. He raised both hands for the thumbs-up this time.

Thank God. "That's good, Pete, nice job. Don't try to move, okay? The EMTs are on their way." He stood up and gestured. "Danny!"

Danny was pale and shaky, but he trotted over obediently, his gaze flicking back and forth between Ty and Pete. "He'll be all right," Ty said gently. "Can you—" He was about to reach for the phone, but then he realized he had Pete's blood all over his hands. "Put it on Speaker?" He waited while Danny held the phone near his face. "Sixteen-year-old male with a tracheobronchial blunt force trauma, trachea is crushed above the C6 vertebra, possible spinal trauma but patient is presenting with no loss of movement. Currently stable after a tracheotomy."

Danny pulled the phone back, took it off Speaker, and listened for a reply. "They say they're ten minutes out."

Ty felt sick. Ten minutes. Would he have made it?

"Great job, Danny. Uh." Ty looked around. Pete's dad wasn't here today. Well, of course he wasn't; he was at his makeshift courthouse, preparing his case against Ty's continued existence in his life. "Is Pete's mom here? Or grandparents or something?"

"No, Coach. Um, I think Coach Tate is calling them, though."

Right, well, in that case they could meet him at the hospital, but— "Do you want to stay with him?"

Danny brightened. "Can I?"

"It'll depend on the EMTs. Henry—uh, Coach Tate—probably has to go in the ambulance. You can see if there's room for you too."

For a second, Ty wondered if he'd guessed wrong. Danny looked back toward Pete with his mouth set and his brow furrowed. Then he glanced back at Ty, knelt next to Pete, and took his hand.

Yeah, that tracked.

Ty stayed with them, monitoring his patient until the paramedics arrived. Eliana looked from Pete to Ty and back again and said, "Jesus, Morris, what the hell happened?"

"Line drive to the throat."

She whistled under her breath as her coworkers got Pete on a backboard. "Lucky you were here, then." She clapped his shoulder. "We got it from here. Good luck today, yeah?" She paused and looked him over. "Uh, maybe change before you go."

Was this thing still going to go forward? Chiu's kid was going to be in the hospital.

But—yeah, he definitely needed to wash up. He was going to traumatize Theo if he kept getting covered in other people's blood.

He tried to ignore the sounds of retching while he was washing his hands in the fieldhouse bathroom, staining the porcelain pink with Pete's blood. It seemed only polite.

Then the umpire emerged from one of the stalls, skin green and waxy. He blanched further when he saw Ty was still cleaning up, and for a second, Ty thought he was going to barf again, but he rallied. "Uh." He didn't get any closer, though. "Think we're gonna call the game."

Oh, do you fucking think? Ty bit his tongue on that comment. "Good idea," he said instead.

He couldn't do much about the shirt. He really would have to go home and change. First, though, he needed to check on Theo and make sure he was all right. He jogged back to the dugout just in time to see the ambulance leave the parking lot.

Ty barely had time to thank Riley before Theo launched himself into his stomach and wrapped his arms around him. "Oof!" Oh jeez. "Careful, buddy, I'm kind of—dirty." If Ollie saw Theo covered in blood he would have an aneurysm. This day had been traumatic enough.

"That was scary," Theo said into Ty's navel. "Is Pete gonna be okay?"

Fuck it. Ty needed a hug too. He wrapped his arms around Theo's shoulders and gave him a squeeze. "He might have a little bit of trouble talking for a while, but he'll be okay."

Theo looked up without loosening his grip. "I'm glad you were here, Ty."

Eyes stinging, Ty ruffled his hair. "Me too."

A throat clearing interrupted their moment. "Uh, Coach." Riley held up Ty's phone, which he'd left on the bench. "This thing has been going like crazy."

He unlocked it to six text messages and four missed calls from Ollie.

Waiting for you at town hall. It's going to be fine!

Damn this place is filling up fast though.

Oh fuck. Shit for brains decided to "move up the agenda" AKA he's planning to start this thing in ten minutes with or without you. Will do my best to stall but get here FAST.

Where are you?

Jesus please answer your phone.

Ty???

Ty took a deep, calming breath. He'd literally just saved a kid's life, but his adrenaline rush had faded. Now he existed in a state of Zen. What could Alan Chiu do to him? Nothing. Ty had literally held the man's kid's life in his hands, and he was going to sit judgment on Ty's existence in town hall not even knowing Pete was in the hospital with a tube down his throat? Or did he know and not care?

Minor emergency, on my way, Ty texted back, and then he shoved his phone in his pocket. "Hey, Riley, can you do me a favor? You know that kid who hit the baseball?"

Maybe-Jeff-Bridges was sitting in the dugout with his head between his knees as his teammates looked on. No one seemed to know what to do with him.

"I mean, not personally?" Riley hedged.

"Just, uh, let everyone know there's someone they can call if they need to talk about what happened, okay? Counseling. Totally free. I'll text you the number." He turned to Theo. "Can you get all your stuff together, buddy? It turns out we're going to be late."

Chapter 21

TY HAD never been to the town hall before, so he didn't know what to expect. It turned out to be a low, modern-looking building with an atrium, a library on one side, and about half as much parking as it needed. Ty parked down the block and prepared to hoof it.

Ollie met him at the door. By the look of him, he'd been pacing a trough in the concrete. "Where have you—*minor* emergency?"

"Long story," Ty said. "Should we go in?"

"Is that *blood on your shirt*?"

"Hi, Dad," said Theo.

"I'm going to go in," Ty said, and he pulled open the door.

Ollie scrambled in after him.

A bespectacled receptionist stood when they entered, her expression alarmed. She took in Ty's appearance and paled. Then her eyes went to Ollie. "We know the way," he assured her as he jogged to get in front of Ty. "Uh, are you sure you don't want to change?"

"Pretty sure," Ty said confidently. "This the place?" Without waiting for an answer, he pushed inside.

If beige was an aesthetic, the Suffolk town hall meeting room fit it perfectly. At the far end of the room stood a long beige oval table with five beige chairs, all facing the door. The beige walls had been adorned with photographs of past and present mayors and council people, who apart from a few exceptions, were also beige. Beige curtains framed a window that looked out onto the beige interior courtyard. In one corner stood a pole with the American and Connecticut State flags.

Ty hadn't expected the room to be so full of people. Fifty or sixty mostly beige Concerned Citizens turned to look as he came in. Many of them were wearing some kind of blue sticker on their shirts. Maybe he was supposed to stop and sign in and get a badge or something. Oh well. No time now—the door at the back of the room had opened, and the town council filed in—the mayor, the deputy mayor, Alan Chiu, and two other council members Ty didn't know.

Alan Chiu was not the mayor, but that didn't stop him from taking the spot at the center of the table.

He did a double take when he saw Ty had managed to arrive on time and was so surprised he made his first mistake. "Mr. Morris— you're here."

Right into the microphone. "Oh yeah," Ty said cheerfully, aware of all the eyes on him. "Baseball game ended early."

He let them make whatever they wanted of that.

The mayor looked sideways at Chiu before and then whacked a little wooden mallet on the table. Ty thought only judges used those. "This meeting of the Suffolk town council will come to order. Before we begin, I would like to remind those present that we are not a court of law and this is not a legal proceeding."

It's just supposed to make me feel *like I'm on trial*, Ty thought acidly.

Alan Chiu cleared his throat. "Mr. Morris, we've prepared a table with a microphone to the side of the room here so that all those gathered present can hear your responses to our questions."

Yep. There it was. A tiny little desk off to the side with its own little mic on a stand. Ty sauntered over and sat down at it. Ollie turned to speak to the people directly behind the table, one of whom moved over a seat so Ollie and Theo could sit close.

Ty leaned forward and said into the microphone, "So this isn't the defendant's chair."

The room behind him tittered. Ty blinked, disconcerted; he hadn't expected them to appreciate the joke.

Chiu waited for the laughter to die down and then continued. "Thank you, Mr. Morris." He made it sound like *die in the gutter, wretch*. "I would like to state for the record that the matter this query pertains to is the sudden death of Eileen Sanford at Hilliard's Grocery on the twenty-seventh day of April of this year. We have asked Mr. Morris, who was present at the scene, while not on call as a paramedic nor currently employed by the Orford Township emergency services, to give an account of his actions."

If he didn't regret giving Ty a microphone already, he would soon. "Was my police report deemed deficient in some way?"

"Your report was thorough. This query is merely to address any outstanding concerns that may be held by members of the community."

Oh, so he was going to turn over the microphone and let the people who hated Ty grill him. Super.

"We will also be hearing accounts from others who were present at the incident."

For a moment Ty had an unbidden flash of Alan Chiu calling upon Mrs. Sanford to give her testimony by Ouija board, but then he gestured to the other side of the room and Ty recognized Jake and Brent, one of the EMTs who'd been on duty, as well as the store manager.

Weird choices, Ty thought. The store manager had thanked him profusely. Jake had a crush on him. Brent had been trying to convince Ty to apply for a job with Orford Township EMS.

Chiu started the discussion by having Jake, who'd been with Mrs. Sanford in the grocery aisle when she collapsed, give his account. When it was Ty's turn, Ollie tapped his shoulder and handed him a sheet of paper.

It was a copy of Ty's police statement.

Ty dutifully read it out loud, trying not to smirk when he noticed Chiu's eyes following a sheet of paper he had in front of himself. Obviously he had his own copy of Ty's statement and had been hoping to catch Ty contradicting himself.

Asshole.

Chiu scowled.

Point for Ollie and Ty.

After Ty, Christie, the store manager, and Brent, the EMT, gave abbreviated accounts: *I got him the defibrillator. He used it but it didn't help. When we arrived the patient was DOA. It looked like someone had attempted CPR and electrical defibrillation without success.*

Short and to the point. Ty appreciated that. He'd worded his report the same way. Nothing subjective; nothing someone could pick apart in court.

Someone had attended the same professional CYA seminar Ty had.

"Thank you, Mr. Patrick. If you could just remain at the microphone for a moment. When you arrived on the scene, what did you note about the patient's condition?"

Brent paused. "Um, not to be indelicate, but do you mean apart from the fact that she was dead?"

Chiu's eye twitched. "What was the state of her attire? Was she bleeding? Were all of her apparent injuries addressed?"

So that was his angle.

"She wasn't bleeding because her heart had stopped beating. Her shirt was open because a defibrillator has to make contact with the skin."

"And was Mrs. Sanford's head wound addressed?"

"If you mean did it look like anyone attempted to stop the bleeding, no."

Finally Chiu seemed triumphant. "Thank you—"

"There wouldn't have been much point, as her heart was not pumping any blood."

The microphone picked up the sound of Chiu's teeth grinding. "You may be seated, Mr. Patrick. Mr. Morris?"

Ty leaned forward. "Present."

A few of the assembled crowd giggled again.

"Mr. Morris, is Mrs. Sanford's death amusing to you?"

No, but this waste of time sure was. "I apologize, Councilor."

"Could you explain the nature of your relationship with the deceased?"

This, unfortunately, was a little trickier. "We didn't have one."

"When you say you didn't have a relationship… you mean you didn't know Mrs. Sanford?"

"I knew her," Ty said. "She didn't like me very much, so we didn't have a relationship."

"And why didn't she like you?" Chiu glanced around the room. "Did you do something previously that would cause someone to develop a negative opinion of you?"

Ty's heart sank. He could either put it in his own words or let Chiu bring it up, but either way, this was going there. "I threw up in her flowerbed once. And…." He wasn't proud of this. "I, uh. I urinated on her husband's grave, by accident. I was drunk."

"You were drunk and you accidentally urinated on someone's grave."

"No, the urinating on someone's grave was on purpose. I thought it was the placeholder for my dad. I had been drinking by my mother's grave. His plot was reserved right next door. Like I said, I was drunk."

"But you don't think that Mrs. Sanford's dislike of you constituted a conflict of interest?"

"A conflict of…?" Ty could guess where that was going, but he wasn't going to steer the conversation that way. If Chiu wanted to go there, he could hit the gas himself. "Could you please explain?"

Chiu's cheeks darkened and his eyes flashed with anger. "It's been suggested that you might not have tried your best to save the life of a woman who didn't care for you."

Suggested by whom? "If I wanted her to die, I could've left the store. Why would I bother trying?"

"By inserting yourself into the situation, you had the opportunity to rob Mrs. Sanford of her dignity in the last moments of her life."

Ty went cold all over. Did this man *listen* to himself? "Mr. Chiu, I have been present at several deaths in my job as a paramedic, and I can tell you one thing for certain. Either everyone dies with dignity or no one does. Mrs. Sanford did not have a visible medic alert bracelet indicating she had a DNR. I tried to save her life because that's what I do, even when I'm not on duty."

He didn't see his misstep until a crazed kind of light came into Mr. Chiu's eyes. "But you aren't on duty, Mr. Morris. In fact, I'm given to understand that you're on administrative leave from your job at the Chicago Fire Department."

"That's correct," Ty began, because that was what bereavement leave was classified under.

But Chiu had finally gotten a clue, because there was a brief electronic pulse and then Ty's microphone went dead.

At that point it seemed ludicrous to shout.

"Thank you, Mr. Morris. Now that we have established the facts, we will move on to the questions submitted to this council—"

"I have a question."

The interruption gave Ty whiplash. On the other side of the room, where Brent and Christie had given their accounts, a woman Ty recognized from the grocery store incident was standing at the microphone.

Chiu looked to the mayor as though expecting her to bang the gavel and crush the woman into silence, but she didn't.

"How long did it take the paramedics to reach the grocery store after the 911 call? Because it *felt* like forever."

The question clearly wasn't being addressed to Ty, so he didn't try to answer it. Chiu's mouth moved soundlessly like a fish's. "I don't have that report in front of me—"

"I do," said Brent. His voice rang out confidently; like Ty, he was used to projecting to be heard over a crowd. "Right here. Brought the official printout." He held it over his head and waved it for the assembly. "Says here seventeen minutes, including the ninety-one seconds it took Dispatch to connect to our station."

"That seems like a long time," said the grocery store lady. "Is there, like, a benchmark we can compare it to, or…?"

"Excuse me," Chiu attempted to interrupt, but even with the microphone, he couldn't compete with Brent.

"There is, actually!" he said brightly. "Statewide, emergency response times are somewhere around the nine-minute mark. A little bit longer for rural towns, a little bit shorter for everybody else."

Grocery Store Lady's eyes went comically round. Ty would have bet half his fortune she'd done community theater and loved it. "Wow, so we're almost twice as slow?"

Someone had fucking scripted this, Ty thought. And he had an idea who.

"Yeah. A year or two ago we would've gotten there faster, but that was before that sinkhole opened in Road 22. Now we have to go the long way around."

Chiu sputtered. "There was no money in the budget—"

A murmur of disapproval rumbled through the room.

"Now wait a minute," said a balding man Ty didn't recognize, standing up in the middle row. "We've been talking for years about getting a fire station here in town. I have a heart condition too! You're telling me I'm just shit out of luck if my heart stops?"

That—that actually *didn't* sound scripted. Unless this guy deserved an Oscar.

Ty wished he had popcorn.

"Council voted 3–2 against the proposed new station—"

Behind Ty, Ollie stood up.

Ty didn't turn around. He didn't see it. But he could feel it happening, could feel Ollie pulling attention from everyone in the room.

Ollie didn't call for attention very often. But he had the kind of bearing that people automatically paid attention to when he did. Maybe it was his military experience. Maybe it was the fact that he was the kind of handsome TV ads used to sell razors.

"Actually, Councilor, those votes are a matter of public record, so we know that you have voted against building the proposed new fire station at 17 Main Street."

The rumbling went through the assembled townsfolk like a wave this time.

"What I'd like to know," Ollie continued in his clear, calm tenor, "is why you didn't recuse yourself from the vote, Councilor, seeing as you are the sole proprietor of the numbered company that owns the adjacent land parcel. Some people might question your impartiality."

Now Ty *did* turn around—he had to. Ollie was having a whole hero moment, and Ty wanted to savor that even more than he wanted to watch Chiu's bluster and confidence crumble into chalk dust.

Ollie looked *good*. Ty had been too distracted to notice before, but he'd gone shopping. He'd picked out a nice pair of well-fitted dark-wash jeans and a crisp dark green polo that brought out his eyes. He looked like the kind of guy you asked advice from at Home Depot. He looked like he could jump-start a car. He looked like a guy who'd aced his SATs.

He looked like he knew something Chiu didn't want him to know, and damn if that wasn't extremely sexy.

Ollie's pronouncement had several members of the assembly room—which had filled completely while Ty was busy answering stupid questions and was now probably breaking some kind of fire code—jumping to their feet, shouting for Chiu to answer the allegation.

Mayor Atkins looked like she wanted some of Ty's hypothetical popcorn. This time she did reach for her little mallet, and she whacked it on its stand several times until the volume returned to normal decibel levels. "This meeting will take a brief recess," she announced into the microphone. Then she flipped it off, but Ty heard her say to Chiu, "Councilor, I'd like to see you in my office. I'll be inviting Mr. Kent. I'd like to hear what he has to say."

Ty turned toward Ollie, fully aware that he had hearts in his eyes. "Please tell me I can come too. And that I have time to get snacks first."

Ollie smiled indulgently and picked up a leather shoulder bag that presumably held all the receipts. "You can be bitch-eating-crackers at home. Come on." He caught his mother's eye over Ty's shoulder. Ty hadn't even seen her approach. "Theo needs some Grandma time."

OLLIE WOULD not have said his time in the military focused much on planning strategy. That sort of thing was mostly above his pay grade. But he must have been exposed to enough of it to pick up a few things, because so far his plan had gone off without a hitch.

Alan Chiu was going to regret the day he decided to mess with Ollie's man.

Mayor Atkins held the door to her office and allowed them all to precede her inside. Chiu was still red-faced and steaming mad, which didn't flatter him at all. Ollie probably looked smug as fuck.

Atkins took the seat behind her desk and turned her cool gaze on Chiu. "Explain yourself."

Chiu damn near exploded. "My interest in the property at 19 Main is *not relevant*—"

"Except that you wanted to turn it into luxury lofts," Ollie interrupted cheerfully. He withdrew a folder from his bag and handed the top few sheets, stapled, to the mayor. "Obviously the plans have not been filed or submitted to the town for approval yet, but they have existed for several years, as you can see from the date of the commission of this drawing."

He didn't really believe Mayor Atkins knew nothing about it. He figured all the council members had to be complicit on some level, whether via taking bribes to look the other way or through some kind of mutual back-scratching agreement. Probably none of them understood the scope of his scheming, though.

"That's—those documents are *proprietary*—"

"Confidential between you and your business partners," Ollie agreed. He wished he'd worn suspenders so he could hook his thumbs in them. He was rocking back on his heels, almost giddy.

His mother would probably say that the way he felt right now was unchristian. But she'd say it while feeling the exact same way, so Ollie was taking that criticism from his subconscious with a healthy heap of salt.

"I admit, I probably shouldn't have seen them," he went on.

Then he put his hand on Ty's shoulder and continued, "But I think your business partner will forgive me just this once."

Ty blinked at him. "*What?*"

Ollie said gently, "You inherited your father's shares, Ty."

"I'm in *business* with this asshole?"

"Not as much as you used to be." Ollie pulled out the next set of documents. "See, some of the business partnerships they entered together had shotgun clauses. Either your dad or Mr. Chiu could offer to buy the other out at any time, but the flip side was the other could buy out their share at the same price plus one dollar. Kind of a stalemate. Until your dad got dementia."

Chiu was sputtering again. "That's absurd." He turned to Atkins as though she were some kind of authority who would stop Ollie from hanging out all his dirty laundry. "How was I supposed to know how bad the dementia had gotten?"

"You paid ten grand to take full ownership of a business that was started with fifty grand of seed money two decades ago and had tripled in size first." Ollie paused. "And which fired me this week, by the way. I take that personally. But I'm going to guess that you wouldn't have sold *your* shares for ten thousand dollars."

Atkins leaned back in her chair, looking back and forth between Ollie and Chiu. "I'm going to give you three the room," she said after a moment. "Try not to burn the place down. I hear the firefighters are fifteen minutes out."

Ollie gave in to the urge and offered her a fist on her way out. She tapped it with her own.

Then the door closed and Chiu crossed his arms. "What do you want?"

Ah, yes. The art of the trade. Ollie looked at Ty. "You're up, babe."

"Me?" Ty shook his head, half laughing. "You did all the work. You didn't get this far?"

Ollie shrugged blithely. "It's your money. I have a few starting suggestions, if you're stuck."

"No, no." Ty shook his head. "You keep your hands clean. Mine are already…." He looked down at his hands and paused. For the first time Ollie noticed the blood under his fingernails.

He really must have had a weird day.

"Mr. Chiu," Ty said when he looked up again, "you're going to resign your position as councilor immediately. You're going to sell me that plot of land you own on Main Street for what you paid for it, plus say five percent inflation. And for that I'll forget about you screwing my father out of potentially millions of dollars and leave your reputation intact. Well. Somewhat."

Chiu balked. "That's it?"

Ollie fucking hoped not. He'd worked way too hard to let Chiu off that easy.

"No." Ty straightened his shoulders. "We're going to have an independent forensic audit done on all the assets you and my father both have an interest in. And then we are going to sell them all. You can buy me out if you want, but I won't remain in business with you."

Ah. He was just waiting to hit Chiu where it really hurt—his wallet. "Those businesses are worth millions. There's no way I can come up with that kind of capital—"

"Then we'll sell them. Or we can sell some of them and you can use your share to buy me out of the rest. Or you can find another business partner to buy me out. Either way, we will never be in business together."

Vindictiveness looked good on him. Ollie would have to tell him so later.

"Fine," Chiu snapped. "Anything else you want while you're at it? Maybe a kidney?"

"No." Ty paused, winced, then said, "Actually, wait. Sit down for a second."

For the first time since before the meeting, Ollie looked at the blood stain on the front of Ty's shirt.

Frowning, Chiu crossed his arms. "What are you trying to pull?"

Ty huffed. "When's the last time you checked your cell phone?"

"I always turn it off during business hours. No personal calls." He cast a sideways glance at Ollie as if to make a point.

Ollie resisted the urge to flip him off.

"You have a *kid*!"

"Yes, and I *also* have a wife."

God, Ollie hated this guy *so much*.

"Who can't reach you right now to let you know that your kid is in the hospital."

Ah.

Chiu took a step back and collapsed into the chair. All the color had drained from his face. "My—Peter?"

"He took a line drive to the throat that collapsed his trachea. He's fine. Field surgery." Ty gave a tight smile. "Even though the EMTs took forever to arrive."

Jesus. Ollie could guess what that had looked like. And the fact that someone could have died—*again*—if Ty hadn't been in the right place at the right time made him absolutely furious.

Chiu's mouth worked soundlessly for the second time that day. Then he managed, "You…?"

"Me," Ty agreed. "Because that's what I do, Mr. Chiu. Don't forget that. And so the last thing you're going to do as part of this agreement? You're going to go see your son in the hospital." He leaned down. "And you're never going to miss another one of his games. You're going to be at every extracurricular event that kid has for the rest of his life—sports, concerts, plays, blood drives, bake sales, fundraiser car washes. All of it, Mr. Chiu. You're going to do that for me because my dad didn't. Understand?"

Chiu licked his lips and reached out for Ty's hand. "Yes. I—thank you. Yes."

Blinking, Ty shook it.

Suddenly Chiu seemed very small and very tired. Ollie cleared his throat and figured, *what the hell*. "Would you like a ride to the hospital?"

Chapter 22

TY LEFT the mayor's office in a daze with Ollie's hand in his.

The past week had all blurred together in his head. Nothing felt real. Maybe it was the sudden relief from the stress of this meeting? From the end of the schoolyear? Maybe—

They stepped back into the main meeting hall, and Ty stopped in his tracks.

No one had left.

For the first time, he took in the full picture. Several people held signs with slogans: Friends of Tyler Morris. Protect Our Good Samaritans. SUFFOLK HIGH SCHOOL LOVES COACH M.

Jenny Darel, who always glowered at Ty when he went to use the copy machine, was there, wearing a button—jeez, most of them had buttons—bearing the EMS symbol inside the Maltese cross.

Ty tried to swallow, but there was a lump in his throat. He managed it on the second try. "Ollie… what…?"

Ollie tugged Ty's hand until he turned toward him, then put his hand on Ty's face. He leaned their foreheads together. "They weren't going to let Chiu chase you out of here without a fight."

They nothing. Ollie organized this. Ty's eyes stung. "Nobody's ever—" His throat closed up again. He couldn't finish.

"They fucking should," Ollie said fiercely. "And as long as I'm around, they always will."

Ty squeezed his eyes shut and let Ollie hug him for a long minute.

Then he wiped his eyes and turned to the crowd. "Uh—"

They descended on him as one with handshakes and thanks—staff from the school, off-duty paramedics, Jake and Peggy and Jason and half a dozen parents, three kids from the baseball team, and the redheaded sixth grader who threw spitballs.

At some point Eliza supplanted Ollie at his elbow, because Ollie was off playing hero to someone else now. He might not like the word, but Ty knew one when he saw one.

"How did he pull this off?" he asked Peggy as the lineup of people began to subside.

"Me, mostly." She smiled sunnily. "Never underestimate the power of a phone tree."

"Hey, I helped," Jason butted in.

"Jason got the buttons printed."

Ugh, Ty hated crying in public. "*Thank you*."

But the parade had not yet finished. At the outside doors, Theo was waiting with Mel, Cassie, and Ollie's parents.

Theo had added a button to his baseball jersey. Cassie's shirt read SOMEONE I LOVE LOVES TYLER MORRIS.

Oh God, their mom was wearing one too. Even Ollie's dad had a button.

"Ty!" Theo broke forward into a hug. "Grandma says you showed that asshat."

Ty could not have stopped the laugh if his life depended on it, so he hoped Mrs. Kent didn't take offense. "I'm so glad I'm not your teacher anymore, bud."

When Theo released him, Mrs. Kent stepped in and tried to squeeze the life out of him. "I haven't seen my son so animated in years," she whispered fiercely. Then she kissed his cheek and released him. "Thank you."

Ty shook his head. "I didn't do anything."

"You loved my son." She pursed her lips. "That's enough."

Ollie's dad didn't say anything about the meeting, but he shook Ty's hand firmly, his right hand clasped on top, as if to echo his wife's words. "That window holding up okay?"

"It's perfect," Ty said. "Thank you again."

The rest of the weekend went by all too quickly. The assembled crowd descended on the local diner for pie and coffee. After an hour Ty begged off to go home, because he needed to have a good cry and then sleep for three hours.

Theo went home with Cassie and Mel for a sleepover. At this point Ty and Ollie probably owed Cassie and her husband about a hundred free babysitting nights.

He cleaned off the blood, faceplanted in his bed, and didn't wake up until almost sunset, when Ollie slipped into the bed with him.

"Hmm," Ty hummed, turning over to face him. "Oh, are we celebrating a victory?"

"Well," Ollie hedged.

He kissed Ollie's chin and then crawled down his body. "Let me thank you properly."

Afterward, when they were lazing in bed, Ty running his fingers through Ollie's hair, he said, "So."

Ollie tilted his head up just enough to meet Ty's eyes without dislodging his hand. "So?"

Ty tugged gently in reproof. "Seems like you found something fulfilling to do." He'd never seen Ollie so animated as he was at the town hall meeting earlier.

With exaggerated patience, Ollie said, "I am not going to be your kept man."

This time Ty's tug was less gentle. "I meant your scheming." He shook his head despairingly. "I can love you for more than your hot body, you know."

Ollie pinched the fat over Ty's hip.

"Ow!"

"Deserved it."

"Hmm." Another tug, gentle but prolonged, until Ollie rolled off of him and scooted up the mattress to share Ty's pillow. "Seriously. You put a lot of work into that. How much time did you spend with Eliza?" *Someone* had to have gone over those contracts with a fine-toothed comb. Ty had no doubt Ollie could've done it, but it made so much more sense for him to bring Eliza in, considering she'd probably presided over them the first time around anyway.

Ollie's cheeks were a bit pink, but it could've been exertion. "Pretty much every waking moment you weren't with either one of us."

"Except for the time you were organizing with Peggy and Jason?"

"And Henry. That man would cross the Delaware for you. And Jake, which was awkward."

Ty smiled and tucked his hand under his head. "I'm sure you managed fine." He paused as something occurred to him. "Wait, do you think Alan Chiu broke into my dad's office to look for evidence or something before I found it?"

"Not *personally*, but the idea crossed my mind. I only thought he might've hired someone to do it after I started digging through the paperwork, though." He said it with relish, even though they'd probably never know for sure if that was what happened. The smug satisfaction looked as good on him in bed as it had at the town hall.

"So what was it that got you? Unraveling the mystery? Or was it putting the bad guy in his place?" Was Ollie destined for a life of private detective work? Ty super hoped he didn't want to be a cop, but he could probably live with it.

"Oh no." Ollie shook his head minutely, his eyelashes brushing against the pillowcase. "It's much more embarrassing than that."

Good. "So?"

Ollie took Ty's hand and laced their fingers together. "It's, uh…. Well, I've watched you do it, you know. Go through life trying to make the world a better place. That's what I wanted to do when I was younger too. I thought joining the military would help me do that, but that… wasn't the right path for me."

Ty kissed Ollie's knuckles and waited for him to continue.

"But this week I got to see, you know, I *can* make a difference. I can make this town better. And suddenly there's a vacant seat on town council. Word has it the mayor's going to call a special election on Monday."

Ty could just see it. Mayor Atkins better watch her back. This whole town loved Ollie Kent almost as much as Ty did, and no way was he going to stop at council member. "And you're going to let your name stand?"

Ollie cleared his throat. His flush darkened. "I already filled out the paperwork. Um. And I… might have looked into taking some political science courses."

Ty could practically feel his excitement. "That's awesome. You're going to be a great president one day."

"Ty."

"I'm serious. You're good-looking, charming, you're a veteran, you're a dad—total package. Where do I sign up? Ollie Kent 2036?"

"That's kind of a tight timeline."

Ty shook his head. "I believe in you." And he was so fucking *proud*. Too bad he wouldn't be around to see most of it.

Or would he?

Ty's flight to Chicago was supposed to leave tomorrow morning at ten. He didn't want to leave Ollie, but he didn't want to give up what he'd built in Chicago either—friends who appreciated him, coworkers who had his back.

At the party this afternoon, Brent had asked if he might reconsider applying to the Orford Township EMS.

And—he could, couldn't he? Ty's father might have stolen this place from him for more than ten years, but Ollie had stolen it back.

A plan formed in his mind, and he smiled. "Hey. Do you think the new town council might finally approve a new firehouse?"

Epilogue

"THEO! WE'RE going to be late!" Ollie hollered up the stairs. Ever since their kid turned ten, he took forever to pick out what to wear. Ollie figured he must get that from Allison, because he and Ty never took that long. "You don't want to keep Ty waiting on his big day, do you?"

"It's not like they can start without you, Dad. You're the mayor."

Unfortunately, the attitude was probably Ollie's fault. "Which is why it's important to be on time."

Finally the door at the top of the stairs opened and Theo stepped out, looking nervous. He was wearing his nice new back-to-school jeans and the sneakers he'd begged for—the ones Ollie had pretended not to see the price of when Ty immediately said yes. He didn't care if Theo was going to outgrow those shoes in two months, and if Ollie pointed out that inevitability, Ty would just say they'd donate them to Goodwill and someone would be glad to have them.

Ollie had learned to pick his battles.

But along with the jeans and shoes, Theo had put on the Nats jersey they'd gotten for his birthday.

"Do you think he'll like it?"

Theo had done a lot of growing up, but his nature hadn't changed. He was still a sweet kid. Sweet… with a definite sassy streak. *That* he got from Ty.

"I think I'm going to have to listen to the two of you bicker about baseball all night again," Ollie said wryly. "And when you wear each other out, I'll tell you why you're both wrong. Come on, let's go."

Theo thundered down the stairs like an entire herd of elephants and preceded Ollie into the garage.

They'd been in the house on Peach Blossom Street for three months. Ollie half couldn't believe how long it had taken for Ty's father's estate to go through probate so he could sell the family home, and half couldn't believe they hadn't been here longer. The bright, cheerful two-story, with its stereotypical white picket fence in front and the in-ground pool Theo loved in back, already felt like home. Three bedrooms, two baths, a two-car garage, and a sun porch on the back of the house that Ty and Theo had turned into an homage to the old games room. They filled it with books and a card table and that ancient couch that was so perfect for midday naps.

Ollie clicked the button to unlock his car, opened the door, and slid behind the wheel.

The Corolla had gone to the big auto dealership in the sky last winter. Ollie had intended to buy himself a nice, sensible used car, but unfortunately he both took too long and forgot he had a birthday coming up, and before he even had time to go looking, Ty had bought him an electric BMW in fire-engine red.

Ollie wanted to protest, but then he drove the car. It was like flying while keeping four wheels on the road. *Pick your battles*, he reminded himself. And then, when they went house-hunting, he made Ty agree to a strict budget and a mortgage, so that they could be equal partners in home ownership.

Ollie suspected he could pay off his share of the house with the BMW, but if he looked into it, he might be tempted to do it, and he really did love the car.

He backed out of the garage and turned left onto the street.

After a prolonged discussion, the council had eventually voted to put the new firehouse not on Main Street, where the garage might occasionally be blocked by traffic, but a quarter mile outside the town proper, just outside Ty and Ollie's new subdivision. It had taken both significant political maneuvering and intense fundraising to get the new station up and running and equipped. Perhaps the biggest surprise for Ollie, apart from how much he enjoyed getting that done, was the fat check Alan Chiu had cut for the project.

People really could change.

"Are Grandma and Grandpa coming today too?"

Case in point. "They wouldn't miss it, bud." His parents had become some of Ty's biggest champions. Ollie didn't know how exactly, and he didn't care. He'd never told Ty what his dad had implied about him at the diner a hundred years ago, and he'd take that secret to his grave. In this case, what Ty didn't know wouldn't hurt him. He'd been hurt enough.

But now?

Ollie pulled into the station parking lot and turned off the car.

For the past two years the town had operated a satellite EMS and firehouse out of the pole barn on Ty's father's property. While sifting through the mountain of paperwork in the office, Ollie had discovered it was actually a separate parcel and registered in Ty's name. But now the new station was finally ready, and it seemed like the whole town had turned up for the grand opening. Right now they were waiting outside, held at bay by a fancy velvet rope Ollie had unearthed in the town hall basement, but as soon as Ollie was ready, they'd drop that and invite everyone inside.

Not that the festivities would last long. The crew had a job to do, after all.

"Dad! Hurry up!"

Oh, now Ollie was the one causing a delay?

"The cops are going to eat all the donuts before we get there."

Ollie was pretty sure his son did not have a future in politics.

He pocketed his keys, ducked under the thick yellow ribbon tied across the garage doors, and walked into the station.

Every surface in the bay gleamed. The cherry-red ambulance, engine, and ladder truck bore the station number, three, in the same font as Ty's new tattoo.

The tattoo wasn't for the station, though—it was for the three of them.

Up above, the station housed a barracks room and rec room. On the main floor, the open-plan kitchen and gathering area was set up to welcome visitors once the ribbon had been cut. But Ollie didn't see what he was really looking for until—

"Beady!"

Theo saw him first.

"Oof!" Ty said as he caught Theo up in a swinging hug. "Hey, you made it. Oh, that shirt, really?"

Theo was still giggling when Ty put him down. "I wanted to look my best."

Brent appeared at Ollie's elbow. "Beady?"

"B.D.," Ollie explained. "Bonus Dad."

"Only title more important than *ambulance commander*." Ty released Theo with a ruffle to his hair and swept Ollie into a kiss instead. "Unless you've changed your mind about First Gentleman—"

"I am not running for president," Ollie said for the hundredth time. "And no one would call you a gentleman anyway."

Brent laughed. "All right, I'll leave you three to it. We'll be waiting outside whenever you're ready, Mr. Mayor. Or should I say First Gentleman of Station Three?"

"Second Gentleman," Ty and Ollie chorused.

Ty's lips twitched as he explained. "Uh, 'cause I'm not the captain."

"Of course you've had this conversation before," Brent said. "In your own time, boys."

He left, and Theo took one look at Ty and Ollie, made a face, and then followed him. "You promised no kissing," he reminded over his shoulder.

That had become a common refrain in their house too, usually delivered in a long-suffering manner, but with an indulgent smile.

"We lied."

Now that they were alone, Ollie gave Ty a proper once-over. His paramedic uniform suited him infinitely better than the nerdy baseball coach windbreaker (though he still wore that to high school games). "Looking good, Ambulance Commander Kent."

Ty walked his fingers up the buttons of Ollie's oxford shirt. "You're not so bad yourself, Mayor Kent. You're gonna give this town a thrill, huh?"

"In a minute," Ollie said. "Right now I'm gonna thrill my husband."

"Be still my heart," Ty joked.

Ollie had never yet managed to kiss the smile off his face, but he didn't think the novelty of trying would ever wear off. "Come on," he said at last, "before Theo starts a rumor we're getting to second base in here."

"As if I'd ever." Ty took his hand as they turned toward the bay doors. "Everyone knows you have to save that for under the bleachers."

Keep Reading for an Excerpt from
The Rock Star's Guide to Getting Your Man
By Ashlyn Kane!

Chapter One

JEFF HAD misgivings right up until he turned into the driveway and the water of the Sound surrounded him on three sides—a solid, grounded, gorgeous blue, with the sky above it bright and clear. This close to the shore, the trees were sparse and the claustrophobia of the rest of the park didn't encroach. The air tasted like relief.

It was probably a good thing he was mostly there for the scenery, because the cabin wasn't much to look at—a solidly constructed square log A-frame, with a wooden porch along the front and a steel chimney out the back. Lots of windows for natural light, and a stack of firewood that'd last him 'til Doomsday. He parked the truck in a carport that also housed a bearproof garbage box and a huge plastic bin for gravel. With a little luck, he wouldn't need that in the next few months.

There was still time for everything to go spectacularly wrong, obviously. Case in point, bear box. Jeff sat in his truck with the windows down, cut the engine, and listened as the waves crashed against the rocks and Gord Downie told some unknown person to shut up about poets.

It didn't feel real yet—no hotels, no bandmates, no studio time, no practice, no interviews. This far out into the middle of nowhere, he might not even run into anyone who knew his name.

Well, not if he hadn't grown up here.

As the song faded out, a green park-ranger vehicle pulled in next to him and Jeff opened the door and got out to meet the driver. She was a young woman, midtwenties, with pin-straight dark hair, sharp cheekbones, and an easy smile. "You must be Mr. Pine?"

God, *Mr. Pine*. She didn't recognize him. He couldn't place her either. He'd probably been a few years ahead of her at school, if she'd grown up here. "Just Jeff," he corrected. "Thanks for meeting me here."

They shook hands. "Kara. And it's all part of the service."

She showed him around the cabin—a single room with a bed, table and chairs, and a kitchenette with a wood-burning stove set against the wall that led to the bathroom, presumably to keep it toasty in the winter.

God, Jeff could imagine staying there through the winter. His balls tried to crawl up into his body at the mere thought.

"GPS can get a little spotty," Kara warned as they made their way back to the cars. "What with the tree cover. Cell signal's only so-so. You probably won't get much data either. I've got a couple extra maps in the truck if you want."

Jeff smiled. "I think I remember my way around. Thanks, though." Sure, they'd probably changed things since he was fifteen, but where were they going to move the grocery? Willow Sound wasn't that big.

"Oh, are you from here?" Kara leaned back against the ranger vehicle.

He'd opened himself up for that one. "Ah, sort of." He shrugged. "We moved away when I was a teenager. I haven't been back."

Mercifully, she didn't ask him about it. Thank God, because he had no idea what he'd have said. *It's complicated*? It was actually just sad and kind of pathetic.

"All right. Well, I get the impression things don't change too fast around here." She pursed her lips around a smile in an obvious tease. "At least judging by how much people are still grumbling about the Tim Hortons that went in ten years ago."

Jeff barked a laugh. "Some things will never change. Small towns' *resistance* to change being one of them."

"So you've *definitely* been here before." Grinning, she reached into the truck and pulled out a park pamphlet. "You probably got one of these at the gate, but just in case." She turned it over and pulled a pen from her ranger cap. "Not saying the solitary life won't suit you, but if you feel like you need some company, there's a pretty good set of programs—learn to fly fish, identify plants and animal signs. There's a stargazing one, and if you're going to be around in August, you should definitely come to that because the meteor shower puts on a good show every year. And of course there's campfire night."

She handed him the pamphlet.

"Campfire night," Jeff repeated, the corners of his mouth turning up. "What, I don't look like I can build my own?" He wasn't offended; he wasn't exactly a hulking guy. He'd never quite made it to five ten, and his T-shirt was too loose to show off his arms.

"Nah, that's not it." Her brown skin flushed just perceptibly, and she shook her head. "It's more… campfire safety, an introduction to park wildlife, and then s'mores and camp songs." The flush deepened. "It's very popular with kids and people who are attracted to men."

Translation—the ranger who ran it was a hotass. Jeff smiled. "Well, who doesn't like s'mores."

She grinned back. "I'm off duty at six, so I won't be there, but tell me about it later if you decide to go. I'm sure I'll be seeing you if you're here all summer."

"I'm sure I'll get into some kind of trouble," Jeff agreed. "Nice meeting you."

She gave him a lazy salute and then climbed into the truck. Jeff watched it rumble away.

Then, absent anything else to do, he unloaded his stuff.

He didn't have much. Most of his things were in his condo in Toronto; he didn't need ten guitars out here. He'd brought two—his favorite electric Gibson Les Paul, a solid blue body he'd fallen in love with in a music store in Salzburg, and a battered old Seagull acoustic, his first love.

The cabin would be cramped enough with the three of them.

On top of that, he had a bag of clothes and toiletries, his laptop, and a heavy spiral-coiled notebook and three packs of pens. Pens were tricky; the moment you turned your back, they did some kind of battle royale until two days later you were down to one solitary ballpoint, and the cap was missing. He probably hadn't brought enough.

He *definitely* hadn't brought enough food. Or, you know, any.

And he should rectify that. One, because as confident as he was in his daytime navigation skills, all bets were off once the sun went down, and two, because if he wanted to check out Ranger Hot Stuff's sing-along, he needed to get going.

Any minute now. His stomach was grumbling. The clock was ticking. Jeff's feet were not moving him any closer to the truck. Instead they deposited him at the kitchen table, where he set his elbows against the scarred surface and dropped his head in his hands.

It had been almost fifteen years since he'd set foot in Willow Sound, but he wasn't afraid to find out it had changed. The conversation with Kara had put paid to that.

No, Jeff was more concerned that it would be exactly the same, Tim Hortons or no, that he'd walk down the street and be able to tell where he was by the cracked sidewalk under his feet or how strong the smell of hot oil from Shinny's was. He was afraid to go downtown and have people recognize him as Jeff Pine, frontman of Howl, and equally afraid they'd see Jeff Pine, the gawky fifteen-year-old who'd fled and never come back. He was afraid he'd recognize someone and equally afraid he'd meet no one but strangers.

And if he ran into Carter—

No, that's stupid. Willow Sound was small, but not so small Jeff had to have an anxiety attack about the possibility of running into his former best friend in the grocery. At least not on the first day. He didn't even know if Carter still lived here. He'd probably left for college. Lots of people never came back.

Jeff hadn't, until now.

Finally his stomach growled, deciding for him. He needed dinner and provisions for tomorrow morning at the very least. After those needs were met, he could schedule time for self-pity.

So resolved, he picked his new keys up off the counter and headed for the door.

WILLOW SOUND might've had a coat of paint or two, but the landmarks were still there. Jeff pulled into the criminally tiny parking lot shared by the grocery and LCBO and found a spot. It felt strange to drive here; he hadn't had a license before they moved. Now he knew why his dad always complained about that stoplight. In fifteen years, they hadn't fixed the timing?

He didn't realize he was sitting in his car, drumming his fingers on the steering wheel, until someone laughed outside and he jerked himself out of it. Too many memories of waiting in this parking lot for Carter to finish his shift at the grocery so they could swim or fish or hang out in Carter's basement and watch MTV. Jeff hadn't considered this complication. It wasn't like he could avoid the grocery store.

He hoped Carter didn't still work here. *That* would be awkward.

As he picked up a tiny cart near the entrance, he cataloged the differences—unlike the exterior, the inside of the store had had a facelift, and it was bright and pleasant. Jeff picked up as much fresh food as he thought he could cram into the cabin's minifridge and a great deal more shelf-stable stuff for those inevitable days when he sank headfirst into his guitar and didn't come up until midnight. He wished the cabin had a freezer, but mac and cheese in a box would have to do.

Small-town shopping had one thing going for it—expediency. The whole took Jeff twenty minutes through the aisles, without a single person asking for his autograph. He was just thinking he might escape unnoticed when he caught the cover of *Hello*, which the cashier had propped open against her till while she waited between customers. Jeff's own face happened to grace this issue, a particularly unflattering shot of him leaving the label's downtown office, freckles standing out too dark against pale cheeks and his dark curly hair mussed from the number of times he'd pulled at it in frustration. He looked like he hadn't slept in three days, for which Jeff credited caffeine, because it had been closer to a week.

He was debating whether to abandon his cart and make a run for it when a familiar voice said, "Georgia White! Is this the work ethic I inspired?" and the cashier scrambled upright, fumbling with the magazine. Her eyes caught on the speaker and she blanched.

"Ohmygosh, Mrs. Halloran. You scared me." Georgia (apparently) glanced at Jeff, then back at Mrs. Halloran, then doubled back to Jeff.

Awkwardly, Jeff turned to Mrs. Halloran as well—only to find he recognized the face as well as the voice. Mind you, last time he'd seen her he'd been looking from a different angle.

He smiled. "Hey, Mrs. H." Never would he have guessed his geriatric fourth grade teacher would be the first familiar face he saw in town.

"That's 'hello,' Jeffrey. I know I taught you proper manners." But her brown eyes danced; she had always loved gently giving her students a hard time. "Georgia, dear, those groceries aren't going to ring themselves up."

Georgia flushed. "Right. Sorry, Mrs. Halloran."

"It's good to see you back around these parts," she told Jeff sincerely. "Did you buy property out this way?"

He shook his head. He'd considered it, but what if things didn't turn out the way he thought? What would he do with it if he was on the road all the time? Cottages needed upkeep.

"Just renting for now." He didn't dare say where, with Georgia listening, and thankfully Mrs. H didn't ask. Jeff didn't know how to explain that the park, the Sound, felt like the place he needed to be, even if he'd had to bend a few rules to make it happen.

"Well, it's good to see you," she said warmly. "Though, if I can make one request? Maybe next album, at least one song I don't have to give someone detention for singing in my class?"

He felt the tips of his ears go hot. Georgia was paying very close attention to Jeff's selection of lunch meat. "Oh, well, I can't promise that." Especially since he didn't know if there'd even *be* another album. "But I'll try."

Mrs. H patted him on the shoulder. "You're a good boy, Jeffy. Your mom would be proud."

Shit, there it was. The first of many shoes he'd been waiting to drop. But he couldn't begrudge Mrs. H, who had worked alongside his mom for close to twenty years. "Thanks, Mrs. H."

She shook her head as Georgia timidly offered the total. "I think it's probably safe for you to call me Linda."

Jeff paid, signed the credit card slip with a pen like it was 2006, and gestured to the magazine.

Georgia squeaked. "Really?"

"If you promise to be this chill next time, absolutely."

Thank God for Mrs. H.

Jeff signed the cover of the magazine, right under his own face, and Georgia looked at him with stars in her eyes as he left with his bags.

JEFF TUCKED the kitchen garbage into the bear box and secured it before he considered his next move. He knew he needed to be here, in the last place he'd felt close to his mother, that he needed to spend some time excavating himself from the strata of rock star and grief. But now that he was here, he didn't feel *ready*. As much as he'd come up here for space, he didn't actually enjoy being alone. He was a social creature. He drew on a crowd's energy. Though he did sometimes get tired of putting on a show… maybe he'd be okay out here.

Maybe he could just be Jeff.

He knew it was overly optimistic when he packed the guitar into the truck, but he couldn't help it.

The sun was setting when he pulled into the lot near what the park welcome pamphlet called the "amphitheater." From the truck, Jeff could see it was just rows of backless wooden benches around an unusually large fire pit, which was already crackling. This early in the season, there weren't many campers to entertain—a handful of retirees, one younger couple, and a pair in their thirties with kids too young to be in school.

He hung back, feeling like the lone goth kid at a Hannah Montana concert. There was an odd number of retirees, though they still made an obvious group.

But he wanted a s'more, dammit, and a chance to play guitar for someone. He hadn't played solo since high school and he needed to decide if he was going to keep doing it if everything went further to shit.

Also he wanted to meet Ranger Hotass.

So resolved, Jeff hefted his guitar case out of the back seat and schlepped it to the amphitheater. He chose a seat all the way to the left, in the second row, where he could keep the guitar case out of sight. On the far side of the pit from him a table had been set up with the necessities—a cooler of water, a fire extinguisher and first aid kit, and a giant bowl of marshmallows. Jeff could almost taste the burnt-sugar goodness.

He didn't see Ranger Hotass. Was he early? That would be a first. He checked his phone. Nope. Ten minutes late. Well, Jeff had kept way more people waiting much longer, and they'd paid for the privilege. But he couldn't sit still. Maybe he'd take a short walk and come back.

The amphitheater was far enough inland to be mostly sheltered from the breeze off the water. The pine and spruce stood inky green against the twilight sky, somehow friendly figures. Jeff wondered if he'd see any moose while he was up here. Deer, definitely. Maybe a porcupine? Hopefully not a skunk.

In his meandering circuit it was just the usual—a chatter of squirrels, a chipmunk darting across the road, a hawk circling overhead before Jeff lost it to the low light. One day soon he might have to admit he needed glasses. Depressing. He should get Lasik. Jeff couldn't pull off the Rivers Cuomo look.

By the time he circled back to the fire, his guitar case was getting heavy and he'd broken out in goose bumps. He'd forgotten how chilly it could get on a May night up here.

The ranger had shown up while he was gone, and he was demonstrating proper use of a fire extinguisher as though people just had these at their campsites. Jeff couldn't make out his features from this distance, not with the firelight behind him, but he could tell the man was tall and fit, broad-shouldered and blond, with longish hair that brushed just below his cheekbones. The Dudley Do-Right type. Jeff smiled and made for his previous spot as unobtrusively as possible as the lecture moved on to keeping the ground around the fire clear of tripping hazards like roasting sticks.

"Can anyone think of anything else you shouldn't do around a campfire?"

This was obviously for the children's benefit, as he turned toward them when he asked, revealing the long line of a Roman nose.

One of the kids' hands shot up. Were all kids like that at that age, so eager for attention and approval? Jeff could hardly remember. He'd been an okay student before his mom got sick, so… maybe.

"Yes?" the ranger asked.

"Run?" the little girl said.

"Run!" the ranger echoed. "Yes, that's a very important one. Good job. What's your name?"

"Lennon."

"Very good job, Lennon," he repeated. Something about the way he said it—it was like an echo of a memory. Probably a flashback from childhood teachers—he'd been having them off and on since he ran into Mrs. H. "What do you say—is it time for s'mores?"

What self-respecting child was going to turn that down?

Jeff was debating how quickly he could get away with getting in line for a marshmallow and keep his respectability when a voice next to him said, "Are you going to play for us?"

Nope, just thought I'd lug around a heavy instrument for the exercise. Jeff bit down on the smartass remark. The last thing he needed was more bad publicity, and it wasn't a question anyway, it was a conversation starter. He was glad he'd held his tongue when he looked up and saw a woman in her early seventies, lilac windbreaker zipped all the way up, Yeti wineglass in hand.

This lady had no fucks to give about what anyone thought of her, which automatically made her way cooler than Jeff.

"The flyer said there's supposed to be singing, right?" he said. He hoped she didn't recognize him. She wasn't exactly his target demographic. "I don't want to step on anyone's toes—"

"Oh, no, you're fine. Smokey isn't fussed about the spotlight."

Jeff's lips twitched as he pulled the Seagull out of its case. "Smokey?"

She artificially deepened her voice and puffed out her chest. "Only you can prevent forest fires." She smiled as she took a seat on the bench next to him and offered her hand. "I'm Gloria."

Hell, Jeff could get away with using his own first name, right? "Nice to meet you, Gloria. I'm Jeff."

He strummed a quick chord to check the tuning. The ranger was still with the kids, helping them and their parents load up marshmallow roasting sticks. Gloria jerked her head at the group of seniors, and they ambled closer. "Don't suppose you know anything from my day?"

Jeff had cut his teeth—or his fingers, at least—on classic rock, sitting in the man cave in his best friend's basement, concentrating on the shift of strings under his skin. "I know a couple." He adjusted the high E, then checked again. Better. He plucked out an opening riff. "You know this one?"

The intro was quick—just ten seconds or so—and then it started in on the first verse. The words to "The Weight" bubbled up like something deeper than memory, like part of his DNA. It was one of the first songs he'd learned once his fingers were strong enough for a bar chord. It felt right singing it too—he'd just pulled in, and he was looking for a place to lay his head.

He looked up and caught Gloria's eye at the chorus, and she came in on cue, so he cued in each of the others in turn. But before he could finish it, someone said, "*Jeff?*"

Jeff's fingers stuttered on the strings and the melody died on his lips. He paused with his mouth halfway open, left hand still curved into a D chord, and looked up.

The man in the ranger uniform—the one whose body he had admired, whose voice had seemed familiar, stood in front of him, close enough to the firelight now that Jeff could make out his features.

Familiar features—square jaw, straight nose, smooth brow, shockingly pink mouth that had been the unwitting object of all Jeff's early fantasies.

Returning now to taunt him at his *second*-lowest moment. Fuck Jeff's life.

Oh shit, was he still staring? "*Carter?*"

Jesus, he looked—he looked like endless summer days outside, and it was like Jeff could see teenage Carter superimposed on this older, broader, even more absurdly handsome version. Which, inexplicably, had surfer-bro hair.

Gloria said, from lightyears away, "Oh, do you two know each other?"

"Yeah," Jeff said, feeling shell-shocked, at the same time Carter said, "No."

Jeff inhaled sharply, feeling the denial like a knife slipped between his ribs. But before he could make an excuse and leave, Carter backtracked apologetically, "I mean, we used to, but I haven't seen him in…." He trailed off, and everything somehow became more awkward.

It had been over a decade, but from his face, Jeff knew he was thinking about the last time they'd seen each other.

On second thought, remembering that day, maybe Jeff didn't know Carter either. "Fifteen years," he supplied. He felt like there was a band around his chest. That made Carter, what? Thirty-two? The years looked good on him.

The looking hurt, though. It brought home that they'd never talked, after. There was just that awful day, capped off with a good rub of salt in the wound, and then Jeff had run out and refused to speak to Carter, and a week later he and his dad moved. They'd never emailed, even when Jeff stopped being mad. At that point what could he have said? It wouldn't have made a difference.

Maybe Gloria sensed the tension, because she cleared her throat. "Well, it's nice that you have a chance to reconnect!"

Reconnect—God no. Jeff's life was already a turtlefuck. The last thing he needed was to mix his childhood trauma with his adult problems. Why was this happening? Was this some sign from the cosmos? *Go back to the city, kid. This place is for a you long dead.*

Except he couldn't escape the feeling that it was the cosmos that had brought him here in the first place.

"Right," Jeff said, instead of disagreeing and running away. He picked out the introduction of the song again to refocus the attention. As long as he had his little stage and his guitar, he was in control. And control was just what he needed. "So—should we try that again? Maybe we'll get through the whole chorus this time."

A few of the retirees exchanged glances, and Jeff saw the younger couple whispering to each other over a cell phone and thought maybe his cover was blown. Especially when Gloria said, afterward, "You have a wonderful voice, Jeff. Has anyone ever told you you sound like that singer from—oh, what's the band—they have that song 'Ginsberg'?"

Jeff pasted on a smile and pointedly didn't look at Carter, who was back with the kids, scooping melted marshmallow onto graham crackers. "Yeah, I've heard that a time or two." He made a mental note not to play any Howl songs. That would only invite trouble.

Not that trouble had ever needed an invitation, he thought as he glanced across the fire. Carter hadn't joined in on any of the songs, he just sat and listened. Jeff found it unnerving and spent longer than he should scrutinizing his song choices. Nothing too angry, too sad, too nostalgic.

Nothing that might give away the monstrous rending of his own heart.

Finally, after a good set, Jeff begged off. "I might be back next week," he said to Lennon, who had been delighted with his half-assed version of "Let It Go." "But I just got in this afternoon and I'm exhausted." And he was. Full-on gritty eyes, heavy chest tired. "If you're still here I'll see you then, okay?"

Jeez. He was going to bed before a three-year-old. *Guess I really do need this vacation.*

He was extra careful navigating back to the cabin in the dark. Even with the headlights, it was challenging to see the turnoff. He might really have to look into glasses. Or stop driving at night.

There was no use dwelling on any of it tonight. He put the truck in Park under the carport and was halfway into the cottage before he realized he never got his marshmallow.

Fucking Carter. That guy ruined everything.

Scan the QR Code Below to Order!

ASHLYN KANE likes to think she can do it all, but her follow-through often proves her undoing. Her house is as full of half-finished projects as her writing folder. With the help of her ADHD meds, she gets by.

An early reader and talker, Ashlyn has always had a flair for language and storytelling. As an eight-year-old, she attended her first writers' workshop. As a teenager, she won an amateur poetry competition. As an adult, she received a starred review in *Publishers Weekly* for her novel *Fake Dating the Prince*. There were quite a few years in the middle there, but who's counting?

Her hobbies include DIY home decor, container gardening (no pulling weeds), music, and spending time with her enormous chocolate lapdog. She is the fortunate wife of a wonderful man, the daughter of two sets of great parents, and the proud older sister/sister-in-law of the world's biggest nerds.

Sign up for her newsletter at www.ashlynkane.ca/newsletter/
Website: www.ashlynkane.ca

Follow me on BookBub

HOCKEY EVER AFTER • BOOK ONE

WINGING IT

Falling for his teammate wasn't in the game plan....

ASHLYN KANE
MORGAN JAMES

Hockey is Gabe Martin's life. Dante Baltierra just wants to have some fun on his way to the Hockey Hall of Fame. Falling for a teammate isn't in either game plan.

But plans change.

When Gabe gets outed, it turns his careful life upside-down. The chaos messes with his game and sends his team headlong into a losing streak. The last person he expects to pull him through it is Dante.

This season isn't going the way Dante thought it would. Gabe's sexuality doesn't faze him, but his own does. Dante's always been a "what you see is what you get" kind of guy, and having to hide his attraction to Gabe sucks. But so does losing, and his teammate needs him, so he puts in the effort to snap Gabe out of his funk.

He doesn't mean to fall in love with the guy.

Getting involved with a teammate is a bad idea, but Dante is shameless, funny, and brilliant at hockey. Gabe can't resist. Unfortunately, he struggles to share part of himself that he's hidden for years, and Dante chafes at hiding their relationship. Can they find their feet before the ice slips out from under them?

SCAN THE QR CODE BELOW TO ORDER!

String Theory

Ashlyn Kane & Morgan James

For Jax Hall, all-but-dissertation in mathematics, slinging drinks and serenading patrons at a piano bar is the perfect remedy for months of pandemic anxiety. He doesn't expect to end up improvising on stage with pop violinist Aria Darvish, but the attraction that sparks between them? That's a mathematical certainty. If he can get Ari to act on it, even better.

Ari hasn't written a note, and his album deadline is looming. Then he meets Jax, and suddenly he can't stop the music. But Ari doesn't know how to interpret Jax's flirting—is making him a drink called Sex with the Bartender a serious overture?

Jax jumps in with both feet, the only way he knows how. Ari is wonderful, and Jax loves having a partner who's on the same page. But Ari's struggles with his parents' expectations, and Jax's with the wounds of his past, threaten to unbalance an otherwise perfect equation. Can they prove their double act has merit, or does it only work in theory?

Scan the QR Code Below to Order!

DREAMSPUN DESIRES

FAKE DATING THE PRINCE

Ashlyn Kane

A royal deception. An accidental romance.

A royal deception. An accidental romance.

When fast-living flight attendant Brayden Wood agrees to accompany a first-class passenger to a swanky charity ball, he discovers his date—"Call me Flip"—is actually His Royal Highness Prince Antoine-Philipe. And he wants Brayden to pretend to be his boyfriend.

Being Europe's only prince of Indian descent—and its only openly gay one—has led Flip to select "appropriate" men first and worry about attraction later. Still, flirty, irreverent Brayden captivates him right away, and Flip needs a date to survive the ball without being match-made.

Before Flip can pursue Brayden in earnest, the paparazzi forces his hand, and the charade is extended for the remainder of Brayden's vacation.

Posh, gorgeous, thoughtful Prince Flip is way out of Brayden's league. If Brayden survives three weeks of platonically sharing a bed with him during the romantic holiday season, going home afterward might break his heart….

SCAN THE QR CODE
BELOW TO ORDER!

DREAMSPUN
DESIRES

HIS LEADING MAN

Ashlyn Kane

He wrote a comedy. Fate directed a romance.

He wrote a comedy. Fate directed a romance.

Drew Beaumont is bored of the same old roles: action hero, supervillain, romantic lead. He's not going to let a fresh gay buddy comedy languish just because they can't find him the right costar. No, Drew bats his eyelashes and convinces everyone that the movie's writer should play Drew's not-so-straight man.

Aspiring writer Steve Sopol has never had a screenplay optioned. Now one of Hollywood's hottest properties wants to be in a movie Steve hasn't finished writing—and he wants Steve as his costar. Turns out the chemistry between them is undeniable—on and offscreen.

Drew swore off dating in the biz, but Steve is the whole package: sharp, funny, humble, and cute. For Steve, though, giving in to the movie magic means the end of the privacy he cherishes. Will the credits roll before their ride into the sunset?

Scan the QR Code Below to Order!

Babe in the Woodshop

Ashlyn Kane
Claudia Mayrant
CJ Burke

When long hours and crushing stress push Bellamy Alexander to his breaking point, he walks away from his consulting job and drives until he runs out of gas. Fortune deposits him in front of Antonio's, a place with decent pizza and an opening for a delivery boy. Even better, he finds an apartment right across the street from his new job. And best of all, Chris McGregor, the property manager who runs the custom furniture shop below Bell's new digs, is super hot—and super into Bell.

It seems too good to be true—and maybe it is. Things aren't exactly going smoothly. Bell avoids telling his mother the truth about his new job because he doesn't want to hear how he should go back to the corporate world. On the other hand, he doesn't think he wants to deliver pizza forever either. He'd like to think about settling down, but Chris runs hot and cold. Between Bell's uncertainty and the hang-ups Chris refuses to talk about, they have their work cut out for them. Fortune may have caused their paths to dovetail, but it will take more than wood glue to hold them together.

Scan the QR Code
Below to Order!

FOR MORE OF THE BEST GAY ROMANCE

Dreamspinner Press
dreamspinnerpress.com